P9-DFT-334

SOMETHING STRANGE

AND

DEADLY

SOMETHING STRANGE AND DEADLY

SUSAN DENNARD

HARPER TEEN

An Imprint of HarperCollins*Publishers*

HarperTeen is an imprint of HarperCollins Publishers.

Library of Congress Cataloging-in-Publication Data
Dennard, Susan.
    Something strange and deadly / Susan Dennard.
        p.   cm.
    Summary: "In an alternate nineteenth-century Philadelphia, Eleanor
Fitt sets out to rescue her brother, who seems to have been captured by an
evil necromancer in control of an army of Undead"—Provided by
publisher.
    ISBN 978-0-06-208326-5
    [1. Brothers and sisters—Fiction.   2. Dead—Fiction.   3. Magic—
fiction.   4. Philadelphia (Pa.)—History—19th century—Fiction.
5. Horror stories.]   I. Title.
PZ7.D42492Som 2012   2011042114
[Fic]—dc23   CIP
                                                                                        AC

Typography by Lissi Erwin
12 13 14 15 16   LP/RRDH   10 9 8 7 6 5 4 3 2 1

First Edition

ACKNOWLEDGMENTS

First and foremost I have to thank my amazing husband, Sébastien. Without you, Seb, none of this could have happened—not the writing, not the ideas, and certainly not the dirty dishes.

A gigantic thanks to my mom for saying ridiculous things like "get 'er done" and to my dad for encouraging me to connect with other writers. You guys always told me to follow my dreams, and guess what? I did, and it's amazing.

I owe so much to my wonderful agents, Sara Kendall and Joanna Volpe. You two understood Eleanor and the Spirit-Hunters from the get-go, and you found the perfect home for her adventures. All the cupcakes and Zelda games in the world aren't enough to pay you back.

Additionally, I am forever grateful to Karen Chaplin and Maria Gomez. Your red pens honed this novel into a finely tuned tale, and I couldn't have asked for better, more supportive editors—or a better editorial team at HarperCollins. I'm honestly thrilled I have two more books for you all to tweak (or more likely, shred).

Special thanks to Katharine Brauer, Holly Dodson, Sarah J. Maas, Meredith McCardle Primeau, and Jennifer Dennard for reading this book in all its various stages of development. You ladies literally made the story what it is today. And to the gals at Let the Words Flow: Thank you for taking me into your ranks and under your wings. I couldn't have asked for a better group of writing friends!

And finally to Asimov, my Irish setter: I'm sorry for making you sit in my office all day long, buddy. You'll get more walks once I finish this series . . . maybe.

To Seb, for walking the dog, making the coffee, and listening to my stream-of-consciousness rambling—all without complaint. *Je t'aime.*

CHAPTER ONE

"Dead!" a woman screamed. "It's the Dead!"

My heart shot into my throat, and shocked cries rippled through the station. The woman sounded nearby—as if she was also in line at the telegraph office.

But . . . this couldn't be real, could it? The Dead? At the Centennial train depot?

The woman shrieked again, and I saw her, four customers behind me, her face white and eyes huge. A breath later, somber bells rang out, and I knew it was all very, very real. That was the Dead alarm.

I'd heard of corpses awakening—hungry and dangerous though still quite dead. The purpose of bells in coffins was, after all, to warn us; but if the word on the street was true, then in the last week more than a few bodies had escaped their graves.

My heart picked up speed, my veins throbbing in my neck. I did *not* want to be here when the Dead came. I'd never seen a walking corpse, and I saw no reason to change that.

"It's the Dead!" screamed a scruffy boy beside me. His shrill voice was barely audible in the panicked crowds. "Get out—come on!"

But I couldn't. Workers and passengers alike pushed and heaved to be the first out of the distant doors.

My breathing turned shallow. I backed up against the wall. The crowd was moving fast, tugging at my skirts and threatening to pull me away like a treacherous riptide.

I glanced around. The abandoned office told me I'd get no telegram today. For that matter, I wasn't even sure I would escape today.

A woman's parasol jabbed into my ribs, and my petticoats ripped beneath an old man's boot. I pushed myself harder to the wall, frantically searching for a gap in the flow of bodies.

A thought flashed in my mind: *I can go in the office.* It was empty and an easy relief from the panic. I could wait inside for the crowds to thin, and then I could make my own escape.

I took a steeling breath and shoved off the wall, aiming for the office entrance. Once I reached the door, I pushed through and slammed it shut behind me. My muscles shook and I had to lean against the door, but I was safe. I could ride out the storm here.

I scanned the tiny cubicle. Before the clerk's window was a desk with the telegraph machine and stacks of paper. One of those stacks was labeled NEW—where my brother's telegram would be if he'd sent one.

He'd been three years abroad, and today was the day he was finally coming home.

Or it was supposed to be, but the blasted boy hadn't appeared on the New York train. And now my wait in the telegraph line—a wait to find out if he'd sent a message or not—had been interrupted.

By the Dead.

Long moments passed. The screams and pelting footsteps didn't fade. This could be a long wait, but at least I was protected from the stampede. Though not perhaps from the Dead.

What did the stories say? The Dead hunt endlessly until they're laid to rest or their bodies are destroyed.

Shivers ran down my spine. Maybe it was best Elijah hadn't come home—though I *did* want to know why he hadn't been on the train. Of course . . . now that I was here, I could get Elijah's message myself.

I shot a quick glance through the clerk's window. The crowds were still packed outside, so I dropped my parasol to the floorboards and grabbed for the papers. After skimming the top message, I moved to the next, and then the next.

But I reached the end, and nothing was for me. When Elijah had missed the train a week ago, he'd instantly tele-graphed. But now something was wrong. I could feel it. There

3

should have been a message from him.

I threw the papers back on the desk. *Where else can a telegram be?*

My eyes caught on a crumpled sheet of paper nearby. I snatched it up, but it was only a newspaper page. The headline read: "Walking Dead Still Rise in Laurel Hill Cemetery." I pushed the paper into my pocket to read later. I'd ignored the recent Dead reports, thinking they wouldn't affect me. Foolish—the Dead were more than just specters to frighten unruly children. The Dead were very real.

And the Dead were *here*. I tried to swallow, my throat pinched tight. I needed to get out!

The frenzied cries of the crowd's escape were fading. Now was my chance to run. I stooped down to retrieve my parasol.

That was when I noticed the smell. The stench of carrion.

My hands froze over the parasol. I lifted my gaze with deliberate caution and met the face that now waited outside the window, where only minutes ago *I* had waited. It was a corpse. One of the Dead.

Time stopped as my mind took in the creature before me. Lidless eyes with creamy, decomposed irises. Half a mouth revealing yellow teeth. The tatters of a brown, wool suit hanging loosely over waxy skin. Brittle, gray hair. And now the corpse lifting his arm.

I shrieked and clambered backward. My feet tangled in my petticoats, and I crashed to the floor in a flurry of skirts.

No, no, no!

Whimpers burst from my mouth as I struggled to stand, but my corset hampered my range of movement and balance. I couldn't draw in a decent breath.

The corpse's arm was now fully extended through the window, its rotten fist only inches from my head. It stiffly unfolded its fingers, and a sheet of paper fluttered to the counter. Then, in a slow, convulsive turn and with shambling footsteps, the corpse left.

Seconds passed and still I could not seem to breathe. Why hadn't it attacked?

I watched the window. Was the corpse coming in the office? Were there more Dead? I listened closely but detected no sounds over the somber tolling of the alarm.

Was the corpse really gone?

The stink lingered, so perhaps it was waiting outside the window. A few flies had hitched a ride on the body, and they buzzed around me. I only gave them a cursory swat. I was trapped in here until—

I heard a loud crack like thunder.

My heart jolted, and my whole body jumped with it. What the devil was that?

Then, suddenly, the alarm stopped. I heard voices from within the depot. Living people.

The danger must have passed; I was all right. But I couldn't stop the shaking in my hands. My whole body felt like jelly.

It took several minutes for my breathing to settle, for my heart to stop its frenzied pounding. It wasn't until a full five minutes had passed and silence reigned in the depot that I trusted myself to try standing.

My legs wobbled, and I pushed my chin shakily forward. I didn't want to approach the counter, but I ached to see what the Dead had left behind. A piece of paper, yes, but what was on it?

I inched closer, seeing it was a letter.

I inched closer again until the words of the letter were clear.

My breath hitched, and I grasped the counter for support.

The paper was for me, and it was from my brother.

When I got home, I went straight upstairs, locked myself in my bedroom, and leaned against the door. The fading, yellow stripes on the wallpaper made my eyes waver, so I stared hard at the floorboards.

I needed simplicity. Calm. And above all, I needed time alone before Mama hounded me. The words from Elijah's letter rang in my mind over and over again. I had scanned the note a thousand times on the walk home and could recite it from memory now.

I can't come. Trouble in New York has caught up with me. Don't tell Mama—it will only worry her. And you shouldn't worry either. If I do what he needs, I can come home.

And that was all it said, except for *Elijah* scrawled at the bottom. When I flipped it around, it was just dirt-covered blank.

I threw my parasol beside my oak wardrobe and crossed to the window opposite me, giving my bed a wide berth—its beige sheets beckoned to me with promises of protection and escape. I stoutly avoided looking at Elijah's picture on my bedside table, and I pressed my forehead against the glass; it fogged with my breath.

This could not be happening. This had to be a joke. Or a mistake. Elijah would show up at any minute, his bony face laughing and his spectacles sliding down his nose.

I fingered the pale scar on my left wrist. A hard-earned reminder of our tree-climbing, game-playing days. Surely, *surely* this was a prank—like the time he convinced me it was a good idea to dress up as ghosts and scare Mama during tea.

My heart dropped into my stomach, and I twisted around to slide to the floor. This couldn't be a joke. Elijah couldn't manipulate a corpse.

The reference to trouble in New York—Elijah had mentioned problems in his earlier letters. He had said people were after his research, but I hadn't understood what he meant. During his travels across Europe, he was always drifting from one museum to the next, and studying old books and ancient artifacts. But theology had never been a topic of much interest to me.

Oh, why hadn't I paid better attention? I'd been so excited

about his return, I'd completely ignored his trouble. And now it had caught up with him in the form of lidless, putrid eyes.

Despite the press of my corset, I hugged my knees to my chest and rolled my head back to the wall. Elijah was right—I couldn't tell Mama.

My mother seemed tough, but it was all an act. When Father had died six years ago, the grief had almost killed her. The stress of a missing son—of a son who was likely taken by the Dead—would be too much.

I whimpered and squeezed my eyes shut. I had no idea what to do . . . no idea why this was happening to Elijah. Other than childhood stories and the occasional newspaper article, I had never paid much attention to the Dead. It had never been my problem before, never been my family affected by a ringing casket-bell and rising corpse.

From my pocket, I yanked the crumpled newspaper and roughly unfolded it.

WALKING DEAD STILL RISE IN

LAUREL HILL CEMETERY

Today marks one week since the discovery of the corpse

of Frederick Weathers, son of City Councilman Thomas

Weathers. Frederick, who had disappeared two days before,

was discovered at the International Centennial Exhibition

as a walking corpse. His murderer is presumed to be the

same person responsible for raising the Dead.

Murder? Oh God—I was going to be sick.

"Eleanor? Let me in!"

I whipped my head up. *Mama.*

I crushed the newspaper in my fist and shoved it back into my pocket. "Let me in!" she commanded.

"Coming. Coming." I climbed to my feet and scrambled across the room.

"Why is this locked?" Mama demanded once the door was opened. She didn't wait for an answer but sailed past me into the room. "Well, where is he?"

I stared wide-eyed. The truth boiled in my throat. I wanted—*needed*—to tell her, but I knew better.

So I blinked.

"Do not just stand there, Eleanor. I asked you a question." Mama's figure was all shoulders and angles, with a mass of curling gray hair on top. And right now she stood puffed up like a triangle, tapering to the ground and demanding authority as if she were President Grant himself.

"The Dead came," I mumbled.

A crease folded down her forehead. "What do you mean, 'the Dead came'? What is that for an answer? What Dead?"

I shrank back, fighting the urge to run past her through the open door. "Th-the walking corpses," I stammered. "The ones people have been talking about. One came to the train depot, so everyone was evacuated."

"What?" She threw her hands in the air. "But this is cause for alarm, Eleanor! If you were in danger—"

"No!" I lunged at her, my head shaking to keep her calm. "No, I'm fine. Elijah wasn't there anyway."

"He . . . he was not there?" Her eyebrows drooped, and she lowered her hands.

"No, but he left a message."

"Where?"

"At the telegraph office."

"I mean, where is the message? Give it to me."

I licked my lips. "I don't have it. I must have dropped it when the Dead alarm rang."

"Hmph." She folded her arms over her ample chest. "What did the note say? Will he be on the afternoon train?"

"No." I shook my head as a story unfolded in my mind. "Not on the afternoon train. He ran into some friends in New York, so he's going to stay. For a few days, or perhaps longer."

She groaned and pressed her hands to her forehead. "Three years away with nary a letter, and now he changes his plans with no warning at all. We need him here—does he not realize this? You explained that in your last letter, did you not?"

"Of course, Mama." I had written to Elijah of our financial trouble long before she had nagged me to. In every letter I had begged Elijah to hurry home and resume our dead father's work.

But Elijah never responded to those passages.

"And what of our party tonight?" Mama insisted. "What am I to do?"

"We could cancel," I said hopefully.

She snorted. "Of course we cannot cancel. The walking Dead must have addled your brain, Eleanor. This is our first party in years—our chance to impress the Wilcoxes. The guests have accepted our invitations, and I will not squander this opportunity."

I cringed. Merciful heavens, a party was the last thing I wanted to endure. To make polite chatter and pretend all was well? It seemed impossible.

After Father died, my family stopped receiving invitations to parties. I'd thought it was Mama's grief that kept our calling card bowl empty. I'd thought it was our year-long mourning that kept us tied to the house. But as I'd gotten older, I'd realized that it was society's decision to ignore us—not my mother's—and I could conjure only one reason for this isolation: the raving paranoia my father had suffered from before his death. His babbling cries of enemies, sabotage, and revenge had frightened my family. I could see how it would frighten other families as well.

"Consider the expense of our party," Mama continued. She began to pace. "All that money for nothing! We cannot waste such food and preparation. Although . . . the entire affair *was* meant for Elijah, which means we must offer our guests some other form of entertainment."

"We must?" I squeaked.

"Yes, yes." She drummed her fingers against her lips. "There are too few guests for a ball and too many guests for cards, and literary debates are so dreadfully dull."

She continued her steps, muttering more solutions to herself.

I squeezed my eyes shut and took the moment to calm my nerves. I had to keep this brittle control in front of Mama or else I would blurt out everything.

"I have it," she said.

I snapped my eyes open. Mama was stopped midstride with a finger thrust in the air. "We shall have a séance." Her face filled with pride.

I was not nearly so pleased with her solution. "Why?"

"Why not? We used to have them all the time."

I swallowed and flicked my eyes around the room.

"What is wrong with a séance?" Mama pursed her lips and squinted at me.

"I-I'm still upset by the Dead at the depot. Contacting the spirits sounds . . ." I trailed off and shrugged.

"Ah." She tapped the side of her nose. "I see. Well, you needn't worry. The séances have never worked before, and we won't have time to hire a medium for tonight. It will be quite casual. Purely entertainment, Eleanor."

"All right." She was correct, of course. She'd conducted dozens of séances, but even with a medium, she'd never been able to contact Father. Besides, my chest was starting to ache from my secrets. I needed her to leave before the truth came spilling out. "A séance will be perfect then."

"Yes, I think so too." She grinned. "It is cheap, and everyone loves the drama. People still talk of Mrs. Bradley's séance." She chuckled.

I tried to laugh with her, but it came out breathy and shrill.

"Are you all right, dear?" Mama asked. "Did the Dead truly disturb you? Did you actually see this walking corpse?" She inspected my face, and I had to fight to keep my body still. Why couldn't she just *leave* already?

"N-no. I didn't see it." I licked my lips. "I'm fine, Mama. It's just so . . . it's so hot."

"Yes, and you are sweating." She stepped close to me and sniffed the air. "I'll have Mary draw a bath. You smell like a guttersnipe."

I merely nodded, no longer trusting myself to speak. Fortunately, Mama chose that moment to leave; and in three long strides, she was gone.

I sucked in a shaky breath and collapsed backward onto my bed. My fingers curled around the familiar beige linens.

How could I keep this a secret when I could barely deal with it myself? The Dead had delivered Elijah's letter. The corpses had my brother!

And before I could stop it, another, much darker thought came. What if Elijah was a walking corpse himself?

CHAPTER TWO

The party around me was a smoky dream. None of it felt real. Not the constriction of my bodice or the poke of my hairpins, not the glittering chandelier or the warm gaslights, and least of all, not the chattering guests.

While our elderly butler, Jeremy, and our young maid, Mary, prepared the drawing room for the séance, the guests and I waited in the parlor. I had successfully deflected old Mr. and Mrs. Moore's attempts at conversation (discussing church sermons was never my favorite subject, particularly when my nerves were screaming for relief); and fortunately, Mr. and Mrs. Cook were wholly occupied by Mrs. Wilcox and my mother.

Meanwhile, the Cooks' fair-haired daughters, Patience and Mercy—whom I called the Virtue Sisters—were focused on the remaining guests: the beautiful Allison Wilcox and her very rich, very eligible brother, Clarence.

I sat alone on the sofa, avoiding company by feigning a great interest in examining my surroundings.

Mama had drained half our remaining bank account to ensure that our parlor was at the height of All Things Fashionable. The wallpaper had recently been redone; the shelves were littered with peacock feathers, coral shards, and a thousand other knick-knacks. The velvet rugs and drapes, recently added for this very occasion, swirled with elaborate patterns.

Mama's greatest pride was the grand piano. It shone in the light of the gas lamps and told the tale of Fitt taste and wealth. It was no wonder she stood beside it to prattle to the Cooks and Mrs. Wilcox.

By the window, where the dour-faced Moores stood, was the mahogany bookshelf built to house all of Elijah's theology books. And behind me was the chess table. *Our* chess table. The one Elijah had gotten so he could teach me to play—and then beat me nearly every day.

My thoughts vanished at the sound of a bubbling laugh.

Through lowered lashes, I peered at Allison Wilcox. She sat in a mauve armchair nearby, and the peach silk of her gown made her pale skin glow and dark hair gleam. In comparison, my own skin looked pasty. Or perhaps Allison's exceptional beauty came from her obvious joy—she basked in the happy warmth I had envisioned for myself.

Her brother, Clarence, had recently returned to Philadelphia after two years at college, and he lounged elegantly against Allison's chairback. He was just as handsome as his sister in his perfectly tailored black suit. The Virtue Sisters no doubt agreed with me, for they hovered nearby. Lanky Patience on one side and squat Mercy on the other, giggling at every word he spoke.

At each of Allison's laughs and smug glances in my direction, I had to bite the inside of my mouth to keep jealous tears away—and to keep from hurling the nearest knickknack at her face. I wanted *my* brother here; I wanted Elijah safe.

Catching my eye, she bounced up and waltzed over to me.

"Where's your brother?" she asked.

"He's in New York," I mumbled. She plunked down on the sofa beside me.

"Yes, I *know*—your mother already said that." Allison rolled her eyes. "But why didn't he come? I thought this party was for him."

Clarence strolled over and settled beside his sister.

"Yes, well . . ." I fidgeted with my lavender dress and avoided the pair's gaze. "I believe he ran into some friends and decided to visit."

"Do you know the friends?" Clarence asked. He slid out a shiny, golden watch from his waistcoat pocket. After glancing at its face, his eyes flicked to mine.

"No," I answered. "I do not."

Clarence was undeniably handsome. The delicate curves of

youth still clung to the strong angles of his jaw; and when his eyes met mine, I caught my breath. They were so dark it was as if they sucked up all the light.

I'd never met Clarence before this evening. He was twenty and, with the recent death of his father, had inherited the Wilcox business and immense fortune. Mama had mentioned something about political ambitions as well, but I couldn't recall.

Though I knew the pair expected me to continue the conversation, I kept my mouth clamped shut. Mama would be horrified at my wasted chance to impress Clarence Wilcox, but I didn't want to talk about Elijah.

Seconds passed in awkward silence. Clarence's head swiveled about as he studied the room. Allison eyed me, and I fidgeted with my amethyst earrings—a nervous habit I'd acquired ever since Elijah had given them to me on my thirteenth birthday.

At last Allison sighed and scooted closer. "So, what's wrong with you tonight?"

I scowled. "Nothing."

"Humbug!" She narrowed her eyes and wagged a finger. "You don't want to talk to me, you've avoided the other guests, and you haven't smiled the entire evening."

"Not now, Allison." I gave her what I hoped was a pleading expression, but I could feel the muscles in my jaw twitch with anger. Ever since Mrs. Wilcox had unexpectedly, and rather abruptly, befriended Mama three months ago, I had been forced into Allison's company far more than I wished.

"Allie," Clarence said wearily, "leave her alone."

"No." Allison straightened in her seat and planted her hands on her hips. "Why are you so dour? Be nice to me. It's not my fault your brother didn't come home."

That was too far.

"Enough," I hissed, grabbing at her. "Shut pan, Allison."

She leaned out of my reach, but Clarence laid a gloved hand on her arm. "I think you've done sufficient harm for one evening, Allie. Go talk to Mother." He tipped his head toward the other side of the room.

To my astonishment and relief, Allison actually obeyed. For a moment, the heavy plumes of depression cleared from my chest. I could breathe.

"I can't believe she listened to you." I turned a wide-eyed gaze on Clarence.

A grin tugged at his lips. "Yes, I imagine I'm the *only* person she'll listen to."

"Well, I'm impressed." A warmth eased through my body. Despite his perfect features, he was not so difficult to talk to.

"No doubt you'd do the same with your brother."

"Not precisely." I smiled ruefully. "To be honest, I don't take orders well."

"Then I shall be sure I never give you any." He winked before whipping out his pocket watch again and glancing at its face.

I arched my eyebrows, and my grin grew wider. "Are you bored?" I teased. "Or do you have some late-night appointment you can't miss?"

He jerked his head up, and my breath caught. His pupils had grown until there was no iris left.

"Neither. Of course." He dropped the watch back into his pocket and slouched leisurely against the sofa. He gave an unruffled smile. "So tell me, Miss Fitt, do you know when your brother will return?"

"No." I wet my lips. "Do you know Elijah?"

He looked off to the right. "I know *of* your brother."

"Oh?"

"Of course." He folded his arms over his chest and returned his gaze to me. "Everyone knows of the Philadelphia Fitts. I even know of *you*."

"You mean Allison told you about me."

His lips twitched. "Certainly."

I stroked my amethysts and made my expression passive. I didn't care one whit about her gossip—though I did wish she wouldn't talk about me to Clarence. I'd prefer if eligible young men learned my faults *after* meeting me.

He flashed his eyebrows playfully, as if knowing where my thoughts had gone. "You needn't worry. She's said nothing unkind. She finds you amusing—she likes to talk, you know?"

"I hadn't noticed," I said flatly. Saying Allison loved to gossip was like saying birds enjoyed flying. It was not so much a hobby as a part of her physiology.

Clarence's smile expanded, and his eyes crinkled. "Apparently there was an insult you gave her a few days ago, though. . . . She had to ask me what it meant."

My face warmed, and I looked away. "I believe I *might* have called her a spoiled Portia with no concept of mercy."

He laughed and hit his knee. "That's right. Portia's speech on mercy in the final act of *The Merchant of Venice*. Allie had no idea what you meant."

"In my defense, she was taunting me—"

"With no mercy?"

"Something like that," I mumbled, embarrassed he'd heard about it.

"Oh, I have no doubt. One of Allie's charms is her childish teasing." He laughed again and shook his head. "Next time, though, I suggest you use less obscure insults. They might hit their mark better."

I didn't know if I ought to laugh with him or stammer apologies, but at that precise moment, the subject herself saved me from my confusion. Allison bustled up and glared down at us. "What's so funny?" she demanded. Clarence only shrugged, putting his hand in his pocket, and shot me a conspiratorial wink.

"Fine," she said. "Keep your secrets. I don't care." She lifted a perfect eyebrow. "Scoot over. I want to sit between you."

"Take my seat, Allie." Clarence rose and slung a smooth bow. "If you'll excuse me." Then he sauntered away.

"Where is he going?" Allison asked.

I didn't answer. My attention was focused on Clarence's hand, in which gleamed the golden pocket watch. He strolled through the parlor door and disappeared.

* * *

The minutes ticked past, and Clarence did not reappear. Either something at dinner had disagreed with his digestion or the man had sneaked off for some other purpose. But what?

When I was a child, Father used to say, "My daughter's biggest vices are curiosity and a fondness for buttered toast." He was right, of course, and that curiosity was now piqued to its fullest.

Clarence was up to something, and I intended to find out what.

I left Allison on the sofa and crossed to the window, where I slid the velvet curtain aside. The parlor lights glared on the window, so although I could make out a few hazy shapes in the garden—the old cherry tree to the left and the bench beside it—I could distinguish nothing more.

I let the curtain fall back. The séance would begin soon, but I still had enough time to peek outside. I casually strolled across the room, darted through the doorway, and softly closed the door behind me.

I crept down the dim corridor that bisected our house and into the high-ceilinged foyer. Voices, deep and low, permeated the front doorway, and I would wager that one of those speakers was Clarence. My heart picked up speed. I gathered my skirts, tiptoed pass the main staircase, and pressed my ear to the front door.

"Two hundred," drawled a male voice with a Cockney accent.

Someone sputtered—Clarence. "That's outrageous."

"Hmmm. Well," said the Cockney man, "if you want his word, you'll 'ave to pay."

"Yes, yes," said Clarence. "And have you had any news on Sure Hands?"

"No, but I brought you this. It's a picture of him—quite old. He's only a boy in it."

"But you're certain the man you saw was he?"

"Aye."

"All right, then." There was a rustling sound, like paper being handed over. "Same time tomorrow night," Clarence added. "I'll be at the Arch Street Theatre."

"Yes, sir."

Suddenly, footsteps drummed toward me.

I reeled back. Clarence hadn't even said good-bye, and now he was coming back inside? The door handle turned, and I scrambled around to flee to the parlor. I only made it four steps.

"Miss Fitt."

I whirled around. "M-Mr. Wilcox. Hello." I bobbed a curtsy.

"What the devil are you doing here?" His eyebrows were angled so far down, they practically reached his nose.

"I was l-looking for you." I gulped. "The entertainment is about to begin." I glanced at his hand. He held a rolled-up newspaper and, at my gaze, he stuffed it into his jacket pocket.

Clarence strode through the foyer and peered down his perfect nose at me. "How long have you been standing here?"

"Only a moment." I fluttered my lashes. *I am as innocent as a baby bird*, I tried to say with my eyes.

"Really." He spoke it as a statement, and frowned. "You know, eavesdropping is most unladylike."

My jaw dropped. "Eavesdropping? I was doing no such thing."

"No?"

"Certainly not, Mr. Wilcox. And false accusations are most un . . . most un-*manly*-like." The retort was a stuttered failure, but I puffed out my chest anyway. "What were you doing outside?"

"Getting fresh air."

My eyebrows shot up as if to say "Really?" He squinted at me, and I glowered back.

At last he cleared his throat and donned a tight smile. "Miss Fitt, while I am delighted to have your company at present, I would ask that you keep our current meeting to your—"

Footsteps clicked on the wood floor, and someone bustled into the foyer. Clarence and I jerked our heads around to find Mary, her eyes practically popping out of her skull. She bowed her head, her chestnut bun bouncing with the force of the movement.

Clarence and I sharing an interlude in the hall? How inappropriate, and how very suggestive of an intimacy that did not exist. I was sure Mary salivated at the thought of telling Mama.

Mary looked back up, her lips twitching with the effort not to smile. "Your mother sent me to find you. The séance is beginning."

"Of course. Thank you." I glanced at Clarence.

He started, and then—as if realizing he was expected to act—he gracefully took my arm and hooked it on his. Together, we marched past the maid and down the corridor toward the drawing room.

"Miss Fitt," he murmured over the whispers of my skirts and the clack of our heels. "I would greatly appreciate it if you would keep our conversation in the hall to yourself."

"Of course," I said primly. "Though I want some explanation of your behavior."

"How about a bouquet of roses instead? Or a new hat?"

"Are you trying to bribe me?"

He chuckled, his cheeks reddening slightly. "I suppose I am. It always works on Allie."

"Well, I am most definitely *not* like Allie."

He smiled. "Yes, I can see that." He whisked me into the drawing room.

Mama, who hovered at the room's center, gave me a look of utter joy. No doubt, like Mary, she assumed my arrival with Clarence suggested a budding intimacy.

My family's drawing room was as lush and bedecked with patterns as our parlor. At the moment, the sofa and armchairs had been pushed to the walls, and an enormous oval table with eleven seats was in the center of the room, ready for the séance. The table's polished surface shone from the three candles at its center, which were meant to attract the spirits. There was also a bowl of bread as an offering.

All the other guests were seated. Mrs. Wilcox beside Mama;

Allison beside her mother; the Virtue Sisters next, followed by their parents; and finally the Moores. That left two seats vacant and adjacent.

Of course Mama had seated Clarence and me beside each other. Fabulous. The man had caught me *eavesdropping*, for heaven's sake, and the last thing I wanted at that precise moment was more time in his company.

Once we were seated, I opened my mouth to beg him for answers, but Mama spoke sooner.

"Let us begin," she commanded.

She gave me a regal eyebrow arch, and I flashed my brightest, sweetest smile. *Clarence adores me.*

She stood in front of her seat, and her hands flourished gracefully as she spoke in a low voice. "Tonight we shall try to commune with the spirit world, so let us use our combined energies to call forth the ghosts of our loved ones."

Since the séances never succeeded in contacting spirits, all of the entertainment was in the presentation. And Mama was an excellent presenter. Shadows billowed from the lone candles and flickered eerily across her face.

"As is customary," she continued in a somber tone, "we must hold hands and chant together in order to summon the spirits' attentions." She lowered herself gracefully into her chair, her head held high. She extended her arms to grasp at her neighbors' hands, and soon each person was locked, gloved hand to gloved hand.

"I would like to begin with my dear husband, Henry," she

proclaimed, "and once we have visited with him, we can move to any other spirits you may wish to see."

A wave of nods moved around the table.

Mama closed her eyes. "Henry, it is your wife, Abigail. I call to you in heaven. Commune with us, Henry, and move among us."

The guests and I repeated her words and waited, our eyes closed.

The scent of the fresh-bread offering wafted into my nose, and my stomach bubbled with hollow hunger. To fit myself in my corset, I'd had to forego most of my supper. Perhaps I could steal a slice while our guests' eyes were closed.

Several silent moments passed, and then Mama led everyone in another chant. I wondered who would be the first to tap the table. On the third round of chanting, I decided it should be me.

I lifted my slippered foot as silently as my skirts would allow, and with a gentle thrust, I kicked the table.

"Henry!" Mama exclaimed, her face a dramatic mask of pleasant surprise. "Is that you?"

I kicked twice—two knocks meant "yes."

Around the table, guests giggled or gasped, though I was certain no one believed it to be real.

"Have you any message for us?" Mama asked.

Someone else knocked once for "no," and everyone twittered.

"Are you certain there is no message?" Mama pressed. Two knocks this time, and I suspected she'd done the tapping herself.

"Do you miss your wife?" Allison cooed. "Or how about—"

A loud whack resounded in the room and cut her off. It was the heavy, hollow bang of a fist on wood. I stopped breathing. It hadn't been the wood of the table—I'd felt the vibration through my whole body. It had rattled my bones and my teeth.

The knock had come from beneath the floor.

CHAPTER THREE

Whack! Another insistent knock on wood, and my whole body flinched. Was this real?

"Henry!" Mama exclaimed, her eyes enormous and filled with shock. "Is that you?"

Whack, whack!

A strangled yell of joy broke through Mama's lips. "My darling!" Her eyes glittered with tears. "My darling, you have never come to my call before."

Whack, whack!

Clarence flinched, squeezing my hand. It startled me, and my breath hissed out. This couldn't possibly be real—Mama must have enhanced the theatrics somehow. But . . . the joy on her face was genuine, as were the shaking floorboards.

The guests' eyes darted around the table, but no one broke the chain.

"Mama," I said. "How do you know it's Father?"

"Because he says so," she replied.

Whack, whack!

My breaths came faster. In the candlelight, I could see steam puff from my mouth. When had the room turned so cold?

"B-but," I quavered, "couldn't the spirit be lying?"

Whack! The whole room shuddered, and the lamps rattled.

"Why would he do that?" Mama's voice was high and quick with elation. There was something else in her tone too. Fear. But was it fear that it wasn't Father? Or fear that she might lose her only chance of meeting him again? Either way, all her concern for presentation or entertainment had vanished. "Of *course* it is your father."

Whack, whack!

"Great heavens, Henry, I've missed you." Her smile gleamed in the candles' glow. "Who would like to invite Henry into our realm?"

No one answered. All of the guests sat stiff and wide-eyed.

"Eleanor, why don't you invite your father in?"

"No, Mama." I freed my hand from Clarence's grasp. Could the spirit still enter if our hands were not connected? Did a spirit's entrance actually hinge on invitation? The rules of the séance were probably all dramatic nothing, but either way, I didn't think the spirit had entered the room yet. Maybe there was still a chance to send it away.

I gulped. "You must listen to me, Mama. Make sure it's Father."

Whack, whack, whack!

Mama blinked at me, her eyes like empty holes. I knew the hollow desperation she felt. What if it *was* Father? What if this was our only chance to see him, to talk with him?

But this was not Father. He was love and warmth; he would never turn the room so cold.

I pushed to my feet. "Mama, please, this isn't Father. We must not let it enter!"

"It *is* Henry," she shouted over me.

"Make sure!" I leaned over the table, my hands reaching for her. "Ask him a question."

Clarence sprang up, and his chair toppled behind him. "Mrs. Fitt, you must listen to your daughter."

"No!" Mama rose and lifted her head high. "I know when my husband is near. I was his wife for fifteen years, and this is my house and my séance. I will invite him in if I wish."

Whack, whack!

Around the table, the other guests watched us, but frightened, amused, or entertained, I didn't know.

"Beloved Henry," Mama called, "know that you are welcome in this house."

"Help me!" I shrieked at the guests. "Stop her!"

"You are welcome to our bread," Mama continued.

"Mrs. Fitt!" Clarence yelled.

Mama clasped her hands to her chest. "You are welcome to move among us."

An icy wind blasted through the room, and with it came the smell of dark, moist, ancient soil. Grave dirt.

The air and the smell cloyed at my nose and slid into my throat. I wanted to gag, but I couldn't breathe. Time had frozen, and it was as if I viewed the room from some distant place. Even the flames of the candles stood still. Then my breath returned with such force that I crumpled back onto my seat. Cries and whimpers burst out around the table.

The spirit had joined us.

Breaking the chain of clasped hands had done nothing, and this spirit felt strong—evil.

I lunged forward and grabbed a candle. What had Mama done? I should have stopped her.

I lifted the flame high and scanned the room.

"You're not welcome here. Go back!" I waved the flame this way and that in search of the spirit's location. "Go back!"

And then I saw it, crouched beside the door, an unnatural clot of black in the darkness—shapeless, sentient, and waiting.

Everyone was paralyzed. My own mind screamed, though no sound escaped. All I could do was stare.

Until it moved. The darkness elongated into the rough shape of man, but thinner and taller, with arms that stretched to the floor. I forced my body to move, my nerves refueled by terror.

I brandished the candle toward the evil, and the flame almost sputtered out.

"Leave," I rasped. "You're not welcome here."

The shape undulated forward—one moment like a man, the next like a gaping shadow.

And it was moving toward me.

A woman screamed. And then another and another until the whole room was a chorus of fear. People began to wiggle and tumble, and chairs groaned with the movement.

"My love!" Mama screeched. "Henry, oh Henry!" She moved forward, but Clarence reached over and seized her by the arm.

"No!" He held her back, half his body sprawled across the table.

I felt a tingle in my ears, through my temples, and down my neck. A shivering, powerful pulse. Was the spirit doing this to me? I grabbed at my ear with my free hand, but the feeling only intensified.

"You must leave!" I shoved the candle forward. The spirit paused.

The shrieks of terror drowned me out, but I shouted again— "Go back!"—and stepped toward the spirit. My strength grew with each inch I gained.

I reached the end of the table. The terrible mass was only a few feet away, a shadow of death hanging motionless. For a moment I thought I was victorious. But my relief drained right back out as the spirit rushed at me in a furious streak of black, and the cold consumed me. It was the harshest chill I'd ever felt, a deeper ache than I thought possible. My mind, my bones, my soul were devoured by this cold.

Then, faster than my mind could process, it was gone.

By the time the room was illuminated again, the panic was out of control. Crying, hysterics, mumbling, and shock had taken the guests. My own hands trembled, and I couldn't keep still. I used my anxious energy to soothe the situation.

"It was all a show!" I yelled. "Just theatrics!"

Some of the guests actually accepted my claims with surprising ease—despite the fact that Mama was collapsed in a dead faint.

She sat limp in her seat, draped across the table with her eyes closed. Though the spirit had scared her, I thought the realization that she wouldn't see Father was what had snapped her nerves.

I was just grateful Clarence had kept her from injury when she toppled down.

For the next few minutes Mary, Jeremy, and I strained to get everyone else out as quickly as possible. Fortunately, they needed no urging.

Once the house was empty and I had gotten my mother's unconscious form in bed, I collapsed in my own and cried.

I cried until my abdomen hurt and my nose was clogged. Until I had cried enough to realize tears weren't making me feel better.

Where was Elijah? Why were the Dead rising in Philadelphia?

34

Why was this happening to *me*? I just wanted my brother home. I wanted things to be exactly as they were three years ago, when Elijah would teach me his lessons from school or read Shakespeare aloud while we sat in our cherry tree. We'd dreamed of seeing exotic places—such as Venice, Verona, or Illyria—and when we dutifully visited our father's grave, we would wander the nearby woods and pretend we were in the Forest of Arden.

I shuffled to my wardrobe and found the walking dress I'd worn that morning. From its pocket, I pulled out the wrinkled *Philadelphia Bulletin* article.

Joseph Boyer of the Spirit-Hunters stated in an interview:
"The Laurel Hill corpses are under the necromancer's
control and do his bidding, but as of yet, we do not know
the necromancer's identity or aim."

The Spirit-Hunters arrived a week ago to protect the
thousands of Centennial Exhibition visitors from the Dead.
They have installed alarms throughout the Exhibition
buildings in case more corpses appear on the grounds. . . .

The Spirit-Hunters. Hired to protect. That was my answer! I scanned ahead. They were a three-man team led by Joseph

Boyer, and their office was in Machinery Hall at the International Centennial Exhibition.

"Spirit-Hunters," I whispered. Chills trickled down my back. These people would help me find Elijah. It was their job to help me, and I felt instantly better armed with this knowledge.

I rubbed at my salty cheeks, and my sense of helplessness subsided. I wasn't lost; I wasn't alone; there were people I could turn to. People who could help me with my brother and with the spirit my mother had invited into this world.

I lugged myself to bed and slid the paper beneath my pillow. I couldn't leave the house tonight, but tomorrow . . . tomorrow, I would see just how good these Spirit-Hunters really were.

CHAPTER FOUR

Saturday morning arrived, and when the sun hit my eyes, yesterday's horrors flooded my brain. The train station, the letter, the séance—they all crashed over me.

I hadn't forgotten my decision to see the Spirit-Hunters, but I also hadn't figured out a way to do it. It was one thing to run household errands alone, but to attend the crowded Exhibition by myself would raise questions.

As Mary helped me dress, I considered whether sneaking away was worth Mama's inevitable suspicion.

Mary gripped my corset laces. "Inhale."

I sucked in, and the corset's whalebones cinched in. "Too tight!"

"Too fat is more like it." She gave one final tug before deftly

37

knotting the laces. Then she helped me layer on the petticoats, bustle, skirts, and polonaise of the same gray gown I'd worn yesterday. It was a walking gown, so the train was shorter and allowed easier navigation of the Philadelphia sidewalks. Plus, the smoky color had the advantage of not showing dust.

"Where is it you're goin'?" Mary asked, her mouth pruned skeptically. "You did the shopping yesterday, and the bank is closed today." As my mother's devoted servant, Mary kept no secrets from Mama—or rather, she only kept secrets when the payment was good.

I ignored her probing and focused on pinning my gray, feathered hat at the perfect jaunty angle. As I was pushing in the last pin, a loud knock startled us.

Mary and I exchanged wide-eyed glances before racing from the room. We reached the foyer just as Jeremy opened the door to find Allison Wilcox, flushed and beautiful in a sky blue walking gown. My eyebrows rose in a combination of awe and envy as she swept past Jeremy into the foyer.

"What brings you here so early?" I asked. A morning call would ruin my trip to the Spirit-Hunters—what if Mama woke up before Allison left?

"After last night, Clarence, Mother, and I were dreadfully worried." She clapped her hands and leaned close. "But it was all a grand hoax?"

I tried to murmur an agreement, but all that came out was a strange gurgling sound. If only it *had* been a hoax.

Allison's eyebrows shot up. "I knew it! Now come with me

to the Continental. I'm just *dying* to have tea and show off my new gown."

I blinked rapidly, at a complete loss for words. She wanted to spend time with me? And at the Continental Hotel no less?

Allison, sensing I needed an extra nudge, added, "I heard the Brazilian emperor is staying there! What if we caught a glimpse? Patience and Mercy would just *die* with envy!"

I forced a chuckle. Emperors? Overpriced tea? This was definitely not how I wanted to spend my morning—to say nothing of my outfit, which was absolutely unfit for luxurious society.

"Um, wh-who would chaperone?" I asked.

She gave a tinkling laugh and shook her head. "We don't need a chaperone, Eleanor! It's not as if we're going to the theater or a party. I go to tea without Mother all the time." She held out her arm and crooked it, waiting for me to slip my own arm through. "Now, are you coming or not?"

No chaperone? But that meant . . . My breath caught in my throat. That meant I had an *escape*! Ugly dress or not, this was a gaping wide opportunity for an unrestrained trip to the Spirit-Hunters!

My lips twitched with excitement, and before Mary could utter a protest, I snatched my parasol from beside the door and scooted outside with Allison.

We scurried to her family's carriage—a well-made, black coach that could easily fit eight people.

Allison slid across the purple satin cushions to a window, tied back the lilac curtains, and then gestured for me to do the same. As I fumbled with ribbons, the horses clattered to a start.

I leaned close to the carriage window and watched the mansions, elaborate fences, and well-tended yards roll past. Usually I navigated the hour-long trek into the city on foot or sat crammed on a horse-drawn streetcar. To ride without dust, mud, or horse manure flying into my face—no wonder Allison could wear such a brilliant blue dress!

I snuck a glance at her beautiful gown and then stared mournfully at my own. My petticoat hems were frayed from all the scrubbing I'd put them through, and they'd long since turned from white to mottled brown. Plus, there was a rather obvious rip from that dratted old man's boot at the depot.

Allison poked me with her parasol. "So how'd you do it?"

"Do what?" I shifted my body to face her.

"The séance, of course! How'd you get the floor to shake and the air to freeze?"

I lifted one shoulder and said casually, "It was all real, of course."

"Pshaw! I don't believe that." She wagged her finger at me. "Your mother used to throw all sorts of séances—*my* mother told me so—but they were never so wild as that."

I frowned. How did Mrs. Wilcox know about Mama's séances? I thought we'd only known the Wilcox family a short while. Strange . . .

The carriage pulled onto the busy Chestnut Street. Hackneys and wagons rattled by, and as we crossed the bridge with the Schuylkill River glittering below, the first buildings of downtown Philadelphia came into view. Shop after shop—all with enormous signs shouting their wares: BOOTS & SHOES, STRAW GOODS, GLASS & SILVERWARE—were interspersed with saloons, banks, restaurants, and offices.

Allison prodded me with her parasol again. "Clarence wants to know if you're available tomorrow."

"Huh?" I grunted.

"He wants to take you for a drive tomorrow afternoon, if you're free."

A strange sense of unreality washed over me, and I eyed her with disbelief. No one had ever invited me for a drive before, so why the dickens would Clarence Wilcox want to?

I voiced my question in slightly politer terms.

"He said he likes your company."

I sputtered a laugh. There was *no way* Clarence had enjoyed my company. Sakes alive, he'd caught me eavesdropping!

Allison scowled. "Why're you laughing? What's wrong with—"

"It's not that," I interrupted. "I'm just surprised is all . . . but also delighted." I grinned.

Handsome Clarence asking me for a drive . . . It was rather surprising, yet my stomach fluttered at the prospect. *And wait until Mama hears this news!*

"So I'll tell him you've accepted?" Allison asked.

"Yes, yes. Tell him to come at half past three."

She squealed and bounced across the carriage to plop down beside me. "I wish young men would call on *me*! Clarence has some rather handsome chums, you know, but he says I'm not allowed to flirt with any of them. Of course, I haven't seen them much lately. . . ." Her words faded, and she gnawed her bottom lip.

"Is everything all right?"

She sighed dramatically. "Oh yes, it's merely curious. They used to come every day because of the election, but I haven't seen any of them in more than a week." She paused and looked out the window. "Oh look!" Her face lit up and she pointed. "Just look at those crowds."

I followed her gaze and saw the Continental Hotel towering over the wide, open intersection of Chestnut and Ninth Streets. The side that faced us was elegant, pale sandstone; and Allison was right: people were everywhere—standing on the sidewalks, meandering around the front columns, and gawking at the top floor.

"They all want to see the emperor too." Allison flashed her eyebrows at me. "But they can't get into the tearoom, and I can. It's so wonderful to be rich, isn't it?"

Allison and I entered the hotel's lobby. Travelers marched past us, their poor footmen lumbering behind with trunks and bags. My heels clicked on the marble floor, and I couldn't keep the smile off my face. The last time I'd been here, Father had been alive and Elijah was still a boy. We were on our way to the library, and Father had stopped by for a quick business meeting. Elijah and I had stared, mouths agape, at the colorful, ornate frescoes on the ceiling, the dangling chandeliers, and the white, ionic columns. Then as soon as Father had left us (with orders to sit quietly while he ran up to a different floor), we'd leaped into action, pretending we were a prince and princess trapped in an enchanted palace.

My smile fell. Elijah was in trouble, and yet where was I? Here. Not out searching for the Spirit-Hunters, and certainly not helping my brother. I had to get away from Allison as soon as possible, but without offending her in the process.

"Oh, don't look so wretched," Allison whined. She grabbed my arm and waved to a glass-windowed storefront. "Let's shop while we wait."

Allison had refused to take the stairs, and that meant waiting for the elevator to deposit its passengers above. So I followed her into Charles Oakford & Sons.

The Continental Hotel's ground floor was filled with expensive shops to entice Philadelphia's wealthiest and most powerful visitors. This particular store held some of the most dazzling products I'd ever seen. Long tables were covered in delicate straw bonnets, feminine top hats, dramatic wide brims—any hat a girl could ever want was for sale in this store.

For sale, and outrageously expensive.

A gray-haired clerk with muttonchops moved to help us, but Allison bypassed him without so much as a glance. Her eyes were locked on a blue silk bonnet that matched her dress.

"This is just *divine*." She swooped the hat off its display. "Let's each buy a new hat! Then we can wear them to tea and

43

stun all the men with our beauty."

I blanched. Buy a *hat*? Just like that with no thought to the cost? "But I already have one." I waved vaguely at my head. "And I can't buy things without my mother's permission."

Her excited expression froze. "What?"

"I-I'm not allowed to buy anything new without my mother to approve it." It wasn't true—not since I'd taken over our family's finances. All the same, it was the best excuse I could conjure.

Her nose wrinkled. "That's silly. I'm going to look stunning in something new, and you'll just look drab in that old thing."

Heat crept into my cheeks. "Well, if I'm drab, then that means you'll look all the more beautiful."

Her eyes popped wide, and a smile flashed on her lips. "True! I hadn't thought of it like—oh look! The vertical train is here!" She tossed the blue hat onto the nearest table. I barely had time to shoot the clerk an apologetic grin before she whisked me out of the store.

Several breathless moments later, I was wedged in the tiny, gilded compartment beside Allison and a set of somber couples. A porter stepped inside and slid a metal grate over the entrance.

"Second floor," Allison chirped. With a shudder, the cubicle began to rise.

I fidgeted with the buttons on my gloves. I'd never been on an elevator—or vertical train, as some people still called it. But when, after several seconds, nothing happened but slow ascension, I heaved a sigh. Outside the grate, I could see the next floor coming nearer and nearer until the great contraption finally stopped. The porter opened the grate.

Allison crooked her arm in mine and guided me down a narrow hall with maroon rugs and shiny mirrors. Before us was an open door from which sunlight shone and voices murmured over the tinkle of silverware.

The Continental Hotel's famous tearoom.

With each step my insides roiled. Mama may have held a successful séance last night and the Wilcoxes may have befriended us, but I still wasn't overly comfortable in high society. It was one thing to learn the rules of the well-bred, but quite another to actually *use* them. All the judging and gossip—I simply wasn't very good at it.

We passed through the door and into a crowded, pastel room lined with floor-to-ceiling windows. The round tables were covered with lacy tablecloths, and almost all of them were full.

A waiter dressed in a prim black suit guided us to a table beside a window, spouted out a long list of items, and then waited for our orders.

My heart plummeted to my stomach. He hadn't listed any prices!

"A pot of tea," Allison said. "The fresh fruit platter, a sampling of your pastries, and some of that French bread, whatever it's called." She glanced at me. "Anything else?"

I shook my head frantically. All the blood had fled my

face. What the blazes did etiquette demand when faced with no money?

Allison nodded at the waiter, and he glided off. Then she picked up her earlier conversation, completely unaware of my inner panic.

I slid my hands into my pockets and tried to feel out how many coins I had. Three nickels, four dimes, and a quarter. There was no way it was going to be enough, and this was not the sort of place that would let me pay on *credit*.

I inhaled deeply, ready to come clean about my "momentary absence of funds," when Allison's constant stream of words suddenly broke off.

Her eyes narrowed to vicious slits; her gaze was behind me. "Those lying ninnies," she said through clenched teeth.

I risked a glance back. It was the Virtue Sisters with two mustached young men.

"They told me they were busy today," Allison continued. "Why would they say that?"

The sisters noticed us, and though their faces momentarily hardened, they quickly brandished fake smiles and strode toward us.

I twisted back to Allison. "What did they tell you?"

"That they were too busy tending to their mother after last night's horrors to join us for tea." She gritted her teeth and then flourished her own false grin.

And in an instant I understood Elijah's favorite line from *Macbeth*: "There's daggers in men's smiles."

When the sisters and their two escorts reached our table, Mercy bobbed a curtsy. "What a coincidence seeing you two here!"

"Quite!" chimed Patience with a curtsy of her own. She waved to the mustached boys. "These are the McClures. This is Tom and this is Luis."

I nodded politely before noticing they were twins—matching dark red hair, olive skin, and perfectly tailored suits. Even their bushy mustaches were identical!

"Imagine seeing you," Allison said icily. "I thought you were busy."

"Oh yes!" Mercy twittered, and avoided the comment. "That séance was so *amazing*, Eleanor! Our mother spent the whole night with a case of the vapors!"

"Where's Mr. Wilcox?" Patience asked Allison with an arched eyebrow.

Allison's nostrils flared. "Clarence is at home with our mother. She's still distraught."

"And your brother?" asked one of the McClure twins, his gaze focused on me. "Is Elijah still detained?"

My lungs grew too large for my chest, and for a moment I had no response. He had asked the very question I still needed to answer myself.

I tugged at my earrings. "He's not back yet. From New York, I mean." I laughed shrilly. "D-do you know Elijah?"

"Oh yes," said the other twin. "We were all at Germantown Academy together."

My eyebrows drew together, and my lips flicked down. Elijah had been miserable at Germantown Academy. He'd been tormented every day by a quartet of devils led by one boy: Junior. Were these boys a part of that bullying gang?

"He was a year ahead of us," the twin added. He smiled kindly, and my frown vanished. Elijah's tormentors had been older boys—not younger.

And honestly, even if I *did* meet Junior one day, what would I do? What *could* I do? Nothing more than what Allison was doing right now: fume silently with a veneer of cold politeness.

"We ought to all sit together," Tom said. His gaze was unabashedly focused on Allison.

Peeps of disagreement broke from the Virtue Sisters' lips. They'd lost the attention of their gentlemen. No doubt this was the precise reason they'd avoided Allison's company in the first place.

"Our treat," Luis added.

"Yes!" I blurted. "Join us!" The Virtue Sisters shot me fierce glares, but I stoutly ignored them and waved the waiter over. If these mustached McClures were so intent on impressing Allison with a show of generosity, I had *no* problem with that!

Soon enough, another table had been shoved next to ours, and the twins had dropped down beside Allison. I was left to chat with Patience and Mercy; and despite the sisters' disgruntled disappointment and my pressing errand, I found myself enjoying them. Maybe it was simply because Mama wasn't there and I could speak uncensored, or maybe it was because, when they smiled, the Virtue Sisters were actually rather fun.

Plus, Mercy ate so many croissants, I didn't feel guilty indulging in a few extras myself.

When the church bells rang noon in a thunderous clamor, I knew it was time to go. I needed to find the Spirit-Hunters and face this situation with the Dead and Elijah's absence.

I convinced Allison I could make it home alone, thanked the McClure twins profusely, grinned broadly at Patience and Mercy, and bid the entire group a good afternoon.

Once I reached the hotel's lobby, I bought a streetcar ticket at the front desk before scampering into the hot sun and boarding the first horse-drawn streetcar that rattled down Chestnut Street.

Free brunch, no chaperone, and a few new friends. Life was the shiniest it had been in years. All that remained to make it perfect was bringing Elijah home.

CHAPTER FIVE

Despite the morbid motivation for going to the Centennial Exhibition, it felt wonderful to be alone—to finally do what I could for Elijah.

When the streetcar reached Lancaster Avenue and the towers of the Exhibition hit my eyes, I hopped off the car. My home was within walking distance, and since my remaining coins would be spent on the Exhibition entrance fee, I would have little choice but to use my feet.

The newspaper had said the Spirit-Hunters were to be found in Machinery Hall at the Exhibition. Like the first world's fair in London, our International Centennial Exhibition was meant to unite the world in a display of technology, culture, and progress.

Iron spires and colorful flags rose up along the Schuylkill

for ten blocks, making the Exhibition look just like a fairy tale. Enormous buildings housed the world's wonders, and not even a whole slack-jawed, wide-eyed week of exploring the gardens and halls would be enough time to see everything.

The sun scorched down and the wind whipped my parasol as I joined the throngs that poured through the turnstiles, paid my fifty cents, and strode into the enormous entrance plaza. It was like a field of daisies with all the parasols twirling and bobbing in the breeze. Bartholdi's bronze Fountain of Light and Water rose from the plaza's center and towered over the thousands of visitors. I paused before it to let the mist spray over me.

I had already seen the Exhibition. I had gasped and twittered with all the other visitors, but even the greatest feats of man lose their luster when one's head is filled with storm clouds.

Feeling cooler, I lowered my parasol and turned. Before me was the most popular building at the Exhibition: Machinery Hall, a long, narrow structure made entirely of wood and glass, and I had to crane my neck to see the top.

I entered the building to find sun pouring in through windows that spanned the walls. Sharp beams of light flew from the machine surfaces packed inside.

Engines, furnaces, sewing machines, locomotives—every example of man's newest creations hummed with life. The hall resounded with the whirs and clicks of a mechanical symphony. Singing with it was the chorus of people's laughter and chatter, and above it all was the percussive boom of a massive steam engine.

It was the Corliss engine, sitting in the center of Machinery Hall and soaring more than forty feet up into the rafters. Two monstrous cylinders spun a thirty-foot wheel, and the energy it generated was enough to power almost every machine in the building.

Yet among all the vibrancy, the alarms hung solemnly on the walls at regular intervals. Fire alarms and the new, but necessary, Dead alarms. I shivered as the horrible clang I'd heard in the train depot played in my mind.

I pulled the newspaper article from my pocket, careful to keep the print off my gloves—dirty gloves would incite Mama's ire—and verified the way to the Spirit-Hunters' office. It should be near the east entrance through which I'd just passed.

I glanced to a narrow aisle between the wall and a locomotive exhibit. It was also the path to the men's toilets. Scarcely the sort of place a lady should see. For that matter, scarcely the sort of place I *wanted* to see. Hesitantly, I continued on, keeping my gloved hand to my nose. The stink of urine was strong in the morning heat, and I fumbled for my handkerchief.

I slunk past the water closet door, cheeks aflame and eyes averted, until I saw a narrow door with a small handwritten note fixed to it.

Please knock. Experiments running.

I took one last stifled gulp, returned my handkerchief to my pocket, and gritted my teeth with determination.

I knocked. As the moments ticked by and no one answered the door, my determination faded and frustration wormed in.

I pressed at the handle to check if the door was locked. It flew open and promptly hit something—presumably glass, judging by its spectacular crash.

This was followed by a furious bellowing, sounding much like I imagined an enraged bull would.

Steeling myself, I stepped inside and peered around the door.

"Didn't you see the sign?" shouted a tall, lanky man with tousled, corn-blond hair. He stood beside a table, his shirtsleeves rolled up and the top buttons of his shirt undone. All his exposed skin sent an embarrassed warmth through my face.

And as if he wasn't already frightening enough, he also wore the strangest set of goggles I'd ever seen. They covered half his face and were made of shiny brass with thick, clear lenses that made his eyes look like grass-green croquet balls.

And he was looking at me as if he expected an answer.

"P-pardon me?" I asked.

"Didn't you see the sign?" he snapped.

I glanced behind. "Well, yes."

"So?" He rolled his hands in a quick, wheel-like movement as if to say "Now what?"

"I knocked," I said sheepishly, "but no one answered."

"Because I'm busy." He stomped toward me, and I shrank back, ready to retreat through the open door should his expression turn any more menacing.

"S-sorry," I stammered.

"You should be," he said. "You've contaminated my grave dirt—look!" He thrust a finger toward the floor. I flicked my eyes down. Soil and glass covered the ground.

I opened my mouth to apologize but clamped it back shut at the sight of his blinking, goggled eyes and sharp frown.

"See that?" he barked. "D'you know how hard it is to get dirt from Laurel Hill? I ought to make you get more! Make *you* face the Dead and . . ."

I stopped listening. His hands flailed up, down, and side to side as he declared me reckless, thoughtless, and I even think I heard rude mentioned.

I took his foulmouthed moment to examine the room, which was no bigger than my bedroom, all the edges crammed with books, flasks, and trunks. There was just enough space at the center for several people to move about (albeit closely). Light shone from a single, tall window at the back. Behind the goggled young man, a table stood covered with wrenches, screws, wires, and other equipment one might find in an inventor's lair.

My breath caught as my eyes rested on a telegraph like the telegraphs at the fire stations—telegraphs that spring to life when a fire alarm sounds. This one must be connected to the Dead alarms.

"And," the young man said, interrupting my thoughts with a forceful fist in the air, "I needed it to calibrate my goggles!" His chest heaved as if he'd just fought a boxing match, and I decided silence remained my best response. After several empty seconds, his hand dropped and he cleared his throat. He slid off

55

the goggles' strap and gently eased the lenses from his face.

I blinked in surprise. The lenses were no longer clear but a murky brown. How had the glass changed color? My surprise grew when I noticed that, with his face fully exposed, the blond man was quite young—perhaps only a few years older than me. He had red dents on his face from the goggles, and his formerly bulbous eyes were now normal and entirely too predatory.

He folded his arms over his chest. "You've ruined my experiment."

I took a weary breath, lifted my hands, and purred, "I'm truly sorry, sir."

He wrinkled his nose. "Why are you talkin' like that?"

"Like what?"

"Like you're a kitten."

"I thought it might calm you."

"I don't need calming," he snapped. "If you'll just leave, that'll take care of everything." He pointed to the door. "There's the exit."

I blinked. Part of me wanted to flee his short temper and take refuge in well-bred manners. But another part of me wanted to let my indignation loose. I hadn't come all this way to let some green-eyed, scruffy-faced boy stand in my way.

Indignation won. "Now see here, I've come to see the Spirit-Hunters." I jabbed my parasol to emphasize each word. "I won't leave until I speak with them."

"What would a lady"—he drew out the word like "laaaaydee" and waved in my direction—"possibly need the Spirit-Hunters for?"

"That is none of your business." I pushed my shoulders back. "I will speak with Mr. Boyer and Mr. Boyer only."

"Is that so?" He rocked his weight onto his heels and examined me from head to toe. My face burned under the scrutiny.

Then he stepped close to me. I had to roll my head back to see his face—he was at least half a foot taller—as he gazed down with barely concealed distaste.

"I have grave dirt to sweep," he said, "so if you'll be stayin' around for Mr. Boyer, could you at least stand somewhere else?" He gripped me by both arms and pushed me backward out the door. I was so shocked to be touched I couldn't even protest. All I could do was skitter back where he directed. Even if I'd wanted to stop, my eyes were locked on the very near and very disturbing open collar and exposed throat.

With his hands still planted on my arms and with his lips curved in a satisfied grin, he drawled, "I'm Daniel Sheridan, by the way." He said it so casually, as if all introductions were preceded by manhandling. "Pleasure to meet you, Miss . . ."

I twisted free. The rascal. The scalawag. I gave him my haughtiest dragon stare. "I am Miss Eleanor Fitt of the Philadelphia Fitts."

He flashed his eyebrows and doffed an imaginary hat. "Why then, you're practically royalty." He whirled around and strode back into the lab. The door slammed shut behind him.

I stood there, my shoulders and neck locked with fiery rage.

I felt as if flames might spew from my fingertips and eyeballs.

Royalty? Humbug! I should have quipped, "And that makes you my subject" or "It's Queen Eleanor to you" or any number of responses more glib than my furious silence.

"Oh dear," said a rich, baritone voice behind me. "I told him to keep his temper in check."

I spun around and found my face two feet from the buttons and collar of a black frock coat. I angled my head slowly up and met the speaker's honey-brown eyes. He was the most elegant young gentleman I'd ever seen. His suit was impeccably tailored, a slick top hat sat upon his head, and his dark skin seemed to glow from within.

"Misyeu Joseph-Alexandre Boyer," he said with a bow. "At your service."

I opened and closed my mouth. My composure was thrown at how unlike Daniel this man was.

Joseph opened his hands in a graceful apology. "Please forgive Mr. Sheridan. I am afraid he works better with machines than with people." He spoke with such poise and his movements were so refined that all I could do was gawk. He cleared his throat and looked decidedly uncomfortable.

"Oh yes," I mumbled. "I suppose I shall forgive him."

"*Mèrsi*."

"You're French?" As soon as I asked, I knew my guess was wrong.

"Creole," he corrected. "There is a difference in how we speak and spell our words."

58

My eyebrows jumped. "Creole? Truly? I've never met a Creole before." I extended my hand. "I'm Eleanor Fitt."

Joseph stiffened, his eyes fixed on my gloved hand, and I realized—too late—that I'd put him in an uncomfortable position. A gentleman simply was *not* supposed to shake the hand of an unmarried woman without a proper, third-party introduction. I was so used to chaperoned meetings that I had acted on foolish reflex.

Then his features relaxed, and a smile passed over his lips. He shook my hand firmly before guiding me back into the cramped lab.

"Come in, come in, *Mamẓèi*." Joseph removed a stool from under the table and gestured for me to sit. "Please excuse the mess. As you know, we are busy people."

I glanced uneasily at Daniel's back. He was bent over the table and occupied with something I couldn't see. I took the offered stool.

"How'd the meeting go?" Daniel asked without turning around.

"Mr. Peger was there." Joseph's voice was a soft growl.

Daniel spat, and the spittle landed beside my feet. Droplets splattered on the hem of my gown, and I recoiled. Had the man never heard of a spittoon?

Joseph chuckled, apparently in full agreement with Daniel's reaction. "Yes, and I will give you three guesses as to what was decided." Joseph placed his hat on top of the alarm's telegraph.

Daniel grunted, hammering at some unseen metal. "My three guesses are no, no, and no."

"Exactly." Joseph squinted at the floor. "You do realize there is soil everywhere?"

Daniel barked a laugh and whirled around to look smugly at me. My whole body ignited with embarrassment. Daniel flicked his gaze to Joseph. "I'm well aware of the soil, but back to the meetin'. What did they give as a reason this time?"

"The usual. They listened with much more attention to Mr. Peger, and so they do not believe we need more reinforcements. They also insist no men can be spared."

"They're gonna regret that," Daniel muttered. "When they see what's in the cemetery, they're gonna wish they'd listened to you."

"Yes, but I think that is enough talk about that." Joseph glanced at me slantwise, and I got the impression that whatever topic they were discussing it was not for my ears. He turned toward me. "Tell me, Miss Fitt, what brings you here?"

"Oh." I swallowed and sat up straight. "It's two things, actually. One . . . well, one has to do with the walking Dead, and the other is about a spirit."

Joseph raised an eyebrow and gestured for me to continue, so I described everything that had happened. I rambled, back-tracked, and fought off tears, but soon information about the corpse, the letter, the séance, and the spirit had all rushed from me. Throughout the speech, Daniel and Joseph shot concerned glances back and forth.

When I had finished, Daniel's lips compressed with distaste. "You held a séance?"

I nodded hesitantly. "Yes. Why do you ask?"

Daniel ignored me and turned to Joseph. "I thought you told the reporters to print warnings against séances."

"I did, but it would seem they chose not to listen." Joseph rubbed his hand over his head and leaned against the work-table. "Miss Fitt, if what you say is true, then I understand your worry."

My mouth fell open. "If what I say is true? What do you mean?"

"People take advantage of us," Daniel said. "More than a few have come here with false or overblown tales. But we're not here to take on their family's two hundred-year-old haunting— we're here to stop a necromancer."

"But I don't have a haunting! I have a missing brother and—"

"And *we* don't have time." Daniel's lips curled up, challenging me to argue.

Joseph intervened. "Miss Fitt, what Daniel says is true. We are extremely busy. This necromancer first raised the Dead in New York, and the police called us in several weeks ago. Several opium addicts were found, well . . . let us just say they were in a rather gruesome state."

"There's no need to censor yourself." I sat up straighter. "I can handle the details. I grew up with stories of the Dead like everyone else."

Daniel choked out a laugh. "Go on then, Joseph. You heard

the lady. Might as well tell her the men were decapitated sacrifices."

Joseph sighed. "Daniel, you have the manners and tact of a gorilla."

"Ha." Daniel shot me a wide grin. I spun my gaze to my shoes. *The ruffian.*

"Continue, please," I mumbled.

"Well, the manner of their deaths"—Joseph flourished a gloved hand toward his head—"suggested the men were killed as a sacrifice for power. The fact that the men were also found as reanimated corpses proved it was the work of a necromancer. But then as suddenly as the bodies had begun appearing, they stopped.

"Or so we thought. We soon heard about a Philadelphia man found dead but walking, and judging by the similarity in . . . well, the similarity in sacrificial methods, we knew our necromancer had moved. Here."

Daniel picked up the story, "People can handle one or two walking Dead—just burn 'em or blast 'em to smithereens—but a whole cemetery's worth? And a necromancer decapitating the living? Not too many chaps are comfortable dealing with *that*.

"So we offered our services to the Exhibition board. Most folks with Joseph's skills"—he cocked his head toward the Creole—"don't leave New Orleans."

"No," Joseph said, "they do not." For a moment his face sagged, but then the expression passed and he gave me a curt nod. "Thus far the Dead have only harassed the Exhibition, and fortunately, these corpses have only been moderately dangerous. The rest of Philadelphia is untouched."

"But it won't stay that way." Daniel slumped against the table, shoving his hands in his pockets.

"No." Joseph's lips thinned. "And though the board has hired us, it is a constant battle to prove the investment is worthwhile. The members cannot see the danger of the situation, and there are politics involved. We have only been hired for show—to soothe visitors' nerves.

"Nonetheless, we have a job to do. We must first protect the Exhibition, and in our available time, we must train the Exhibition patrolmen to fight the Dead. Fire will not do in a place that ignites easily." He waved his hands toward the Main Building, which could be seen through the window. "But most important of all, we must stop this necromancer.

"And so, Miss Fitt, if the corpses and the spirit are not directly threatening you, then I see no reason we should strain ourselves further."

"No threat!" I jumped to my feet. "What of my brother? They have him!"

Daniel scoffed. "There's no proof of that."

"What about the spirit? It was *evil*." My voice came out loud and filled all the space in the tiny lab. "I know it—it touched me!"

"Miss Fitt." Joseph stood stiff and straight, his jaw clenched. "There are many spirits free in Philadelphia. Hauntings happen all the time, and most are harmless. My job is here, where the

63

most danger exists for the most people."

"Besides," Daniel inserted, his lips pressed into a grim line, "if the Dead *do* have your brother, he's probably dead himself."

My stomach flipped. It punched the breath from my lungs. I toppled forward, grasping for the table. Both men jolted. Joseph, who was nearer, caught me and slid a supportive arm under my elbow. He eased me back onto my stool.

"Just because a corpse delivered your brother's letter," he murmured gently, "does not mean the Dead have him."

I nodded, unable to speak. Daniel's words repeated over and over in my head. *Probably dead himself. Elijah. Dead.* No—I couldn't believe it. It was too soon to give up.

Joseph must have understood my thoughts. "Ignore Daniel. Please, *Mamzèi*. Perhaps if you bring us your brother's letter tomorrow, I will see what I—"

A rapid clanging erupted outside the lab and cut him off. The telegraph leaped into action.

It was the Dead alarm.

CHAPTER SIX

Daniel reacted instantly to the peal of the alarm.
He dropped to the floor and towed a machine from beneath
the table. It looked like a spinning wheel attached to a wooden
platform, and it was as tall as my knees. Rather than wooden wheels
for making thread, though, this machine had two glass wheels for
making . . . I hadn't the faintest idea. The glass wheels were connected by gears and a handle, and at both ends of the platform,
metal spindles shot up over the glass.

Joseph flung off his coat and gloves and then turned a hardened face to me. "Stay here." He knelt at one end, and Daniel
crouched at the other. They lifted the apparatus and rushed awkwardly from the room. The door slammed shut behind them.

I scrambled up and clutched my parasol to me like a weapon.

The clanging of the alarm masked all other sounds. I peered through the lab window to find people fleeing the building.

I stepped to the door and pressed my ear to the wood, straining to detect something—*anything*—through the alarm. I felt the hum of machinery more than I heard it. No other sounds came through.

How long would the Spirit-Hunters need? Should I help? And what was that machine they'd taken for?

The air in the room shifted suddenly.

The hairs on my neck shot straight up. In the next instant, the damp scent of soil hit my nose, and my heart hurled into my throat.

It was last night all over again, and I forced myself to turn around. To face it. And then there it was: the clot of black oozing in front of the window and consuming all light.

Before fear could paralyze me, I tore open the lab's door and scrambled into Machinery Hall. For once my legs and skirts worked in concert, and I didn't trip over hems or lace. I just ran. I knew that the spirit was following because of the icy sheen that formed over the machines as I raced past.

I reached the east entrance and pummeled into the door, expecting release, but I was thrown back. The door shook but remained solidly shut. I was locked in!

I twirled around and frantically scanned for an escape. The spirit had blocked my path.

"Go away," I shrieked, my throat snapping with the words and strength tingling through me. I swung my parasol at it—"Leave!"—and somehow that worked. I didn't understand how or why, but now was not the time to question my luck.

The spirit slithered away. I forced my feet to run back through the hall, and I had almost reached the center when the reek of decay alerted me to the corpses. I could sense the cold behind me, though, so I didn't slow. It wasn't until I reached the giant Corliss engine towering in the hall's center that I actually saw the first body.

It shambled south, leaving a rain of dirt behind it. Most of its skin was gone, and the tattered remains of bone and muscle barely clung together.

I observed all this in a flash, but I did not pause. The piercing chill that followed gave me no choice but to move forward. Logic told me that following the Dead would lead to the Spirit-Hunters. I veered around the engine in pursuit of the skeleton but then skidded to a halt.

Corpses were everywhere, stumbling like drunks in a thick mass toward . . . I blinked in surprise. They were heading for the Hydraulic Annex, an extension of Machinery Hall that housed a giant, fountained pool. Even from here I could see the hazy mist that meant the fountain's pumps and waterfalls still ran. But why would the Spirit-Hunters go there?

The closest corpse, a skeleton of gleaming bone and shredded flesh, tottered to a stop. Its exposed skull rotated toward me, and though its sockets were empty, I knew it sensed me. Four more Dead, each in varying stages of decomposition, slowed and turned to face me. My chest convulsed at movement crawling on a fresher one's skin. It even wore a dress like my own.

I lifted my parasol defensively before me. The corpse of the woman staggered closer. It was recently dead and more coordinated. When it was only three feet away, it lunged, both hands outstretched.

I swung with all the power I could muster, and the parasol connected with the corpse's arms. It sent a shock up my limbs but hardly affected the Dead. I stumbled back, the urge to scream rising in my chest, and I swung again.

This time its elbow cracked inward and drove into the other outstretched arm. The corpse was momentarily slowed, but did not stop its attack. And now the other corpses were near and approaching from different angles. With the Corliss engine at my back, I knew I was trapped.

A small figure snaked through my vision. Bones crunched and flesh slapped as the Dead crumpled around me. The corpses continued to grab and claw, but they couldn't reach me. Their legs were shattered, and they could gain no ground.

An Asian boy stood before me, his fists at the ready and stance low. He was Chinese, judging by his long, black braid and half-shaved head. Yet he wore clothes like an American boy: brown knickerbockers and a waistcoat.

He jerked a thumb toward the Hydraulic Annex, and though his lips moved, his words were lost in the clanging of the alarm.

When I did not stir, he wrenched me along with him. In five long strides, we reached the end of the Dead parade.

The boy ran to the closest body, kicked the side of its knee, and pushed it over in a fluid, flat-palmed movement. He was a blur of feet and hands, repeating the same maneuver with each corpse. The key, I saw, was in destroying their legs, so I rushed forward and hurled my parasol at a corpse's knee. The joint splintered and rolled inward; and before the Dead could grasp at me, I shoved it with my parasol. Down it went.

Then the alarm stopped. Only the vibrations hanging in the air gave any indication that it had sounded. My ears adjusted in moments, only to be filled with the scrape of bone on bone and the rip of straining flesh. Beyond that was the crash of waterfalls.

It was at that moment that I noticed the oppressive weight of summer heat. No more icy air or steaming breath. The spirit had left.

"Jie!" a male voice bellowed. "Hurry!"

It was Daniel, but there were still many Dead blocking our path to him. So we worked faster, a frenzy of attacks. We targeted the corpses directly in our way. My muscles protested and my elbows popped under each impact. Our progress through the rancid Dead was a surreal blur of flesh and bone.

Then the first misty droplets brushed at my face. We had reached the pool of the Hydraulic Annex.

I stared, momentarily surprised by the view before me. The pool was as wide as my house and twice as long, with a wooden guardrail surrounding it. At its back, a giant waterfall crashed. Along the sides, smaller pumps and cascades rocketed water in an amazing display of hydraulic art.

But what stunned me was that in the middle of it all stood Joseph. His arms were outstretched, his eyes were squeezed shut, and the water reached his waist.

A hand grasped at my skirts. I spun around, and in the same movement, my parasol connected with something. It made a jellylike thud. I had toppled the body of a child dressed in a blue gown, and it was now clawing at me from the floor.

The burn of bile rose in my throat, and I staggered back until I hit the fence surrounding the pool.

The Dead shuffled forward. They were impeded by rows of benches that surrounded the pool, but there was something else—something more. These corpses moved as if they slogged through waist-deep mud. The corpses I'd first encountered hadn't been nearly so slow.

"Joseph needs the machine," Daniel rushed to tell the Chinese boy. "You have to hold 'em off while I get it running." He spared a quick glance for me before dashing to a bench on which sat the glass machine.

"Time to fight," the Chinese boy said to me. Then he moved to intercept the nearest Dead.

I stood, momentarily lost. What was about to happen? We couldn't smash kneecaps indefinitely—there were just too many.

A sharp *pop* sounded beside me as blue flashed in the corner of my eye. It was the machine, its wheels spinning and electricity sparkling.

"Joseph!" Daniel roared. "The machine is ready."

So there *was* a solution, and that machine was somehow it.

The realization spurred me to move.

I swiveled back toward the pool. Joseph moved to the edge, swaying dangerously with each step. His hand reached out as if grabbing for help. I rushed to the guardrail, my hand extended; and with much heaving, I dragged his sopping figure from the pool. The instant his feet left the water, the stampeding sounds of the Dead grew louder.

The corpses were no longer slow. In fact, they shambled forward at a brisk walk—too quickly for the Chinese boy to stop. I raced to help as Joseph ran to the popping machine.

But there were too many. Fingers and teeth and waxy flesh were everywhere. I swung and shoved and swung and shoved.

Daniel's voice howled over the fray, "Now!"

The Chinese boy whirled around, seized me, and lugged me behind a bench. Just before I dropped, I saw Joseph shove his hand directly into the machine's electricity.

A bright, blue light exploded overhead, and a thunderous boom cracked through the annex. Then came the thud and slap of corpses as they hit the ground.

I craned my neck and peered over the bench. The walking Dead had collapsed where they stood.

It took several moments for me to comprehend that it was over and I was safe. I eased painfully onto the bench. My muscles screamed their exhaustion and had already begun to stiffen from overuse.

The Chinese boy rose from our spot on the floor. He looked

down at me. "Thanks for helping." His voice was high and soft. He poked his thumb at his chest. "I'm Jie."

"Eleanor," I answered, gesturing wearily to myself. "Wh-what do we do now?"

"I go get people to help clean up before the flies come. You help Joseph, yeah?" He bounded off without a glance back, and with no regard for his feet hitting flesh and bones.

I winced, glad that the roar of the water blocked the sound of his footsteps. The cool mist also kept some of the rotten scent at bay. I pushed myself up and shuffled toward Daniel and Joseph, who both lay in a heap on a bench nearby.

"What just happened?" I asked. "With the machine? And why were you in the fountain?"

"Now's not the time," Daniel grumbled. He rose, slid an arm under Joseph, and helped the bedraggled man rise. I lurched forward and added support to Joseph's other side.

"*Mèrsi*," Joseph murmured. His eyes were glassy and his breathing rough.

We shuffled from the pool and benches and approached the first of the collapsed Dead.

"Hold your nose," Daniel said. "And you probably don't wanna look down."

I gritted my teeth and kept my chin raised high. Like Jie, I didn't—couldn't—avoid stepping on the corpses. My ankles and heels rolled and sank as we progressed forward.

Daniel tipped his head around Joseph to peer at me. "What are you doin' here, Miss Fitt? We told you to stay in the lab."

My heel poked through skin with a rip and a thud. I pressed my lips firmly together and forced my eyes to remain up and forward. "I couldn't stay," I said.

Joseph cleared his throat. "There was a spirit."

"Yes." I glanced at him, my eyes wide. "How did you know?"

"I could feel the cold."

"You could?" I asked. "How? You weren't near."

"When I stand in water, I can connect more easily to spiritual energy."

"T-to what?"

Daniel answered. "It's like electricity. Everything that's—" He broke off and flinched. His foot was tangled in a corpse's dress. He shook his leg free, wrinkled his nose, and then continued. "Everything that's alive has spiritual energy. You call it soul."

We reached the giant Corliss engine, and though the air still stank of putrid flesh, the ground was clean. Joseph paused our slow trudge forward and straightened. "I can go alone now, thank you."

Daniel wiped his brow. "Like I was sayin', souls are made of electricity."

His words clicked with something Elijah had taught me. "Water's a conductor," I said slowly. "Is that how it works?"

"Right." Daniel flicked his eyes toward me, and I thought I saw a glint of respect. "So when Joseph stands in it, he can connect to the spiritual energy."

"And so," I pressed, "when he was in the water, he could control the bodies?"

"Not control," Joseph said, "but *affect*. You might have noticed a difference in the corpses' speed when I stepped from the water. My ability to affect the corpses weakened when I left the water, so their speed and coordination improved."

Daniel nodded. "We're lucky the Hydraulic Annex has such a big pool. We're even luckier the corpses followed us there."

"*Wi*. It makes me think we were the target of the attack."

"I don't know if that's good or bad." Daniel glanced toward the annex. "I should go back and get the machine."

"What is that thing?" I asked. "It made sparks."

"It's called an influence machine. It makes static electricity from spinning the glass wheels. And when Joseph touches the spark, he uses it to blast all that corrupt soul back into the spirit realm. Kinda like a cue ball smashing apart all the other billiard balls."

"Oh," I said, not entirely sure I understood.

"But that machine wasn't easy to make, and it can sell for a pretty penny. So I ought to retrieve it. Jie can help me carry it to the lab."

Joseph bowed his head, granting permission, and then he turned to me. He tugged at his dripping vest—as if his messy appearance was somehow the fault of his own poor taste.

"Shall we?" He gestured toward the lab, and we resumed our march through Machinery Hall. "You see, Miss Fitt, I could feel the spirit while I stood in the water—it is quite strong." He swallowed and fidgeted with his cuffs. "What was most worrisome was that it knew my range—how far I can reach to affect souls—and it hovered just outside."

I sucked in a breath, and the hairs on my neck stood on end. Was that why it stopped following me? But how would it know something like that? And for that matter, why had it even come here?

"Mr. Boyer," I said, "that's the spirit my mother let out last night."

His lips compressed. "You are certain?"

"Positive." I shuddered, and hugged my arms to my chest. "It smells . . . it smells like dirt, and it's so cold."

"Ah." Lines etched their way over Joseph's brow. "Then it is a very powerful spirit indeed."

"Mr. Boyer!" a Cockney voice shouted. I glanced down the nearest aisle of machinery and saw a cluster of men striding toward us.

"Reporters," Joseph spat, his nose curling. "Even worse, Mr. Peger. He only writes half of what I say, and never the important half."

My mouth went dry. I shrank behind Joseph. "I'm not sure I want to see reporters."

Joseph gave me a concerned glance and opened his mouth to speak, but the men were upon us.

"Hello, ma'am," said one of them, tipping his hat. "Were you trapped in the building during the attack? Did you see anything? Are you connected with the Spirit-Hunters? Did they rescue you?" He sang out question after question, leaving me no time to answer.

I faltered back several steps. I couldn't be in the newspaper. Someone would certainly see mention of me, and then Mama would find out I'd been with the Spirit-Hunters; she'd know I'd been with people of "low society" and, worst of all, that I'd been there because I needed help dealing with the Dead.

I lifted my hands defensively and shook my head as more of the reporters approached me. Nearby, Joseph fared no better.

A squat, square man with shimmering golden curls had attached himself to Joseph; and despite the reporter's much smaller size, the Spirit-Hunter somehow seemed the tinier of the two.

When one of the reporters requested my name, I made a decision. I'd had quite enough, and what were a bunch of reporters compared to an army of the Dead? I lowered my head, lifted my skirts, and pummeled through.

It wasn't until I was several blocks away, gasping for breath and coated in sweat, that I realized I stank like the Dead.

CHAPTER SEVEN

Thank the merciful heavens Mama was away when I reached home. She was calling on all our guests from last night—no doubt to explain away the evening's unusual events.

I bribed Mary to help me wash the dress. Her price was steep: a pair of kid gloves. But a lost pair of gloves was easier to explain than a foul-walking dress. Fortunately, Mary had been so pleased by her payment she hadn't bothered to ask about my need for secrecy, or my smelly dress.

Several hours later, just as the sun was beginning its descent, Mama returned and cornered me in my bedroom, clucking with joy over Clarence's invitation for a drive. Apparently Mrs. Wilcox had shared the news—*and* invited us to the opera the following Saturday.

It was actually the best possible turn of events, for now Mama *had* to let me leave home without an adult (for how else could I go join Clarence?), she couldn't be angry over my morning escape with Allison (woo the sister while wooing the brother), and she was so delighted by our opera invitation she seemed unable to think of anything else.

The only thing that *didn't* work in my favor was that I couldn't sneak back to the Spirit-Hunters lab on Sunday morning as I'd hoped. Mama and Mary pounced the minute I'd finished my breakfast. While Mary brushed my pistachio silk carriage dress, Mama tugged the laces of my corset as tight as they would go. She grunted and I groaned, and we sounded like the giant hogs I'd seen at the zoo—except that, rather than play in the mud and eat to my heart's content, I was forced to sit daintily in the parlor without lunch. For two hours. With my mother for company.

I was so grateful when Clarence finally arrived, I practically swooned with relief. After an awkward reception, he and I left for our afternoon drive. He drove a luxurious carriage with navy bench seats. It was pulled by two chestnut horses, and today he drove it with the top folded down.

My hat and dress were conspiring against me as we traveled past the lavish homes of the neighborhood. I was forced to constantly adjust my position lest I crush the many plaits and ruffles that adorned my gown.

To pile on the agony, once we reached Shantytown—a collection of shacks around the Exhibition that fed off the scraps of rich tourists—the ribbon on my bonnet decided today was the day it wanted freedom. It dangled before my face in a taunting display of rebellion.

I tried to focus my attention on the summer sun and afternoon breeze, the rattle of the wheels and the beat of the horses' hooves as we crossed over the Schuylkill, but my pent-up tensions and fear would not be rejected so easily.

"So, Miss Fitt," Clarence said once we turned onto a tree-lined road beside the river, "you are no doubt wondering why I invited you out."

I swatted the ribbon from my eyes. "And here I assumed it was my unsurpassable good looks."

He chuckled. "That was, of course, part of my motivation."

"Only part?" I slid my gaze left and watched him from the corner of my eye. "Well then, the rest of your reason must be that bribe you mentioned the other evening."

"Something like that." He smiled sheepishly. "Quite simply, I must beg for your discretion regarding Friday night's . . . um . . ." He seemed to be searching for the right word.

"Rendezvous?" I suggested.

He snorted. "I suppose you could call it that."

"Well, you needn't worry. I haven't told anyone." I fingered the mother-of-pearl buttons on my gloves. "Though I am curious why you're so keen to hide a trip for fresh air."

"Yes, well, that is my private affair." He spoke lightly, but his eyes were hard.

"And," I continued, ignoring him, "why did you have that newspaper?"

"Miss Fitt, you know curiosity gets men killed."

I grinned. "Then I daresay it's good I'm a woman."

He groaned—an amused sound. "No wonder Allie finds you confusing. You've a retort for everything."

"No, only for Wilcoxes."

He rolled his head back and laughed. "All right, all right. If you promise to keep my secrets and enjoy this drive"—he opened his hands to gesture at the sun-dappled carriageway before us—"then I will explain."

I blinked. Really? All it took to get an answer was a witty turn of phrase? If only it were that simple with men like Daniel Sheridan.

"Well, go on," I urged.

"I sent my footman to fetch a newspaper because . . ." He clenched his teeth and took in a shaky breath. "Because Frederick Weathers was my friend."

My eyes widened. Though his response made no sense in the context of the conversation I'd overheard, it was startling news all the same.

"The man found headless?" I gripped at his sleeve. "He was your friend?"

Clarence nodded once, his face tightening with pain.

"Oh, Mr. Wilcox, I am sorry."

He gently removed my clenched fingers from his sleeve. "Yes, Miss Fitt. Now, if you'll please keep this information to yourself."

"But don't most people know? It's in the newspapers."

"Yes, but his family wants it kept quiet. Allie doesn't read the papers, so she doesn't know yet." He gazed into the distance, as if considering what to say next. "And it's more complicated than just one man . . . one man dying. There are elections coming up, and Frederick's father has withdrawn from them."

"His father . . ." I thought back to the newspaper article. "He's on the city council?"

"Yes, and he no longer wishes to hold office. That interferes significantly with my own campaign for city council." He flicked his gaze to me for several moments, his mouth curved down. But in an instant his lips were back to their fetching smile. "Now, if you would kindly keep this to yourself."

"I am sorry for the loss of your friend," I offered. This secret was hardly as sinister as I had expected—or hoped. Perhaps my own curiosity was really no better than Allison's appetite for gossip.

"Have you spoken with the Spirit-Hunters?" I offered. "Perhaps they can help."

"No." He tipped his face away. "I would rather not deal with them. They're low-life—disreputable, I've heard."

I frowned. Joseph Boyer seemed about as honest as men came—a true gentleman if I'd ever met one. "But," I said hesitantly, "if they're so disreputable, then why did the Exhibition board hire them?"

"Because they volunteered? Because they're cheap? I can't say." He lifted a shoulder. "Everything about the situation is worrisome, Miss Fitt." He glanced at me, assessing. "Worst of all, I hear all the corpses in Laurel Hill have come to life."

I shivered and hugged my arms to my stomach. Laurel Hill was a graveyard on the steep, rugged hills beside the Schuylkill River. Because it was several miles north of Philadelphia, it had always been undisturbed and peaceful. Though, if all the corpses had risen . . . Well, that meant hundreds—perhaps even thousands—of Dead.

And if the Dead came from Laurel Hill, then it seemed likely the necromancer was there as well. And if Elijah was trapped with the necromancer, then . . . then he could be in the cemetery.

And he might be a corpse too. My skin crawled, and I heaved the thought aside.

"Take me to Laurel Hill," I said.

Clarence whipped his face toward me, his expression revolted. "Why? What a horrible request."

"Please, Mr. Wilcox." I scooted toward him. "It is not so great a detour to go there—it's on our way into the countryside. I just want to peer through the gates."

"Give me one good reason to comply with such a morbid desire."

What could I say? I didn't want him to know about Elijah. "My . . . my father is in Laurel Hill Cemetery," I muttered at last. "You said all the bodies have risen, and I wonder if he is among them."

My words were not entirely false. My father *was* buried in Laurel Hill, and I *was* curious if his corpse had risen.

"Ah," Clarence said. He clenched the reins in one hand and

massaged his forehead with the other. "I have asked myself that same question. About my own father, who is also buried there." He narrowed his eyes a fraction and studied me. "All right, Miss Fitt. You win. But consider this your bribe to keep my secrets." He shot me a half grin. "We will only stay a moment." Then he flicked the reins, and we picked up our speed.

Minutes later we rounded a shady bend in the road. The long, white-columned gatehouse that marked the entrance to Laurel Hill Cemetery moved into view. The gates were closed, and there was no one around. This was usually a place of wandering couples, visiting families, and rattling carriages, all there to view the forested cemetery grounds. Now it was silent and empty—no, not empty. Empty of the living.

"We stop here," Clarence said. "I don't want the horses getting skittish."

We jerked to a halt, and I lurched forward in my seat. Clarence hopped to the ground and offered me his hand. "I do not wish to stay long, Miss Fitt. We shouldn't be here, and . . ." He swiveled his head left and right, reminding me of a frightened squirrel. "Well, the Dead are reason enough."

"Yes," I murmured, clumsily climbing down. My lips were dry, and my heart thumped against my ribs. I had seen the Dead twice now, and they didn't scare me anymore. No—what scared me was the possibility of seeing Elijah. Of seeing him dead.

Soon, Clarence and I stood inside the gatehouse's archway. My fingers gripped the gate's iron bars, and my face was pressed against them. Upon the hill that rose quickly before me were the statues of Old Mortality and Sir Walter Scott. But beyond those stone men, I detected no signs of the Dead.

"There's nothing here," I said, accusation in my voice.

"You've got to be patient. We haven't been here long." Clarence glanced at me. "Trust me. The Dead are in there—I saw them from the river a few days ago."

"Oh."

"Be grateful. What I saw was horrifying. I instantly regretted my curiosity."

I sniffed haughtily and wished etiquette didn't force me to bite my tongue. One would think, after Friday evening, he would know I was not prone to hysterics.

Clarence swallowed. His eyes were locked on some distant point. "Look."

I followed his gaze. At the top of the hill, a figure shambled by. I knew that gait. The stride of long-dead bones.

I clutched at the iron bars. "Where do you suppose it's going?"

"I don't know."

"North," I murmured. "Perhaps we can see it through the fence."

"No. It's overgrown." Clarence waved toward the nearest stretch of bars. Though the outer edge of the fence was bare of brush, the inside was bordered by thick forest.

"But there might be a break somewhere. Come on. Let's follow it." Before Clarence could stop me, I gathered up my skirts and hurried out of the gatehouse. I sped along the road until I reached the iron fence traveling north.

Clarence's footsteps were close behind, but he made no move to stop me. It would seem Mr. Clarence Wilcox wanted to see beyond the fence as much as I. Yet, just as he had declared, I could find no opening in the shrubs within the cemetery.

"Miss Fitt," he said after several minutes of searching. "Our risk of being noticed by the Dead rises each moment we linger." His tone was friendly, but there was a harsh edge to his words. "I have fulfilled my end of the deal. Let's return to the carriage."

"But we've seen nothing." I smacked my hat's ribbon from my face. "Just a bit more. Please."

"No." He planted his feet and shook his head once. "Was the spirit on Friday not enough for you? You don't want to see a corpse. I can promise you it's a horrible sight, and I don't want to carry you home in a faint."

His words rankled me. I wasn't like the silly girls he was used to, and I was tired of him treating me like . . . like *Allison*.

I stepped toward him, my chin tipped high. "Mr. Wilcox, I have seen plenty of corpses. I've been present twice when the Dead alarm rang." I thrust up two fingers. "I want to know how many Dead walk in this cemetery. I want to know if . . . if . . ." My words faded.

Clarence wore an entirely unexpected expression: amusement. His mouth turned up in a smile. It wasn't his usual polite grin—this one was completely genuine, and it transformed his already handsome face into a beautiful one. All I could do was stare, mouth hanging open like an idiot.

Clarence pressed a gloved hand against his lips for several moments before a soft bark of laughter broke free.

"You're nothing like your brother, are you? You're bold—brave even."

I reared back, all thoughts of his good looks gone at those words. "What did you say?"

His smile fell. The color drained from his face.

"You *do* know Elijah," I said. "Why didn't you tell me? You said you only knew *of* him."

"Yes, well . . ."

My temper flared to life. "You lied."

He lifted his hands in a rigid movement, as if it took a great deal of control to remain calm. "It's not like that."

"Then what is it like? You said you didn't know him."

"I didn't know him—not well, at least." He licked his lips and slowly lowered his hands. "He was the year behind me at Germantown Academy."

"And?"

"And nothing."

"That's it? How do you know he's not like me, then?"

"I-I saw him during the school breaks and at events. He always looked scared. But honestly, I never really knew him. If we'd been chums, don't you think our mothers would know?"

I took a long breath and considered his words. Was I being overly suspicious? *I am seeing monsters everywhere.* I let my stiff posture soften. "Why didn't you say that on Friday evening? Why lie about something so trivial?"

"It's . . . well . . . it's quite simple, really. I felt sorry for you."

"Sorry for me?"

He nodded quickly. "Yes. I was sorry that Elijah hadn't returned. I-I thought if we talked of him, you might grow upset. I can see now that you're not that sort of lady."

I lowered my arms and eyed him for several moments. I didn't know if I believed him or not. But really, did it matter if he'd known Elijah?

"Please, Miss Fitt, accept my apology." He leaned into a bow, his head hanging low.

"Of course." I nodded curtly. More and more strange confessions were piling up between Clarence and me. If I didn't watch myself, he would soon be uncovering mine.

Suddenly, something caught my ear—the sound of rustling underbrush. I went to the fence. There was a distant and rhythmic thrashing in the cemetery. I glanced at Clarence. "Do you hear that?"

He frowned, and his eyes unfocused. "Yes," he said. "It's getting louder. Closer."

He was right. I could distinctly make out footsteps now, coming at high speed, pounding along with snapping branches and shaking leaves.

"It sounds like a wild animal," Clarence said. "Come away from the fence."

I pushed my face against the bars. "But I hear two feet," I answered. "Like a person running." Could someone in there be alive? Could it be Elijah?

Whoever it was, they were close now. The beating footsteps crashed loudly in the forest.

"Come away from the fence," Clarence repeated.

It was definitely a person running, but what sort of person could race through dense shrubs and trees like that?

"Come away!" Clarence roared. He clasped my arm and yanked me back, wrenching my shoulder.

Then it crashed full speed against the fence. A corpse.

It shook the bars and sent a low clang echoing in the air. Its gleaming skull pressed against the bars where my face had been only moments before. It was the corpse of a Union soldier. Its old bones were clothed in the tatters of a uniform. Its teeth clacked as it bit frantically, while bony arms reached between the bars. It clawed at the air, trying to push far enough to reach us on the other side.

Clarence shoved me behind him. We retreated slowly, our eyes never leaving the frenzied body. We stopped fifteen feet away and watched in dumb horror. This corpse was nothing like the stiff and shambling ones I'd seen before. No, this corpse had unbridled energy and moved with the speed of the living— perhaps faster, even.

"Let's go." Clarence's voice was rough and quiet over the rapid clatter of the corpse's jaw.

I could only grunt my agreement. My eyes were still locked on the bony wrists and empty eyes. Clarence gripped me by the waist and twisted me around. My mind resumed thought, and I needed no more urging to flee.

We galloped down the road, back to our carriage and skittering horses.

"We should tell someone," I said. "About this."

"I will." He hoisted me into the carriage. "You should keep quiet, though."

"Why?"

"We shouldn't be here." His words were sharp, and his hands shook as he lifted the reins. He was scared. "I don't want anyone—especially our mothers—finding out." He gave me a slit-eyed glance. "Can you *please* keep quiet, Miss Fitt?"

I gulped and nodded. Though I didn't understand Clarence's panic or his secrets, I knew he would tell no one what we'd seen. Yet someone needed to know—at the very least the Spirit-Hunters. It was their job to deal with such horrors.

I *could* keep quiet. But that didn't mean I *would*.

CHAPTER EIGHT

First thing the next morning, before Mama was even awake, I trekked to the Exhibition to give Joseph the letter from Elijah and tell him of the rabid corpse at Laurel Hill.

Other than some questionable streaks on Machinery Hall's floor, I could see no signs of the recent Dead attack. All those corpses—where were they now? And how had the hall been cleaned up so quickly?

Perhaps with so much money spent on the event, the city could afford to keep it running like clockwork no matter the interruption. Or perhaps it was the other way around: the city *couldn't* afford any interruptions when thousands of international visitors were clamoring to get in every day.

I made my way through Machinery Hall to the Spirit-

Hunters' laboratory. Except the Spirit-Hunters weren't there. Their door was shut, and this time no note was on it. I hesitantly tried the handle, but it didn't budge.

After considering my options—Come back later? Leave Elijah's letter?—I crouched in an awkward mass of skirts and bustle and slipped the note through a crack between the door and floor.

Wait—will they even know the letter was mine? Did I mention Elijah's name to them? Well, too late now. I'd have to sort it out tomorrow. Besides, I wanted to go home and read through all of Elijah's letters. In light of everything that had happened, his words might contain a critical clue.

Yes, I could come back tomorrow and offer everything I knew about my brother's predicament. I rose stiffly, my dress rustling back to its full expanse.

"Won't help you, will they?" said a man's voice in an affected Cockney accent.

I whirled around to see the speaker exiting the men's water closet.

He was a short man, no taller than me, but barrel-chested and solid with muscle. Beneath his derby hat gleamed blond curls that matched his broad, wax-tipped mustache. Something about him struck me as familiar, but I couldn't place where I knew him.

"They never seem to be around when people need them," he said.

"Pardon me?"

"They"—he jerked his thumb toward the Spirit-Hunters' door—"can't help you. I've seen you here before, and I suppose they have refused to do their job. They've done that with everyone so far."

He sauntered toward me, inspecting his tan coat cuffs. "What excuse did they give you? Too busy? Not enough money?" He flicked his gaze to mine. "Or is there a new reason I've yet to hear?"

I hesitated, intrigued by his accurate prediction. Joseph had said he would look at my letter, but where was Joseph now?

The man brushed his cuffs and then folded his arms over his chest. "I thought as much. These Spirit-Hunters are here to help, but aren't actually helping anyone."

I squinted. "I'm not sure I follow."

"Well, Mr. Boyer and his team have been here since May twenty-fifth; but rather than solve the Dead problems, the problems have been getting worse." He lifted a hand and fingered the tip of his mustache. "Seems to me they could march into Laurel Hill and end the whole situation once and for all—but they don't. Why?"

I gulped nervously and glanced around to check for listeners. I hoped the din of the hall drowned out our conversation. "I thought it was because they had no means. No one to help them."

"Perhaps." He lifted his shoulder in a lazy shrug. "Curious, and quite a coincidence, though, don't you think? These Spirit-Hunters leave New York, and the trouble ends. They show up here, and the trouble begins. Maybe there's a valid reason the Exhibition board is unwilling to hand over men or money."

I blinked. That was a different spin on the same tale Joseph had given me. "Who are you?"

He swooped off his hat and swung into a bow. "Nicholas Peger, with the *Philadelphia Bulletin*."

Now I remembered where I'd seen him. He had cornered Joseph after the Dead attack. "A reporter," I said blandly.

"Investigative journalist," he corrected. "And in charge of all stories pertaining to the Dead." He popped his hat firmly atop his head. "Also an occasional detective, and also at your service."

"Yes, well, a pleasure to meet you." I nodded my head and turned to go. In a blur of speed, he pounced in my path, and I reeled back.

"I failed to catch your name," he drawled.

"Because I did not offer it." I scooted back several steps and pulled my parasol to my chest. "Please stand aside, sir."

He cocked his head. "Do you perhaps need a detective? Missing persons are my specialty."

"I-I beg your pardon?" How did he know about my brother? I glanced around, and my eyes lit on the water closet nearby. My jaw dropped, and I spun back. "Do you eavesdrop on the Spirit-Hunters? From the men's water closet?" My voice was high-pitched with disbelief.

"Nay, nay. I can't hear a thing in there." He twirled his mustache and smiled pompously. "I simply made a good guess, and then you confirmed. Detective, remember?"

I swallowed a cry of indignation, yanked up my skirts, and, with my fiercest glare, strode toward him. "Good day, sir."

He sidled away, and I stormed past, my chin held high and my focus straight ahead.

"You can't trust them," he called after me.

Though I hated myself for doing it, curiosity got the best of me. I slowed and glanced back.

He doffed his hat. "If you decide you need my help, just find Nicholas Peger at the *Philadelphia Bulletin*."

"Where have you been?" Mama demanded. She was standing in the center of my bedroom when I walked in. My cheeks were still pink from heat and exertion.

I reached up to unpin my hat. "At the Exhibition," I said, trying for nonchalance. Rather than pretend to run long errands each day, I had decided evasive honesty was my best tactic. As such, I had prepared a story for this eventual question.

I laid my hat gently in its box and turned to face Mama. She wore her silk dressing robe, and her hair fell loosely down her back.

"And what, pray tell, brought you there?" She lowered herself onto my bed.

"The Women's Pavilion." It housed inventions by modern women—and she knew it was one of my favorite buildings.

"Women's Pavilion?" Her frown faltered. "Whatever for?"

"They needed volunteers for one of their exhibits." The words sounded tight. Why is it that no matter how realistic or rehearsed a lie is, it always rings false in the teller's ears?

She gasped, pressing her hands to her cheeks. "Eleanor," she hissed. "You cannot *work*! What will people say? They will think you belong to the lower class!"

"But Mr. Wilcox," I blurted, ignoring her question. "He loves charitable women. In fact, he told me that on Sunday."

"Really?" She sucked in a pleased breath. "Did he say that on your drive?"

"Yes, ma'am."

Her lips curved up. "Clever girl." And with those two words, all my anxiety washed away.

She patted at the bed. "Sit."

I moved to the bed and plopped beside her. To my surprise, she opened her arms and pulled me into an embrace.

"Mama?" I said. What was this? I couldn't remember the last time she'd hugged me.

"My dearest daughter has found a rich man." She stroked my hair. "I am so pleased. Your brother may have abandoned us to poverty, but you can still save us."

I kept my lips tightly together and my eyes screwed shut. What the dickens was I supposed to say? That no, in fact, the rich man was only bribing me for silence; and *no*, Elijah was detained by walking corpses? Hardly.

And how long was she going to squeeze me?

"I thought," Mama continued, "we could receive the Wilcoxes on Wednesday. Perhaps for cards or tea." She twirled a finger in my hair.

I paused only a moment before saying, "All right." I could stand Clarence's glower a bit more for Mama's sake.

"You know," she said, "your father would also be proud of you. A rich man to marry *and* a charitable use of your time. He was such a generous man himself. He used to give all sorts of money to the hospitals, the schools, the poor. . . . That was why he wanted to run for city council, you know. To revitalize our government." She sighed, and I could hear the tears that hovered in her throat.

Father had died when I was ten. He had been a busy, bearlike man who ran a supply business for the railroad. Whatever the Pennsylvania Railroad needed, he got them.

But six years ago, a dynamite shipment he was supposed to provide exploded at our local factory. The railroad company turned to another supplier, and Father lost the contract. It was the start of his ruin, and he died shortly after.

"How I miss him," Mama whispered. "I will feel much better when Elijah returns."

My throat clenched. I nodded into her chest. I wanted to say that I was doing everything I could to bring him home. I wanted to promise he'd be back soon and that all our problems would be solved. But I couldn't, of course.

"Well," Mama said with a loud exhale, "let us hope Elijah has grown more like your father these past three years—he certainly forgets to write like Henry did." Her lips twitched with amusement, and she squeezed my shoulders. "We shall see him soon enough, no?"

Tears burned behind my eyes. The sight of my mother's hope was almost too much. I pulled free from her embrace and turned away. "Yes, Mama. Soon enough."

Once Mama left my room I rubbed at my eyes, wiped my nose on my sleeve, and set to work. I needed to find every important phrase or word in Elijah's letters. I needed something to offer Joseph Boyer. Something to force him to take me seriously.

But I'd barely read two sentences when I was interrupted.

"Miss Fitt?" Mary called from downstairs. "I need help with dinner."

I sighed and hauled myself off the bed. Life still needed living even if there was something strange and deadly going on in Philadelphia.

I met Mary at the bottom of the stairs, and we walked through the hall to the kitchen.

Our kitchen was the one room Mama had not splurged on to redecorate since, of course, no one but our family would ever see it. The floor was worn down into familiar paths. The white paint had lately turned to a gray brown, and the iron stove in the back of the room often smoked up the house. Our icebox was really of no use in the summer—it had a hole from which the sawdust had been slowly leaking for years—and that was why we needed almost daily market trips during the warmer months.

Mary pointed at an assortment of vegetables laid out on a long, wooden table. "You said to make a stew, but there ain't any meat."

"I know, but we have to make do." The party had eaten up our budgeted food allowance, and I'd had to lighten our diets for the rest of the month to compensate.

I took a wide knife and moved to the table. "I'll take the vegetables. You get the water boiling."

I set to chopping cabbage. The *clack, clack* of the knife was soothing, and soon my thoughts drifted.

Clarence—why had he lied about Elijah? And why did he insist upon my secrecy but then constantly divulge more? It was as if he played at some game of intrigue but had yet to learn the rules or get the knack.

The thought tickled my brain—I had heard that phrase spoken before, but by whom? And when?

I stared sightlessly at the cabbage, and a vague memory emerged in my mind.

An argument. Between Father and . . . and a dark-haired man.

I'd been only a child, but I could distinctly remember the

man's shouts—"We will live like kings!"—and the slamming doors that sent shudders through the house.

"I promise you, Clay," Father had screamed, "no good shall come of this!"

A dark-haired visitor named Clay and a game of intrigue . . .

I sliced the last of the cabbage and turned to ask Mary, who peeled potatoes beside the stove.

But no. She wouldn't remember; she was only a year older than me, and she'd only just started working as our scullery maid before Father's death.

It was back when my family had a whole houseful of servants. But one by one, all of them had left except for old Jeremy and young Mary. I had always assumed the other servants had found better jobs with more popular families, but perhaps it was merely better jobs with less crazy employers.

When Father's business and city council campaign fell, his sanity fell too. Father claimed it was sabotage, that his enemies sought to destroy him; but I never knew if his paranoid ravings were true. Either way, a few months after Father was forced to withdraw from the election, he died.

But things would look up again. Soon. Somehow I'd make it right again—I just *had* to.

I huffed out a heavy breath and moved to the celery. When I finished dicing it and the stew pot had water bubbling, I gave Mary directions for the rest of the meal and then I dashed upstairs to my room.

It was late afternoon, and I had to use what remained of the day's sunlight to read Elijah's letters.

I settled onto my bed and started with the first letter. For the beginning of Elijah's travels in 1873, he'd been in London. He had scoured ancient texts before traveling to a bookseller's in Paris, and so his letters had focused mostly on these old books. Next, he'd explored sunny Egypt (sending few letters), and then in July of 1875, he'd traveled to New York City.

In each of his letters I underlined his scratchy words to note the parts I thought strange. Such as, the old man in the pyramid, Oliver, or Honorius. Who were they? Authors of the ancient texts, I supposed, but still no one familiar.

In France, Elijah kept referring to some soldier, but who he meant, I couldn't even begin to guess. And in one of his letters from Egypt, Elijah had mentioned "missing pages," but he never named the text or why it mattered.

And what the blazes was the Gas Ring? In a letter he'd sent from New York, he mentioned, "The Gas Ring will see its errors, and Father will be most proud."

Except Father was dead—*would* be proud was what he'd meant. Elijah had never gotten used to referring to Father in the past tense.

I mopped my brow with a handkerchief and set the letter in the growing stack of marked pages. The moist summer heat was suffocating in the room. And reading these letters one after the other made all the strange references more obvious than when

I'd read them with months in between.

I skimmed the next letter in my hand; it had been sent several months ago from New York.

> ... *The missing pages from Cairo are in a museum here, but the curators are not cooperative. These are such exciting times, my dear sister! I have begun experiments that I believe will impress you. Unfortunately, they have impressed others as well, and they are not the sort of people I want around.* ...

People. He'd attracted negative attention from people—plural. Necromancer . . . or necromancers.

Curious, and quite a coincidence, though, don't you think? Mr. Peger had said to me only hours ago. *These Spirit-Hunters leave New York, and the trouble ends. They show up here, and the trouble begins.*

I swallowed over a tight lump in my throat, and with trembling hands I yanked up the next letter. It was dated May 20, 1876.

> *I am coming home on the train scheduled for next Friday (May 26). These people continue to harass me, and I feel my research will run more smoothly in Philadelphia.* ...

Oh no. What had I done by overlooking these words? I had whooped with joy and tossed the letter in the air after the words *I'm coming home.*

It was the last letter in my stack, but there should be one more correspondence: a telegram we'd received that I had never read. Mary had relayed its message to me; and without a doubt, I knew, *knew* this telegram mattered.

I shot off the bed and scrambled to the door. My feet banged full speed down the stairs, and I raced to the back of the house. I burst into the kitchen to find Mary hunched over the stove and stew.

"Elijah's telegram from a week and a half ago! Do you still have it?" In three long steps I crossed the old wooden floorboards to stand next to her. Salty steam billowed up from the pot, mixing with the sweat on my face. "Well, do you?"

"Maybe," she said slowly, her gaze distant. "It'd be in the calling card bowl, if we—"

I didn't wait for her answer. I rushed to the foyer and lunged at the bowl beside our front door. It held those rare cards left when we had callers. Beneath two elegant envelopes, I found a wispy scrap of paper.

It was a crumpled telegram dated May 25, 1876.

Delayed. Will arrive June 2. Much love. Elijah.

And in a scribbled mess on the Received From line was written: *Philadelphia.*

He'd already been in Philadelphia when he sent this. A fresh wave of heat washed over me.

Then another horrifying realization hit. I staggered to the front door and heaved it open, gasping for air and leaning against the frame for support.

May 25 was also the day the Spirit-Hunters had arrived in Philadelphia.

CHAPTER NINE

The next morning I rose at dawn to help Mary with breakfast. I worked quickly and snuck away again before Mama awoke. Simply because I had her tentative permission to wander the Exhibition alone did not mean I ought to tempt her.

I reached the Exhibition right as the gates opened and all the church bells rang nine o'clock. It turned out I could use my ticket from days before and the frazzled men at the turnstiles didn't even notice, so I marched in, more determination in my posture than was actually in my heart. I reached the Spirit-Hunters' door and hovered nervously outside.

Oh, don't be a coward.

Sucking in a fortifying breath, I tapped my knuckles against the door.

It swung open a heartbeat later.

"Miss Fitt." Daniel looked at me blankly. His sandy hair stood at all manner of bizarre angles, while his green eyes were sunken in.

"Mr. Sheridan." I bobbed a curtsy. "I've come to see Mr.——"

"Me." Joseph stepped in front of Daniel, his top hat on and his gloves in hand. "*Bonjour*, Miss Fitt. I am afraid you have come at a bad time. I must leave." He spoke quickly and without meeting my eyes.

"Oh." I swallowed. "I just wanted to know if you'd found my letter. I left it, and I wasn't sure if you knew it was mine."

"*Naturèlman*. We figured it out." He slid on a glove and flexed his fingers. Daniel lounged behind him, his gaze darting from the clock to Joseph to me.

"Did you . . ." I swayed and swiveled my head, trying to connect Joseph's eyes to mine. "Did you discover anything?"

"Some, but we have not yet had time to examine it properly." He pulled on the second glove.

"And what of the spirit my mother——"

"Come back later," Joseph interrupted. "This evening perhaps."

This evening, when there were fewer people. I winced and tried to pump some assertion into my voice. "I don't see why you can't discuss it now. I'd like to have my letter back."

His nostrils twitched, and he finally stared at me full-on. "We need more time to inspect it, *Mamʒèi*, and I haven't the time

106

to talk. I must go." He glanced back at Daniel. "You have your orders."

"Best hurry," Daniel said, tipping his head toward the clock. "Jie's probably already there."

Joseph nodded once, and then in a rush, he stepped from the lab and flew past me. I turned to Daniel to plead my cause, but the door swung at my face. I jumped back as it banged to a close.

What excuse did they give you? Those had been Mr. Peger's words, and now here I stood in a cramped hallway after the Spirit-Hunters had yet again fobbed me off with an excuse.

My eyes widened. Maybe they *were* the necromancers, and they'd taken my letter to destroy the only evidence I had of Elijah's disappearance.

I shook my head, and my curls bounced against my neck. I had to stop this foolish paranoia. I had no evidence of anything. Yet.

I pushed my feet into action. My hand automatically reached for the amethysts at my ears, to feel their delicate shapes. I still needed to go to the market—Mama had complained about last night's bland stew, and I'd promised to splurge on pork cheeks.

I reached the end of the aisle where it intersected with Machinery Hall's main transept and lifted my skirt to join the flow of visitors.

But something whispered in the back of my mind. The nagging sense of eyes watching me from behind.

I glanced over my shoulder and saw Daniel, his face now

shaded by a gray flat cap, and a full, lumpy satchel leaned against his legs. When our eyes met, he spun his face away and focused intently on locking the laboratory door. I whisked my head around, scurried into the crowd, and moved from his view.

That had been an enormous bag—it had practically reached his thighs. What was in it? And where was he going with it?

I can follow him. I can find out.

I swerved from the throng of visitors and pressed myself against the nearest exhibit: a sleek locomotive. It gleamed in the morning sun and bathed me in ethereal light. A boiling thrill at my decision tingled over me. Sweat beaded on my skin.

I slunk left along the locomotive and craned my neck to peer around the shiny engine. Daniel marched into my view, hunched over with the sack hoisted on his back. And something poked from the sack—something that made my heart slam into my ribs.

It was the tip of a boot.

I lurched back. A boot. A heavy bag. I pressed my hands to my face and tried to breathe over my heart. It felt as if it rammed against my lungs with each beat. *Oh God—what did I just see?*

I inched around the engine once more, and this time Daniel was at the exit. He trudged through the building's eastern door while people parted and streamed around him. It was now or never. I had to go while I still held a chance for pursuit.

I steeled myself and then surged through the oncoming people. They weren't as willing to move from my path as they'd been for Daniel, but soon enough I reached the entrance and scrambled into the bright sun. I saw no sign of the sandy-haired boy in the crowded plaza. I scanned for the bulky sack and his gray flat cap. Nothing.

Then the satchel bounced at the edge of my vision. The Bartholdi Fountain had hidden him from view. He was already on the other side of the exit gates! How could he move so fast with such a . . . such a . . . I refused to think the word.

I scooted after him, but by the time I entered the mass of people outside the Exhibition, he was boarding a black hackney. I shoved toward the lines of waiting carriages, all the while keeping my eyes locked on the one that now carried Daniel.

I had a handful of coins in my pocket, so when I arrived at the first hackney for hire, I waved for the driver's attention and darted into the concourse. Before the driver could climb down from his seat, I shouted, "Stay there! I can get in alone."

A frantic search showed Daniel's carriage leaving the concourse. I clambered into the buggy and pointed. "That way. I'll tell you where to go once we're out."

He nodded, and with a flick of the reins, jolted the horse into a rattling chase. I plopped down and shaded my eyes. My heart throbbed in my throat, and the tip of the boot flashed in my mind.

Then I spotted the black hackney. "Turn right at Girard," I yelled up.

"Yes'm."

We clopped down the avenue and onto the Girard Avenue Bridge. It was packed with carriages, and I lost sight of Daniel's hackney.

I stood in my seat, my knees wobbling with the movement of the wheels. Though the breeze of the river whipped at the ribbons of my bonnet, it offered no relief to the scorching sweat that dripped down my back.

"Oi, miss!" snapped the driver. "Sit down!"

I glanced behind. "Do you see a black hackney?" I pointed ahead of us.

"Yeah—about twenty. Sit down. It's not safe if you want to go fast." As if to prove his point, we suddenly veered right, and I tumbled sideways. I clutched at the edge of the cab and slid to the end of my seat. I tried to peek around the powerful horse before me, but my view was only obstructed by other horses.

Oh, please don't tell me I've lost him already. Oh, please, please.

We crossed the river, and the end of the bridge came into sight—but no black hackney. Daniel could go anywhere in the city now, and I wouldn't be able to see. I puffed out a breath of frustration. I was so sure I'd almost uncovered something about the Spirit-Hunters. Something significant.

And then there it was, below the bridge! Daniel's tanned face was focused straight ahead as his hackney trotted by—in the opposite direction. It traveled along a tree-lined leisure path parallel to Girard Avenue. How had it gotten there so *fast*?

"There!" I bolted up and pointed wildly below. "There— we must go there!"

"Then sit down. Now!"

We jerked left, and I fell sideways into the seat. As we catapulted through the oncoming traffic, drivers shouted their fury and horses whinnied. Then, in a bone-jarring bounce, we clattered off the bridge and onto the dirt path.

The reins pulled back and we slowed to a steady trot. I jumped up once more.

"This is too slow," I declared. Bonnet ribbons slapped my face. "You must go faster."

"I can't, miss." He wiped his brow and glared down at me. "This is for slow traffic only."

"B-but . . ."

"But nothin'." He scowled and stroked his beard. "You know, Miss, followin' someone costs double fare."

"Oh." I gulped. Of course he was lying, but what choice did I have? I couldn't pretend that I *wasn't* pursuing the other hackney, and I couldn't hope to find another driver this far into the chase. I just had to hope I had enough money. "All right then. Double fare."

"In that case," he said with a twist in his lips, "is that your hackney there?" He pointed, and I scanned ahead until I too saw the familiar gleam of black. It was disappearing around a bend ahead.

"Yes! That's it!"

"Then I'll keep my eyes on it," he answered. "Now sit down."

I tumbled back in my seat. My heart had begun to ache

from overuse, and the morning heat was suffocating beneath my gown. Later—I could relax later.

The horse trotted my cab north with the river at our left and a forest at our right. The carriages, riders, and passers-by had thinned out, and now my cab and Daniel's were the only two still on the dirt road. Fortunately, Daniel remained far ahead.

"We'll have to be stoppin' right soon," the driver announced.

I leaned forward and tilted my head up to look at him. "What do you mean? Why?"

"Because," he said with a meaningful jump of his eyebrows. "No one's allowed past East Fairmount Park no more—that's where Laurel Hill is."

My eyes widened. Of course. Laurel Hill Cemetery. In the blur of the carriage chase, I'd paid no heed to what direction we traveled.

"S'past that landing there." The driver gestured with his whip to a small dock to the left of the road that extended into the Schuylkill. Ferries carting cemetery and park visitors usually landed there, but today the dock was abandoned. Though the occasional vessel still moved up and down the river, now that I observed it closely, I could see that each one hugged the opposite bank. Clarence *had* said he could see the Dead from the river.

Daniel's hackney slowed, and my driver tightened the reins on our horse.

"Here, Miss?" he asked.

"Y-yes, please." My throat suddenly felt tight. *You can do this*, I told myself. *Elijah would do no less for you.*

I rose and offered the man my coins—seventy-five cents worth of change. I shoved it into his expectant hand. "Will this cover it?"

He smacked his lips. "Is that a dollar?"

I stepped unsteadily from the cab and then stared up at him, my jaw set. "No, it's not a dollar, but it's all I have, so take it."

He protested, but I didn't listen. He *was* cheating me, after all. Before he had time to stop me, I gathered my skirts in one hand and my parasol in the other and hustled after Daniel.

He was already plodding down the path toward Laurel Hill, and I picked up my pace to a brisk clip.

The dust of the path muffled my footsteps and rose up to cling at my petticoats. The woods at my right were part of East Fairmount Park, and though the road stayed flat, the ground on which the woods stood grew gradually steeper—so much so that in the distance, the road along the river was lined with rocky bluffs.

Daniel trekked before me on his long limbs, and my own short ones had trouble keeping up. Yet having him so far ahead meant he couldn't see me stalking behind. Besides, the quick pace calmed my nerves.

As I passed the vacant dock, Daniel rounded a bend in the path, and the forests and hills blocked him from view. When I reached the trees, I slowed to a hesitant creep. I inched toward the road's curve and peered around.

The iron bars of Laurel Hill and a gate, chained firmly shut, were directly before me. The fence took a sharp turn up, following the curve of the land.

But there was no sign of the lanky blond.

He must have left the path, moved onto the hill and into the trees beside me. I stepped forward, flicking my gaze around as I went. Where was he?

Branches from a wide-trunked sycamore floated above, shading this portion of the path. These woods were still part of East Fairmount Park, so had Daniel entered the park or had he gone into the cemetery?

I wiped my hands on my skirt, hoping my gloves would soak up the sweat on my palms, and I tried to moisten my dusty mouth. The cemetery loomed before me, and the emptiness around was silent—too silent. With each passing moment, my certainty grew: I had made a dangerous mistake by coming here.

Suddenly, something fell on the path before me, thudding to the road, and yellow dust puffed up around it.

A boot!

My heart exploded into my throat. I glanced wildly about and spun, clutching my parasol to my chest. All I could see were shadows and leaves and dust, yet I knew it must be Daniel—he was here, somewhere, watching me.

Then a figure dropped from the overhanging branches. His feet hit the ground with a heavy thump that sent fresh dust pluming up.

I cried out and reeled back, my eyes locked on the young

man crouched before me.

Daniel straightened. "Well, if it isn't her Royal Highness," he drawled, lifting his right arm. Sunlight flashed on metal, and the beams blinded me. When I finally saw what he held, my knees turned watery.

It was a sickle, and sunlight flickered on its long, wicked blade.

Chapter Ten

I wanted to scream, to run, to do something, but I couldn't move. I just stared, mouth agape and eyes bulging.

Daniel swung the sickle like a pendulum. It was the sort used for harvesting hay, and the blade was the length of my forearm. Back and forth he swung it.

"Do you have a death wish?" He cocked his head and pinched his lips thin. "Or do you visit such deadly places by accident?"

"Don't hurt me." I lifted my parasol with both hands and scooted back several feet. "I'll scream."

"You scream, and we both die." He spat onto the road. "I ain't gonna hurt you, Princess, so stop the hysterics."

"Hysterics," I screeched, waving my parasol at him. "You're

holding a blade and threatening—"

Daniel darted forward and snatched at my parasol. Before I could suck in air for a panicked shriek, he slung me around and clamped a firm hand over my mouth.

"Not a word," he breathed in my ear. "If any of the Hungry are in there, they'll come in seconds, and you'll get to see what this sickle is really for."

I struggled to breathe. My heart sprinted in my chest; the sound echoed in my head. His hands smelled like metal, like the cool tang of machines.

"I'm gonna drop my hand," he continued, "and you'd better keep quiet. Go running back to your mama or jump in the river—I don't care, so long as you don't scream."

My eyes moved from the tanned wrist pressed near my face to the glinting blade held at my chest. I gave a frantic nod of my head, and he withdrew his hand from my mouth.

I sucked in summer air. The scent of metal clung to my cheeks. "You ought to wear gloves," I hissed, hoping to mask my fear with insults.

"And you ought to be more careful." He still stood behind me. His breath tickled at my neck, and goose flesh bristled down the side of my body. He moved away then, and my skirts rustled back to their full width.

I twirled around, harsh whispers on my lips, but he had already marched off. He reached the enormous sycamore and circled behind its ancient trunk.

I lifted my skirts and scurried after him.

"Why're you still here?" he asked.

I ignored him. "The Hungry," I said in a low voice. "You mean the Dead—the quick, rabid ones."

"Yep." He tugged his flat cap from his pocket and slid it atop his head. "When a corpse *isn't* under a necromancer's control, it's desperate to feed. Like the ones that wake up on their own—the Dead that casket-bells warn us against."

So it *was* like the scary tales about rabid Dead that escape their coffins. The jingling bells that warn of Death were created for those occasional corpses who, somehow or other, were sparked with life though their bodies were still dead. Sparked with life and this desperate hunger.

"But," Daniel added, "rather than a corpse or two a year, we've got a whole cemetery's worth."

My fingers tightened around my skirts. "So . . . is the whole graveyard Hungry?"

"Not yet, but if the necromancer has lost control of one, it stands to reason he'll lose control of more." He bent down and slung the familiar satchel off the ground—no boot peeked from it now.

I suppose he'd used the boot to cover his sickle. And up close, I could see the sack was jagged and angular. There was clearly no body within.

"How do you know about the Hungry?" he asked.

"I-I saw them." I shuffled closer and pointed to the iron bars. "Through the fence."

He sighed. "Can't say I'm surprised you were here. You have

the curiosity of a cat and the common sense of a goldfish." He stared at me for a moment, the muscles in his jaw pulsing. Then he turned and strode toward the cemetery gate. I followed.

When he was several paces from the iron bars, he set down the bag and knelt beside it. With concentration, he removed the bag's contents and laid them out in an orderly manner on the ground. An enormous spool of copper wire, a wrench, some wooden stakes, glass jars, and a series of black stones—perhaps magnets. As he continued to remove various mechanical apparatuses, I sidled closer and closer.

"What's it all for?"

"Dead alarm." He didn't pause his careful unpacking. "A telegraph cable to connect to our lab."

"Why?"

"One of the Hungry got out last night. They're just so damn fast—too fast. It killed a man and two horses before we got to it." He gestured to his tools. "If what I'm trying actually works, then when something Dead—a spirit or a corpse—passes through the gate, its spiritual energy will complete a circuit. That'll set off our telegraph, and we'll know somethin' bad is on the loose."

"Oh." It was all very logical—clever, even.

Daniel twisted his cap to the side and then turned his attention to his sleeves. With meticulous care, he rolled them to his elbows. I turned away and scanned the iron bars of the fence. They were too close together to allow a person in or, rather, to allow a corpse *out*.

I looked back to Daniel and found him eying me, his expression dark. "You were following me, weren't you?" He yanked the final fold of his sleeve into place.

Embarrassment flamed through me. "Yes." I stared at the dusty path. "I-I'm sorry, Mr. Sheridan."

He grunted.

"I thought . . ." I paused and peeked up at him. "Well, I thought perhaps—"

"I know damn well what you thought." He dropped to the earth and yanked at the spool of copper wire. "You're all the same in this blasted city—you want our help but don't trust us. You think we ought to save you just *because*. Well, as far as I'm concerned, the Dead can have the whole lot of you."

"So why help us then?" I frowned. "Why don't you just let the Dead kill us all?"

"Because . . ." He shut his mouth, and for several moments he twisted the wire off the spool with more force than needed. At last he spat on the dirt and tried again. "Because Joseph won't let the Dead kill you. He does the right thing, so I do the right thing with him."

"But why? Why do you work for Mr. Boyer?"

"What's with all the pestering, huh?" He shoved out his lower jaw. "Listen, I got . . . Well, I got a lot of making up to do, and there ain't a nobler man than Joseph Boyer."

My mouth fell open at his gruff confession.

He wagged a warning finger. "Don't think I'll look after you, though—the world would be better off with one less princess."

"I'm not a princess," I huffed, beating my brain for some worthy retort.

"A queen then?"

"No! That's not what I meant—"

"Oh, an *empress*. I see. Pardon me, Your Majesty." He swooped into a crouched bow, and when his torso sprang back up, a smile floated at the edge of his lips.

"N-no, not an empress either. I-I'm just . . ." The more I stuttered, the more pompous his smile became. "You're exasperating," I finally groaned.

"Look, you don't have to like me, and I don't have to like you. But Joseph? Well, he's the only man around who can help you, so you'd best start trustin' him."

"I never said I didn't." I was grateful when Daniel didn't contradict me. "So will Joseph—er, will the Spirit-Hunters help me?"

"Yeah, yeah." Daniel waved at me as if brushing away a fly. "Your letter was covered in spiritual energy. Joseph was gonna offer to help, but you . . . well, you got there at a bad time." He dragged a thumb slowly across his neck. "Another one was found."

"A headless man?" I squeaked.

"Yeah."

My chest constricted, squeezing all the air from my lungs. A headless man? Elijah—what if it was Elijah?

I stepped dizzily to Daniel and grasped at his shoulder. He flinched.

"Land sakes, Empress." In a single, fluid movement, he sprang up and slipped a sturdy hand beneath my elbow.

"D-do you think," I tried to say. "Is it my—is it m-my . . ."

"It's not your brother." He lowered his face toward mine, and although his grass-green eyes were hard, his words were soft. "This boy's family found him."

"But . . ." My fingers dug into his bare forearm. "It could still . . . it's possible that h-he could, Elijah could show up like that . . ." I knew the answer, but I searched Daniel's face for some other reply.

"Yeah, it's possible, but it hasn't happened yet."

I clutched at my belly and forced myself to swallow. It wasn't Elijah—my brother was still all right. Certainly I would know if he was dead. I would sense it. The part of my heart that belonged to him would somehow know . . . wouldn't it?

Daniel drew me closer. "Don't worry. If your brother's got even half the grit you've got, then he'll be fine."

I nodded, moving my head a fraction of an inch. Elijah was fine. I would save him.

"Yes," I breathed. "Yes."

Daniel's eyes went distant, and his lips parted. With his free hand, he stroked the rough skin of his jaw, where new hair broke through. It made a scratching sound, like walking on dry sand.

Did his face smell like machines too? Or his neck? My gaze flicked to his white collar and exposed skin, then back to his face. For a moment, despite the stubble and the angles of his jaw, despite the mocking air and belligerence he always wore, Daniel looked vulnerable.

And there was something else in his eyes—a glint of interest I'd seen in other men's stares (though never directed at me). Perhaps even . . . but *no*, he couldn't possibly be attracted to me . . .

Could he?

Then he blinked, and the spell was broken. I squirmed away, instantly hot and unsettled. How had I fallen into such easy closeness with a boy I barely knew?

"Right. Well . . ." He cleared his throat and fidgeted with his cap. "Right."

"Yes." I shifted from foot to foot.

He flexed his arms and turned away. "Well, if you're gonna stay here, you might as well help—especially seein' as you owe me and all." He pointed to a glass jar. "I need some more grave dirt."

I choked. "Grave dirt? You can't possibly be serious."

"I'm always serious." He swooped down and picked up the jar. "There's a nice little spot near the river—that's where I got my sample last time."

"No." I laughed hollowly. "No."

"After all this," he drawled, opening his arms wide, "and you don't wanna go into the cemetery?"

"No." I bustled over to my parasol, still lying in the dusty path, and I bowed down to retrieve it. Then I brandished it at Daniel. "Going into Laurel Hill is certain death."

"Why, Empress, that's the first logical thing I've heard you say." He grinned, baring all his teeth. "Maybe next time I won't have to rescue you."

"Rescue me?" I squawked. "Rescue me from what?"

"From yourself." He drummed his fingers against the jar and then shoved it in his pocket. "If you interfere in my affairs again, I'll personally feed you to the Dead."

I scoffed. *And if you ever get in my way, I'll personally feed you to my mother.*

I shoved my chin as high as it would go. "Good day, sir."

Then I stalked past him and toward civilization. I might have to trust Daniel Sheridan, but I didn't have to like him.

What had been a brief hackney trip along the Schuylkill was a much longer journey by foot. By the time I reached Girard Avenue Bridge, my feet were screaming for mercy and my petticoats were suffocating from the dust. To pile on the agony, my arm ached from holding my parasol aloft.

Well, at least I knew a bit more about the Spirit-Hunters. I wasn't entirely convinced I could trust them, but I was willing to give them a chance.

When I finally reached the Exhibition, I barreled through the entrance. I was becoming quite adept at navigation by force, and soon I stood before the lab door.

It was open. Joseph was within, his back to me. His hat was on as if he'd just returned—or was about to leave. Words rushed from his mouth, and he spoke to Jie, who lounged on the windowsill.

"The Sutton family has been uncooperative on all levels. They refuse to print this in the papers." He lifted his hat and ran a gloved hand over his scalp. "Not that I blame them, *naturèl-man*. Losing a son, especially in such a horrifying manner . . ." He tapped his hat back on. "All the same, the public should know the danger they face. Listen: if Daniel has not returned by four, you must retrieve him. He must finish plans for the pulse bomb so I may propose it to the mayor."

Jie's dark eyes locked with mine, and he cleared his throat. He pointed to the door—to me—and Joseph whirled around.

"Miss Fitt." Joseph glided toward me and swooped an elegant bow. "You are back so soon, yet I am on my way out once more." Sweat glistened on his skin, and his face hung with exhaustion.

"It will only take a minute," I said, stepping into the lab. "It's about—"

"Your letter?" His eyebrows flicked up. "Speak with Miss Chen, then—she can help you. I really cannot stay. I have a meeting with the mayor and Exhibition board."

"Speak to whom?" I tilted my head.

"Miss Chen." He pointed to Jie. "Did you not meet her the other morning?"

"Oh, w-well, I . . ." Heat rose through my neck and face. Jie was a *girl*? Blazes! "We, uh, we weren't properly introduced," I finally managed to stutter.

Jie slid off the windowsill and addressed Joseph. "I can introduce myself. You should go."

"*Wi.*" He doffed his hat, his feet already carrying him away.

"*Orevwar*, Miss Fitt." He bolted into Machinery Hall and was gone.

I gulped and turned my attention to Jie. Now that I knew he was a *she* it seemed obvious—the soft curve of her face, the grace in her tiny hands, and the definite roundness near her bosom. But then why the dickens did she dress like a boy?

I stared at her linen trousers and matching blazer. She even wore a cherry-red necktie at the nape of a white shirt. And if that wasn't masculine enough, her hair was braided down her back while the front half of her head was shaved completely bald.

"You done admiring me?" she asked. Her voice was a sweet soprano, and only the faintest accent clung to her words.

"I, uh—"

"You never seen a Chinese person before?" She shoved her hands in her pockets and scowled.

"W-well, I . . ." I shook my head. "Not like you."

She narrowed her eyes, and I had to fight the instinct to cower back. She was like a wolf with hackles raised and, merciful heavens, she was scary.

"You dress like a boy," I blurted. "But you're not."

"It's easier this way." She sauntered over to me. "In case you hadn't noticed, Chinese girls aren't popular in this country."

It was true they were rare. I'd never seen a Chinese woman before—Jie was the first.

Jie coughed and waved a hand in my face. "You still here?"

I turned sharply away. "Yes," I mumbled. Heat ignited on my cheeks once more.

"So you want my help or not?" she asked.

"Yes. Please." I bowed my head and gazed at the ground.

"All right." She jerked her thumb to a stool. "Sit."

I swept my petticoats and skirt aside and then lowered myself onto the stool. My corset creaked like ancient floorboards.

Jie snickered and flung herself back on the windowsill. "That's another good reason to wear trousers." She gracefully swung one leg up and squeezed her knee to her chest. "Can you do this?"

My jaw tightened, and I fought the urge to glower. She could taunt me all she pleased. Mobility was probably overrated.

At Jie's not-so-subtle cough, I reeled my mind back to the matters at hand. "Mr. Sheridan told me my letter was covered in spiritual energy."

"Yep." She nodded once. "And you said that a corpse delivered it?"

"Yes, that's right." I relayed my experience at the train depot to her. Then I slid Elijah's messages from my pocket, excluding the one I'd left with the Spirit-Hunters. "I've read all his letters, and I think he was researching something important. He mentions books by Solomon and Honorius. I don't know what books, but I thought . . ."

Jie's eyes were wide, and her lips parted. "Solomon and Honorius," she repeated to herself. "Grimoires?" She pressed her fingers to her face, and the knuckles popped loudly. Then her eyes focused on me, and she dropped her hands. "Your brother, was he studying grimoires?"

"I don't know. What are . . . grimoires?" The word rolled off my tongue, strange and unknown.

"Books of power. Black magic—like necromancy." She sighed. "I don't know much—Joseph could tell you more. What I do know is that grimoires can be bad." She rose and stepped to Daniel's worktable.

"What do you mean 'bad'?" Ice spread through my chest.

She lifted a hand to silence me. Then she opened a wooden box and removed the bizarre brass goggles Daniel had worn at our first meeting. She slid them on her head and inspected the packet of letters I'd brought.

"Yep," she muttered. "Spiritual energy. Not much, but it's there." She pulled the goggles back off and flashed a warning look in my direction. "If you tell Daniel I used these, I'll kill you, yeah? He doesn't like it when people touch his inventions."

At my rapid nod, she returned the goggles to their box and strode back to the window.

"Please." I leaned urgently toward her. "You said bad. What did you mean?"

"Those names—Solomon, Honorius. I know those names. They wrote grimoires for dark magic." She hugged her arms to her chest and squinted at me as if considering how much to say.

Finally, she licked her lips and began. "Joseph had a friend once. Marcus. They studied with the Voodoo Queen of New Orleans."

"Voodoo?"

"Yeah. Like magic to ward off spirits and methods to contact the spirit realm. But Marcus wanted more, yeah? He wanted to know magic that stops illness—that raises the dead." She lowered her voice to a whisper. "He wanted the magic that kills people."

I pressed a hand to my stomach. "What happened?"

"From what I remember," she said, her gaze hazy as though she rummaged through her memory, "he used grimoires. He used them to learn the magic, and he started to kill people— same thing this necromancer is doing. He grew stronger and turned to darker and darker magic."

"So . . . could this necromancer be Marcus?"

Her head fluttered side to side. "No. Marcus died. See, Joseph found out about it all. He didn't know much about necromancy, but he could tell things weren't right with his best friend. So he followed Marcus one night and confronted him in the middle of a ritual."

"What kind of ritual?"

"Marcus was trying to bring a lotta corpses back to life. He wanted to attack the Voodoo Queen and take her strength, yeah? But when Joseph showed up, Marcus got distracted. He lost control of the bodies, and the corpses attacked. Joseph tried to save Marcus, but the Dead were too fast and too hungry."

Fast. Hungry. Like the ones in Laurel Hill.

"But how did Joseph survive?" I asked in a hushed voice.

"The Voodoo Queen. She came just in time, and they laid the bodies back to rest." She shook her head. "It was bad. Very

130

bad. Joseph survived, and the guilt eats at him—like maybe he should have noticed and stopped Marcus sooner. Like his friend's death was somehow his fault." She frowned and stared at her hands. "Joseph never talks about it."

"Yet he told you?"

She turned away. "Once. He spoke of it only once. So I'd understand why he does what he does, why we fight against the Dead. And so I'd understand how the spirit power can corrupt and consume." She exhaled heavily and a silence settled on the room.

Grimoires, spirit power, and voodoo. It was more horrifying and fantastic than I'd ever imagined. And what was Elijah's connection to it all? Why the devil would he study such dark theology?

Jie twisted her gaze back to me, a thoughtful expression on her face. "You said your brother was in New York, yeah?"

I nodded.

"When did he leave?"

"I'm not sure. He was supposed to arrive on May twenty-sixth, but he sent a telegraph saying he was delayed." I took a ragged breath, and the rest of the telegram tale poured out of me, ending with Elijah's arrival on or before the twenty-fifth of May and his telegram sent from Philadelphia.

Jie slouched forward and planted her hands on her knees. "Listen. The Dead were rising in Philadelphia before we got here on May twenty-fifth. That's why we came, yeah?"

"Right," I began slowly, "and before that you were in New

York because the necromancer had been there."

"Yep." Her eyebrows tilted up. "So maybe this necromancer was bothering your brother in New York, yeah? Maybe your brother came here, and the necromancer followed him. And then we"—she patted her chest—"followed the necromancer."

The door banged open. Jie and I jumped and twirled around.

Joseph sailed in. "Where is my list of volunteers?" Sweat was heavy on his face. "I need to show the Exhibition board that some of the guards are willing to train with us."

"Aren't you in the middle of the meeting?" Jie asked, grabbing a paper off the worktable.

"We haven't begun yet. They wish to take tea first." He took the list, and his eyes slid to me. "Miss Fitt, are you all right?"

I clamped my mouth shut—apparently I'd been gawking. "I was hoping to speak with you. I have questions."

He shot a glance toward Jie, his eyebrows jumping high.

She shrugged. "I couldn't answer them or I woulda."

"Ah." The lines around his mouth and eyes softened. He ran his hand along the rim of his top hat. "I can, I believe, spare a few moments. If you would be willing to walk with me." He glanced out the window and then back to me.

I nodded, excitement building in my chest. Curiosity is a strong fire, and once ignited, it is not easily put out.

"Please understand," he added. "I may not be able to answer all your questions, but I will do my best." He bowed his head and then marched through the door.

* * *

The bright afternoon sun hit the Bartholdi Fountain and shot beams of light off its bronze form. Rather than walk to Joseph's meeting in the crowded Main Hall, we had opted to stand in the fountain's refreshing mist.

All around us, couples promenaded arm in arm, ragged children scampered past, and many out-of-town visitors were rooted to the ground, scanning their guidebooks.

I squinted and popped open my parasol. Then I set my jaw and asked my first—and most important—question. "Mr. Boyer, will you help me?"

Joseph's gaze locked on my face, and for several heartbeats he did nothing but appraise me. Then at last he said, "I can stop the walking Dead, Miss Fitt. I can stop wicked spirits, and I can save those who need saving from the darker parts of the spirit world." He drew his shoulders back. "I use my abilities for good by helping those who need it, and so, yes, I *will* help you find your brother."

Gratitude swept over me like a cleansing rain, and my body swayed from the relief. Yet I didn't know how to express my feelings. A firm handshake seemed absurd, and a hug was utterly inappropriate. So I resorted to a blubbery "Thank you," tugged forcefully at my earrings, and moved on to the next question.

"Have you learned anything about the spirit my mother let in?"

"No." He frowned. "It is strange. Such a wicked ghost, yet no sign of it since Saturday. I cannot say if that is a good thing or a bad thing, for I have no idea what it seeks or how it became so strong."

"Can you stop a spirit like that?"

"Yes, in the same way I stop the walking Dead. I magnify an electric spark and break apart the soul."

I nodded and turned to the fountain. I stared with unseeing eyes into its splashing waters. I still had one desperate question I had to ask—though, heavens, I was scared of what his answer might be. I inhaled deeply and forced the words to come.

"Mr. Boyer . . . if my brother was studying grimoires, then that was probably bad, wasn't it?" I angled my head to watch him from the edge of my eye.

He clasped his hands behind his back. "Miss Fitt, grimoires typically teach black spells, but not . . . not *always*. A person can certainly study a grimoire without trying to master the rituals within."

That made sense. Elijah was a scholar through and through—action was not his style. I couldn't imagine his fascination with this type of theology being anything but academic.

I swiveled around to face him again. "So whatever my brother learned, it must have been something dangerous enough to attract the necromancer's attention."

"I have had little experience with grimoires," Joseph said, his chin lifting, "but I can think of no other reason for kidnapping your brother. This necromancer will not let your brother leave—that was plainly written in the letter—so whatever your brother may have learned, it makes him valuable. As long as he is valuable, he will stay alive. You must remember that."

I winced. I knew Joseph meant his words kindly, but I could take no comfort in them. What if Elijah stopped being valuable? Then what?

Joseph pulled a pocket watch from his waistcoat, and then his eyes flicked up to meet mine. "I must be going, *Mamzèi*."

I wet my lips. I didn't want him to leave. His presence made me feel safe, certain that at least one person knew what to do. I understood why Daniel and Jie trusted him so completely. He was solid.

Joseph slipped off his hat to bow, yet before he could say parting words, I rushed to speak.

"One last question, Mr. Boyer. Then I promise to leave you to your meeting and to trust your judgment without question."

He hesitated, but only for a heartbeat. Then he waved his top hat in the air. "Ask."

"If . . ." I gulped and steeled myself. "If this necromancer is sacrificing people to build his power, will you and the Spirit-Hunters be strong enough to stop him?"

Joseph's lips compressed into a tight line. Finally, he said, "I do not know, Miss Fitt. Let us hope that we are strong enough, *wi*? Let us hope." And with that he gave me a curt bow and spun on his heel toward the Main Building.

CHAPTER ELEVEN

The next day, the Wilcoxes came to tea.

I had refused to don a petticoat with this gown—the flounce and ruffles gave it sufficient girth, not to mention my own liberal padding in those lower regions. Besides, the dress's violet faille and black camel hair were simply not suited to a Philadelphia summer.

We were in the parlor, and the heat was especially stifling. The fringe of my collar scratched against my moist skin, and I knew a rash would await me later.

Mama and Mrs. Wilcox sat in high-backed armchairs, the tea tray between them. They chattered about the séance and future parties. I sat at the grand piano, plunking aimlessly at the keys, and Allison babbled cheerfully beside me.

Clarence sat on the sofa. He looked dreadful. His skin was greenish white and his eyes were ringed with puffy, black circles. Sweat shone at the edges of his face, and he dabbed at his brow with a handkerchief. He seemed sick or as if he hadn't slept in days.

He was probably just overworked. After all, he had taken on the family's business recently. Funny, I didn't actually know what that business was. Perhaps it was political? Clarence was running for city council, after all.

I flicked my gaze out the window and into our grassy yard. A bulky figure loafed against our cherry tree—the same tree from which I'd fallen and broken my wrist as a child. It was Willis, Clarence's footman. His black coat and trousers blended in with the shadows. The bench only feet away was also protected by the tree's shade, but the footman did not sit. As I watched, he detached himself from the trunk and strolled into the sunlight.

He reminded me of a patrolman who prowls the Philadelphia streets at night, but for what Willis prowled, I couldn't guess.

I returned my attention to the piano and found that Allison had stopped speaking. She eyed me through half-lowered lids.

I lifted my brows. "What is it?"

"Are you wearing makeup?" Her voice was accusatory.

"Of course not." I hit the highest white key, and it plinked sweetly. "Why would you think that?"

"You look . . . *different*. Almost pretty even."

I smirked. "Are you jealous?"

"Pshaw. Don't be stupid." She flipped a dark curl over her

shoulder. "I would never be jealous of *you*. Though"—she dropped her voice to a whisper—"you will have to tell me how you colored your cheeks."

I gritted my teeth. "It's quite simple, Allison. It's called *sunshine*."

At that moment, Clarence stood and cleared his throat.

"Miss Fitt, I don't suppose you'd like to go outside for some air. I fear the indoors do not suit me today."

"Yes please." I smiled gratefully and rose.

He turned to Mama. "Mrs. Fitt, would it be acceptable if I took your daughter for a stroll in your garden?"

"Of course." Mama's lips puckered. I knew that pucker—poorly masked smugness. She fluttered her lashes and turned to me. "Be sure to take your parasol, dear."

"Can I come?" Allison asked eagerly. She slid to the edge of the piano seat.

"No," chimed three voices. Clarence, Mrs. Wilcox, and my mother formed a stout chorus of refusal.

Allison's face fell. "Fine." She glowered at the ivory keys and pounded a low, plaintive note.

I took Clarence's offered arm, and we sauntered to the parlor door. Someone moved in the corner of my eye, and when I glanced back, I found Mama mouthing something, her eyebrows high.

"Greee-shenn beeend." Her lips moved with exaggerated care.

I whipped my head straight, and Clarence guided me

139

through the parlor door. Mama wanted me to remember my Grecian bend. It was the most popular stance for ladies these days: bottom thrust back and high, chest pushed forward and low. Supposedly, it was an enticing pose to the modern man. I couldn't imagine why since it made us look like camels who expected at any moment to be ridden by our masters.

Ah, but of course. That was no doubt *precisely* where the enticement lay. Heat rose in my face as the scandalous ideas connected in my mind, and I decided that ignoring Mama was my best course of action.

Clarence and I stepped onto the front porch, but Clarence wobbled unsteadily down the steps to the yard.

"Are you ill?" I asked him. "Or losing sleep?"

"No," he murmured. "I'm fine." He squinted and lifted a gloved hand to block out the sunlight.

"Really?" I stopped walking, and since we were linked, he was pulled to a halt as well. "You don't look well, Mr. Wilcox. I'm truly concerned for how . . ." I gestured vaguely toward him. "For how you are."

He clenched his jaw. "And I'm truly concerned for how red your skin is. You ought to use your parasol or the spots on your nose will spread all over your face."

I huffed in disgust. A tired and grumpy walking companion—fabulous. Although . . . my skin *did* feel overwarm. I popped open my parasol, a beige, Indian lace affair. Though it didn't match my dress in the least, it would protect me from the dreaded freckles.

After we resumed our stroll, Clarence pointed to the cherry tree. "Let's sit in the shade, shall we?"

"I'd rather walk."

"And *I* would rather sit." He clasped my arm and tugged me toward the shaded bench.

"Why are you so ornery?"

"And why are you so stubborn? I'm tired, and I want to—" He broke off, for at that moment Willis stepped around the edge of my house. The footman's eyes ran over Clarence and me. Then he planted his feet shoulder width apart and locked his gaze on mine, as if I were somehow a threat to his master.

I gave the burly man my fiercest glare before turning it on Clarence. "I'm going back inside, Mr. Wilcox."

"Why?"

"Your rude behavior. And also your . . ." I twirled my hand in the air, searching for the word. "Your thug over there."

Clarence turned to Willis and nodded, and though the footman doffed his derby hat and relaxed his stance, he did not depart.

Clarence rubbed his neck, and his chest heaved as he pushed out a long sigh. "Please stay, Miss Fitt. I . . . I'm sorry." He pointed again at the bench. "I promise to be civil."

"Civil enough to explain your mood?" I arched my eyebrow.

"Yes, yes." He offered his arm, and I hooked mine in. We shuffled awkwardly to the bench, and he helped me sit before easing himself down. He leaned exhaustedly back and then laid a limp hand over his eyes.

"You're right," he murmured. "I haven't been sleeping."

I straightened. "Why not?"

"I have . . . things . . . on my mind."

"What sort of things?"

He dropped his hand and gazed at me. The tightness of his lips showed none of his usual charm, and the rest of his face showed a bone-deep weariness. He shook his head, as if to say he was too tired to even deal with his own emotions.

After several moments, he finally said, "Another friend of mine passed away, and I've been having a difficult time with it."

"Oh," I breathed, suddenly wishing I had let the man be. As usual, I had pestered in the precise spot I could do the most damage. "I . . . I'm sorry, Mr. Wilcox."

"Hmmm." He let his head roll back. I thought for a moment he'd fallen asleep, but then he stirred and rubbed at his eyes. When at last he faced me again, I saw a fresh redness tingeing them.

"A close friend from Germantown Academy. James." He drawled out the name, as if savoring its taste. "James Sutton. A good man. The funeral was quite small—he deserved more."

I flinched as Joseph's exact words came flooding back to me: *The Sutton family has been uncooperative on all levels.*

I stared at Clarence, a new sort of pity in my chest. It had to be the same Sutton—there was no way it was just coincidence. The poor, poor man. He'd lost two friends to gruesome deaths—what were the chances? Two former schoolmates from

Germantown Academy taken and murdered.

My stomach turned to stone, and I fell back against the seat. Elijah was also a schoolmate. Elijah was missing. It was connected—the two decapitated men and my missing brother were connected. The necromancer hadn't just targeted Elijah, but other boys from their academy as well. Boys who were now men . . . men who'd met grisly deaths at the hands of a necromancer.

Oh God.

My recent helping of buttered toast churned its way out of my stomach and into my throat.

I threw my parasol on the grass, clapped my hand to my mouth, and bounded dizzily toward the hibiscus beside the front porch.

Clarence jogged to me, his expression horrified.

No doubt I resembled a toad: eyes bulging and chest ballooning with each desperate gasp. In and out, in and out until the revolt in my stomach subsided.

I wiped at my sweaty face with my sleeve.

"Let me get your mother," Clarence said. He held my parasol in his hand, and I snatched it away.

"No." I shook my head frantically. I needed to speak to the Spirit-Hunters—they needed to know this connection between the headless men and Elijah. Such news could not wait. Or rather, *I* could not wait with the knowledge boiling in my brain. "No. I . . . I must go."

He reared back. "Where?"

"The Exhibition," I mumbled, dabbing at the moisture at my hairline. I staggered away from the porch.

"Why the devil do you need to go there?"

"Fun."

"Fun?" He grabbed at my elbow. "Enough of this nonsense. You're ill!"

"No." I slipped from his grasp. "I'm going to the Exhibition. Now." I headed toward the street. I swayed with each step, but my legs were sturdy by the time I left my front yard. I opened my parasol and held it high.

My feet pounded a quick rhythm on the road. My stomach's rebellion had passed as quickly as it had come, and the only remaining effect was the acrid taste of bile in my mouth. My first reaction of sickening fear had been replaced with relentless determination.

My steps faltered. If the Germantown Academy boys were in danger, then that meant Clarence could be too. Did he realize? Should I say something?

No. I ought to wait. I should hear the Spirit-Hunters' opinions first. No need to frighten the man unnecessarily—he looked stressed enough already. Besides, he had the bulky Willis to look after him. Elijah had no one.

Clarence trotted up behind me on the street.

"Who will tell our mothers where we've gone?" he asked, his voice breathy. My pace was beyond his current physical capacity.

"You could tell your footman." I tipped my head backward,

certain the man trailed behind.

Clarence made a gurgling sound, and I gaped at him in surprise. Somehow his pale face had gone even paler. "No. Willis cannot go," he insisted. "H-he must stay with me."

"Why?"

Clarence fidgeted with his necktie. "Reasons. Personal ones."

I compressed my lips in a tight line. Maybe he had already sorted out that he was in danger. Perhaps that was why Willis always hovered nearby. The man was not a typical footman— following his master around, glowering at young damsels, and no doubt doing all sorts of other bizarre duties.

"Then *you* could go back," I suggested.

"To our mothers' shocked disapproval? I think not. And you can't get rid of me that easily, Miss Fitt." He lengthened his stride, a new glimmer in his eyes. "Whatever mischief you're up to, I'll be there for it. Besides, someone must ensure that you behave like a lady."

I skittered to a stop. "Like a lady? Which is how exactly?" My voice was shrill. He had picked a poor moment to antagonize me.

"Biddable."

"Biddable? Biddable!" Somehow my pitch was even screechier than before. I kicked my bottom high and dipped my chest low—a perfect display of the Grecian bend. "If it's a camel you wish to have, sir, then you are on the wrong continent!"

I straightened, pleased by his astonished expression. Then

I swiveled on my heel and resumed my race to the Centennial Exhibition.

I must have set a personal speed record, for it felt as if only minutes of half jogging and half walking had passed before Clarence and I reached the Exhibition. It was likely a personal sweat record as well, for my hair was painted to my face and my gloves were soaked straight through.

We entered Machinery Hall through the east entrance. Willis wasn't too far behind, and when we paused at the locomotive display, the footman paused nearby.

"What's in here?" Clarence moaned with no attempt to hide his annoyance.

"I want to see the fountains. I thought it might be pleasant on such a hot day."

"It *is* devilishly hot in here." He waved a hand at his face. "Let's get an ice cream soda, shall we?"

"Oh yes! There's a place that way." I pointed toward the Corliss engine. "I . . . I need to use the necessary. Perhaps I can meet you in the Hydraulic Annex?"

Clarence's lips quirked up slightly. "Yes, all right. Use the water closet and then meet me in the annex." He bowed slightly, then stepped backward and moved into the crowd.

I waited until he was out of sight before I pivoted right toward the Spirit-Hunters' lab. I had only made it two steps when a shiny blond head caught my eye. Crouched behind the nearest steam engine, exactly as I had hidden the day before, was

Daniel Sheridan. I reached his side in less than a second.

"Why are you hiding?" I demanded.

He rose and craned his neck, his eyes darting around the exhibit. "I'm not hiding."

"Then what *are* you doing?"

"I was . . . I was heading back to the lab, and I dropped something." He tried to move past me, but I sidestepped and cut him off.

"What did you drop?"

"Nothing. Stand aside, Empress."

"So you *were* hiding."

He set his jaw, and I noticed his face was freshly shaved. It made his skin look soft.

"I've places to be," he growled. "So if you don't step outta my way, I will move your imperial figure myself."

I had no doubt he would, so I skittered aside. He stalked past, but I chased close behind—we were headed to the same place, after all.

He lengthened his stride. "Don't do that."

"Do what?" I picked up my pace too.

"Follow me."

"But I'm going where you're going, Mr. Sheridan."

"What?" He twisted around, his hands snaking out, and he grabbed my wrists—not hard, yet tightly enough that I had no alternative but to go where he led. He slung me into a narrow space between two locomotives and released his grip.

He blocked my exit, and his shoulders were hunched

practically to his ears. His usually tanned face was bloodless and white.

My pulse quickened. I inched back, trapped between the gleaming machines, and inhaled a proper lungful of air—I would scream if I had to. But then he spoke.

"Does he know where you're going?"

My scream died. "Huh? Who?"

"Wilc—" He broke off and swallowed. "Your beau. The man you came in with."

I narrowed my eyes. Why did Daniel care about that? "No. He doesn't know I'm here."

"What did you tell him?"

"That I was going to the water closet. Why are you asking—"

"That's it?" Daniel interrupted, his shoulders dropping an inch. "That was all you said?"

"Yes."

"He doesn't know about me? About the Spirit-Hunters?"

"No—not from me, at least. He does know about the Spirit-Hunters, though. Everyone does. You're in the newspapers."

He ran a hand through his hair and eyed me warily. "If it's just the papers, then it's fine."

My heart slowed, and intense curiosity supplanted my fright. "Why do you care if Mr. Wilcox knows about you?"

"That's none of your affair, but don't you ever mention my name to him." He dipped his chin and looked at me from the tops of his eyes. "Got it?"

"No." I was wretchedly tired of men declaring what I could and could not do. "I don't 'got it,' Mr. Sheridan. You can't act like this and not explain yourself. So . . . so unless you answer my questions properly, I'll make a special point to tell Mr. Wilcox exactly—"

Daniel clamped his hand over my mouth and pressed me against the engine. "You'll do no such thing." He spoke softly into my ear. It didn't frighten me, but had my full attention.

"For your own safety and mine," he continued, "you will keep that tongue of yours still." He slid the hand from my mouth and planted it on the engine beside my head. His mouth still hovered beside my face, and his breath tickled along my ear.

All the hairs on my neck and arms pricked up.

Then the reality of the situation hit me. He was entirely too close—both for proper etiquette and my composure. I punched the inside of his elbow with all my strength.

"Ow!" he howled, stumbling back.

"Varmint!" I spat out the first word I could find and prayed he couldn't see my scarlet flush. "You rude, low-class varmint! Don't you *ever* touch me again."

He gripped his elbow to his stomach, massaging the joint and muttering under his breath.

"What's that?" I demanded. "What are you grumbling about?"

His lips curved into a frown. "I said I ain't a varmint, and I ain't gonna hurt you."

"Aw," I simpered, pouting my lower lip dramatically and

trying to hide my own discomfort. "Did I hurt your feelings? Well, you shouldn't take it personally, Mr. Sheridan. No one cares about my opinion."

Daniel's frown vanished, and the angles of his jaw eased into a gentle sadness. "Maybe I care."

His words astounded me, and a strange flutter whirled through my chest. Had he just *complimented* me?

For several moments I was too flustered to speak, and the air was thick with our silence—as if the words I wanted to say were there, but invisible. Daniel shifted his weight, his eyes still on mine.

At last he flashed a grin, and the strange moment passed. He gave a mocking bow. When he lifted his head back up, his face was somber once more.

"Empress, you must not tell Clarence Wilcox that you know me." His voice was low, and he inched closer. "Please. That man can't know I'm here."

The sincerity in his face and the quiet desperation in his words convinced me to keep his secret. "I wasn't going to tell anyway," I said primly, tilting my head away. "I don't exactly want him to know I'm working with the likes of you. I'll keep your secret, Mr. Sheridan, though I expect an explanation one day."

He nodded. "And maybe one day"—he reached out and flicked my chin playfully with his thumb—"I'll give you one." He sauntered backward until he reached the edge of the machine. Then he leaned out and scanned the area.

"Oh, and one last thing, Empress." He turned his light eyes on me once more. "You might want to reconsider your suitors."

"What does that mean?"

"It's a warning." He glanced over his shoulder and then back to me. "I'm almighty scared of Clarence Wilcox, and if you've got any sense in that pretty head of yours, you'll be almighty scared of him too."

CHAPTER TWELVE

Joseph ran a hand over his bare head and leaned against the window of the Spirit-Hunters' lab. I had followed Daniel to the lab, and then he and Joseph had patiently listened to my rushed explanation of the Germantown Academy boys. Jie was away, though they wouldn't tell me where she'd gone.

"And you do not think it is merely coincidence?" Joseph asked.

I shook my head. "How can it be? Two boys from the same school as my brother, both decap—" I faltered and swallowed. "Both decapitated. Both walking Dead."

Daniel scooted a stool out and plopped down with his knees angled out. "I see why a necromancer might be interested in your brother, but what about the other boys? Where's the logic behind that?"

"I don't know. I simply came to tell you because it seemed important."

"Yes," Joseph said, "and I think you were right to come here. We were not aware of this connection. And perhaps . . . well, perhaps such information will sway the city officials in our favor."

"Yeah." Daniel chuckled, a hollow, derisive sound. "All these rich boys showing up headless? Their families may want to keep it quiet, but eventually someone will notice, and that'll attract attention from the international visitors."

"Yes, and so . . . wait . . ." I shook my head. "I don't understand. Why doesn't the city government help you?"

"They help some," Daniel said. "I mean, they let us install Dead alarms, and they've given us a handful of Exhibition guards to train, but . . . "He sniffed and pointed out the lab window, where people in colorful gowns and dapper suits meandered beside the majestic Bartholdi Fountain. "They aren't as helpful as they *could* be because of all that."

I frowned, baffled. "What do you mean?"

"The Centennial Exhibition is a fantasy, Empress. An illusion. It gleams like diamonds and distracts the eye from the rotting parts of America—like Shantytown." He tipped his head in the direction of the shacks on Elm Avenue. "The amount of money spent to keep this Exhibition spotless reeks of dirty politics to me, and from what I can see, the local politicians aren't out to help anyone but themselves."

"Daniel is correct," Joseph said. "Mayor Stokely and many of the Exhibition board members are focused on the upcoming political elections. None of them wish to draw attention of *any kind* to themselves. Too much focus on the Dead or decapitations might bring attention to some of their shadier dealings. Every American politician is under scrutiny now because of the Whiskey Ring."

"The Whiskey Ring?" I picked at the buttons on my glove. "You mean that group of Republicans, right? I don't see how that's related to any of this."

Daniel pressed his lips into a grim line. "Because those officials were using taxpayer money for their own misbehaving. And your local politicians aren't any nicer. They rig the votes, keep tax money, and don't want any of the visiting federal workers or foreigners to notice."

I pressed my hand to my forehead. "I still don't understand. If there's so much danger from the Dead, wouldn't the whole city want you to have the resources you need?"

"You'd think." Daniel ran his tongue over his teeth. "But the board's convinced we can keep the problem contained until the end of the Exhibition."

"But that's not for months!" I cried.

Joseph winced. "*Wi*, but with the elections coming up, the politicians need to make the Dead appear to be a minor problem."

"Plus," Daniel hastened to add, "they don't wanna spend precious campaign and bribery money on some worthless Spirit-Hunters."

Joseph nodded. "Money that is also needed to pay for all this grandeur." He flicked his wrist toward the window. "We, the Spirit-Hunters, have made progress, for we are training Exhibition guards to disable corpses, and it looks as though Mayor Stokely may also provide some police. This helps, but it is not enough. I am still the only person who can lay hundreds of Dead to rest at once."

"So what do you need?" I asked, glancing around for a clock. There was none, but I was certain enough time had passed to raise Clarence's suspicions over my extended absence. "If people aren't enough, Mr. Boyer, then what is?"

Joseph grimaced. "Money, equipment, and when the time comes, more men. Many more men."

"The time comes?" My eyes flitted between Joseph's frown and Daniel's glower. "Time for what?"

"Entering Laurel Hill." Joseph spoke so low I could scarcely hear the words. "To stop all the Dead at once."

Daniel huffed out a sigh. "But first I gotta finish my newest invention. And . . ." He dragged out the word and rolled his hands, as if the next step in his explanation was obvious.

But it wasn't obvious to me, and I wagged my head. "And what?"

"And I *can't* finish it."

"Why?"

"I don't have access to research. I need more information on electricity, explosives, chemicals, and the like."

I wrinkled my forehead. "Why don't you just go to the library?"

"We don't have the right subscription." Daniel scratched his jaw. "Sure, I can waltz into the Mercantile Library downtown whenever I fancy, but it does me no good if I can't get into the private collections. And the Exhibition board does not seem keen on sharing that sort of subscription."

Joseph spread his hands, palms up. "The city does not allow just anyone access to potentially dangerous information. It is for the safety of the citizens."

Private collections. The Mercantile Library. Excitement bubbled through me—I could help! I'd spent many a childhood afternoon in that very same library, squeezed together in a chair with Elijah or exploring endless shelves. It was several miles east of the Exhibition, directly in the center of Philadelphia.

I stepped toward Daniel. "Do you mean the Mercantile on Tenth?"

"Yeah." Daniel picked at his fingernails and avoided my eyes. "Why do you ask?"

"Because I can."

"You can what?"

"I can go in the private collections!" I scurried toward him. "My father had a lifetime subscription, Mr. Sheridan, and not just that, but he had special privileges. I'm certain I could use his name to get you into the private collections."

Daniel's jaw fell. "Why didn't you say so before?"

"What?" I recoiled. "How was I supposed to know you needed it?"

"We could've gone ages ago!"

My enthusiasm transformed into outrage. "In that case, why didn't you say you needed it?"

"Because I didn't know you had a subscription!"

"Aha!" I cried, thrusting a finger at him. "Your argument's a circle!"

Daniel sprang up. "We wasted all this time—"

"Silence!" Joseph roared. "You are like squawking parrots, and I have had quite enough. Miss Fitt, I would ask that you take Mr. Sheridan to the library immediately. Daniel, I would ask that you keep that big mouth of yours silent."

My shoulders drooped, and all my indignation washed away. "I-I can't go now," I replied meekly. "I'm here with someone, and I'm afraid . . ." I stopped my words and gulped.

Daniel's face lost all color. "She's right. Now won't do. Tomorrow morning, first thing." At Joseph's questioning eyebrow, he added, "I'll explain later."

"So tomorrow morning, then?" I twined my fingers around my earring.

"*Wi*." Joseph bowed his head. "Though I beg you to come quite early. We lose valuable time as each day passes."

After a soft good-bye, I shambled into Machinery Hall and struggled to conquer my resisting heart.

Daniel's words would not stop repeating in my mind: *I'm almighty scared of Clarence Wilcox.* But I had no reason to fear Clarence, right? Whatever Daniel's reasons, they were his and his alone.

I tipped my chin up and drew my shoulders back. *I merely visited the water closet—I must pretend that. Easy as pie.*

Soon I saw the mist from the Hydraulic Annex, and the crashing of its waterfalls grew louder with each step. When I reached the rows of benches surrounding the pool, I scanned about for Clarence.

Then I saw Willis. He slouched against the pool's rail, but his attention was focused elsewhere. I followed his gaze, and what I saw made me stop.

Clarence was talking to Nicholas Peger, and judging by their dark expressions, animated movements, and close proximity, the men knew each other—very well.

CHAPTER THIRTEEN

By the time I reached Clarence's side, Peger had slithered off into the crowds. It was probably best, for I didn't want the blond reporter to recognize me. I prodded Clarence with casual questions about Peger, but Clarence insisted the man had only stopped to ask for the time.

Funny, because now jutting from Willis's pocket was a rolled newspaper—the same sort of newspaper Clarence had acquired during his mysterious rendezvous on my front porch.

I let the subject drop, though, and I drifted into my thoughts. Clarence seemed focused on his own sad musings, and we spent the remainder of the hour wandering the rows of Machinery Hall in somewhat companionable silence.

When I arrived home later that afternoon, Mama cornered

me, her mouth spewing questions. They weren't angry questions, though. She wouldn't stop clapping her hands and demanding specifics on my conversations with Clarence. It seemed it was all right for me to misbehave and run off with no warning so long as I did so with a wealthy bachelor.

The next morning I woke early and rushed to the Exhibition. As Joseph had said, there was no time to waste.

The three Spirit-Hunters awaited me at the Exhibition turnstiles. They'd been forced to abandon their lab when Peger had arrived demanding interviews.

Joseph pointed to the horse-drawn streetcars that clattered to and from the Exhibition. We clambered through the throngs to reach the concourse.

"I do not like leaving the lab." Joseph fidgeted with the rim of his top hat. He held a black leather case in one hand much like a doctor's bag, and it swung with each of his gliding steps. "Peger is like a spider who spins my words against me."

"Aw, it's good we're all going," Daniel said. "Three can work faster than one, and when we get back, the spider will be gone."

"Four," I corrected. I had to pump my legs to keep up with the team's trotting gait.

"Huh?" Daniel glanced over his shoulder at me.

"There are four of us," I said.

His stride slowed until he walked beside me. "I'm not sure you count, Empress."

"Why not? I can scour the library as well as any of you! I

162

have a brain and am perfectly . . ."

He was grinning wide. The rascal was teasing me! And before I could summon a worthy retort, he whistled brightly and sauntered ahead of me.

Blazes, he was cocky. And entirely too dashing for his own good—or for *my* own good, rather.

Moments later, and with no time to dwell on Daniel's easy smile, I clambered onto the streetcar.

"Fare?" the mustached driver demanded.

"Oh, what is the—" I shut my mouth as he plucked a coin from my gloved hand. It was like magic! I had no idea how it had appeared there.

Jie gripped my now-empty hand and towed me to an open-air window. I was squashed by the other passengers, but at least I could breathe.

"Two for the price of one." She snickered. "I gave you my quarter. The driver didn't even see me get on."

"Really?" So it wasn't magic, then. Just Jie's unnatural dexterity. I huffed out a jealous sigh. "So you managed to sneak on *and* slip money into my hand? How do you do it—move like that, I mean? Where'd you learn it?"

Her dark eyes crinkled with pleasure, but she didn't reply. I inhaled for a dejected sigh, but gagged on the stench of people and horse. I thrust my head out the open window and sucked in air.

The horses heaved, and the streetcar rattled to a start down Elm Avenue, east toward downtown. Jie swung out the window beside me. Over the trotting hooves, squeaking wheels, and crunching gravel, I shouted, "You're nothing like any girl I've ever met." I couldn't keep the envy from my voice, and my face was likely as green as my words.

But honestly, I *hadn't* ever met anyone like her. She could go where she pleased, do whatever she wanted, and no one was scandalized by it. And most impressive of all, she could fight.

She rubbed the bald half of her head. "It's because I have no hair. In China we say, 'The girl with the full hair is not as free as the girl with the bare head.'"

"What?" I tried to ask, but the dust plumes from the road flew into my mouth. All I could manage was a wispy choke. I pulled back into the streetcar and coughed my throat empty. I tried again. "What does that saying mean?"

She twisted back into the car too. "It means that as long as I still shave my hair, I'm free. See, in China, girls keep their heads bald like the boys, yeah? Then when we're the age to become a woman, we bind our feet and grow out our hair."

"So . . ." I frowned. "Does that mean you're not a woman yet?"

"Yep." She flashed her eyebrows and pointed down to her boots. "My feet are still big and ugly."

I cringed. Foot-binding was a practice that seemed barbaric to my Western sensibilities. Breaking one's foot and wrapping it so it stopped growing? Of course, if one paused to consider, was binding a woman's waist and forcing her to stand like a camel any less barbaric?

"Why haven't you had your feet bound?" I asked. "You're older than me, aren't you?"

"If I were still in China, I would've." She cracked her knuckles against her jaw and stared out the window. "See, when I came to America, I was real young. My uncle had to pretend I was a boy. It was safer that way, yeah? Things here . . . they aren't good for people like me, and it's even worse out west. As a boy, my chances were better. And that way my uncle and I could both work."

But what had happened to her uncle? I wanted to ask. In fact, I had a thousand questions I wanted to ply her with—about her past, about her culture, about her strength—but I didn't. I couldn't. Not when her face looked so distant.

"So how did you meet Joseph?" I asked, hoping to change the subject.

"We were all three at the same saloon."

My eyelids shot up. "A saloon?"

She chuckled and waved in Daniel's direction. "He got cheated at cards, yeah? And a fight broke out. Joseph saw the whole thing, and when the police came, he vouched for Daniel."

I rolled my eyes. The story certainly fit what I knew of Daniel—and I almost wished I could have seen it.

"And you?" I prodded. "What were you doing there?"

She grinned wickedly. "I was the one who cheated Daniel."

I barked a laugh. Now I *really* wished I could have seen it.

"So now you see?" she asked. "With my hair like this, I'll be free forever." She poked at my bodice. "Why would I ever want to put this on? Squeeze my guts and deform my ribs? It's not natural."

I snorted. "You wouldn't want to wear it. I certainly don't."

"Then why do you?"

I scrunched my forehead up at the absurdity of the question. "Because I don't have a choice."

She shook her head and gazed at me with sad eyes. It made me uncomfortable.

I turned away from her disappointed scrutiny and watched the Schuylkill River flowing beneath the Girard Avenue Bridge.

"Eleanor, you have a choice," she said softly. "You *always* have a choice."

Half an hour later, the Spirit-Hunters and I paraded through the arched doorways of the Mercantile Library. The moment my foot crossed into the cavernous room, calm blew over me.

Before me, the high, curved ceilings of the library rose over aisle after aisle of bookshelves. The morning sun poured in from windows spanning the entire length and height of the walls. It layered shadows over the western half of the room. A small fountain bubbled at the entrance, and the soft murmur of the library's patrons traveled over it like a melody.

I hadn't visited this place since Elijah had left, and I couldn't imagine why. So many happy days had been spent here. My chest clenched with regret. I had been Elijah's outlet from his bullies, and he had been my escape from Mama's expectations.

Yet without Elijah in my life, I'd bowed to Mama's demands.

I had done no studying, and most of my intellectual thinking had involved coin counting and haggling.

I guided the Spirit-Hunters to a circular desk at the center of the room. After verifying my father's subscription, the pretty, black-haired librarian slipped a brass key from her pocket.

"The entrance is there." She pointed to a chestnut door at the back of the room. "If you wish to take any documents home, you must sign them out first."

I took the key, and we moved through the people and shelves toward the back room. Once I'd unlocked the door, Joseph turned to Daniel.

"Take these." Joseph slipped the brass goggles from his bag and thrust them into Daniel's hands. He swiveled to me. "What year was your brother at school, Miss Fitt? And what was the name?"

"Germantown Academy, and he started in the mid-sixties." I wrinkled my forehead. "Why do you ask?"

"Yearbook. I'd like to see a list of all the boys who attended, if possible." He spoke with no hint of command, only a straightforward efficiency. Joseph had a job to do, he expected us to help, and he tolerated nothing but obedience. The Spirit-Hunters worked together like the gears of a clock—orderly and focused.

Joseph inclined his head toward Jie. "You heard Miss Fitt."

Jie nodded and stalked off toward the bookshelves in the main room. Joseph went into the private room, and I followed.

Daniel was already inside, his lanky form draped on a

ladder as he scanned the highest shelves. The square room that housed the library's private collections was also lit by enormous windows, and the walls were lined with colorful book spines, newspapers, scrolls, and loose pages. In the center were tables and studious-looking, straight-backed chairs. It was a haven of knowledge.

I cleared my throat and moved to Joseph, who was systematically plucking books from the shelves. "Mr. Boyer?"

Joseph did not move, but his eyes slid sideways to peer at me. "Yes, Miss Fitt?"

"Do you need me?"

"No, I think not." He looked back to the shelf and flourished his gloved hand toward the door. "We have enough hands on deck. You may relax, if you wish, and we should be finished quite soon."

I curtsied, but hesitated to leave. "Um . . . have you learned anything about the spirit yet? There's been nothing in the papers about it, so I wondered if perhaps . . . it had vanished?"

"*Non.* I doubt that it would leave—not if it tried so desperately to enter the earthly realm." He waved to the shelves. "I intend to search for a history of Philadelphia's hauntings, but there is little else I can do. Unless this spirit appears before me, I cannot possibly find out what it wants—or hope to stop it."

I inhaled slowly. I supposed he was right. What could one possibly do about an absent, faceless spirit?

"We have not seen it since Saturday," Joseph added. "Let us hope its business with us is finished."

After a murmured thank you, I left the private collections room and bustled back to the circular desk at the center of the library. I had my own research to conduct. I now knew to whom the strange names in Elijah's letter belonged, but the meaning behind the other odd phrase in Elijah's letter still eluded me.

"Do you know anything about the Gas Ring?" I asked the pretty librarian sitting at the desk. "Or where I can research it?"

She narrowed her eyes. "I've never heard of it. Do you mean the Whiskey Ring?"

"No." I gave her a tight grin. "Thanks." I strolled back toward the private collections room, but when I reached the door, I turned right and headed down the hallway for a red velvet armchair—a chair I knew well.

I took my time adjusting my petticoats, fidgeting with my bustle, and squirming in my bodice. Then I eased down and set my parasol on the pine floor. This had been the chair Elijah and I had shared when we waited on Father. It was just as I remembered it.

Sunbeams pierced the air around me, illuminating the hidden world of dust that floated like the finest of snow. I grinned and tapped the armrest. A fresh army swirled up. The first time Elijah had shown me that trick, I'd been seven and he ten. We'd sat here, and he'd read aloud from *A Midsummer Night's Dream*.

A figure moved at the corner of my eye. It was Daniel, leaving the private collections room. He held books and papers in one hand and the goggles in the other. He stared at the floor, either inspecting the wood grain or deep in thought. I presumed the latter.

"Mr. Sheridan." I stood, my gown rustling. "Did you find what you needed?"

His head snapped up. "Empress." He hunched his shoulders. "Yeah, I got some books for my invention."

"And those will help?" I angled my head and read a title. "*Annalen der Physik und Chemie.* Do you speak German?"

"Some. I've had to figure it out, Germans being the masters of engineering and all."

"Oh." I was impressed. I gestured to the goggles. "And is that one of your inventions?"

He grunted his acknowledgment.

"What do they do?"

"Well, uh . . ." He swayed from foot to foot, as if he wasn't sure how to proceed. "Land sakes," he finally grumbled. "Just take 'em. See for yourself."

My eyebrows shot up. "You want me to wear them?"

"Yeah. And tell me what you see." He set the books on the ground against the wall and, taking my hand, he put the goggles in my open palm. His face tightened. "But do be careful."

I slid them on and scanned around me. The lenses were heavy and thick. They pulled at my ears and pressed on my nose. I studied my hand; the white of my gloves was barely visible. "It's so dark," I said. "And blurry. It feels as if I'm staring through muddy water."

"That's good. It means there is no spiritual energy here. If there was something Dead around, the lenses would clear up."

"Why?" I tried to examine his face, but all I could make out was the general shape of his head.

"The goggles operate on a simple principle. They rely on magnetic energy—electromagnetism, to be precise." He spoke much like Elijah would when explaining his latest theological find: animated and articulate.

I slid the goggles down and peered over the tops. I watched the curve of Daniel's lips—delicate, round, and at odds with the angle of his jaw. I caught glimpses of his tongue as he spoke.

What was it about mouths that made them so fascinating? I had read of kisses (Shakespeare was fond of them in his plays), but I'd never seen one. And I'd *certainly* never experienced one. Did people merely touch lip to lip . . . or was there more to it?

Has Daniel ever kissed anyone?

My whole body stiffened when I realized the direction my thoughts had taken. I scrunched my eyes shut. This was not the sort of curiosity I should indulge.

When I lifted my eyelids, I realized I'd missed Daniel's entire lecture.

"Could you repeat that last bit?" I prayed he wouldn't notice the tremor in my voice.

"I said there's fluid between two pieces of glass." His tone was disapproving, as if my lapse in attention was an insult. "That fluid has a magnetic powder in it."

"And?"

"And since electricity is magnetic, the magnetic powder moves within the lenses according to the energy around. Come on—the particles are easier to see in the sunlight."

He pushed the goggles up my nose and over my eyes again. Then I felt his hand clasp my elbow. He guided me toward the eastern wall on the right. We walked, my footsteps careful and controlled, as he continued to explain.

"All free energy leaves a residue behind—something traceable. I calibrated the goggles with grave dirt, so now the magnetic particles are attracted to spiritual energy. That way when something Dead has been in the area or touched something—"

"Like the letter the walking corpse delivered?" I interrupted. "You said it was covered in spiritual energy." I strained my neck this way and that, scanning everything we passed. We turned around and walked back toward the armchair and private collections room.

"Yeah, like your letter. The magnetic powder moves toward the residue, and the fluid clears up."

"Does it work?"

He sniffed. "Of course it works."

I stopped walking. "Then why don't I see you?" I squinted and tried to make out his features. "Don't living people make the powder move since we have spiritual energy too?"

"Good question," he said. "The general principle is that our spiritual energy is attached—it's woven into our bodies. When we die, the spirit and the body split apart. One half heads to the other realm while the other half goes into the ground."

The hairs on my arms pricked up beneath the faille of my gown. "So that spirit my mother let in, it's just pure spiritual energy?"

"Exactly. And the walking Dead, they're mostly just rotting corpses with a bit of energy to animate 'em."

I lowered the goggles and gazed at him. "And that energy isn't attached, so it leaves a residue."

"Right again." He measured me with a narrow-eyed stare, and then his lips quirked up with pleasure.

My mouth went dry. I shoved the goggles back up. That smile was unnerving.

I stepped hesitantly back toward the private room, searching around as I'd done before and taking comfort in the blurry darkness of the lenses. At least now I couldn't see Daniel's face. Except the darkness wasn't so dark anymore. In fact, the fluid wasn't muddy at all. I could distinctly make out the bookshelves to my left, the wall to my right, and the velvet armchair ahead.

But no—I couldn't actually see the armchair. All the magnetic powder had clumped where the chair should have been in my vision. The more I gazed at the fuzzy blob where I knew the chair stood, the more everything else came into focus. Something magnetic was pulling the powder toward the chair.

"Mr. Sheridan." My voice came out husky with shock. "Mr. Sheridan, come quick."

He appeared in my field of view: messy blond hair, bright green eyes, and concern wrinkling down his brow. He and the rest of the library looked exactly as they would without the goggles. Only the armchair remained dark and indistinguishable.

"What is it?" he asked.

"I think . . . I think . . ." I dropped my voice to a whisper. "I think the Dead were here."

Daniel slid the goggles off my face, brushing his fingers along my jawbone in the process. I gasped in surprise. His fingers were rough and warm.

He pressed the lenses to his eyes and whistled softly. "You're right."

My heart thumped with a nervous hope. I grabbed at Daniel's coat sleeve. "Maybe my brother was here," I breathed. "This was our chair, and . . . all his letters had energy on them, so maybe Elijah's covered in residue too and leaving it behind."

He removed the goggles and stared at my hand on his sleeve. Then his eyes shifted to my face. "It'd be possible if he was around it, but . . . but still, it shouldn't leave such a strong signal. The magnetic powder is clumpin' so tight that it's like a walking corpse is sitting there now. This is a lot of energy, and it's fresh."

"Come on then." I ignored his bark of surprise and hauled him by the coat toward the circular desk. Perhaps someone had seen who had been there.

I asked the same librarian from before. "Did anyone sit in that chair recently?" I pointed back. "The red one near the private collections room."

Daniel planted his hands on the desk. "Someone within the

last two days. And whoever it was would've been there awhile."

She gnawed at her lip. "Yes, I do recall a man there yester-day."

"What did he look like?" I asked.

"He was young. And big." She tapped her shoulders. "Broad."

"Bigger than him?" I cocked my head toward Daniel.

The librarian assessed my companion and then flashed him an approving grin. "Oh yes, this man was bigger." She ran her tongue over her lips. "But you're taller."

"Did he have spectacles?" I pressed.

"No. No spectacles." Her eyes stayed locked on Daniel.

"Is there anything else you remember?" I demanded.

The woman puffed out her lips and ignored me, clearly flirt-ing with Daniel.

I glanced at Daniel, hoping he would back me up, but all I found was a smug lift to his eyebrow.

"Focus!" I banged the desk with my fist, and they both flinched. Did they not see the importance of this situation? I trembled with anxious energy, and I needed answers. "Was there anything else distinguishing about this man?"

"Well . . ." Her eyes roamed around, but at last she nodded primly. "Come to think of it, yes. The man was filthy."

I leaned over the desk. "How filthy?"

She sniffed and curled her lips. "As in, I doubt very much he had bathed in the last year. He was covered in dirt, his suit was abominable, and he *stank*."

Daniel and I exchanged a wide-eyed glance. What she described sounded like one of the Dead. A fresh corpse perhaps. Elijah's? No, no. A big man, she said. Elijah was small. No extra girth like his sister.

"What was he reading?" Daniel asked.

"He took all the information we have on the Centennial Exhibition."

Daniel's brows drew together. "Did he ask for it?"

"No. He simply took the books we have laid out for Exhibition visitors. Then he went and sat in that chair." Her eyes thinned and hardened. "Why are you asking so many questions?"

I didn't answer, for I had spotted the display of Exhibition books on the desk. "He took those?"

At the woman's nod, I swept them up and scampered back toward the armchair. The Dead had been here, and we were onto something! I could feel it. We were about to discover some critical piece in all these puzzles. My energy overflowed, and I didn't care if I looked like a fool frolicking through the library.

Daniel trotted beside me, and when we reached the chair, I tossed the books haphazardly on the seat to inspect their titles. They were all guides to the sights, buildings, and items of the Exhibition.

"So the necromancer wants something at the Exhibition," I murmured.

When Daniel offered no response, I glanced up to find him rubbing the goggles against his coat and gazing toward the center of the library. I whipped my head that way. The librarian was at the receiving end of his stare.

A choked yell broke from my mouth, and I launched a book at his chest. "Help me!"

"Oi!" He jerked around. "Watch it! You almost broke my goggles."

"And you're wasting time! We have work to do."

His back stiffened and his face turned pink. "Why are you so ornery all of a sudden? I'll work in my own sweet—" He broke off midsentence, and the storm vanished from his face. He eyed me knowingly. "I see how it is. Her Majesty is jealous."

I stamped my foot, ready to declare my exact opinion of *that* comment, but my words froze, trapped in my throat.

A film of frost was forming on the goggles.

"Spirit," I tried to say, but the bone-deep cold reached me then, snaking under my gown and stabbing into my flesh.

I stumbled into Daniel and clutched at his shoulders.

"Spirit," I tried again. "Here."

His pupils grew, consuming the green of his eyes. He said only one word: "Run."

CHAPTER FOURTEEN

Daniel heaved me back toward the center of the library.

"Dead!" he roared. "The Dead are here! Get out!"

First came whimpers, then shrieks as the people near us flew for the exit. Their feet stampeded on the pine planks.

I yanked free of Daniel and ran to the nearest fire alarm, which dangled on the western wall between two rows of shelves, just out of reach above my head. My eyes caught on a footstool nearby, and I scrambled to it.

"Dead!" Daniel continued bellowing, and then Joseph's voice joined in.

I dragged the stool to the wall, but a sudden blast of cold surged behind me. I froze midstep and turned my head slowly.

There it was. The bodiless, lightless creature my mother had let loose. It was far worse than I remembered. Blacker, deeper, and radiating death.

I threw myself toward the nearest shelf as splinters exploded. The spirit had smashed into the stool. I bolted out of the aisle and ran for the entrance, where I saw Joseph run and leap into the fountain.

A plaster bust whizzed past my head, missing me by inches. It smashed to the floor and sprayed white dust everywhere.

I didn't pause, but ran faster toward the front of the library. A sound like agonized fury followed me. It ripped through the air, so high-pitched it barely registered in my ears yet set my skin crawling.

I reached the fountain just as Jie skidded to a halt beside me. Joseph stood as he had the other day, arms extended and eyes squeezed shut. The spirit was nowhere to be seen.

"It moves between the realms," Joseph said through clenched teeth. "It jumps back and forth. As long as it hovers in the spirit realm, we cannot see or touch it."

"But how can it do that?" I asked.

"The spirit is strong—stronger than before. The curtain between worlds is no longer a barrier for it."

"But I can see it," Daniel said. "With the goggles—I can see it even though it's in the other world. There!" He pointed back to the circular desk in the center of the library. "It's there."

"How do we stop it?" Jie asked.

"I need electricity," Joseph said. "I can do nothing without a source."

Daniel yanked off the goggles. "This place ain't powered. We've gotta find something else."

The black clot formed like a sudden thundercloud over the desk. Daniel shoved me behind him.

Books flew off the desk and hurled toward us. Jie sprang up and intercepted them with fists and flying kicks, and the books pounded to the floor one after the other.

The darkness winked back out.

"It must stay in our realm," Joseph murmured. Sweat beaded on his brow, and his face was twisted with concentration and effort. "Lure it out or I cannot affect it."

"Here." Daniel shoved the goggles in Jie's hands. "You cover us." He turned to me. "You look for quartz. Like a prism or part of a small decoration."

"Quartz?" The word tasted heavy on my tongue—I didn't see the logic. "Why do you—"

"It's a power source," he snapped. "D'you know of any here?"

"N-no."

"Then you have to look around. Maybe it's part of a vase or some other bauble."

"What will you do?" I asked.

"See what other electricity I can find. Now go." He shoved me toward the western side and darted off toward the east.

I jumped into action, scrambling to the first aisle of shelves, but a quick scan showed only books.

A thump and the flap of pages resounded behind me. I whirled around just as a dictionary thudded at my feet. I jerked my gaze up and saw that Jie had stopped it. But only barely. I had to trust her instincts to protect me.

I rushed from that row and on to the next.

"Down!" Jie screamed, and somehow I reacted. I dropped to the floor, and a crash suddenly filled my ears. Shards of plaster and white powder rained down around me.

That figurine would have killed me.

The thought set me moving again. I raced to the next row of shelves and spared a glance across the room. Daniel seemed no better off than I. He was covered in soil as if he'd survived a potted plant attack.

I skittered into the next aisle, but the spirit was already there. Waiting, its shape like a twisting shadow in the hazy light.

I tried to stop, windmilling my arms to keep from tumbling forward.

In that moment as I fought for my balance, time seemed to stop. This couldn't end here. Not now, not after we'd finally found a clue about the Exhibition guides and the Dead at the library.

I grasped at a shelf, and my eyes lit on a book spine.

The Nature and Presence of Amethyst.

I knew, deep in the back of my mind, that this meant something. But what?

Darkness consumed my vision, and the stench of grave dirt invaded my nose. Time surged back to its racing pace.

Before me, the spirit grew into a hulking, long-armed shadow. It slithered forward. Death. A creature of fear.

Then it clicked into place. Amethyst. Quartz. They are the same. Elijah had taught me that.

I wrenched around. I didn't check to see if Death pursued—I just bolted.

"My earrings!" I screamed. "Amethyst!"

Joseph's eyes flashed open. My feet drummed on the wooden floor as I hurtled toward him and the fountain.

"Amethyst! Quartz!" My voice broke as I strained to run and scream.

"Squeeze them!" Daniel bellowed from the back of the library. "Squeeze them!"

I reached the fountain. I searched over my shoulder, and though I couldn't see the spirit, I knew from the chill that it hovered in the spirit world nearby.

"Come out!" I whirled around, thrusting my head forward and my shoulders back. "Come and get me! I'm right here!"

The spirit winked into being directly before me. Piercing cold and corrupt darkness. The high-pitched shriek stabbed at me again, burning into the crevices of my brain.

I faltered, tripping backward. My calves hit the lip of the fountain, and then a hand planted against my back.

Joseph, standing in the fountain, ripped my hair aside and clasped my earring.

Instantly, a ripple like hot, thick oil ran under my skin from my earlobe. My muscles started to twitch, and my heart beat faster and faster. A weak blue light snaked across my vision, filling the air with a crackling pop. The light flashed again—stronger and booming like thunder. It hit the spirit but was sucked in.

Again the blue lightning. Again it was consumed.

I felt as if my veins would burst, as if my brain were too large for my head. The agony bit into my bones so deeply that I thought they would surely snap. And still my heart beat faster.

Another blue crack, but this time it hit the clotted shadow and remained a flowing line of electricity. A thousand veins of blue sizzled over the spirit and down to the floor.

Just as my brain screamed for this hot oil to leave my skin, for my heart to slow, that I could take no more, a howl of pain erupted from Joseph's mouth. The lines of blue lightning stopped. The darkness was gone.

Joseph and I lay on the floor of the library entrance, leaning against the fountain's lip. Beneath his legs, a pool of water grew as his trousers dripped dry.

I brushed halfheartedly at the white powder on my gown. It must have come from the plaster bust that had nearly smashed my head in.

"What did you do?" I asked. "With my earring, I mean."

"I cannot say." Joseph smiled weakly. "I do not know how it worked, but squeezing your earring gave me a source of electricity, and I used it."

Daniel knelt before us. "Quartz is piezoelectric. Mechanical stress creates an electric current."

I reached up and stroked the amethysts. "Oh." He made it sound so simple.

"Although," he added, "I never expected that much power. How were you able to magnify it so much, Joseph?"

"I do not know," Joseph said. "I was also surprised by the strength of the electric source." He tapped his chin and gazed at me. "I wonder . . ."

"Empress, are you well?" Daniel peered at me with concern.

"Yes," I answered, though I wasn't sure that was true. I felt . . . fuzzy.

Daniel leaned toward me and placed a hand on my forehead. "You just got electrocuted. You should tell us if you don't feel right."

Jie stumbled up and plopped to the ground. A slur of unfamiliar words spouted from her lips, and I could tell by her ferocity that they were not meant kindly. Her knuckles bled, her clothes were shredded, and a ripe, red bruise swelled on the side of her face. Her dark eyes shone with fury. "I hope you sent that spirit back for good."

Joseph shook his head. "I do not think so. It was strong, and I fear it will return."

"What does it want?" I asked. "Why would it attack us here? Now?"

Joseph opened his hands. "I cannot say."

"I can," Daniel said. "I think it wants those Exhibition guides just like the other Dead that was here. It's the only explanation I can conjure." He quickly described the discovery we'd made right before the spirit's arrival. When he finished the tale, Jie hopped up and strode off. She soon returned carrying the guidebooks to the Exhibition.

"I don't get it," she muttered, gazing at the volumes. "Can a spirit do much with these? Maybe it just wanted to kill us."

"*Wi*," Joseph said. "Or perhaps both. There is something about this spirit. I can sense its desire. Its power is wholly focused on some deep-seated want—though what that want is, I cannot say."

Daniel sniffed and scratched his nose. "Well, let's take the books and look at 'em in the lab. Maybe we can figure out what all these Dead are after."

"Perhaps we should leave a note." My brain hazily insisted something about a subscription and checking out books.

"Eleanor." Jie crouched beside me. "You don't look right. We should get you home."

"No, no." I waved the comment aside. "I'm a mess . . . and I've lost my parasol. I haven't the slightest idea where I put it. Mama will kill me, and we can't spare the money to buy another." I huffed a dramatic sigh. I felt like I had at Allison's birthday party, when I had drunk too much champagne. Blurry.

"Eleanor." Jie scooted closer. "Stay awake."

"Just a little nap," I insisted.

My eyes fluttered shut, and I let my body slump. Right before I wandered into sleep, someone caught me. I hoped it was Daniel.

When I awoke, I found myself layered beneath blankets. It was my bed, my bedroom, though I couldn't think how I'd gotten there.

My tongue felt fat and dry, like an overcooked slab of sausage. I kicked away the covers. They were soaked through with my sweat, and my nightgown clung to my skin.

Amber light shone through my window. Evening. My head hurt, and I wiggled my fingers and toes experimentally. My muscles felt as if someone had pummeled them.

I'd been electrocuted. That's what Daniel had said. I shuddered. Bad enough the Spirit-Hunters had battled a spirit, but then they'd had to bring an unconscious lady home.

Merciful heavens, had they met Mama?

The door flew open, and the dragon herself sailed in. She settled on the edge of my bed, her face severe and her nostrils flaring. "Well, dear, no more Women's Pavilion for you."

"Huh?" I propped myself onto my elbows. These were not the first words I'd expected.

"I will not have my only daughter working and then fainting from the heat."

The heat. A clever explanation.

Mama lifted her chin. A queen declaring her law. "It is utterly unacceptable for a lady of high society to lose consciousness in front of such crowds."

"It's not the Women's Pavilion that made me overheat," I muttered, "but all the petticoats—"

"Do not blame your clothes." Her eyes thinned. "You have put yourself in a very improper position, and it will require the utmost delicacy to mend." She sighed dramatically. "To be brought home by such ilk."

"Wh-what do you mean? By what ilk?"

"A young *man* carried you home, Eleanor. A filthy young man. Do you realize the talk that could come from this?"

It must have been Daniel who had brought me home, for Joseph could never be called "filthy." *Good. I don't want Joseph tarnishing his reputation with swooning girls. Daniel, at least, has no reputation to tarnish.*

Mama rose and began pacing. Her feet pounded a slow rhythm that echoed miserably in my aching skull. I fell back onto the bed and draped an arm over my eyes.

"But he helped me," I argued wearily. "Why would the gossip be anything but grateful?"

Mama clucked, a sound filled with condescension. "Naive little girl. Working-class men have one intention and one intention only. They want you for this." She waved to my body and raised a single eyebrow.

"That's not true." I heaved myself back up. As if any man would want me for *that*. Even if I were a beauty like Allison, I

188

still knew Daniel wouldn't want me in that way. He would never treat me as if I were . . . as if I were a *camel*.

"How can you think that, Mama? You don't even know the boy."

She paused midstride. "Do you know him?" Her voice was low, and her eyes gleamed with awareness.

I flicked my gaze right and stared at the stripes on my wallpaper. "No, of course not."

Mama didn't reply, and I wondered if she suspected. But then she sniffed, and I knew my secret was safe.

"So . . . this young man," I said, trying to sound casual. "How did you repay him?"

Mama flicked her wrist. "Jeremy dealt with him. I could not invite him into the house."

"What?" My breath quickened, a combination of shame and anger growing in my chest. "You were rude to the man who rescued me, *and* I'm forbidden to attend the Exhibition?"

"Exactly." She gave me a withering glare.

"I *promised* to work there," I said through grinding teeth. A tense fire had begun to burn in my shoulders.

Her mouth tightened. "Are you arguing with me, Eleanor? This is most unlike you."

I clenched the moist cotton of my nightgown. I could conjure a thousand reasons to argue, but none I could speak to Mama. *Breathe, Eleanor, breathe.* Raising her suspicions would not serve me well.

I heaved my breath out in a single, long exhale. All my fury shot out with it, and I deflated back onto the bed.

Mama's lips twitched with satisfaction, and she resumed her pacing. "Now, about Mr. Wilcox. Tomorrow when you play croquet with him, you must do your best to hold his attention." She droned on, but I stopped listening. I traced my fingers on the worn fabric of my linens. I was hot, and thirst raged in my throat. Mama could prattle all she liked about marriage, money, and men, but it would stay far from my mind.

The necromancer and his pawns were still intact, a spirit wanted to kill me, and all I knew was that there was something special at the Exhibition—something the necromancer and the spirit had not yet found.

"Are you listening?" Mama stomped to my side. "I said you are lucky to have Clarence's affection."

"I don't have his affection."

"You most certainly do, and stop mumbling. You are luckier than you can imagine. A handsome man like that could have any woman he desires, and you are hardly the sort of woman for whom most men pine."

I stopped tracing the sheet and glowered up at her. "I *don't* have his affection, Mama."

She slapped my hands. It was a stinging reminder of who ruled this house. "Enough of this, Eleanor. He has clearly shown an interest in you. And if you continue to enchant him, an engagement—"

"Engagement?" I asked. "Mama, I'm only sixteen!"

"And we are out of money, Eleanor." She hunched over me,

an urgency in the hard lines of her face. "He may not be interested in you forever, and our fortune has shrunk to the point of poverty. Soon there will be nothing left. We will be on the streets! Everything depends on you—including *me*."

I shrank back, frightened by the intensity on her face and in her words. She was desperate.

"Yes," I whispered. "I-I'll try."

The wrinkles on her face relaxed. "Good," she crooned. "For now, you need your beauty rest. I'll take this"—she bent and lifted a frilly white parasol—"and dispose of it."

My jaw dropped. "What's that?"

"That man grabbed someone else's, I daresay."

"No," I murmured, my eyes fixed on the parasol's white lace.

She snorted. "Yes. This parasol is certainly not yours. It is cheap."

"Give it to me." I lurched forward and ripped it from Mama's hands. Her eyebrows flew up, and I swallowed. "Er, I-I'll just see if there's a name inside. Perhaps I can return it and get mine back."

She peered at me, disbelief clear in her eyes. "All right." She gave me one final glare and then strode from the room.

Once I heard the bedroom door shut, I eagerly examined the parasol. I was certain it was meant for me. I stroked the white lace and flounce. It was not something I would select, and Mama was right: the quality was lower than anything she would ever buy.

But I didn't care. It was lovely, and I popped it open. A slip of paper fluttered out from the folds of lace.

Sorry you lost yours.

Daniel

A thrill of pleasure ran down my body, and I couldn't stop the grin dancing on my lips. For all that Daniel hated me, maybe he liked me a little too.

CHAPTER FIFTEEN

Despite the leafy richness of East Fairmount Park, its flower-lined paths and sunny slopes, I could not cheer up. I simply did not want to be here playing croquet.

Allison, Clarence, and I were with the mustached McClure twins and the Virtue Sisters. The twins showed little interest in anything but flirting with Allison. Meanwhile, the Virtue Sisters showed no mercy to poor Clarence, and they were clearly trying his patience with their incessant chatter. The end result was that I was left to myself. I didn't mind in the least, for my humor was, to put it politely, *foul*.

Despite my white lawn dress—which was supposedly meant for outdoor play— the sun roasted me. I couldn't enjoy the beautiful blue sky or the gentle breeze. We were on a wide, flat yard surrounded by woods. The whole park covered miles and miles, but this was one of the few lawns suitable for croquet. As such, the area was crowded.

Barely even a mile north of us was Laurel Hill Cemetery, yet here the people played, oblivious and carefree.

Nearby, a restaurant sent a salty perfume on the breeze that made my stomach growl—it did *not* improve my mood to be hungry.

Mama forbade me to attend the Exhibition after an overheating spell, yet she insisted I gallivant in the park in the midafternoon sun. I almost wanted to pass out again just to spite her.

I smacked at my ball and watched as it rolled across the grass and passed by the nearest wicket.

"Damn!" I cried. It was the fourth time I'd missed.

Clarence sputtered a laugh, and I pivoted toward him. His dapper white suit and straw boat hat were at odds with his exhaustion.

I gulped and scanned everyone's faces. Their eyebrows were collectively high and their jaws collectively low.

"Pardon me." I coughed weakly. "There must be something stuck in my throat. If you'll excuse me." I stomped off the course, all the while continuing my cough and enhancing its severity for dramatic effect. I was determined to cough up blood if it would wipe the startled expressions off their faces.

I would have to be more careful. It was all fine if I wanted to cuss in front of the Spirit-Hunters, but not here.

It was Allison's turn, and I kicked past her, stoutly avoiding her eyes. But she clutched at my arm. "What's wrong?"

"Nothing, of course."

Her eyebrows drew together, and I realized she was actually concerned for me. I forced a taut smile. "Honest, Allison. I'm just hot."

"Then you ought to rest in the shade." She pointed with her mallet to a nearby chestnut tree.

"Yes, I think I will. Thank you."

Her face lit up with a sparkling smile, and she turned back to the game.

I moved to the wide-limbed chestnut that spread its branches over the edge of the field, grateful that Allison had suggested it. I wanted to be alone.

My mallet swung side to side in my hands, ticking and tocking as my brain sorted through my black thoughts. What had happened yesterday with the Spirit-Hunters? Had they taken the Exhibition guidebooks? Had they discovered anything new? And where on earth had Daniel gotten that parasol?

With my eyebrows jutting down, I gazed at the grass beneath my white patent leather boots.

"Miss Fitt," said Clarence.

I snapped my head up. If I thought he'd looked unwell Wednesday, it was nothing compared to today. Not even the sun could add color to the deathly pallor of his cheeks, and his eyes were rimmed with such darkness, it looked as if he'd rubbed them with charcoal.

Willis was planted on a bench across the field and had taken on some of his master's appearance. I was certain neither of them had managed to sleep since I'd last seen them.

"Are you all right?" Clarence asked. His voice was gravelly, and his eyes were sad.

"Yes, quite." I gave him a false grin.

"I don't believe you." He approached slowly.

"I promise, it's just . . . it's just the heat."

"Then I'll keep you company in the shade."

I bit back my urge to groan and tossed my mallet on the ground. He winced at the thud, and then gently laid down his own.

He folded his arms over his chest and considered me for several moments. "Have you perhaps had . . . have you had bad news? Have you heard something?"

"No." I flicked my gaze away. "I told you, it's just the heat. I . . . I had a fainting spell yesterday, and I'm still not entirely myself."

"You fainted?" He frowned, a pinched expression that gave his skin a papery look—as if it might tear at any moment. "What are you doing here, then? You should be in bed."

"Mothers." I flashed my eyebrows and turned away. Looking at him disturbed me. How could this be the same beautiful prince I'd met last Friday?

"Wait," I murmured, whirling to face him. "Have *you* had bad news?"

He grunted and dropped his hands. "No."

"Don't lie." I advanced on him. I was certain another headless man had been found.

Clarence stalked from me, circling around the tree trunk and away from the other players. I followed.

"That's why you seem sad," I pressed. "You've had more bad news—Mr. Wilcox, has someone else died?"

He stopped and rubbed his eyes. The muscles in his jaw pulsed. "You're entirely too clever, Miss Fitt."

"Who was it? Another boy from the academy?"

He nodded once. His lips and nostrils trembled, and I could see the battle he fought to keep tears away.

"I'm so sorry, Mr. Wilcox."

"Then damn it, stop pestering me! This is—" His voice broke, and he blinked rapidly. "This is an incredibly difficult time for me."

I yanked my handkerchief from my pocket and shoved it in his hands. "Truly, I'm sorry. I shouldn't have bothered you, but I . . . I just knew somehow and . . . Does anyone else know?"

"No." He thrust my handkerchief back at me. "I have my own."

"Of course," I murmured, stuffing it in my pocket. "Do you want to talk about it?"

"No." He dabbed at his eyes with his fingers. "And I expect you to not talk about it either. Not even the newspapers know. This man, Clinton Bradley, he was . . ." His words faded, and his eyes went distant.

"Was what?"

"Was my closest friend from childhood. His father, my father—we grew up together. We had . . ." He ground his teeth. "We had plans for the coming elections."

"Oh." I knew that name—Clinton Bradley. His mother had thrown the famous séance my mother had wanted to outshine. It was truly tragic he'd met with a gruesome death. I shivered and hugged my arms to my stomach.

"Have you heard from your brother?" Clarence asked.

I choked and faltered back several steps. What was this change in subject?

"Answer me." Clarence took a single, long stride, closing all distance between us. He gripped my wrists and hauled me close. "Look at me. Look at me, Miss Fitt. Have you had any news from Elijah?"

I stared with wide eyes. "No."

"Write him." He leaned toward me, and the tree's shadows covered his face in menacing swirls. "Write him and tell him things aren't safe here. He must stay in New York."

Clarence dug his fingers into the soft flesh beneath my wrists. "Tell Elijah we're *all* in danger. I-I don't know who's next. Tell him to stay away from Philadelphia. Tell him that!"

"Yes."

"Promise." He yanked me closer until his face was inches from mine. "Promise!"

"Yes, yes, I promise!" My wrists burned where his fingers dug into the skin, but I was too stunned to do anything but stare.

His eyes roved sideways and then back to my face. They were red rimmed, like angry wounds.

He wrenched me even closer. "Something follows me! I sense it around me at night . . . hovering, waiting, hiding in the shadows. It means to kill me, like it did the others. But I won't let it. I'll do whatever it takes to stay alive—to keep my family safe! Whatever it takes!"

My hands throbbed in time to my banging heart, and numbness crept into my fingers. All the blood was being squeezed out. What was happening to Clarence? Who was this man, and what was he capable of?

"Hello?" Allison trilled. "Clarence? Eleanor? Are you going to play?" She would circle the wide tree at any moment.

"We're coming," Clarence barked over his shoulder.

"All right," she called, "but hurry." Her skirts rustled, and I knew she'd trotted back to the game.

Clarence released me. I staggered several steps backward, and my pulse echoed loudly in my ears. I rubbed at my wrists, but I couldn't massage away the growing red welts. My hands pricked as blood soaked back into them.

"Miss Fitt," Clarence said, his voice hoarse. "I'm sorry." He stepped toward me, but I scrambled away.

"Stay away. Don't touch me."

"Please, Miss Fitt—I'm so sorry." He shook his head and wiped at his eyes. All of the fire had burned out. He seemed even wearier than before.

He lifted his hands like one might do to a frightened puppy.

"Please, I won't hurt you again. I'm sorry. You're a good sister, a good woman. I didn't mean to lose my mind like that—I'm tired and scared. All my plans for the future are falling apart as my friends are killed. I fear for my family." His words were tight, as if tears lurked in his chest, and his eyes were filled with pleading hope. "Please," he whispered. "I'm sorry."

I nodded hesitantly but kept my distance. Now he seemed harmless. As if he was nothing more than a man who'd suffered more than anyone should ever have to. Someone who wanted his family kept safe just as I did.

"All right." I swallowed. "But Willis isn't enough protection if the Dead want you. You should speak to someone."

"Like who? The Spirit-Hunters?" He shook his head. "I don't think . . . well, I have it on good authority that they're not the sort of people I want protecting me."

"Then the police," I said.

"Yes . . . I've considered it." He licked his lips. "I don't want Mother or Allison to find out though. They don't need to worry. And with the coming elections, I can't attract much attention."

"Why do you still care about the elections? Your friends are dying!"

"You don't understand." He tipped his chin up and stared down his nose at me. "I must carry on my father's dream. It is the duty—and the burden—of sons." He looked away. In a low voice he added, "I *refuse* to be killed."

The intensity behind his vow was sincere. I had no doubt that his means for survival would be as desperate as his words.

"Clarence, come on!" Allison shouted. "You're ruining the game!"

He gazed into the distance for a moment, and then he turned and shambled away. I waited, unwilling to follow.

I had never imagined Clarence as dangerous—he'd almost always worn his mask of well-bred charm. Had this insanity always been there? Hidden deep within? Or was it sparked by his exhaustion and fear?

I didn't know, and for that matter, I didn't *want* to know.

Dark clouds flew in from the east and cut off our game. I was more than grateful to shorten my time with Clarence, but he foiled my relief on the ride home when he took a sudden detour to the Centennial Exhibition.

"I've quick business," Clarence said to Allison and me. "So please wait in the carriage, and I'll be back in a few minutes." He brandished a finger at us and then hurried into the Exhibition crowds. Willis trotted at his master's heels.

I watched Clarence's boat hat bob away. Once it was out of view, I turned to Allison on the seat beside me. "What sort of business does he do?"

"He's a Gas Trustee." She gazed out the window, boredom evident in the droop of her eyes and sag of her lips.

"A what?"

"Philadelphia Gas Works." She slid her eyes toward me. "What our father worked with. He and some other men run the company. They're called the Gas Trustees."

At those words my chest tightened. It felt as if my ribs pressed against my lungs, and I couldn't take in a full breath.

"Like the Gas Ring?"

"I've never heard it called that." She shifted her body to face me.

"Well, what do you know about it?" I forced myself to stay calm, though I was desperate for answers.

"Nothing. Papa never talked about it, and Clarence doesn't either. Whenever I ask him about work, he says, 'Don't worry your pretty little head. We live like kings, don't we? Now, would you like a new hat?'" She spoke in a deep voice, mimicking Clarence. Then she giggled and clapped her hands. "So if I ever want new clothes, I make sure to ask!"

I couldn't keep a wry grin from twitching at my lips. Perhaps Allison was shrewder than anyone gave her credit for.

She rubbed her nose and yawned. "Why are you asking so many questions?"

I slouched back on the seat, trying to inhale deeply. "I'm just wondering why we're here." I stared out the window. Her words triggered a memory—the same memory of my father and his argument with the dark-haired man. With Clay.

My heart jumped back into action. I spun to Allison. "What was your father's name?"

"Clarence."

I scooted closer. "Did they call him Clay?"

"Yes." She furrowed her brow, clearly confused by my questions.

The names couldn't be mere coincidence. But what did that mean? Why had our fathers fought? Had it been over this gas company?

I leaned toward her. "When did your father join the Trustees? How long ago?"

The lines on her forehead deepened. "Not long after the war, I think. I was only six or seven. He was in railroad something or other before that."

"And who are the other Trustees?"

"I don't know," she whined.

"Remember," I snapped.

She recoiled and pressed her back to the carriage wall. "Mr. Sutton, I think. And . . . and Mr. Sutherland and Mr. McManus." She chewed her lower lip. "Oh, and Mr. Bradley and Mr. Weathers—but why do you care, Eleanor?"

I didn't answer. The three decapitated men weren't only Germantown students, they were also connected to the Gas Trustees—as was Clarence. "Sutton, Weathers, and Bradley?" I asked.

She nodded slowly, and I forced myself to slide away from her. My mind exploded with thoughts and memories and confusion. I knew there was something I was missing. Something important that I couldn't see, something to do with this Gas Ring and my father and . . . and a game of intrigue that no one knew how to play.

I groaned and massaged my forehead. Whatever the connections were, they hovered out of my reach.

"Are you all right?" Allison asked. "Does your head hurt?"

"Yes," I lied. "I hope your brother hurries." I pressed my face against the glass of the carriage window. I could see the nearest turnstiles, but no sign of Clarence.

Allison sighed dramatically. "I'm bored. I wish I'd brought my book."

"What book is that?" The first raindrops splattered on the road outside.

"*The Quaker City*," she whispered, her tone conspiratorial. *The Quaker City* was famous for its lewd and horrifying tales.

I twisted my face toward her. "Does your mother know you're reading that?"

"Pshaw." She sniffed. "Of course Mother doesn't know— and you'd better not tell! The original copy is here, you know." She waved toward the Exhibition. "There's an entire display of old books and manuscripts and scrolls and stuff."

"Really?" I squinted at her. "Have you seen it?"

"Oh, yes." She nodded rapidly, warming to the conversation. "Mother made me go so we could look at an old Bible from the Middle Ages—it's in the Main Building. And that's where I saw *The Quaker City* for the first time. You remember Mercy read it? There's a little ogre on the title page, and it looked positively horrifying, so I went to the library . . ." She continued babbling excitedly, but I had stopped listening.

An old book exhibit. That was intriguing. If they had Bibles, mightn't they have other ancient texts? Ancient texts such as *grimoires*? It was possible, and an Exhibition guidebook would tell me.

Exhibition guides such as the ones at the library.

"I'll be right back." I shoved open the carriage door and clambered into the rain.

"But Clarence—"

"I'll be right back!" I slammed the door shut and galloped through the crowds to the entrance. I didn't actually need to go in. I just had to find someone selling guidebooks.

Giant raindrops sliced through the air, cold and hard when they hit my skin. I found a covered stall selling, according to the hand-painted sign, "All Things Exhibition." I squeezed between people who took cover from the storm, and within seconds I found stacks of *International Exhibition, 1876: Official Catalogue.* I scooped up a catalogue for each building—the Main Building, Machinery Hall, the Art Gallery, and so on. I emptied my pockets of all my change, and then I scrambled back into the wet.

I hugged the flimsy papers to my chest and tried to keep my white skirts from the fresh mud. Now the rain was really coming down.

Someone grabbed my arm and whirled me about. I inhaled, prepared to shout my alarm, but I promptly clapped my mouth shut.

"Empress," Daniel said. He dropped his hand from my arm. His cap was soaked through, and water dripped off the edge. He must have been standing in the rain since it started. He slid his brown coat off and draped it over my shoulders, speaking all the while.

"Your beau—he's back, and he's lookin' for me."

"What?" I huddled under the coat and hefted it over my head. The rain hadn't sneaked through its sturdy wool. "Clarence?"

"Him, yeah." He nodded and tugged his cap low over his face. "You haven't said anything, right?"

"No, of course not. But your name must be in the newspapers, and I've seen him talking to Mr. Peger. It won't be difficult—"

He lifted a hand to cut me off. "That's fine—I know all that. Just remember—"

I mimicked his gesture and cut him off. "I won't say your name. Don't worry, Mr. Sheridan."

He wiped the rain from his face. "All right." He reached for the coat but paused, his arms outstretched over my head and his eyes scanning my face as if to memorize me. "You may not be seeing me around for a while 'cause of all this. I'll be lying low."

"Oh." A maelstrom of feelings passed through me. Sadness, curiosity, anger, regret, and an aching hollowness in my chest. I didn't want to *not* see him.

"I learned something," I rushed to say before he could run off. "The murdered men weren't just schoolmates. They're all connected to the Gas Trustees."

Daniel balked and let the coat drop back over me. "The Gas Trustees? What do you know about them?"

"Nothing. I think they might be called the Gas Ring too,

206

because Elijah mentioned it—"

"Don't mess with the Gas Ring." He grabbed my chin and forced me to look into his eyes. "I can't stop you from seein' Wilcox, Empress, but stay the hell away from the Gas Ring."

"Why? What is it?"

"It doesn't matter. It ain't your affair, so don't dig your nose in any farther."

"What if it *does* matter? For the necromancer?"

"I'll deal with it." He wrenched the coat from me. "Hurry. Your man's back."

I needed no prodding. I pivoted toward the concourse and raced through the pounding rain. I could see Clarence at the carriage, and a derby-hatted, golden-locked reporter jogging away. I stuffed the catalogues in my pocket and threw a glance behind me.

Daniel was gone. I scanned all about, but I saw no sign of his corn-blond hair or drenched flat cap. Only the lingering scent of metal and the earthy smell of summer rain proved I hadn't imagined the entire thing.

The sun sank in the western sky. Red rays peeked through the piling rain clouds. I scrambled from the Wilcox carriage to my house, fierce droplets falling on my skin.

I rushed upstairs. My mind swirled with thoughts of Daniel and Clarence, and my body shivered from the wet. Clarence had clearly been annoyed at me for leaving the carriage at the Exhibition, but he'd refrained from expressing it. Likely he felt guilty over his earlier outburst.

I shuffled into my room and fumbled with my hairpins. But then I stopped, frozen midstride. A letter lay on my dressing table. A grimy slip of paper—folded, wrinkled, and addressed to me. I threw myself forward and ripped at the fragile sheet.

Dearest Sister,

You must stop searching for me. You must stop seeing the Spirit-Hunters. You hurt me by being with them, and worse, you put yourself in danger.

With all my love,

Elijah

It was like a punch to my stomach. My breath flew out. My lungs heaved and clenched and heaved and clenched. I crumpled to the floor, ignoring my gown. Tears burned my eyes and then dropped down my cheeks.

I made no sound and simply let the tears fall.

I had wasted time worrying over Daniel and Clarence, playing on the croquet course, and arguing with Mama. I had neglected what was most important: Elijah. He was alive and he had been here, in my room. I had to find him.

I squeezed the white folds of my dress, held my breath, and counted my heartbeats. One, two, three, four. I eased the air from my lungs and let my body relax. A final shudder, and I was in control once more.

My brother was *alive*—thank God—but he was still in danger. The necromancer clearly still had him. But . . . I looked at the letter again, now stained with tears. I hurt Elijah by searching for him? Why? Because the necromancer felt threatened? Yes. That had to be it.

The Spirit-Hunters and I were getting close to solving the mysteries of what the necromancer wanted at the Exhibition, of why he wanted the Germantown boys. The Spirit-Hunters were building devices to destroy the Dead, and now the necromancer was scared. He—or perhaps she or they, since we really did not know who this person was—must have forced Elijah to send this letter.

Yes, this necromancer was scared, and that meant I had an advantage. Fear made people act irrationally, made them misstep and forget to cover their trails. Like at the library.

I scrambled clumsily up and to the window, where some stormy light still came in. Then I pulled the Exhibition catalogues from my pocket.

I started with the Main Hall since that was where Allison had seen the ancient texts. I flipped through and saw that it was organized by nation or state. I hadn't a clue who displayed the old books, so I started on page one. I scanned for anything noteworthy; but after several pages, I realized the book was almost entirely advertisements. In fact, many exhibits weren't listed or were given no detail at all.

Official Catalogue? Humbug.

I searched the pages anyway, until my eyes burned from straining. It felt like hours, but I finally found Allison's book exhibit. There was nothing on display that sounded like a grimoire. All the same, I was certain my hunch was leading me in the right direction. If only I could sort through all these blasted advertisements!

I tossed the catalogues aside in frustration. This must be why a corpse had gone to the library—to find more reliable inventories.

I went to the window and pressed my face against the cool glass. The rain splattered in loud drops and filled my nose with its scent. I held my right hand against the window's glass, and with my eyes screwed shut, I imagined Elijah's letters.

"Something took him to Cairo." I nodded my head with each word as the lines formed in my mind, connecting clue to clue. "And he referenced Solomon . . . but he said pages were missing. So he traveled to New York because the pages were in a museum."

That's what I needed, wasn't it? Those pages.

I raced back to the Exhibition catalogues and fell to one knee. I clawed at them, searching for any items listed from New York.

Maybe Solomon's pages had been moved. Maybe they were *here*, in Philadelphia, at the Centennial Exhibition. The necromancer had followed Elijah to find them!

I found it on page seventy-seven of the United States

Government Building's book, listed under New York's collection of museum novelties.

Original pages of Le Dragon Noir, a scarce companion to the Grand Grimoire, supposedly from the pen of King Solomon. On loan from the New-York Historical Society.

There it was—a book of magic at the Exhibition. That was what the necromancer wanted and possibly what the spirit wanted too.

I laughed a shrill, panting laugh. I had to tell the Spirit-Hunters.

And we had to find this grimoire.

CHAPTER SIXTEEN

At nine o'clock the next morning and without Mama's knowledge, I waited with a grim face for the Exhibition to open. I was the first through the turnstiles, and I fled instantly to the Spirit-Hunters' door.

"*Bonjour.*" Joseph waved me into the lab. I skidded to a stop at the sight of Jie wrapped in a blanket on the floor.

"Is she asleep?" I whispered.

"*Wi*, but do not worry. She worked on the railroad, so she can sleep through anything."

"Why is she here? Why not in your . . ." I furrowed my brow. "Well, wherever it is you sleep."

He chuckled and spread his hands. "*This* is where we sleep." He tapped his foot on the floor. "This is our bed."

"You mean the city never gave you lodging? A house or a hotel to stay in?"

His eyebrows rose. "Are you offering your own?"

I opened and closed my mouth, my face flooding with heat. "I . . . um . . . No."

At that moment the door screamed on its hinges and banged into the table behind. Daniel stormed in.

"They won't give it to us." He slammed the door shut. I flinched at the violent whack. Jie jerked awake.

"I ran into one of the officials," Daniel continued, "and he said the city can't trust us with dynamite." The muscles in his neck strained, and his body was tense with fury. He pounded his chest. "Us. The ones who've done nothing but risk our lives."

Joseph lifted his hands. "Calm yourself."

"How can I be calm?" Daniel shouted. "They treat us like a bunch of dogs, and we put up with it."

Jie stretched her arms overhead. "It's true—" A jaw-cracking yawn overtook words, and she tapped at her mouth. "It's true," she tried again. "They want us to save them from the Dead, but then they don't help us." She drew herself gracefully to her feet.

Daniel opened his mouth to speak, but Joseph laid a warning hand on his shoulder.

"Settle down."

Daniel ground his teeth and stomped to the window. He pressed his hands against the glass and leaned, his gaze moving to some distant spot outside. Judging by his labored breath, he was trying to keep his temper under control.

I gulped. The Spirit-Hunters needed dynamite? Why? I had to admit I'd be wary to hand over explosives to just anyone. Except the Spirit-Hunters *weren't* just anyone.

Jie shifted her head side to side, and her neck popped loudly. "We can't fight the entire cemetery, you know."

"I know," Joseph answered. "But if the city will not let us have dynamite, then there is nothing we can do."

She spoke her next words casually. "We can take it, Joseph. We just break into the factory and take what we need. It'd be fair enough to—"

"No," Joseph and Daniel snapped in unison.

Daniel dropped his hands from the window and inched around to face Jie. "No stealing. Especially not that."

I spoke up, my voice breaking. "I-I know what the Dead want."

Three heads spun toward me.

"It's one of the grimoires—*Le Dragon Noir*—and it's on display here. I saw it listed in the Exhibition catalogue."

Joseph sagged onto a stool. He rubbed his head and then he slung out another stool. "Sit. Tell me everything from the beginning. This . . . this is startling."

So I did as he asked. I began with Elijah's most recent letter and ended with the New York listings in the Exhibition catalogue.

Joseph stared at me, his whole body stiff and his lips pressed thin. "*Le Dragon Noir*," he murmured. "This is very bad." He jumped up, massaging his forehead.

"What is it?" Jie asked.

"I asked the Exhibition board about this title." Joseph dropped his hands, and his eyes shone with anger and fear— something I'd never seen in him. He spoke faster, his voice rising. "When we first arrived here, I'd mentioned this title and many others. I thought perhaps the museums would display their valuable pieces. The board insisted there was nothing. Promised me. They must not realize what they have—not understand what someone with the proper training could do with a handful of these pages."

He hung his head and stared at the floor. His hands trembled as he clenched and unfolded his fingers. When his head lifted, he met three sets of wide eyes. "*The Black Dragon* has spells that are especially seductive to a dark magician—to a necromancer. It teaches how to bring a soul from the dead to animate a body. It is like . . . well, imagine if the spirit, the one your mother let in, were able to take over a human form. Or if every corpse in the cemetery were given a new soul."

I shuddered. "So the spirit must want the grimoire too. That's why it was at the library."

"*Wi*. That must be so—which is an even greater cause for concern."

I tipped my head to Daniel. "And now you need dynamite. Why?"

"It's an invention." He reached under the worktable and slung out a metal canister the width and length of my forearm. It was fixed at an angle to a flattened piece of tin, giving it the look of a toy cannon. A copper wire coiled around the canister and glowed bright red in the morning light.

"It's a special explosive." Daniel held up a metal rod the size of my fist and dropped it in the tube. It clunked at the end. "When this magnet shoots through this cylinder, it creates a pulse of electromagnetic energy. A big wave." He spread his arms wide. "I call it a pulse bomb."

Joseph cleared his throat. "It would affect the Dead as I do, Miss Fitt. The explosion of electromagnetic energy would destroy spiritual energy. It would stop many corpses at once."

Daniel grunted and set the device on the table. "The problem is, the magnet has to be propelled somehow—like a bullet."

"Or a cannonball?" I asked.

"Yep. But the magnet has to go almighty fast to make the electromagnetic pulse, and it won't move without an explosion—a *big* explosion."

"Dynamite," I murmured.

"Yeah." He pushed the miniature cannon toward me, and I ran a gloved finger down the copper wire. Clacking jaws and rabid hunger filled my mind. If there were more of those corpses or, heaven forbid, an entire cemetery of them, then no one in Philadelphia stood a chance.

"And this is our only hope?" I held up the canister. "An invention that can't be finished?"

"It can be finished," Jie said. She marched between Joseph and me. "We're wasting time talking about it. If you won't break

217

into the factory, then I'll do it myself.

"When the Dead come, we won't be able to stop them. They will cover this city, and the Hungry will kill and kill and kill. That's much worse than jail time, yeah? I thought it was our job to stop the Dead. Isn't that what makes us the Spirit-Hunters?"

Joseph closed his eyes. "Jie, I do not think you see—"

"No, you don't think! You're not thinking at all, yeah? You just found out the Exhibition board has lied to you and put a grimoire on display. They don't care about protecting the people here, but that *is* what we care about, Joseph. That's our job. What matters more? Stealing something we deserve anyway or letting the entire city be slaughtered by the Dead?"

Joseph's brow wrinkled. He stared at the floor, and his gaze turned hazy.

"I think Jie's right," I said. "You don't owe the city's officials anything—not after they've treated you so rotten." I waved my hand around me. "This tiny lab, their unwillingness to help because of some election, and now this problem with your invention. I don't understand why they even hired you to begin with."

"At first they believed in us," Daniel said. "Then Peger came on the scene and stirred up a storm."

Jie threw her hands up. "It doesn't matter if they trusted us before or if they'll ever trust us again. What matters is *now*. We have to finish your invention, yeah? And that means we have to take the dynamite."

"It's the only solution." I pushed to my feet and looked at

Joseph. "Don't you see? All of us have to do as much as we can to stop this necromancer, and if it means breaking the law then—"

"That's easy for you to say," Daniel snapped. "You won't get your rich fingers dirty."

I launched my chin up. "I'd go if you'd let me."

He towered up to his full height and glared down at me. "If you're so willing, then why don't you mosey on down there and do it for us?"

I winced. His words hurt, and I didn't understand why he was so keyed up. "That's not fair—"

Joseph's hand shot up between us, his palm flat. "Hush. I have heard quite enough." He planted his hand on Daniel's chest and pushed the sandy-haired boy away from me.

"Tell me," Joseph said, "do you remember the factory's layout?"

Daniel's face fell. "No. Please, don't do this."

"I did not ask for your desire. I asked if you remember it or not."

Daniel's face contorted, and he squeezed his eyes shut. His chest heaved, and I couldn't look away. What about the factory could bring such pain to the surface? For that matter, why did Daniel even know the layout of the factory?

But then Daniel swallowed and pushed his shoulders back. He opened his eyes. "Yes. I can get into the factory."

Joseph bowed his head. "Then you and Jie will go tonight. In the meantime, I will go retrieve this grimoire. It must be destroyed. Now you should leave, Daniel, before anyone sees you here." He pointed to the lab's door.

Daniel nodded once and tugged his flat cap low. "Right. I'll be back later." He stalked past me toward the exit.

I reached out and clasped his sleeve. "Daniel—I mean, Mr. Sheridan." A blush ignited on my cheeks.

"Empress?" He gazed at my hand on his arm.

"I forgot to thank you. For my new parasol."

The edge of his lip twitched. "Anything for Her Majesty." He drew his eyes up, and he held my gaze. Green eyes, clear and alert. Then he wrapped his hand around mine and removed my fingers from his sleeve.

He gently lowered my hand before stalking through the door and out of sight.

After leaving the Spirit-Hunters' lab, I navigated the maze of Machinery Hall. My mind whirred with housekeeping duties—market shopping, bank accounting, and the like—but the cogs kept sticking and wandering to Daniel

I tugged at my earrings. *Focus, Eleanor.* Hadn't I vowed to think only of Elijah?

I was almost to the central transept and the booming Corliss engine when a man's voice called out, "Miss Fitt."

I twirled around, searching for the source among the throngs of visitors. Nicholas Peger materialized before me, his hat at a jaunty tilt and his mustache shining.

"Eleanor Fitt. That's you, isn't it?" he asked. "Of the Philadelphia Fitts?"

I stared. No words came to my lips. How had he found out my name?

He sauntered closer and slid a small notebook from his waist-coat pocket. He flipped it open. "Parents are Henry and Abigail Fitt. You're sixteen years old. Formally presented to society . . . hmmm. Not yet." His eyes flitted to my face, though his head stayed still. "I take your silence as confirmation."

"Well, you shouldn't," I snapped, my mind kicking back into gear. "I haven't the faintest idea who that girl is, and I do not appreciate you trying to discover who I am."

"Don't excite yourself," he drawled. "I'm not being paid to investigate you—although I'm rather certain *someone* would pay to find out about your little excursions." His eyebrows bounced up, and he jerked a thumb in the direction of the Spirit-Hunters' lab.

I narrowed my eyes, trying to hide the trembling in my veins. If Mama found out, or Clarence, or anyone, they would be horrified. What if they went to the police or it reached the press? If the necromancer felt more threatened, what would happen to Elijah?

I brandished my parasol at him like a rapier. "You, sir, are an abominable scalawag of a man, and I'll be damned if I let you threaten me."

He clicked his tongue and rolled his eyes. "Such language doesn't suit a lady of your breeding. Course, neither does spending time with those low-life Spirit-Hunters. You know that Boyer fellow was a necromancer back in New Orleans? He even killed his best friend. That's why he skipped town."

I sneered. I already knew about Joseph and how he'd stopped the necromancer Marcus. "I don't know why you dislike the Spirit-Hunters as much as you do," I said haughtily, "but I won't listen to your filthy lies."

"Fine, fine. Maybe you can help me, though." He tucked his notebook back in his pocket and slid out a newspaper clipping. He waved it in my face. "Recognize this boy?"

I glanced at the faded image before me, and fought to keep a straight face. The picture held a dirty, long-haired boy—perhaps twelve or thirteen years old—who had clearly been neglected. Yet the lines of his jaw and the sharpness in his eyes were unmistakable. It was Daniel Sheridan.

"No, of course not," I lied.

Mr. Peger pursed his lips. "This boy would be a young man now. His name is Sure Hands Danny. He's an escaped convict, and I imagine you'd want to help me find him."

"Convict?"

"Aye, from Philadelphia's own Eastern State Penitentiary."

"Wh-what was he arrested for?"

"Murder."

My heart punched against my ribs. "Murder?"

"Aye. Murder." He shoved the paper back in his pocket. "He was also responsible for an explosion at a factory. Maybe you heard of it, hmmm? Happened six years ago, and I gather it caused Fitt Railway Supply a lot of trouble."

I bit the inside of my mouth until I tasted blood. That was

the explosion that caused Father to lose his contract. It was the explosion that killed his company.

Mr. Peger twirled a finger in his mustache and watched me.

Despite my wavering confidence, I forced myself to speak steadily. "I don't recall such an explosion."

"Really? Well, no matter. I've a pretty good idea where Sure Hands Danny is hiding. The word is he's here—mighty foolish of him, considerin' his past and all. He may have gotten away before, but Sure Hands Danny can't hide from *me*. Not at the high price my client is willing to pay. I'm going to find him. So"—he leaned toward me—"if you happen to see this man, tell him he can't hide from me much longer." He doffed his hat. "G'day, Miss."

I hugged my parasol to my chest and watched him amble off into the crowd. I staggered to the Corliss engine, desperately needing a moment to catch my breath and gather my emotions.

When I reached a narrow set of iron stairs that soared dangerously upward, I plopped onto them. They led to a series of catwalks meant for aerial viewing of America's greatest mechanical triumph, and though I wasn't allowed to ascend—boys and men only—surely there was no harm if I simply sat.

Had Mr. Peger spoken the truth? Was Daniel a murderer? Had he destroyed the factory? Destroyed my father?

I couldn't believe it. Not Daniel! His temper was short and his manner crude, but he had never hurt me. If anything, he'd been protective. I trusted him. I believed him to be good.

But . . . but maybe it's all an act. Just like Mama pretends we're still wealthy. Like Clarence pretends his life is fine. Like I pretend to fit in with the high-society girls.

I rocked forward and back. Who was good? Who was bad? And if there was no one I could trust, did that mean I was all alone?

I pressed my hands to my face. No, I wasn't alone; I still had Elijah. Elijah was good. Elijah I could trust.

Soon, I will find him. Soon.

CHAPTER SEVENTEEN

"But Mama!" I cried. "That's not appropriate!"
I stood in my bedroom, dressed only in my underclothes. After I'd arrived home from the Exhibition, my mind spinning with questions about Daniel and my mouth sputtering lies of a failed trip to the market, Mama had swept me off to the dressmaker (for the final fitting of a dress she had failed to mention she was having made) and then shoved me into Mary's hands to go back home for preparation.

Going to the opera was drab Eleanor's chance to shine—or at least it was in Mama's eyes.

It didn't take long before my head began to ache from the multitude of hairpins scraping at my scalp and straining at the tightness of my coiffure. After two hours of me being primped and curled under Mary's none-too-gentle hands, my patience was entirely spent, and Mary was sent away.

Mama left the doorway and crossed to me. She still wore her robe, and her hair was untended. She waved a letter in my face. "Neither of the Wilcox ladies will be attending—do you know what sort of opportunity this is? It is great luck they are ill."

"What a horrible thing to say." I clenched my fists. "How can you even consider not joining? I am only sixteen, Mama. This isn't some casual drive—it's the *opera*. Everyone will see me alone with him!"

She snorted. "I thought you would be delighted to spend time alone with your sweetheart."

"It's actually the last thing I want, and he's not my sweetheart." The absurdity of the statement, of the situation, of my mother! I *had* to convince her to call the whole evening off. I had no desire to see Clarence Wilcox and his brewing insanity. My wrists were still tender from yesterday's outburst.

Plus, if she canceled our opera attendance, then maybe I could sneak away. Maybe I could go to Machinery Hall and help the Spirit-Hunters get their dynamite. More importantly, maybe I could confront Daniel. I refused to believe Peger's word until I heard Daniel's own explanation.

Mama gripped my shoulders and wrenched me around to face her. "Mr. Wilcox had better be your sweetheart, Eleanor."

"And what will you do, pray tell, if Clarence isn't interested in me at all?"

"Clarence?" A squeal erupted from her lips. "Do you call

him by his Christian name? Oh, Eleanor!" She flung her arms about me and squeezed.

"No, Mama." I battled the embrace and backed away. "I do not address him as Clarence. We're not nearly as close as you imagine."

"That is not what Mrs. Wilcox said." She lifted a single, accusatory eyebrow. "Mrs. Wilcox said Clarence speaks of nothing else. Of how different you are."

"Different? That's hardly flattering."

"It is a compliment."

"It is ridiculous. That's what it is." I pulled my shoulders back. "I will *not* go without you."

"You will. What more could you possibly want?"

"Anything!" I threw my hands up. "I'm only sixteen. How can I know what I want yet? Maybe I'll want a tall man with . . . with blond hair. A-and green eyes."

Mama hissed and her eyes bulged. The reaction fueled my rant further.

"And maybe a man who isn't afraid if I say what I want, who doesn't care about . . . about etiquette and fashion and stupid, stupid Grecian bends—"

"Enough." She took quick, shallow breaths, her nostrils fluttering. "I do not know what this little revolt is, but be certain of one thing: I am your mother, and you will obey me." She straightened to her full height. "Mr. Wilcox honors you with his attentions. He comes from a wealthy family. His father and your father were friends once upon a time, and if my Henry considered

227

the Wilcox name a worthy connection, then so will you.

"And, Eleanor, keep in mind that when I am dead, you will have no one left to care for you."

"Elijah—"

"Elijah?" She shook her head slowly. "Where is my son *now*? He does not even care enough to return home. Your only hope lies in a husband. Only he can love and provide for you. Only a marriage and children of your own will ever offer you a chance at happiness." Mama's eyes lost focus, as if she stared into some other realm only she could see. "Trust me."

I swallowed my sharp retort and turned away. She had no pity from me. Once I might have clung to her, I might have believed her words and fretted over her desires; but I no longer did—I no longer could. I was capable of thinking for myself, and at that moment, my mind was reciting her earlier words: *His father and your father were friends.*

"When?" I blurted. "When were they friends?"

She blinked. "Who?"

"Father and Clarence's father. They stopped being friends, didn't they? When? Why?"

"I scarcely remember—it was so many years ago. Something to do with business. Mr. Wilcox and some other men wished to leave behind the railway industry, and Henry did not like it." Her eyes squinted with suspicion. "Why do you ask?"

"So . . . so I don't say anything inappropriate in front of Clarence—in case he still harbors his father's attitudes."

"If he still harbored his father's attitudes then he would not

228

be spending time with us. Luckily, his mother recently wanted to reconnect with me. If our luck continues, then the other families will also be as generous."

"What families?"

"The Weathers, the Suttons, and the Bradleys, of course. Do you ever listen to anything I tell you?"

Frederick Weathers, James Sutton, and Clinton Bradley. Three quite headless and quite dead young men.

I lurched at Mama and grabbed her robe. "The Gas Trustees? Did they offer Father a position in their business?"

"Yes, but Henry refused." Mama pushed me away. "Why do you ask?"

I ignored her question. "Why did Father refuse?"

"Eleanor, calm yourself!"

"Just tell me," I pleaded.

"I do not know why he refused. All he ever said was that he did not want to play their game."

My excitement deflated, and I stumbled to my bed. Once again the strange game of intrigue—but what was it?

"What *game*?" I groaned. "I don't understand."

"And I do not understand why you are so curious."

I picked at a fingernail and avoided her gaze. "I just want to know about our connection to the Wilcoxes . . . so I can understand Clarence better."

Mama examined me for several seconds, considering my words. At last she said, "I always assumed it had to do with politics. Perhaps . . . perhaps *dirty* politics—the sort of thing of which Henry would never approve."

"So . . ." I winced as the nail ripped off too far. "You want me to spend time with the people who ostracized Father because he wouldn't play dirty politics? Who ostracized you because Father wouldn't work with them?"

"The past is of no consequence. Your father's business *collapsed*, Eleanor, and with it went his sanity and his family's fortune. All that money wasted on a city council campaign." She massaged her temples. "Soon our funds will be completely spent. The Trustee families are the highest in Philadelphia's society. Powerful, rich, and—"

"Dead," I mumbled.

"Pardon me?"

"Nothing." I pinched the freshly exposed finger. I needed silence in order to work out this new information. I knew what game of intrigue my father had refused to play—dirty politics—though I still didn't understand the game itself.

Daniel had said he would deal with the Gas Ring part of the puzzle, but I didn't know if I could trust Daniel anymore.

"You are behaving very oddly this evening," Mama said. "You had better collect yourself. I will not have you acting like a lunatic with Mr. Wilcox."

I almost laughed. She had no idea how close to lunacy Clarence and I both were these days.

"I-I'm nervous," I stammered with what I hoped was a shy expression. "About tonight."

"Ah, I understand." Mama tapped the side of her nose.

"Well, I will call Mary back in to finish your hair."

"Yes, fine." I waved her away, too lost in my thoughts to care about her satisfied smirk.

"Miss Fitt," Clarence murmured, bowing when I greeted him in my family's parlor. The dim, yellow glow of the gas lamps layered him in flickering shadows, hiding the haggard expression I knew he wore.

"You look simply stunning," he added.

"Thank you, Mr. Wilcox." The dress was a lavender silk lined with white lace and miniature roses, and it trailed at least three feet behind me. It did enhance my plain looks to a passable pretty. But no matter how much it flattered my figure, it could never be worth the three hundred dollars Mama had paid for it—or rather had bought on credit.

"You look nice as well," I told Clarence with a wave to his crisp black suit and gleaming patent leather shoes.

He offered me his elbow, and I hooked my arm in his. Despite his obvious exhaustion, he gracefully escorted me to the carriage.

A rough breeze kicked at my curls, and I pulled my black velvet cloak tightly to me. Rain would ruin my elaborate hair and cover the gown's train in mud. *And how will rain affect the Spirit-Hunters' mission?*

I nodded to Willis, who sat with the driver on the back of the Wilcox carriage. He tipped his hat.

Clarence swung open the carriage door and hefted me

in. I started when three leering faces emerged in the darkness before me.

Clarence guided me to a seat, plopped on the bench across from me, and slammed the door shut. "I took your advice, Miss Fitt," he said. "Allow me to introduce my newest guards."

I squinted to see them. They were tough-looking men. Though all three wore shiny top hats, they looked more like men one would find patrolling the streets at night. Broad shoulders, bushy mustaches, and stiff postures.

"They're Pinkertons," Clarence explained. "The best of the best."

"Ah." The Pinkerton National Detective Agency was well-known for its top-notch private security. Its motto was We Never Sleep. Even President Lincoln had hired them. Although, that hadn't worked well for him in the end.

"How appropriate," I murmured in a syrupy voice. "The men who never sleep to guard the man who never sleeps."

Clarence laughed hollowly. "Well, perhaps now I *can* sleep." He slouched back in his seat and rested his hands behind his head. "I've also decided to send Mother and Allison on a trip to our seaside cottage. They are at home packing as we speak. You were right to suggest more protection, Miss Fitt. Why, I haven't felt this at ease in two weeks!"

So the Wilcox women were not ill at all. The carriage rattled to a start. None of the Pinkertons moved or even flinched.

"I'm glad I could help," I said dryly.

"Yes. It's wonderful to relax." Clarence's tone was light, and he was almost like his old charming self. If three stone-faced guards weren't with us in the carriage, I might have enjoyed him again.

As if in response to my musings, Clarence said, "I must admit, Miss Fitt, I actually enjoy your company."

My eyebrows darted up. "You sound as if this surprises you. Some people *do* like me, you know."

He only laughed again. "Yes, yes, of course. Pardon me—I merely meant that although you have a vexing habit of never acting quite as I expect, I still enjoy my time with you. Perhaps that's precisely *why* I like you . . . or perhaps it's because you are the only person who knows of my situation. Either way, it makes your mother happy to have me around, and it makes my mother happy to see me showing such interest in a young lady—even one such as yourself."

"Honestly, Mr. Wilcox, do you *hear* yourself? You insult me at every turn."

He grinned and leaned toward me, setting his elbows on his knees. "Yes, and you're a wonderful sport about it."

I sighed dramatically. "Are we still going to the opera?"

"Of course. And these men will be joining us. The three extra tickets shan't go to waste."

"Oh."

We descended into silence. This evening was turning out far different than I'd imagined. I couldn't even dream of escape—not with those Pinkertons there.

I tried to concentrate on something else, to lose myself in the clack of the horses' hooves, the rattle of the wheels, and—land sakes! Snoring!

I leaned forward and peered at Clarence in the darkness. The man had fallen asleep. I wilted back onto my seat, and the Pinkerton nearest me said, "I reckon he's tired. Don't wake him."

Pshaw. I glared at the man and then turned my stare out the window. Why had Clarence even bothered to take me out if he intended to sleep the entire time? As intriguing as he might have been, a sleeping companion was utterly useless. I doubted our mothers would be particularly pleased to know he'd left me to make conversation with the Pinkertons.

A quarter of an hour passed, and we clattered to a stop on Arch Street. Clarence twitched to life and dragged himself from the carriage. He tugged me out with him, and I fought the urge to resist. As he spoke to Willis and the driver, I hugged my cloak tight and glanced around.

Families and couples in lavish evening attire traipsed all around the street. Women in pastel gowns shimmered under streetlamps, and their dragging skirts whispered like a symphony of moth wings. The men, all dressed in their long black coats and black top hats—identical copies of Clarence—guided their ladies to the granite steps and tall white columns before the Arch Street Theatre's entrance.

Carriage after carriage rattled up and deposited the beautiful and the wealthy of Philadelphia. And, like me, they all examined everyone else. Yet, if they sought familiar faces or merely wished to critique their neighbors, I couldn't say. Either way, I was suddenly very grateful for my new gown. For the first time since leaving girlhood and frocks behind, I felt I was a match for my society.

"Eleanor!" A girl's voice shouted.

I twirled around to see Mercy nearby, her sister, Patience, still climbing down from a carriage. I waved.

Mercy daintily lifted her skirts to approach me, but then she paused. Her smile wavered and fell.

Fingers grasped my arm, and I flinched. But it was only Clarence. I gave him a tight grin—the Virtue Sisters would be delighted to know he was here!—and I glanced back to the street.

Patience had joined Mercy, and they glared at me. The hatred and envy was so thick, I staggered back.

Clarence steadied me. "Are you all right, Miss Fitt?"

"No—yes . . . yes. I'm fine. Let's go in." My voice broke over a lump in my throat.

Here I was unwillingly on the arm of Clarence Wilcox, but all the Virtue Sisters would see was Eleanor Fitt of the fallen Philadelphia Fitts on the arm of the most eligible bachelor in the city.

Maybe these people would talk with me and play croquet, but they still lived by the judgmental rules of class and wealth. And for a very brief moment, I wished I could go back in time to when Mercy had smiled.

But then I set my jaw and pulled back my shoulders. If their friendships were based on such meaningless things as name, then did I truly want them in my life?

Clarence and I reached the top of the steps. The grooved columns towered up beside us, and cheerful light poured from the open theater doors.

I peered back at the street. The Virtue Sisters were nowhere in sight, but my gaze hit on a small figure lounging against a gas streetlamp. My breath hitched. It was Jie! *Jie!*

What was she doing here? She nodded at me, and I nodded back. All my concerns over society vanished, for here was someone I knew I could call friend.

A fresh energy pumped through me. This evening wasn't ruined yet. There was still time to do what needed doing. Pinkertons, Clarence, Patience—none of them mattered. I still had a chance. A choice.

Porters bowed as we passed through the theater doors. Glistening crystal chandeliers greeted us, and for the first time I was able to fully inspect Clarence's newest bodyguards. They each wore ill-fitting black suits and well-fitting black scowls. They reminded me of those Russian dolls that all fit inside one another, for the three men could have been triplets if it weren't for their differences in size. Small, medium, large.

They looked dangerous and dependable, but I knew I could handle them.

Clarence guided me through the theater's entrance hall. Our feet clicked on ornate marble floors and up the main staircase.

On the second floor, we walked silently down long, bloodred carpets until we reached a private balcony. Once inside, Clarence plopped into a seat and lounged back. Two men settled into seats, and one stationed himself at the balcony's entrance. A single vacant seat was at Clarence's right, but I avoided it. I was too excited to stay still.

My mind buzzed with curiosity over Jie's presence outside.

I hustled to the balcony's edge and gazed at the theater's ceiling, a painted dome that reflected the gas lights and bathed everyone in yellow warmth.

I felt good—not happy per se, but in control. No one and nothing could stand in my way. This was my life.

When the first strains of music began, I moved to my seat. I glowered at the small Pinkerton who sat at my right. He offered me a flimsy, paper program, and I snatched it from his fingers. I flipped through the pages, only pretending to read them.

I needed a plan.

"Have you the time?" I asked Clarence.

He eased out a pocket watch. "Five after nine."

I peered in the program. The first intermission was in an hour. Would Jie still be standing there at ten? I had no way of knowing since I didn't know precisely why she was here in the first place. I tugged at my earring and forced my mind off the subject. I could do nothing at the moment.

The lights dimmed, and the opera began. Clarence quickly slumped over into a heavy sleep. None of his guards drifted into slumber, of course.

The first act passed at an excruciatingly slow speed. I constantly adjusted my train or massaged my scalp, and the performance did nothing to keep my mind from wandering.

I used to love the opera. Much like I swooned over Shakespeare's exotic lands, I longed to see the magical worlds of Mozart's *Die Zauberflöte* or Wagner's *Die Walküre*. To see Germany and Austria—the lands that had inspired such beautiful music and tales.

But not tonight. Perhaps never again, in fact. How could I dream when I knew I could *act* instead? And with all the strange and deadly things in the world, what was there even worth dreaming about?

Elijah. No matter what Mama said, I knew that Elijah cared about me. But sitting here watching a silly opera was not helping him. I had to leave. I had to talk to Daniel and get answers. I had to get away from here and put my mind and body to use.

Not soon, but now. Enough waiting.

"I must go to the necessary," I murmured to Clarence, but he didn't budge. I shook him lightly, but the only response was a sputtering snore.

I turned to the squat Pinkerton. "I must go to the necessary."

"I'll eth-cort you."

I almost laughed at his squeaky lisp. It was so unexpected. Instead, I puffed out my chest and wrinkled my nose.

"You'll do no such thing. Have you no manners, sir?" I snorted and jumped up. "I am not the one in need of protection.

You must stay with your employer."

I scurried into the hall. Willis was there.

"My head pains me," I told him, my chin held high. "I will hire a hackney home."

He moved toward the balcony door, presumably to wake Clarence.

I caught his arm. "Leave him. He sleeps soundly, and he needs the rest."

Willis narrowed his eyes, and my confidence wavered. I couldn't let him wake Clarence. I was so close to escape.

"I daresay this is as safe a place as any for him to slumber." I pursed my lips and arched a single, prim eyebrow. "You may tell Mr. Wilcox to call on me in the morning. I expect him to inquire after my health. Thank you."

I swiveled, my gait as imperial as I could make it, and I marched down the carpeted hall out of the footman's sight. When I reached the stairs, I ran. My blood pounded in my ears. For all my bravery, I was terrified of discovery. Clarence's outburst yesterday had been as unpredictable as a summer storm, and if I slowed to let my mind think, I'd be lost to cowardice.

I raced through the now-empty main hall. My footsteps echoed off the marble tiles. The porters at the front doors exchanged shocked glances. I could imagine the sight I must have presented—a flushed ball of purple silk and rustling skirts. No matter. I whisked past them and flew out into the Philadelphia night. My feet thudded on the theater's stone steps. Despite the stormy breeze that hit me, I sweated beneath my gown.

Jie lounged against the same streetlamp, and at the sight of me she straightened.

I jogged to her. "What're you doing here?" My ribs heaved against my corset as I strained to catch my breath.

"I was waiting for you. Your maid isn't so nice, yeah? I went to your house to find you, but she wouldn't tell me where you were."

"What'd you do?"

"I said I'd rip out her eyes and knock her teeth loose if she didn't tell me." She scowled, and the bruise on her cheek from the library attack made her look positively menacing.

I laughed a full, bubbling, stomach laugh. It was the first time I'd done that in weeks, and it felt good.

"I need your help," Jie said when my chuckles subsided. "I don't think I can trust Daniel tonight."

Fear flapped into my throat like clawing bats. *Daniel is a murderer.*

"Wh-why?" I gulped. "Is there something wrong with him?"

Jie popped her knuckles. "Just something funny. I dunno. This factory makes him . . . makes him skittish. We need another hand in case things go wrong."

"And you thought of me?" The fear in my throat eased back.

She shrugged. "Why not? You got legs and arms like the rest of us—you just need some trousers."

I couldn't keep the smile off my face. "All right," I said. "But let's get away from here before I'm caught."

"The men you came with." She pointed to the theater. "Where are they?"

"Occupied."

She flexed her arms. "Perfect. Let's go." She grabbed my hand and towed me into the street. "I'll hail a hackney. Since you're wearing that silly dress, we can't *walk* to the Exhibition."

"No one wears silly gowns in China?"

"Oh yes," she said. "We have silly clothes too."

"You'll have to show me one day."

She heaved open a hackney door and shot me a toothy grin. "That's a deal. But first we have to survive tonight."

CHAPTER EIGHTEEN

"I fear you have wasted your time by coming,"
Joseph said a half hour after I'd fled the opera house. His lips
pinched together. "I don't know what Jie has told you, Miss Fitt,
but we do not need you."

I huddled under my cloak, wishing Joseph would turn his
worried gaze elsewhere. He, Jie, and I stood in the lab. A lone
lantern flickered from the worktable.

"She'll be a lookout," Jie said. "We go in the factory, and she
stays outside."

"No."

"We need her help." She waved toward me. "What if Daniel
loses his nerve?"

Joseph stood taller. "Daniel will be fine with only you. I

trust him. And this is not Miss Fitt's job, but it is *our* job." His gaze flicked to me. "You have been a great help to us before, but there is too much risk for you this time."

"But—" I started.

"Please." His lips twisted down with apology. "I appreciate the offer. Truly, I do, but you should leave."

"No." I felt like an idiot standing in the middle of the laboratory dressed in layers of silk with a trail of lies snaking behind me. "I can help. Besides, it's my brother who's missing. I have to do everything I can to save him. It's my duty."

Joseph shook his head. "Miss Fitt, we are in a difficult place right now. The Dead grow strong, our help is limited to men who run and scream at the sight of a walking corpse, and we are about to break the law—something I have never done before."

"Which is why I can help."

His eyebrows drew tightly together. "No—do you not see? Ultimately, your presence here only complicates matters. You are a woman of . . . well, of high society."

I inched toward him, winding my fingers in my skirts. "And? You're a gentleman, so you must understand that society has nothing to do with the Dead!"

His shoulders sagged. "You misunderstand. The *consequence* of injury to your person—it outweighs the need for your help. Daniel will be fine with only Jie."

"No," I pleaded, though I saw the logic of his argument. "No."

"Miss Fitt, we do not need your help, and I think it best you go. And this is not a request now. It is an order."

I dropped my eyes and swallowed. My breath shook as I tried to keep my exterior calm. I had thought—no, I had *hoped* Joseph would want me here just as Jie did.

Bricks of defeat hung over my shoulders, threatening to drop at any moment and crush me. I'd made a risky escape for nothing. Daniel wasn't even here for me to question. Joseph did not need me, and I would succumb to frustrated, useless tears if I did not keep breathing.

I turned and shuffled from the lab into the empty darkness of Machinery Hall. I didn't even bother to lift my gown from the floor.

I would have to hire a hackney home and sort out my newest tales of deceit. Clarence would need to be dealt with. Mama too . . .

A figure formed in the shadows. My heart jolted, and I threw my hands up, ready to fight. But it was only Daniel.

"You scared me," I said.

"I'm sorry." His voice was so soft I could barely hear it.

His gaze roved over me. "You look . . ." His eyes stopped at the open expanse of my neck and chest, and he twisted his face away. "You look different."

My heart bounced, and for the second time that evening I was pleased with my gown. "I was at the opera." I smoothed at my bodice. "Evening attire, you know."

"No, I reckon I don't." He stepped toward me and slid his hands into his pockets. He inspected me again from top to bottom, and I inspected him right back. I searched for signs of wickedness. In the faint glow of moonlight that trickled through the hall's windows, all I could see was the lanky young man I'd grown accustomed to.

"What did you mean," I asked, "when you told me you had a lot of making up to do?"

"When did I say that?"

"At Laurel Hill the other day."

"And why're you asking me this now?" He sauntered two steps toward me. "If you've got something on your mind, Empress, then spit it out."

I hesitated, but only for a moment. "Are you Sure Hands Danny?"

He stiffened. "Where'd you hear that?" He slipped his hands from his pockets and opened his arms wide. "Actually, it's of no consequence 'cause I can guess who told you. There's no sense in protesting what you can clearly see is true."

He crossed one leg in front of the other and pivoted around, slinging off his cap on the way. Then he bowed low like a performer basking in applause. "Sure Hands Danny, at your service."

"You're a murderer." I skittered back several steps. "You blew up the factory."

He shot up. "So you've heard the whole tale then, have you?"

"No." I forced myself to meet his eyes. "No. I haven't heard *any* of the story. I was hoping you would contradict me. That you'd tell me it was a lie."

"I can't contradict the truth."

My throat tightened. "So you're a murderer? You ruined my father's company?"

"Now hold up. I don't know nothing about your father." He slapped his cap back on. "But I did kill a man six years ago. I'm an escaped convict, Empress." He said it so simply, as if he were declaring himself a carpenter or locksmith.

"Does Mr. Boyer know?" I asked.

"Joseph knows parts."

"A-and is that why Peger wants to find you? Is that why you're hiding from Clarence Wilcox? Because you killed someone?"

"Something like that, but it doesn't matter. It's a long story, and the end goes like this: I got a lot of making up to do, and one of my duties is to go back into that same damned factory tonight." He scuffed past me.

"Wait." My lips and mouth had gone dry, and despite his confession, I couldn't accept it. I didn't want to. I still had so many unanswered questions. "Can't you tell me the whole story, Mr. Sheridan? Maybe it was—"

"A justified murder? Does it matter?"

"Yes." I wet my lips. "It does matter. To me."

He opened his mouth, but whatever he was about to say was lost. At that instant the Dead alarm went off, a distant bass clang that echoed from some other Exhibition hall.

Daniel snatched my hand and hauled me to the lab. We

247

barreled in to find Jie and Joseph already dragging the glass-wheel influence machine from beneath the worktable.

Joseph started when he saw me. Likely he thought I had left by now.

Daniel bolted to the telegraph. "It's the alarm in the U.S. Government Building."

My knees wobbled and I grabbed at the door frame. "Have you destroyed the grimoire yet?"

"No," Joseph said. "It is not easy to destroy a book of magical power. It takes time. I have hidden it." He knelt to heft the electricity device onto the table.

Daniel moved to help him, but Joseph shook his head violently. "No. You must go to the factory."

Daniel recoiled, his eyes widening. "What? Now? You can't be serious. We can go another night."

"Your job is at the factory."

"But you can't fight the Dead alone." Daniel flung his hand in the direction of the U.S. Government Building. "What if the necromancer has come for the book? It could be the whole cemetery out there."

"Yes, and if you stay, will that improve our chances?" Joseph straightened, his eyes glowing in the dim light. "Without that dynamite, we are lost."

"No." Daniel swung his head. "I can't abandon you to the Dead."

"You won't be." Joseph spun to Jie. "You will stay here, Jie. You are our best fighter, and I will need you to lead the guards in defensive maneuvers . . . if any of the guards are able to help, that is. We will do what we can until Daniel's return." He paused, and his eyes flew to me. For several long moments he watched me. Then he nodded once, as if settling a debate in his mind.

"Miss Fitt," he said. "You must go to the factory."

"What?" Daniel threw himself between Joseph and me. "Are you crazy? She can't come! She doesn't stand a chance, and she's not one of us—"

Joseph slid Daniel aside with a single, cool hand. He stared at me. "She has proven her worth on more than one occasion. It is our turn to trust her. Will you go, Miss Fitt?"

I nodded. "Yes."

"No." Daniel's hands flew to his forehead. "Please, no."

"Listen to me." Joseph's tone was firm and final. "We will fail without dynamite."

"But the risk to her—"

"Daniel, if you do not succeed in your task, then at least she will be left to alert us. She need not be put in danger, but she must be there in case you fail. She knows the risk, and we must rely on her." Joseph pivoted to me, his chin raised high. "You were right, Miss Fitt. It is your duty, and you must do everything that you can. We all must. Now hurry."

Jie dropped to the floor and flung clothes from a trunk. She shoved a pile in my arms. "These are Daniel's smallest clothes, and here's a wrapping for your chest, yeah?" She set a piece of white linen on top of the clothes. "You'll have to wear my boots, though they'll probably pinch." She gave me a tight smile and added, "Good luck." Then she moved to help Joseph with the electricity machine.

I clutched the clothes to my chest. "Should we ring the fire alarm—would it bring more help?"

"Perhaps," Joseph answered. "And the Exhibition guards may be of some use."

"And what about the police?"

"Stop talking," Daniel snarled. He advanced on me, his face lined with anger. "Get changed."

I stumbled back. "Yes."

He pushed me toward the door. "And one more thing. You will do *exactly* as I say, do you understand?"

"Yes."

"Then stop standin' here, wasting time. Get dressed. We have work to do."

We went north for several miles until the sounds and lights of the city were long gone. The Schuylkill River at our right was barely visible in the clouded moonlight, but I could smell its aroma. A jumble of mud and river water laced with the spice of impending rain.

The trousers were both strange and liberating, as was the replacement of my corset with a linen wrap. I didn't feel bare as I'd first feared. Instead I was keenly aware of the strength and flexibility in my legs, the ease with which I could breathe. I could run, jump, kick, *fly*. The thousands of opportunities that erupted with the unlacing of my corset were now stretched before me.

But I stuck with the path that needed me most. One foot in front of the other with Daniel's back ahead.

"Listen," Daniel whispered. He had two empty burlap sacks slung on his back. "When we get there, I'll need to scout a bit before I head in. There's a fence around the property, and the factory sits right on the river's shore. It's constantly under guard, and if it's like it used to be, then there'll also be guards outside the fence. They circle every thirty minutes, so I don't wanna try to jimmy the lock until I know their locations."

"You said, 'before *I* head in.'" I patted my chest. "What about me?"

"You're going to stay outside."

"Why can't I come?"

"You're backup, remember?"

I clenched my mouth shut.

"That's what I thought." He stopped walking, though he still bounced from foot to foot. Something flashed from his pocket, and he placed a warm piece of metal in my palm.

I looked down at a knife, glinting in the dim moonlight.

"Now if anything happens," Daniel continued, "you run—like if I ain't back in an hour or you hear a commotion. Find a patrolman or go into a saloon if you have to. Offer money. Just get help for Joseph." He knelt, rolled up my trouser leg, and slipped the knife in my boot. "And don't mention he's a Negro or that you're a girl."

I licked my lips. "Yes."

He rose, and we resumed our trek. I was careful with my

steps—Jie's tiny boots were tight and had rubbed blisters along the sides of my toes. Plus, Daniel's constant fidgeting made me nervous.

"If it works out right," Daniel said, "then I'll be in and out in an hour." He pressed his palms to his eyes as if he was trying to hold something in. Whatever that something was, he looked miserable.

"Tarnation," he swore. "What was Joseph thinkin' by sending you with me? I can't do this again."

"Do what again? Please, Mr. Sheridan. Tell me."

"Daniel. You can call me Daniel." He slipped off his cap and ran his fingers through his hair. Then he flopped the cap on my head. "Here, you ought to wear this. It'll cover all those lovely blond curls."

I stuffed my hair beneath the gray wool. The cap smelled like him. "Tell me. Please, Daniel. There are so many mysteries that I can't solve, and for once I'd like to know the truth about someone."

He inhaled a long, hissing breath. Then he blew it out in a single puff. "I'm from Chicago, Empress. I had me a real nice setup over there. I was a darn good safe blower."

"A what?"

"Safes. I've got a way with mechanics, and no lock stands a chance against me." He grinned and wiggled his fingers at me. "I used to say, 'If there's a special lock that needs picking, I'm the special picker to unlock it.' They called me Sure Hands Danny, and since I was still a kid—tiny and thin—I was perfect for jimmying my way into banks and hotels and houses."

He shoved his hands in his pockets. "*Used* to. I don't do that low-life stuff anymore. It ain't . . . well, it's not who I wanted to be. Something I realized pretty quick after a few weeks in Eastern State Penitentiary."

I shivered. He started to walk faster, and I scampered to keep up.

"So six years ago," he continued, "a few thugs picked me up outside a bar and brought me to their boss's slick black carriage. A few turns around the block, and I learned exactly what this Philadelphia boss wanted. He needed an out-of-town kid to do a job for him. Someone the local coppers didn't know. Someone with the surest hands and a lotta grit. This boss said he needed me in Philadelphia, and that I was the only person to do it. I was flattered. Clay Wilcox wanted *me* to do a job."

"Clay Wilcox?" I gripped Daniel's sleeve. "Clarence's father?"

"Yep."

I drew back my hand and pressed it to my lips. "Keep going. Please."

"Well, Clay Senior paid for my fare, so I hopped on the first train to Philadelphia and did some snoopin' about. I wasn't so cocky as to trust my new employer completely. But all I could discover was that he was some bigwig called a Gas Trustee. The local low-lifes referred to him and the other Trustees as the Gas Ring.

"Clay and his ring controlled just about everyone in the city,

253

and they were riggin' the vote for upcoming city council elections. From what I gathered in saloons and on street corners, no one liked the Gas Ring's power. But the gas company controlled five thousand jobs, which meant the Ring controlled five thousand votes. And once Clay Senior and his fellow Trustees landed those council seats, they'd control almost every job in the city.

"Well, none of that business mattered to me. If those rich men wanted votes, so be it. They were paying me a small fortune to do this special job for them."

"And what was the job?"

Daniel scratched his jaw. "I broke into this same Nobel Company factory we're going to now. I went down to the storage warehouse, loaded up my sack, and then on my way out, *bang!* Two guards jumped me. They'd been waiting the whole time.

"We fought and I knocked one over—*hard.*" He pointed to his temple. "He hit a big rock, and well . . ."

I cringed and tried to keep my stomach from spinning.

Daniel looked out over the river and rubbed the nape of his neck. "I realized the guard was dead. Worst moment of my life, Empress. I was stunned and . . . and numb."

He took a deep breath. "I'd seen people die, but never by my hands. I didn't realize how much . . . how much *weight* murder carries. On your soul. And the blood—oh God, the blood . . ."

He hung his head. "The other guard brought me back to my senses. He was going crazy and babblin' about the plan. He kept telling me I had ruined everything, that I was gonna pay for it when Clay found out. That was when I realized they were supposed to blow it up."

"Blow it up?"

"Yeah. Big explosion, and I was supposed to go up with it. Then my charred body would make an easy explanation for the whole nasty situation. Soon as I figured out the plan, I skedaddled, and even though I didn't die, I was still a good scapegoat for the whole thing. Do you remember it? You'd have been young when it happened."

"Yes. I remember the explosion—not you, though. I-I never knew about you." I swallowed and tugged at my bare ear. Of course I remembered it. I would never forget. "My father had a dynamite shipment of his blown up that night. He was a middleman for Pennsylvania Railroad. He ran Fitt Railroad Supply. Well, the railroad needed a lot of dynamite, and Father had lined it up for them. He spent half of his company's money to buy it all. But then, *poof.*"

I mimicked an explosion with my fingers. "Without the dynamite, the railroad moved on to Father's competitors. Then no one else would hire him. Worst of all, Father was campaigning. He'd just started gathering support. He was running as a Democrat for the city council."

"The Trustees are all Republicans."

And that was when it all made sudden, perfect sense. Tears burned behind my eyes, and my voice shook when I spoke. "Now I understand."

"What happened?" Daniel's tone was gentle. He slowed to a stop, and I halted beside him.

"He died. My father *died*." I hugged my arms to my chest. "The stress and the grief. He went crazy with it, Daniel. Always talking about sabotage and his enemies. We all thought he'd lost his mind, but . . ."

I turned my gaze on Daniel.

"But what?" he asked.

"The thing is, Father and Clay Wilcox were friends. They worked together until Wilcox joined the Trustees. My father refused to follow. And since he was running *against* Wilcox for city council, Wilcox must have turned on him."

Daniel whistled softly. "Clay Senior planned the whole thing just to bring down your pop."

"I guess." I lifted a shoulder. "What other reason could there be? Father had to pull out of the election because his company had collapsed as a result of the explosion. And since you would take the fall, there was no obvious link to Clay."

"But I didn't die in the explosion as planned, and I wound up in prison pretty fast." Daniel ran his tongue over his teeth. "I was gonna be hanged for that whole affair. Luckily, I managed to figure out Eastern State's locks the day before my necktie sociable."

"But then why'd you come back here if it's so dangerous for you, Daniel? It's not even your home."

"I work for Joseph now. I go where he needs me. Besides, I

stupidly thought, with Clay Senior passed on, no one would care about me."

"But you're an escaped convict."

He snorted. "It's been six years, Empress. I'm grown up now, and I figured they weren't searching for me anymore. I sure didn't think the same reporter who covered my case back then would be coverin' the Dead now."

I blinked. "Peger?"

"Exactly. It seems he recognized me from my picture. Of course, I recognized him mighty fast too, so after one encounter, I made sure our paths never crossed again. But he had picked up the scent by then. I reckon he started askin' around to see if anyone was still interested in finding me."

"And Clarence Wilcox was." I massaged my scalp beneath the cap. "You're a threat to his election. If people found out the truth, he might not get that council seat."

"I doubt too many people would believe my story, Empress."

"All the same, he must be scared. Peger told me Clarence is willing to pay a lot of money to find you." I trudged forward, my feet dragging in the soft earth.

Just before he died, when Father's rants had been their worst, he used to shriek to Elijah, "We'll show them! You and I, son— we'll show them." It had scared me, it had scared Elijah, and it had upset Mama too. The shouting, the stomping, the wild eyes.

"Blazes," I said in a rough whisper. "All this time, Daniel, I thought Father meant his railroad competitors had sabotaged him. But no . . . he meant exactly what he said. His enemies. My father wasn't crazy. He was justified."

Daniel scooted closer to me. "And now Junior wants to court you? That's real sick."

"Junior?" My eyes grew wide. "Clarence is called Junior?"

"He was six years ago."

"Oh my God." I rolled my head back and stared at the cloudy sky. Junior. Elijah's bully. It was as if the world flipped. As if I'd been holding a picture upside down, but now I'd figured out which way was up. Junior had been my brother's main tormentor—the one Elijah cursed the most.

Oh, why had Elijah never *told* me? Surely he knew the connection between the Wilcox family and our own. And why had Father never protected his son? Why had Mama and I been shielded from all the secrets?

I forced my thoughts aside—now was not the time to worry over Clarence's lies.

The fence that spanned the factory came into our view. High and long, it stretched off into the night's darkness and hid the river. The road continued beside it and out of sight. Though this branch of Alfred Nobel & Co. was considered tiny, it still spanned several acres along the gentle riverbank.

Over the wind and insect chorus, I heard the rhythmic beat of horses.

"Listen," I said. "What is that?"

The ground began to vibrate. Then came the clamor of wild laughter and shouting—not the usual sounds accompanying late-night travelers. I glanced down the road. I could make out the dust rising in the distance.

"Road agents," Daniel hissed. "What the devil are bandits like that doing so close to the city?" His head spun about. "There's not a place to hide anywhere around here. Come on." He grabbed my hand and heaved me into a sprint.

We dashed alongside the river, speeding over the soft riverbank until we reached the factory's fence and raced beside it. By the time Daniel slowed, I had to gasp for breath and muffle the noise in my sleeve. I squinted and saw the faint shape of a door.

"New plans," he said. "I don't know what those bandits are looking for, but a pretty girl is not the sort of thing to leave out for 'em." He tossed the empty sacks at me and slid a leather wallet from his pocket. It unfurled to show gleaming metal wires and keys. He chose two pins and shoved the wallet into my hands.

"I also don't know how long we've got before the next guard rounds that corner." His pins scratched in a lock.

"To pile on the agony," he continued, "I don't know how many guards are on the inside, but I think our chances are better in there. Normally, the guards don't carry firearms 'cause of the explosives. But I *know* those bandits have pistols or some kind of barking iron."

The lock clicked, and he exhaled sharply. With aching slowness, he pushed the door inward and peeked inside. Then he reached back and yanked me with him through the fence door.

Before us, a grassy hill sloped gently down to the Schuylkill River. Three long, low structures stood on the bank, a hundred feet between each. Daniel pointed left, and we crept along the fence until we reached a line of covered wagons. We ducked behind the first.

He grabbed the sacks from me. "I'll break into the warehouse, and you'll sit here," he whispered. "First I gotta wait until the guard down there"—he brandished his thumb toward the nearest building—"makes his round. Or . . ." He trailed off, his mouth parted.

The hoofbeats were loud now. Hooting and laughter rang out. The road agents were almost to the factory fence. Daniel crawled to the edge of the wagon and peered down the hill.

"Perfect. The guards are all leaving their posts." He pointed, and I followed his finger. Sure enough, four men in scarlet uniforms were jogging to the middle hut. They converged for a few seconds, and then they all hiked up the slope toward the fence. It was then that I noticed an enormous gate in the fence. It was beside the door Daniel and I had just sneaked through, and the guards were headed straight for it.

Daniel scuttled back. "Well that's a stroke of luck."

"What?" I strained to see him in the darkness. He was fiddling with his leather wallet, flipping it open and shut, open and shut. The noise of the road agents was outside the fence now, passing by at a slow meander. They were anything but quiet, and it sounded as if there were at least ten of them—maybe more.

"I'd warrant the guards and those agents have a deal going down tonight. This factory is rotten to the core." Daniel's teeth gleamed in a shadowy grin. "Now, listen, I'm gonna slip down

260

while everyone's distracted. You just sit here, all right?"

"But if they're distracted, I can go with you. Two people can carry more than one."

He didn't answer. The heavy creak of enormous hinges snaked through the racket of the bandits. The guards were opening the gate.

"Just stay here." Daniel lurched out from beneath the wagon, shot a glance up to the gate, and then launched off down the grassy slope.

Blasted boy. I scuttled to the edge of the wagon, hoping to spy on the guards, but my foot kicked something in the dirt.

I knelt and picked up Daniel's leather wallet. It was the one with all his lock picks. Did he need this? If so, there wasn't enough time for him to run all the way up the hill and then down again.

Drat, drat, drat, what should I do?

I spared a glance for the guards. I couldn't see them, but raucous laughter drifted through the air. Meanwhile, Daniel was huddled at the nearest hut's door. Wouldn't he have broken in by now if he had the tools he needed?

I sucked in a breath—I had to risk it—and then launched into a run.

CHAPTER NINETEEN

This must be how mice feel when they run from the hawk. The emptiness of the factory grounds and the open gate spurred me on. I had chosen this path, and now all I could do was follow it. Thank heavens the grass was still damp and soft from yesterday's rain; it soaked up the pounding of my feet.

Though not enough that Daniel didn't hear me. He whirled around, his fists up, but at the sight of me, he blanched.

"Empress, I told you to stay," he hissed. His head twisted toward the gate.

"Your tools." I held up the wallet. "I thought you needed them."

He snatched it from my hand. "Sake's alive . . . I thought I'd dropped that in the field somewhere and the guards would find it." He gazed at me. "Thanks—though it was still mighty stupid."

After several long moments of metal scratching on metal, he rolled his heel against the door and it inched open. Then his hand snaked out and he hauled me to him. We wedged through the narrow space of black, and then he eased the door shut.

"I told you to obey my orders," he murmured.

"I'm sorry." I strained to see in the total darkness of the hut. "You should be grateful, though."

"I am . . . honest, I am. Now shut pan, Empress."

A yellow glow appeared, faintly illuminating Daniel and the immediate surroundings. I gaped at the light and waited for my eyes to adjust.

The light came from a jar in Daniel's hand, and whatever emitted the glow resembled a squirming mass of something alive. "Is that light moving?"

"Yeah. Glowworms. Can't risk fire near the dynamite."

It was so clever, so *typically* clever of Daniel.

His rough hand slid into mine. "Come on," he murmured. "Don't touch anything, and I'll find what we need. Looks like they rebuilt the warehouse exactly the same."

We moved away from the door. I focused my attention on the ball of light and on my steady footsteps over the earth floor. Around me, I had the sensation of open space.

I leaned close to Daniel's ear as we walked. "What's in here?"

"Tables. It's where they put the dynamite ingredients into

cartridges. We're going to the end where they load the finished stuff onto riverboats—that's where any complete dynamite will be."

"What's in the other two huts then?"

"The middle hut is where they make an absorbent that soaks up the nitroglycerin. And then in the last building they make the nitroglycerin. That's what causes the dynamite to explode." He lifted his arms and spread them wide. My arm rose with his, our fingers still clasped, and the light of the glowworms beamed around the room.

"They brew it in huge vats," he said. "All it takes is a teaspoon of the stuff to blow you to pieces, and there's hundreds of gallons in that building. The vats keep the nitroglycerin cool, so it doesn't explode. The safety of everything and everyone in that building depends on a thermometer. Seventy-two degrees. Nitroglycerin's gotta stay at that temperature."

The echo of our steps died, and we stopped our slow creep through the room. I realized we had reached the end of the building. Daniel raised the jar of glowworms and scanned the area.

"There." He pointed to a waist-high crate. The yellow light showed a label.

STUMP

"What is it?" I asked.

"It's dynamite for clearing farmland." He set the jar in my hand and tossed the empty sacks beside the box. "And it'll do perfectly. We need a hammer or—"

"A crowbar?" I gestured to a metal rod set next to the crates.

"Yep. Help me get this open."

Soon, after many smothered grunts and much creaking wood, we had the crate's top off. Inside, wrapped carefully in straw, was stick upon stick of explosive dynamite. They were small cylinders, no longer than my hand. How could so much power fit into something so tiny? It reminded me of Jie.

"You hold the bag open." Daniel pushed a sack into my hands. "I'll put this stuff inside."

"How much are we taking?"

"As much as we can carry."

The minutes passed in silent packing until the bags were full. Each sack held twenty sticks of dynamite packed securely in paper and straw. We knelt to heft the lid back on the crate.

Daniel suddenly froze midway. "D'you hear that?" he whispered.

I held my breath and listened.

Then came a shout. Unmistakable. It was a man's cry of alarm, and he was outside the building.

"Shit. You left footprints, didn't you? Shit, shit." Daniel heaved the bags on top of the crates and shoved me into a narrow crevice between the boxes. "Shit, shit, shit, Empress."

My heart began to beat frantically in my ears. "What's going on?"

"Shh." He set the jar of glowworms into my hand. "Joseph was right to say I might need you. I do. You gotta get the bags, or at least one of 'em, back to the Exhibition. I'll distract the guards. If you can't get to the fence door, wade in the river." He backed away from the faint light until he was part of the darkness. "I'm sorry, Eleanor. I promise I'll keep you safe."

His footsteps thumped loudly away, as if he wanted to make as much noise as he could. I slid the jar of glowworms inside my shirt.

It was all too fast for me to understand. What was Daniel doing? Was he turning himself in?

Over my wild pulse, I barely heard the hut's door swing open. There was a slapping thud like flesh hitting flesh. Then came shouts, feet scuffling on the dirt floor, grunts, more thuds, and finally calm. I cowered in my corner, my breathing so shallow and my heart racing so fast I thought I might pass out. I kept my shirtsleeve over my mouth to muffle the whimpers that threatened to escape.

"He broke my nose!" yelled a whiny voice.

"Shut pan and get him outside," rumbled another voice.

"I ain't going nowhere—" Daniel's words were cut off by crunching bone and a desperate howl. He was hurt.

A cry writhed in my throat, but I bit my tongue until the pain filled my brain.

"You're in for it now," said the whiny man. "I reckon you saw somethin' you shouldn't have seen, and we can't have you tellin' no one. So dead meat for you."

There was the scraping sound of a body being dragged along packed dirt. Then the door slammed shut, and no more sounds seeped into my ears.

My hands trembled uncontrollably as I eased the jar of

glowworms out from my shirt. My lungs worked overtime, sucking in and shooting out air. It was a strange feeling that coursed through my whole body. Intense heat, intense cold. Up and down, as if my body didn't know what season it was.

For a moment the world around me vanished. I only heard my heart and my breath. I only saw the jittery glowworms. Then the world resumed, and I latched on to reality before insanity could paralyze me anymore.

I did as Daniel had ordered, and I hoisted a sack on my back. I tried for the second, but it was too much. Twenty sticks would have to do.

I crept through the hut. My toes were numb from the pinching boots, and one of the blisters had popped and now burned.

Once at the door, I pressed my ear to it and strove to catch any movement or sound. Nothing came but the faintest patter of rain.

I could do this. Daniel needed me. The Spirit-Hunters needed me.

Cracking the door, I peeked outside. No one! So I ran silently, through the rain and up the hill. I didn't pause, look, or think. I just ran.

When I reached the wagons, I skidded behind and peered out at the three buildings on the river. Where would the guards be? Was Daniel still alive?

I couldn't leave him. Yes, it was my job to get the dynamite to Joseph, but it was also my fault Daniel had been caught. I was the only person who could save him, and he would die if I left him here.

In the space of a breath I made a decision. I did not consider it as carefully as I should have—I didn't consider it at all, really. I was giddy with a sense of invincibility. It ran through my arms and legs.

This is a dangerous place. A dangerous place means an alarm. An alarm is something I can sound. An alarm will draw the guards away.

I hid the sack and glowworms beneath one of the wagons and then watched the huts. No one appeared. With a deep breath and a silent prayer, I raced back down the slope. I went to the middle hut, but the door was locked. The rain picked up speed and intensity, and as I scooted along the outside wall, it filled my ears and sank into my clothes. It also masked the sound of my footsteps, and this time I was careful not to leave tracks.

At the back of the building I tipped my head around the corner. Nothing. I bolted to the next hut. The closer I got, the more a caustic reek burned in my nose. Hadn't Daniel said this was the nitroglycerin hut? A pipe the width of a man and at least twenty feet long spanned from the hut to the river, and I knelt beside it.

For several seconds I waited, allowing my ears to adjust to the raindrops on the river and my nose to accept the sharp nitroglycerin scent. There had to be an alarm in this building—anything as explosive as Daniel had described would have some warning system.

A door groaned nearby, and I slung myself beneath the pipe. *Please don't let anyone look my way.*

Three sets of red feet with a fourth set—brown and stumbling—passed by me. I bit my tongue and fought to keep my breathing under control.

"In the river," said the whiny man. His voice was muted, and I risked a glance out. The man had a rag pressed to his nose. Daniel must have gotten in a good punch.

"Come on then," said a gruff voice. "Don't make us club ya first. Drowning is so much more fun ta watch."

Drowning? I had to act now.

I rolled out from under the pipe and darted toward the door—or at least where I had heard the groaning sound of a door. It was at the center of the building, and once I reached it, I gave a quick look—the men hadn't seen me—before pushing inside.

My hands shook as I moved within, but I kept them aloft and defensive. The room was longer than sixty feet in either direction and lined with chest-high vats. It was like the Centennial Brewery; but rather than the yeasty, sweet scent of beer, my nostrils were overwhelmed with the burn of acid.

My breathing seemed loud and harsh, and the single light that hung in the center of the room hurt my eyes. But I prowled onward, seeing no one and hearing nothing but the gentle whir of pumps. My eyes watered from the sting of nitroglycerin, and I pulled my shirt collar up over my nose. A glance at the door for guards showed it was still shut. That was when I glimpsed the alarm.

It was a large bell with a handle for turning, like any fire alarm. It hung over the door, and it was too high up for me. Blast it!

I sniffed and wiped my eyes. A stool was beside the nearest vat, so I scooted to it. It was heavy, meant to stay in one place, and as I lugged it backward, it scratched and moaned across the ground.

Until my back hit something. I whirled around to find the glowing scarlet of a guard. The door was wide-open, and a shadowy face leered down at me. Before I could react, he grabbed me by the collar and shouted, "There's another."

The man hauled me from the building to the river with no effort.

"Look! It's a girl." He snatched the cap off my head and then kicked me toward the other men. I tumbled to the muddy ground.

I dragged my eyes to Daniel. His hands were bound, and a gag was stuffed in his mouth. Though one of his eyes was almost swollen shut, hurt and fury still burned bright in his gaze.

The gruff man yanked me back to my feet, and the guard with the rag against his nose sauntered toward me.

"You're a bit fleshy, ain't ya?" He licked his lips. "That's good. I like 'em fleshy." He thrust at me. I flinched, and the three guards guffawed.

"Well," the whiny one continued, tossing his bloody rag aside. "Fleshy or not, a knife will go in ya all the same." He leaned close to me. The bones of his face were sharp, half his teeth were missing, and he had the sallow skin of a consumptive. "Got any weapons, darlin'?"

"No—yes." I swallowed, desperately trying to wet my mouth. "I do have a weapon. A knife."

"Where?"

"In my boot," I said.

The man knelt, and as soon as his knees hit the earth, I moved. I heaved my left leg backward at the knee of the man behind me. My foot connected with the edge of the kneecap. His leg rotated and crunched inward. I pushed my hips against him, and he fell back.

With my right leg I jerked my knee against the kneeling guard's face and cracked his nose.

It all happened so fast—too fast for the third guard to react. I wormed away and barreled to the nitroglycerin hut.

The nitroglycerin has to stay at seventy-two degrees, and that means it needs a cooling system. If I can change the temperature, the guards will have something else to worry about.

I went to the first vat in the building. There was a thermometer with a knob marked

DO NOT ADJUST.

Footsteps beat nearby. My time was up. This knob had to be it. With all my force, I turned it.

It broke off in my hand. I had expected resistance—not for the damned thing to break!

"She's turned off the water!"

I jerked around and found two guards, eyes enormous in the dim light.

We all reacted at once.

I dropped the broken knob and scrambled from the vat. The two men bolted for the hut's door. I dashed after them, away from the cloying stench and the now-broken knob. We skidded into the rainy night.

The guards roared a warning down to the riverside—"It's gonna blow! Run!"—before fleeing toward the distant gate. Their red uniforms glowed in the drizzly darkness.

I sprinted to the shore and scanned for Daniel. He was still bound and gagged, struggling to stand on the slippery grass.

I dropped to his side and yanked the cloth from his mouth.

"What've you done?" he asked, his voice rough. Blood oozed from a gash in his lip, and his left eye was now completely swollen shut.

"I tried to scare the guards." I reached for his bound hands. "I-I just wanted to pretend. To act like I changed the temperature, but the knob broke."

He jolted away from me. "What temperature?"

"The nitroglycerin."

"Did you turn off the cooling?"

"The knob broke."

"What do you mean it *broke*?" He blinked rapidly and tossed his head to get the rainwater from his eyes. "Did you turn it off first?"

"Yes."

For a half second he stared. Then the whites of his eyes bulged, and he redoubled his efforts to stand. "Get me up!"

"I need to untie—"

"There's no *time*! Get me up!"

At the raw panic in his voice, my heart dropped into my belly. What had I done?

"Now!" he shrieked, and this time I did as I was told. I heaved him to his feet, and we broke into a run.

We sped over the grounds of the factory, past the nitroglycerin hut and up the long slope toward the gate. The factory's fence formed before us, growing higher with each pounding step but still seeming so far away.

"Faster!" Daniel screamed, and I tried to accelerate. My feet slammed into the damp earth. I ran faster than I'd ever run before, but even with bound hands, Daniel sprinted ahead.

We reached the wagons. A voice in my mind nudged me to get the stolen dynamite. After all this terror and loss, I couldn't leave the prize behind. I veered right and surged toward the nearest wagon. I slid underneath. The sack was just where I'd left it, dry and safe from the rain.

"Eleanor!"

I darted back out. Daniel was searching for me, his eyes wide and wild.

"I'm here!" I bounded toward him, the sack slung onto my back.

We flew through the still-open gate and bore left down the long, empty road toward Philadelphia.

I experienced it all in a half-numb frenzy. The slats of the factory fence blurred as I streaked past, the rain hit my skin and soaked my clothes, the awkward weight of the sack banged against me with each step, and my lungs burned in desperation for more air.

But nothing happened. No explosion, nothing. We reached the drawbridge a quarter mile away and still no fires or booms blazed in the distance.

We stumbled to a stop inside the covered drawbridge, and I collapsed to my knees, certain I would vomit. The nausea rose heavy in my throat, and my bladder felt excruciatingly tight. My feet were raw from all the blisters—they had to be bleeding by now.

Beneath the bridge, the Schuylkill River flowed lazily by. No carriages, no people in sight, only the gentle rain tapping the wooden roof. The calm of it all clashed with the chaos that still blazed inside me.

Daniel's breathing rasped nearby, and a glance showed him slumped to his knees. I crawled to him and began to pick at his ropes.

"You must not've," he said between gasps for air, "turned the right knob."

The words echoed without meaning in my brain. My wet clothes clung to my skin, and I shivered with cold and exertion. My single line of coherent thought was focused on the task of loosening his ropes, on mustering more dexterity into my numb fingers.

Minutes ticked by, and at last the knots came free. I slid my hands beneath the ropes. Daniel flinched—I had stroked raw skin.

"You're hurt." My voice cracked.

"I'm lucky that's all that happened." He pushed unsteadily to his feet. "You could have killed us."

"But I saved you."

"No." He bent and hoisted me roughly to my feet. "You almost killed me."

"I didn't!" I tried to break free, but he pulled me closer.

"I told you to leave," he snarled. With his face only inches from mine and glowing white in the darkness, I could make out lines of fury scored into his face. His swollen left eye and bleeding lip only made him look more anguished.

"They almost killed you," I said hoarsely.

"And they almost killed you too!"

He dropped me, and I stumbled back until I hit the bridge's wall. He thrust a finger in the direction of the factory. "Do you know what should have happened back there, Eleanor? Do you?"

"I just meant to scare the guards. I didn't mean to break the pump." The hot ache of tears burned in my throat.

"Joseph sent you as backup—in case things went wrong." He strode to me, his hands bunching into fists. "Well, things went wrong, and your job was to leave. To stay safe."

"And you'd be dead in the river if I had."

"And what if *you* had died too? Did you think of that?" He gave a strangled groan and stomped away, clenching and flexing his fingers as if trying to keep the violence to himself. "You didn't think at all, did you?" He whirled back around. "Tell me—did you?"

"Yes!" I shouted. "I *did*. And I made a choice! If you're worried about Joseph, then we should go. We have the dynamite, and we can still—"

"This isn't about Joseph or the dynamite." He spoke in a low growl. "Leaving was your only job, Eleanor, so why didn't you go when I told you to?"

"Because, Daniel." My voice was raw with bitterness and hurt. "You . . ." My voice broke. I swallowed to try again. "Because, Daniel, no matter what you say, I know you would have done the same for me."

His breath burst out. He tumbled backward as if I'd slapped him. I used the moment to escape, shoving past him and slinging the sack onto my shoulder. Without a glance back, I sprinted through the bridge toward Philadelphia. My footsteps were loud and hollow.

Tears fell now and mixed with the raindrops. But despite the sobs that hovered in my chest and threatened release at any moment, I refused to succumb.

Joseph needed the dynamite, and Daniel was right: I had a job to do.

"Wait!"

I looked back. Daniel was rushing toward me through the rain. In half a heartbeat he was beside me and tugging me into his arms. His lips parted, but if to speak or to kiss, I never found out.

The sky lit up as if a flash of sunlight pierced the night. A sound like thunder, black and heavy, cracked through the rain.

It was from the factory, and a shock wave shuddered over the earth. My knees, already weak, buckled from the impact. I fell onto Daniel, and we toppled to the ground.

The factory had exploded.

It was the impetus we needed, the reminder that life and death still hung in the balance in Philadelphia. In seconds we were back on our feet and bolting toward the city. Toward Joseph at the Centennial Exhibition—and toward the walking Dead.

CHAPTER TWENTY

The lab was destroyed.

When we finally straggled back over an hour later, we found nothing intact. Joseph's papers were shredded, Daniel's inventions were torn apart, and everything was covered in grave dirt and bits of jellied corpse. I stood frozen at the door.

In the middle of the room, Jie held a slumped and barely conscious Joseph. Daniel lunged forward and eased Joseph to a stool.

"It was a trick," Jie said. Her voice was raspy and thin. "The necromancer tricked us from the lab. We went to the U.S. Government Building, and we fought the Dead. But this"—she waved at the room—"is what they came to do."

My breath shot out, and I eased the sack of dynamite to the

floor. "You mean the necromancer lured you away to destroy your equipment?"

"What other reason can there be?" Her eyes were hollow. "Without our things, we cannot fight back."

"The . . . the influence machines?" Daniel asked, examining his destroyed equipment. The only unbroken item in the room was the table.

"We still have one." Jie flicked her eyes to a blanket-wrapped mound. "The other was gone when we got back."

Daniel rubbed his eyes and nodded wearily. "How many Dead?"

"Over a hundred."

I choked. "A hundred? And Joseph stopped them?"

"Yes." Jie's shoulders drooped. "But he's exhausted . . . he's not even in his head right now."

I stared at Joseph. He leaned against the wall, his eyes half open and unseeing.

Everything had gone wrong, Daniel's capture, my attempt at rescue, the explosion, and now this. Guilt ate at my neck and shoulders—a stiff, heavy question: had I made the right choice? Maybe if I had left Daniel and brought Joseph the dynamite, then the lab would still be intact. By saving Daniel, had I endangered the entire city?

"Will he wake up?" I asked.

Daniel planted his hands on the worktable. "Yeah, he'll wake up." He hung his head. "He'll need sleep, though—a lot of it."

I pointed to the sack beside my feet. "The—"

"Not now." Daniel turned toward me with a single shake of his head. "Leave it there. Go home."

Jie turned to me, her gaze intense. "It's three in the morning. Your mother will wonder where you are."

My mouth went dry. Mama, Clarence, the opera . . . I screwed my eyes shut. I had to face them. I'd known that all along.

"I-I need to get dressed," I said.

"I'll help." Jie picked her way over the floor and joined me at the door. She glanced back at Daniel. "You hire a hackney for her, yeah? She can't waste any more time here."

My silk gown on once more, but with my hair a tangled mess down my back, I rode home in a hired hackney. My mind was filled with lies and half-truths to tell Mama. The black guilt that plagued my shoulders and neck now descended over my whole body. I had single-handedly annihilated a factory, I had lied to Mama and Clarence, the Spirit-Hunters' equipment was ruined, and I was still no closer to finding Elijah. I wanted to cry, to give in to the hysteria of the night, but I found myself too numb with exhaustion to even think properly.

I paid the hackney driver and hurried through the gate into my front yard. No lights shone in the windows, and I prayed the servants had gone to sleep. I held my skirts high, but it was no use—such an excess of flounce could not be protected from the dirt and puddles. And though the rain had stopped, my slippers still sank into the muddy path, making a sucking sound as the heels pulled loose with each step.

"Miss Fitt," said a man's voice.

My heart heaved. I froze. A figure emerged from the shadows of the cherry tree. It was Clarence Wilcox, striding toward me.

I tugged my cloak tightly to me.

"What is it?" He folded his arms over his chest. "Is it opium? Were you at an opium den?"

My fear melted. "Opium? *Opium?*"

"Yes. Opium. It's a substance that induces a euphoric—"

"I know what opium is." I threw my hands wide, not caring that my cloak slipped to the earth. "How dare you accuse me of that."

"One of the Pinkertons saw you leave with a Chinaman."

I advanced on him. "Well, it was not opium, Junior." I spat the name with all the disgust I could muster. "I know all about the Gas Ring. About what your father did to *mine*. Don't look so surprised. I know your secrets now. So stop flinging your pathetic accusations at me."

Clarence staggered away to the cherry tree's bench. I slung my cloak off the mud and followed. My rage grew with each step.

"Your father killed my father—did you know that? He blew up the Nobel factory and ruined Father's business."

"I know," Clarence mumbled. He dropped to the wet bench and buried his face in his hands.

"Clay ruined my father's council campaign. He killed my father!" My body was so tight, I could barely move. I wanted to slap him, to shoot my energy and fury out in violence. Why

282

didn't he respond? Why was he so calm? "Answer me!"

"I know what happened. I wish I didn't."

"Wishing won't help!" My shout was muffled by the moisture in the night air, but it was loud enough to wake my house. I lowered my voice, though it shook with emotion. "You and those other boys from the Germantown Academy—your wicked Gas Ring—you were all my father's enemies!

"And," I said, bending down and pushing my face in his, "you were my brother's bully."

Clarence dropped his hands. His eyes were thin.

"What?" I snarled. "Did you think I wouldn't find out? That I'd be so blinded by your stature and image that I wouldn't care? You're a bastard." I shoved him, and he toppled back in his seat.

"The almighty Junior. I can't believe I didn't see it sooner." I lunged at Clarence, but he grabbed me by my bruised wrists. He twisted my arms and bolted out of his seat.

"That's enough, Eleanor—enough!" He towered over me. "Yes, I knew your brother. He was always cowering and crying. And yes, I thought him a sickly, ridiculous thing." His nostrils flared as his breath came out in great gusts. "Then after your father refused a spot in the Gas Ring, Fred, James, Clint, and I did exactly as *our* fathers told us to do. We made your brother's life a living hell."

"Bastard."

"Hush. You've no right to say such things, and it doesn't suit you. Behave like the lady you are." He bore down on me and forced me to sit. "I am not proud of how I treated Elijah. It was easy and even fun as a child, but now, as an adult, I wish it hadn't happened."

"Don't lie."

"I'm not—I have every intention of making amends when he comes home. I hope to offer him a position among the Gas Trustees."

"Why? Why would you do that?"

"I don't agree with everything my father did. I . . . I regret the enmity between our families." He released my wrists and thrust his chin high. "However, I am a dutiful son. I follow my father's footsteps and carefully laid plans because, well . . ." He spread his hands. "What choice do I have?"

"You always have a choice," I growled.

"No. That's not true. This was the life given to me, and I honor my father's memory by faithfully living it. I run for city council because he wanted me to. He made no mention of your family, though, so I have taken it upon myself to help."

"How generous of you."

"Everyone can see you fake your wealth." He grimaced with a mixture of pity and distaste. "Of course, with a mother like yours, it's not hard to see where it all gets wasted."

"Don't talk about my mother like that. You know nothing about us."

His eyebrows jumped up. "I know she raised an unruly daughter, whom, despite it all, I *like*. A daughter who must be married off quickly and taught some manners. I know she raised a weak son who has abandoned his family when they need him most—"

"He hasn't abandoned us." I launched myself at him and pounded on his chest. "He hasn't! You don't know anything."

Clarence wrestled me off. I didn't resist—I couldn't resist. Somewhere in my pummeling, I had started to cry.

"Calm down," he said. "You must calm down. You will wake your house." He pushed me onto the bench and sat beside me. "Eleanor. Miss Fitt. Calm down."

"How can I?" I whimpered. "How can I be calm when *you're* Junior a-and my brother has been taken and I-I ruined the Spirit-Hunters lab and my brother is going to die—the whole city . . ." I laid my face in my hands and sobbed. I knew my behavior had turned hysterical, but I couldn't rein in my emotions. It felt as if my brain were separated from my body by a wall. I could think logically, but I couldn't act it.

"Eleanor." Clarence yanked my hands from my face and made me meet his gaze. "What do you mean your brother has been taken? And what about the Spirit-Hunters—have they found Elijah's body?"

"No. He's not dead. The necromancer has him."

"How do you know?"

"Because I just do! Now let me go!" I wrenched free of his grasp. He reached for me, but I scrambled off the bench. "Stay away from me."

The muscles in his jaw twitched. "No. Explain. It makes no sense." He sprang up and chased me, his eyes huge and white.

I retreated clumsily, wiping at my eyelashes and damp cheeks. "Wh-where are your bodyguards?"

"Around," Clarence said. "Don't worry. I'm safe. Even if you don't see them, they're lurking nearby."

I laughed, a breathy sound. "I'm not worried for you. I'm worried for me."

"I don't intend to hurt you."

"Then why don't you leave?" I pointed toward the gate. "I don't want your company."

"Absolutely not," he snapped. "There are quite a few questions that need answering. How do you know of your brother? Where did you go tonight? And, most importantly, who told you about the Gas Ring and your father's company?" He advanced on me.

"Stay away!" I hefted up my skirts and tried to flee, but all I could manage in the mud and petticoats was a quick hobble. He clasped my arm and whipped me around. I toppled into him and had to clutch at his coat.

"You had better cooperate, Eleanor. There are many lives at stake, including my own."

"The devil can cite Scripture for his purpose."

"And the foolish can cite Shakespeare," he snarled. "Enough with your childish behavior. Answer my questions or I will tell your mother of all this."

I gasped. "No." He couldn't tell Mama. Everything I'd

worked for would be ruined—she would lock me away and probably lock herself away too.

Clarence snorted. "Finally, a sensible response. Now satisfy me with answers or I'll tell."

"Not tonight." I licked my lips and searched for an excuse. "I-I'm so tired. In the morning. If you call in the morning, I'll explain everything."

"Why should I trust you?" He cocked his head and gestured to my gown. "You're deceitful."

"And you're a corrupt, murdering bastard."

"Ah." His eyebrows rose high. "Back to your charming self, I see."

I wrenched away from him and spat at his feet. It splattered on his patent leather shoes. If I could handle a dynamite factory, then Clarence Wilcox should be nothing.

Clarence's lip curled.

"Spare me, Eleanor. Truly, you only embarrass yourself. I'll be here in the morning. Early. Until then, your little secrets are safe with me."

I stared, suddenly tongue-tied. He held all the power. I had to do as he asked or he'd tell Mama. If she learned her only son was gone—possibly dead—and that our chances of redeeming our wealth were gone too . . . I couldn't imagine the consequences. I had already lost one parent to devastated mourning and insanity.

With one hand Clarence twined his fingers in mine. With the other he brushed an errant curl from my face. I didn't flinch, though I wanted to.

"You could be such a fine lady if you would only try." He released me and backed away. "I shall see you tomorrow, then."

As Clarence wandered into the night, I saw a figure detach itself from the shadows beside the gate. It crept after him.

One of the Pinkertons, I thought. *So now at least two people know all my secrets. Can things get any worse?*

When Mama discovered my late night with Mr. Wilcox, she was aghast. But that reaction lasted less than an hour. Then she realized it was actually what she'd wanted all along: Alone Time with an Eligible Bachelor.

Her mood flipped like a coin, and she bubbled with delight. She doted on me, all the while singing of betrothals, wedding gowns, and wealth. She even indulged my desire for a second helping of toast.

And I hated all of it. The serpent of guilt that lived in my chest now wound into my stomach. It writhed with something else too, something much darker.

Powerlessness. Dread. My whole life rested within Clarence's hands, and with it laid Elijah's. If Clarence decided to tell Mama about my time with the Spirit-Hunters, about Elijah's disappearance—as far-fetched as it all sounded, I knew she would believe him. Her esteem of Clarence, of *Junior*, was too high. As was her suspicion of my "rebellion."

I knew I would have to tell Clarence everything. I would lie with all my heart about Daniel's part in the puzzle, though.

If I had to, I'd say Nicholas Peger was the one who'd shared Clarence's secrets with me. But I couldn't hide the truth of Elijah and his letters. And perhaps the part of Clarence's character that I liked—the young man with the fetching smile who loved his family—would find it in himself to help me.

With each passing minute of the day, my paranoid anxiety only worsened. I scrawled a note to Clarence after breakfast, but I received no reply, and by midafternoon he still hadn't called.

To make matters worse, the explosion of the dynamite factory was on the front page of the Sunday paper. I read the entire article four times, my chest growing blacker and heavier each time. There was no mention of Daniel or me—no description. Likely the guards feared we'd rat out their own wrongdoings. But that didn't make me feel better. So much destruction because of me.

Daniel probably felt tenfold worse. He'd been forced to relive the worst night of his life, and yet I was so very glad I hadn't left him to die.

And poor, poor Joseph. Had he recovered from his exhaustion? *Could* he recover from the loss of his lab?

I paced the parlor, my leg muscles screaming from overuse and my blisters still burning. The knickknacks, the flowered wallpaper, the velvet curtains all shouted at me, sucked the air from my lungs until I had to flee the house and walk in the yard. But once there I couldn't stop staring at the bench, couldn't stop replaying Clarence's words.

And then Daniel would flash into my mind, his lips parted

and pulling me to him. A strange ache would flare through my chest, and I would think of his lips, of his fingers. And then those thoughts would mix with the guilt and the darkness like some chemistry experiment gone wrong. My whole body would shake.

What was I doing? Truly, things could get no worse.

I gave a strangled cry and dashed back into the house, up to my bedroom. I desperately wanted to go to the Exhibition, but I couldn't. I had to wait for Clarence. Wait to see if he meant what he'd said.

I burrowed myself in my sheets, and I let my emotions overtake me. Clarence didn't come that day.

The next morning was Monday, and my composure was on the verge of shattering. I was so tired that my nerves throbbed. If I had to hear another pleased exclamation from Mama, I would crumple to the floor in a weeping heap.

I needed to talk to Clarence, and then I had to see the Spirit-Hunters. I placed my green bonnet firmly on my head. Shadows ringed my eyes, and I pinched my cheeks to induce some— *any*—color into my lifeless face.

I wore an old dress that barely reached my ankles and didn't require a bustle, and after wrapping the blisters on my feet with linens, I donned my sturdiest walking boots. Fashion and appearance be damned. If I was lucky, my clothing might frighten Clarence into helping me.

Best of all, I could breathe, having foregone my corset. I had fought furiously with Mary until she'd run away on the verge of melodramatic tears. But I had won the war, and no corset confined my waist today. If the suffragists could do it, why couldn't I?

As I descended the steps into the hall, a knock resounded at the front door. The black dread exploded in my stomach. I raced to it and flung it open, expecting Clarence. But it was Allison, flustered, crimson cheeked, and sweating.

"Oh Eleanor!" She rushed inside and clasped at my hands. "Have you seen Clarence?"

"No. Why?"

A cry escaped her lips, and she threw her hands to her mouth.

"What is it?" I demanded.

"H-he hasn't come home."

My pulse thumped in my ears. "Since when?"

Allison only shook her head and whimpered. A tear rolled down her cheek.

"Allison! When did you see him last?"

"S-Saturday."

My breath froze. Oh no, what had happened? "He never came home after the opera?"

"N-n-no!" she wailed. "We were supposed to leave town, b-but . . ."

"Calm yourself. You must explain."

She didn't respond but rocked and wept into her hands.

For a lack of anything better to do, I dragged her into the parlor and thrust her on the sofa.

"Get a hold of yourself." I knelt and gripped her chin. "Look at me. What is going on?"

Allison took in a shaky breath. "He never came home, and Willis said he came here after the opera. B-but when Willis came to pick him up, Clarence wasn't around, and his security men didn't know where he'd gone."

I crumpled to the sofa. I had seen a figure following him and assumed it was a Pinkerton, but it must have been . . . "The Dead," I breathed. "Oh no, oh no. I've got to find him."

"What? Y-you can't do that."

"Of course I can." I pushed to my feet.

Allison pawed at my hand. "We've tried." She gazed up with puffy, red eyes. "Mother went to the police and the firemen."

"And no one would help?"

"It's not that they won't, but they *can't*."

"Why?" My voice was harsh and loud. "Damn it, Allison. Say what needs to be said."

She howled again and flung her face into her hands. "H-hostages. Hostages at the Exhibition."

Ice spread through my body all the way to my fingers and toes.

"What do you mean?"

No answer came, just more crying. I yanked her by the shoulders and shook her. "This is no time for hysteria—tell me what is going on!"

"The Dead!" Allison jerked out of my grip. "It's the Dead! Th-they've taken hostages at the Exhibition."

CHAPTER TWENTY-ONE

The streets around the Exhibition were almost impenetrable. Shouts were on everyone's lips, and violence was in the air. I could feel it like shimmering electricity that connected us all.

This is how riots begin.

I shoved my way through the crowd, ignoring angry protests, ignoring my sore muscles, ignoring the terror that churned in my belly. I had left Allison to Mary's care—the maid would make sure Allison got home safely. I had to get to the Spirit-Hunters *now.*

I reached Elm Avenue and the train tracks that ran alongside it. Wagons were lined up before the Exhibition entrances, and interspersed between these barricades were Exhibition patrolmen. Black plumes of smoke twirled up from inside the grounds, and the scent of burning was in the air. It was as if war had come.

I marched up to the nearest patrolman. "I must go inside."

"The Dead have taken over the whole Exhibition, lady—hostages and everythin'. No one in or out. Now back away."

People clambered behind me, jostling and screaming. "How many walking Dead?" someone yelled.

"Dunno. Thousands, maybe." The officer waved his pistol. "Get back!"

"If there are so many, why are you here?" I pointed at the barricade. "Why aren't you doing something?"

"Our job is to keep people out. The hostages will be killed if we don't."

"And what about the firemen?" I demanded. "Where are they?"

The patrolman blinked his eyes rapidly. "They're in there. The Dead started fires in the state buildings."

Many nations and states had their own structures on the Exhibition grounds. That meant at least forty buildings were up in flames. The firemen would have their hands full for hours—maybe even days.

I hugged my arms over my chest. The necromancer had prepared for everything. He had stopped the Spirit-Hunters by destroying their lab. He had stopped the police and Exhibition guards by taking hostages. He had stopped the firemen by igniting the state buildings.

The patrolman glanced uneasily at the crowds behind me. They heaved closer and closer. "Besides," he called out, "what're we gonna do? We can't kill the Dead."

"No," I snapped, "but we could set the Dead on fire! Explosives—anything!"

"And that'll destroy the Exhibition. Not to mention put the living at risk."

"Then break their knees—does no one pay any attention to the Spirit-Hunters?" I thrust my shoulders back. "Let me through."

"No."

He swung his gun at the nearest protesters. "All of ya! Back off or I'll shoot!"

Like an ocean wave, the crowd pulled back, including me.

Well, I tried diplomacy and that failed. So distraction and speed it will have to be.

I turned to face the crowd. "Listen. Listen to me!" I shouted. "I've got loved ones in there too. If we want to keep them safe, we have to do as the police ask." I glanced back. The patrolman had lowered his gun. He gave me a nod of approval. Perfect.

In a single movement I spun and leaped at the officer. His mouth dropped and he tried to lift his pistol, but I was already on him. I jabbed his arm aside and sped between the wagon barricades.

I didn't look back. I held my skirts high and pumped my legs as fast as I could. I raced through the turnstiles.

A gunshot popped. I prayed it wasn't at me. The cries of the crowd swelled to a roar, and I knew the police would have their hands full soon—if they didn't already.

I flew across the main square, past the Bartholdi Fountain, and toward Machinery Hall's eastern entrance. Another shot rang out, but I couldn't tell if it was intended for me. Either way, I was too close to stop.

I slammed into Machinery Hall's entrance. Two more shots fired. One cracked into the wooden door frame just above my head. I barreled inside.

The Spirit-Hunters' lab door was open, and I skittered through. Daniel was at his table. He whirled around, his fists bouncing up and his stance dropping low.

He froze. "Empress. Why are you here?"

"To help." I gulped in air and wiped sweat from my brow. "I heard about the hostages."

Daniel had healed some since Saturday night, though not much. The skin around his left eye was purple and green, and the gash over his lip was a ragged scab.

"What's happening?" I asked.

"It's bad. Two thousand people are trapped in Agricultural Hall."

I gasped. "Two *thousand*?"

"Yeah. And the necromancer gave us a note—delivered by one of his corpses. We've still got the book hidden for now, but if we don't hand it over soon, the necromancer is gonna let some of his Dead loose to feed on the hostages."

My breath shot out. I swayed back, but Daniel lunged

forward and caught me before I could fall. For a moment he held me, his arm looped around my waist and his eyes gazing hard into mine.

"Eleanor." He swallowed and wet his lips, his eyes roving over my face. But then he pulled back and released me. "You shouldn't be here. There's nothing you can do."

"No. I have to help." I reached out and clutched at his sleeve. "Where's Joseph? Jie?"

"Agricultural Hall. They're trying to get through the lines of Dead."

"Lines?"

"Yeah. The necromancer's got hundreds of them in rows, like an army. They attack if you get too close, but otherwise they just stand there."

"Have you seen the necromancer?" I wanted to ask if he'd seen Clarence, but I held my tongue. Now wasn't the time.

He swung his head sharply. "No. His corpses do all the work for him." With a yank, he freed his arm from my grasp and turned back to the table. "Whoever he is, he picked the perfect moment. He took us apart bit by bit, and now we can barely fight back."

"Are you going to give up?" I demanded at his back.

"Hell no, Empress."

"Are you going to give him the book?"

"Maybe. Probably."

I wedged myself between him and the table. "What's the plan?"

Through clenched teeth he said, "We're going to try to save the hostages without givin' him the book, but there are fires burning everywhere." He threw a hand toward the window. "There are corpses crawling all over the place, Joseph is exhausted, and I'm havin' to start all over with my pulse bombs.

"Worst of all, the necromancer is losing control of his army. Joseph says the spiritual energy that animates them is unraveling. If we hand over the book now, maybe the necromancer and his army will leave before it's too late."

"You mean before the whole army turns Hungry?"

"Yeah."

"But the book—won't it give the necromancer more strength?"

Daniel lifted one shoulder. "We're going to hold off on handing it over as long as we can, but the Dead have all the power right now."

I screwed my eyes shut and turned away. "Let me help, Daniel."

"No." He pressed his palms to his eyes. "Not after . . . not after the last time."

"This time I'll listen," I pleaded. "I'll do exactly what you tell me. I learned my lesson."

He gripped the sides of my face and stared at me, his jaw set. "That's not what I'm talking about. It's your safety that bothers me."

"The Devil take my safety!" I jerked away from him. "Tell me what to do!"

He eyed me for several breaths. Then he slowly nodded. "All right . . . I'll send you to do my job—to retrieve the hidden book— but I can't come with you. My first priority is to make pulse bombs—*now*. D'you know where George Washington's camp trunk is?"

"Th-that's in the Government Building."

"Right, and the book is hidden in that trunk in the Government Building. So, you take that"—he pointed to a baseball bat leaning next to the lab door—"and go get the book. Then you take it to Joseph at Agricultural Hall."

I pushed back my shoulders. "Yes."

"And you run, Eleanor, d'you understand? Run as fast as you can until you reach the Government Building. And if you see a corpse, beat the hell out of its knees and then keep on running. If there are too many Dead for you to get through, then you come straight back to me. None of your stupid bravery, got it?"

"Yes."

He reached across the table and plucked up the brass goggles. "Take these, and wear them any time you're indoors."

"Why?" Icy fear clutched at me. "Is the spirit here?"

"Could be. This is its kind of party, don't you think? And if it can still jump between worlds, well . . . you need these to see it when it hides in the spirit realm." He shoved the lenses into my hands. "We've been trying to learn all we can about that spirit, but we haven't found a damn thing. For whatever reason, it hasn't made any more appearances since Thursday. I reckon it's waiting for the perfect moment."

"The perfect moment for what?"

"For getting that grimoire." He pointed to the goggles. "Put 'em on. Get to the book. And go to Joseph."

I nodded and slipped on the goggles. Then, before my mind and my fears could stop me, I raced from the lab.

I crept through Machinery Hall, clutching the baseball bat. The goggles were heavy on my nose and shrouded the exhibits in murky darkness. When I had entered, I had been too rushed, too desperate to notice that everything in the hall was different. No people spoke, no engines whirred.

During a normal day one's footsteps went unheard, but now the high-ceilinged hall echoed with each click of my heels. The exhibits, the machines, and the looming Corliss engine were no longer feats of man's ingenuity but places for the Dead to hide.

At last I reached the north exit with no sign of the spirit. Zooming into the hot sun, I shoved the goggles into my pocket and let my eyes adjust. A scan of the Exhibition grounds showed chaos.

Black smoke billowed, and flames flew at the firemen. The burning state buildings. And far in the distance, Agricultural Hall reached to the sky like a cathedral. Its gothic spires and stained glass windows were just visible above the trees and buildings before it.

I could see a long line of figures, and though these beings were too distant to clearly discern, I knew they were the Dead. With my skirts in one hand and the bat in the other, I kicked up my feet and ran toward the main road.

I reached the ice-water fountain in the middle of Belmont Avenue and dashed around its white pavilion before skidding to a stop. There it was: an endless row of putrid corpses strung down an intersecting avenue. The smell of decay burst into my nostrils.

Like Daniel had said, the bodies simply stood. They were unmoving sentinels covered in buzzing, hungry flies. I marched onward and searched for a gap between them. There was none, so I chose the closest, most decrepit body in the wall as my target. I hefted the bat high and darted forward.

It was like a trigger went off once I got close. The corpses nearest me convulsed to life. Their decomposed limbs lifted, and they lurched at me.

I filled my lungs with air and focused on my target—a skinless skeleton held together by gristle. I swung back, and with a full-forced exhale, I let the bat fly for the skeleton's knees.

It crunched immediately to the ground. No secondary attack was needed. Without a pause, I leaped over the crumpled bones and sprinted down the road. The shuffles and plops behind me meant the corpses followed, but I spared no glance. Nothing blocked me from the Government Building.

I pushed through the double doors of the Government Building's northern entrance then I slammed them shut and slid the baseball bat between the door's handles. If any Dead followed, I hoped that this would keep them out.

With my back pressed to a door, I gauged my surroundings.

The Government Building was shaped like a large cross with two central transepts for exhibits from the federal departments of the United States. Directly before me was a tall lighthouse covered in prisms. It sent light beams and rainbows bouncing across my vision, and it illuminated the dust fairies dancing in the air.

Hanging from the rafters throughout the entire hall were American flags—some dating back to the American Revolution. The flags were still, and the silence was complete.

I was alone.

With my skirts held in one hand, I crept forward. I moved around the lighthouse and into the main walkway of the building. Where was the trunk? I knew I had seen the George Washington exhibit when I'd first visited the Exhibition weeks ago, but where?

I glanced right and left. The American flags made blurry stripes in the corners of my eyes. Sunlight glinted on glass exhibit cases. I smelled the mustiness of mounted animals. All sorts of creatures were displayed through this building, and the scent prompted my memory. The George Washington exhibit was near the stuffed, mounted polar bear.

I squinted, and at the southern end of the building, I could just make out an imposing white mass. That had to be the bear.

I inhaled deeply. Then I walked slowly and carefully toward it. I didn't like the beady, sightless eyes of all the stuffed animals. They sent chills down my back.

As I passed an aisle of plaster fishes that hung on a low wall, the hair on my neck pricked and I froze midstep. I jerked my head right. Fins and tails streamed down the aisle and stopped at a glass case filled with jars of preserved fish. I fumbled in my pocket and yanked out the goggles to check for spiritual energy. When I stared at the case, my vision was dark and hazy. Good. I exhaled a breath I hadn't realized I was holding.

But then the vision began to clear, and my heart began to pound.

I tiptoed to the case until I was only feet away, and I paused. My vision through the goggles was now fully clear—except inside the case. Specifically around each jar of preserved fish. There was definitely spiritual energy here.

A tap came from inside. My heart shot into my throat.

Another tap. Then more and more, getting faster and faster. I stared, paralyzed.

A loud crack splintered down the center of glass. The case shattered outward. Fluid sprayed and fish flew. I was doused in ancient preserving alcohol. Its sweet, noxious scent covered me. Bodies flapped against me, and fins sliced into my dress. At least the goggles protected my eyes.

I staggered back and then I bolted. Fish flopped on the floor around me. How was this possible? These things had been dead for years. It could only mean the necromancer was nearby.

I sped into the main transept, but I immediately stopped.

It wasn't only the fish waking up—it was *all* the animals. Everything was awakening and lurching out of the displays. Directly before me, two oxen creaked into action. They were just as tall as I was, and with horns the length of my arm.

I sidled right and then threw myself onward. I heard stiff, heaving footsteps behind me, but I dared not look back. I needed a weapon—some protection. Why had I left the bat in the door handles?

The vision in my goggles had returned to its dirty blur. I ripped them off as I sprinted to the end of the building. I reached the aisle I needed, steered left, and scrambled to the exhibit. It was George Washington's camp from the Revolution.

I shoved aside pots, lanterns, and clothes until I reached Washington's leather camp trunk. I swung it open. It was filled with multiple compartments and packed with his belongings.

The commotion from the animals thundered through the hall. I was running out of time.

I grabbed the tin plates, forks, lamps, and medicine bottles and threw them aside, coming at last to a small black velvet bag. A peek inside revealed folded yellow pages, and without another thought, I pushed the bag into my pocket.

The floor shuddered now. The beasts were approaching fast. I searched for some sort of defense, and my eyes lit on a long, thin blade. Washington's sword. It was meant for thrusting, not hacking, but it was my only hope. I dove for it, and just in time. When I whirled around I was faced with a terrible wall of white. The polar bear.

Behind it came the oxen, the elk, and the slithering heap of a walrus, but it was the bear that consumed my attention.

I retreated, lifting the sword, but my feet tangled in an overturned chair. I toppled to the floor and scuttled backward, unable to stand but desperate to move away from the approaching bear. Its head was so close now that I could make out individual teeth gleaming in the sunlight. It swung a paw and hit the chair I'd fallen over, smashing it in two and sending wood splinters flying.

I crawled as fast as I could, my sword no weapon against such a beast. Faster, I had to crawl faster.

My back hit something. It was an American flag draped against a wall. I was trapped.

Panic filled my mind. No more thought, only action. I hoisted the sword, prepared to stab and claw with all the strength inside me, but then a new fear impaled my chest.

Frost climbed down the length of the sword, and frigid air blasted into me. All I could smell was grave dirt.

"No," I whimpered. "No." I swung the sword at the polar bear. The blade was dull. It stuck in the bear's jaws.

The white beast rose, jerking to its hind legs. I flew up with it, clinging to the sword's hilt. I used the momentum to jump to my feet. Before the bear could crush me, I darted around it— straight into the oxen's wicked horns.

"No!" I shrieked. I searched for an escape. Then I realized the oxen weren't moving. None of the animals were moving. I glanced back to the polar bear. It was stiff and upright. Yet something shimmered above it.

The spirit winked into existence. It hovered over the bear, a warped human shape, and pulled out the sword. Then winked back out.

"No, no, no," I whispered.

The air had turned to ice. It was so cold it cut into my skin and instantly numbed my fingers.

I tugged the goggles out and pressed them to my eyes. They were frosted over, but I could see. The particles in the lenses writhed and clumped into a sinuous, long-limbed shadow that floated overhead.

It held one arm high, and I craned my neck to see what was clasped in its dark fist.

Washington's sword.

At any moment it would flash from the spirit realm into mine and strike me down. The dull blade would smash through my skull. I stopped breathing. My heart stopped pounding. My mind went blank. The whole world waited.

"*Siste!*" A male voice echoed through the building. "*Siste! Siste!*"

The sword dropped.

CHAPTER TWENTY-TWO

The sword fell toward me.

I leaped forward between the oxen as the sword clattered to the floor. I glanced back. The spirit was gone. The particles in the lenses swirled apart like silt in a pond.

I fell to my knees, shaking and overcome with relief. *I'm alive. Thank you, thank you, thank you.* I tugged off the goggles and patted my pocket. The grimoire was still there. But who . . . who had called off the spirit? I'd heard an oddly familiar voice.

The beat of running footsteps hit my ears. I slid beneath the nearest ox. It sent dust flying from its fur. Between the legs I peered and waited. The footsteps galloped louder. The speaker wasn't Joseph or Daniel. What if it was the necromancer? Who else could control a spirit? Was I safer now or were things even more deadly?

The steps slowed, and I stretched my neck to see who came. An imposing figure stepped into the aisle. The sun illuminated him from behind, so I could make out no features. All I saw were broad shoulders and hulking height. He faced me silently for several moments. He could see me. He was *inspecting* me.

And then he let out an exuberant whoop. "Eleanor! Eleanor!"

My heart fell like a brick into my stomach. I knew that voice. I *knew* that voice! I scrambled out from beneath the ox. The man barreled toward me, his auburn hair glowing. A sob of relief flew from my mouth. I stumbled toward this giant of a man I barely recognized but instantly knew.

"Elijah! Oh, Elijah!" I flung myself into his arms. "It's you! You're alive—oh God, Elijah!"

I forgot everything around me. He was here after all this time, and he was alive! I buried my face in his chest, and hot tears poured down my face.

"You're so big." I laughed through my sobs. "And so dirty! Mama would die if she saw you."

"She would, wouldn't she?" He laughed and clutched me tighter.

"I missed you so much," I said, still weeping. "So much, Elijah. I was so worried."

He pressed his lips to my hair. "I missed you too." He squeezed me once more. "Come. We must go."

"Why?" I tugged away from him. I patted my pocket—the pages were still there. "It's dangerous out there."

"It's not safe here either."

I gazed up at his face. Something was off. Elijah had become a man since he'd left, square-jawed and whiskered. His voice was so much deeper than three years before, his frame so much larger, and . . .

"Your spectacles," I said. "Where are they?"

"I don't need them anymore."

"Why not? How is that possible?"

"Now's not the time for talk." He grabbed at my arm, but I skipped out of reach. "Listen, El, I can't hold that spirit off for long. Any moment now it will return, and its army of animals too."

A warning whispered in my head. "H-how did you fight the spirit? And why are you here?"

"I'm here because I was following that spirit." He folded his arms over his chest. "Lucky for you, isn't it? Now come on."

"Why were you following it?" I slid my hand into my pocket and stroked the velvet bag.

"I thought it would lead me to something I want." He narrowed his eyes and watched me for several long seconds. "Something I *need*, actually."

My stomach hitched. "Wh-what is it you need?"

"I think," he said, emphasizing each word, "that you know the answer. And judging by your movements, I think what I seek is in your pocket."

"I don't understand." I shook my head violently. "Y-you

mean the necromancer needs it, not you."

"No." His brow furrowed. "It's for me. *I* want the book."

"But you're with me now—y-you don't have to go back to him." I rushed to Elijah and clasped his hands. "You're with me now, and I'll get you out of here."

He wrenched free. "I'm not sure what you mean. I'm quite fine as is." He waved a hand up and down his body. "You don't need to care for me anymore, El. I'm not that weak, pathetic thing from before."

"I didn't mean it like that. I just want—"

"Enough." He gripped my arm and yanked me toward the exit. "This spirit is powerful, and I'm losing control."

My mind rioted and my body resisted, but he was stronger. He was unnaturally strong, and he hauled me easily to the exit. Past the American flags and the prism-filled lighthouse. We left all the displaced animals behind. At the door, Elijah paused and gave me a warning look.

"There are a lot of Dead out there." He tipped his head toward the door. "No hysterics."

"I'm not afraid of the Dead." I clenched my teeth. "I don't need taking care of either."

He shrugged. "If you say so. Now come—please." He pushed through the doors.

The sunlight blasted me, and the stench rolled over me. I gagged and whipped my sleeve to my mouth. I tried to see through the spots in my eyes.

The Dead, organized in regimented rows, were spread

310

before me. Tall, short, decayed, fresh. The only movement was the buzzing blanket of flies.

I reeled back and smothered my cries in my sleeve. I could see no escape. "Elijah—what do we do?"

He merely chuckled and lifted a shoulder. "Well, El, we're going to stand here a moment, and you're going to tell me where the grimoire is."

"I-I don't know what you mean. What's a grimoire?"

"You've already lost the game." He tapped the side of his nose. "You blabbed about it before."

"But I don't have it."

His eyebrows bounced up. "Then why did the spirit want to kill you, I wonder." He hauled me to him. "Enough excuses now. You know what I want, and I know you have it."

"Why do you want it?" I shrank within myself, but he heaved me even closer.

A smile twisted at his lips. "Isn't it obvious?"

I waved vaguely toward the corpses. "The necromancer?"

He chuckled. "Yes, the necromancer." His nails, dirty and crusted, bit through my sleeve and into the bruises Clarence had left. "Now give it to me."

I knew with sick certainty what the answer would be, but I had to ask anyway.

"Who is—" My voice broke. I tried again. "Who is the necromancer?"

"The only man clever enough and strong enough to perform such a task." He grinned triumphantly. "Me."

"No. You didn't do this." My voice was rough.

"What do you mean?" He flung down my arm. "Of course I did."

"My brother would never do something so sick."

"Sick? Sick?" He recoiled. "But this is revolutionary, Eleanor! I will make history with this army." He slammed his fist to his chest. It made a hollow thump as if nothing were inside. "I have made myself strong by commanding this army of the dead. I will show the world my power with this army. I will have my revenge. And"—his voice dropped to a confiding whisper—"I will bring back Father with this."

My eyes bulged and my mouth went slack. Bring back Father? Was he serious? Father had been dead for six years.

Elijah smiled, a single eyebrow arched high on his forehead. "Mama will be pleased, no doubt. I will bring him back and show him the man I have become." He opened his arms. "And together we will topple the Gas Ring and take the council seat that is rightfully ours."

"H-how will you bring Father back?"

"With the pages in your pocket—the grimoire." He extended his hand. "Now give them to me."

"No."

"This is not a request, El. This is a command. Give them to me *now*."

I swung my head side to side. *Stall for time, Eleanor. Stall for time.* The Spirit-Hunters would appear at any moment. Their pulse bombs would explode the corpses, and Elijah would realize the futility—the evil—of his course.

"How have you become so big?" I sputtered. "And where are your spectacles?"

He growled a laugh. "Oh, you will like the answer to that, El. It solved a problem for me, and it solved a problem for you." He fluttered his fingers as if playing some invisible piano. "And, best of all, that evil man finally got what he deserved."

"What do you mean?"

He turned to his army and shouted, "*Venī*! Come!" At first nothing happened. Then a tornado of flies began to move over the rows of Dead. Something was coming.

"Elijah, what have you done?"

"You'll see."

"Tell me!" I tore at his dirt-covered sleeve.

"I dealt with that pest," he spat. "Exactly as I did with the other boys from school." He shoved me from him. "The ones who tortured me. The ones whose fathers killed our father." He ticked the names off on his fingers. "Fred, Clint, James, and Junior. Though Junior was the hardest one to nab." He turned an accusing eye on me.

My throat was so tight I could barely breathe. Elijah hadn't only targeted Gas Ring members; he had targeted his bullies. His campaign wasn't only for Father—it was for his own revenge.

"Junior?" I asked. "What do you mean 'hard to nab'?"

"He was always with you, and I couldn't take him then." He snorted at the thought. "No, no. But then he foolishly left behind his little bodyguards."

"You," I croaked. "It was you who followed him from the garden."

"Yes," he said simply "And now I am stronger than ever before."

"How?"

"A sacrificed life can work many wonders with the right spells." He gestured to his body. "Cure illness, ward off death, and, of course, increase magical power."

A sacrificed life. Decapitation. "What have you *done*? Tell me!"

"I can show you." He pointed to the corpse army.

I spun my head where he directed. The Dead were parting amid furious flies. A body shambled through them. Where the head should have been there was a raw, crusted stump with part of the spine jutting out. And in the corpse's hand, gripped tightly by the dark hair I had once admired, was Clarence's head. It swung back and forth with each jolting step forward. The once fresh, white skin was now waxy and gray.

My stomach heaved upward into my throat. I toppled to the ground and vomited. I could take the corpses, the nameless faces, but this one . . . this one I had cared for.

This one had been my *friend*.

Sweat and tears mixed on my face. I couldn't stop my stomach's revolt.

This wasn't real. It couldn't be real. Elijah was a necromancer, and Clarence was dead. A walking corpse.

Seeing Clarence like this, knowing he was—despite

everything—not a bad man, I realized just how important he was to me.

Now . . . now it was too late.

"Eleanor," Elijah said, his tone gentle. He had crouched beside me, and even in my sickness I could feel his genuine concern. Some of my brother still lived inside this man.

"What is it?" he asked. "So many Dead and yet this one disturbs you?"

"He was *not* a bad man," I rasped, my throat scorched raw from the bile. "He meant to make amends to you! He didn't deserve that, Elijah! No one deserves that." I wiped at my mouth and hid my face in my hands. *Please let this end. Please, God, tell me it's not real.*

But it was real, and my brother, my Elijah, was the cause of it all. He was the necromancer, and he had killed Clarence. I risked a glance over; the headless body of Clarence was still there.

I pushed Elijah away from me and tried to stand. "You're a monster."

He blinked and shook his head. "But I saved you."

"How? From what?" I wobbled, almost falling again. Elijah lurched up to help, but I fought him off. "Don't touch me!"

His mouth bobbed open and closed, and his eyes darted side to side. "But Junior . . . he and those boys—*they* were the monsters."

"How?"

"They weren't good people." He tugged at his hair. "Their fathers destroyed our—"

"So?" I shrieked. "So? Does that make it all right?" I lunged at him. My fists connected with his chest. "You're insane! How could you? *How could you?*"

He wrestled me, and I was no match for his immense power. His false, evil power. He threw me aside easily.

Then an explosion boomed through the air.

Elijah whipped his head toward the sound, toward Agricultural Hall. "Not today," he snarled, whirling back to me. "I've not come this far to be stopped by them. By you."

"I'm your sister," I quavered. "Your best friend."

"And so I won't hurt you." He pointed toward Agricultural Hall. "But don't think I'll be so generous with those people. I don't care about them, and I can always use more strength. There's no limit to the power I can take from the blood of the living."

I believed him. "If I give you the pages, then you have to promise you'll leave."

"Yes." His tone was dismissive, his attention focused on the approaching blasts.

I grasped at his sleeve. "All the Dead. Take them with you. Promise."

"Yes, yes." He shoved his open hand out impatiently. "Give it here."

I reached into my pocket and slipped out the velvet bag. Was this right? Was this what I was supposed to do? I scrunched my eyes shut and tossed it to him. I heard a slap as he caught it mid-air. Then came a jubilant cheer.

I opened my eyes.

"*Vāde*! Go!" he roared, and in one sickening movement, the Dead turned and shambled away. "Checkmate," he said to me with a gloating grin. "Strategy never was your strength, not even when we used to play chess. You're too impulsive and too quick to—"

Another boom—a close one—cut him short. I craned my neck and saw smoke billowing from the outermost rows of the corpse army. The Spirit-Hunters were here.

A growl burst from Elijah's lips. Without another word he bounded off, directly into the center of his retreating Dead army. Clarence's wretched corpse was the last to leave.

I crumpled to the ground, a useless heap. It had all gone wrong. Everything was wrong.

Another explosion rocked the earth, and I heard the flesh splatter as bodies fell. When I lifted my head, I saw that Clarence had toppled too.

Daniel raced through the haze of smoke, dust, and flies. He staggered to a stop, his attention on Clarence. His face wore shock and revulsion, but he paused only for a moment.

He broke into a sprint. He was going to destroy the Dead— to hurt my brother. I couldn't let him. There was still a chance for Elijah; I could still save his soul if I tried hard enough.

I hoisted myself to my feet, darkness clouding my vision as blood rushed in my ears. Once steady, I chased after Daniel.

Through sparse trees, barren paths, and empty grounds, I sped. I passed many marching Dead, but they were unconcerned with me. Elijah had kept his word. When I reached the back Exhibition entrance that led into Fairmount Park, a massive clump of decaying bodies came into view. Row after row were protecting Elijah. Daniel, who was a full hundred feet closer than I was, slowed to a stop. I could see that a flame blazed in his hand. His arm wound back. Then his hand snapped forward and from it sprang the thick coils of copper that held the newly made pulse bomb. Through the air it went, faster than the marching of the Dead.

Whether or not Daniel meant to hit Elijah, I was certain the explosion would reach him.

"Run!" I screamed. I careened past Daniel. I was only twenty feet from the edge of Elijah's barrier. "Run!"

The pulse bomb clattered to the ground near me, the fuse burning. I sailed forward and grabbed it. Then in one final surge, I left the Dead and my brother. I thrust the bomb with all my might into the nearest trees.

But I was just a few moments too late. The dynamite detonated with a black boom and a bright light.

It hurled me back. I slapped against the ground like a broken marionette, and pain erupted all over me. A fierce sting scraped at my skin. My bones felt crushed.

Then everything faded. I couldn't move, I couldn't hear, I couldn't see. The world vanished in a hazy void.

CHAPTER TWENTY-THREE

My eyes fluttered open. A shadow formed before me and shifted into Daniel's face. Tears fell from his eyes, leaving dirty streaks that dripped into his open mouth. His lips moved, but if he spoke, I couldn't hear the words. I sank back into the painless nothing.

But the pain came back, a knocking in my skull. I lifted my eyelids once more. Daniel's face again, but close. *He must be carrying me,* I thought, but I couldn't sort out why.

His eyes locked on mine. He spoke, but still no words entered my ears. I thought perhaps I should answer him, but the task seemed impossible. I closed my eyes.

When I opened them again, the pain was gone. My family's doctor hovered above, his features basked in a glow of fuzzy warmth.

My tongue felt enormous. I wanted to laugh.

I turned my head, straining to look around. Where was I? My bedroom, perhaps, but then . . . why was Daniel here? Why was Mama throwing her hands up and bellowing? Why did Daniel let her scream at him so?

And why couldn't I hear any of it?

The laugh bubbled up. I coughed and choked on it. Mama stopped her wild gestures, an expression of joy flooding her face. She rushed to me. Her blurry figure left trails across my vision.

I gazed at Daniel. His face was twisted with pain, and that wrung my heart with guilt and yearning. His beautiful face. I wished I could make him feel better. I parted my lips to tell him, but the doctor poured a cloying liquid in my open mouth.

Bitter! It was so bitter. I sputtered, swallowed, and a new wave of warmth spread over me.

Laudanum. It must be laudanum. How nice.

I awoke with the sunlight streaming into my bedroom. It hurt my eyes, piercing my skull, and I had to squint to see.

That sun meant late afternoon. But what day? I blinked, and though I successfully cleared the haze from my eyes, my mind remained cloudy.

I smacked my lips. The taste in my mouth was rotten, as if someone had stuffed cotton balls between my tongue and gums and then left them there for days.

Despite the burning protest in my muscles, I heaved myself onto my elbows. The movement made my stomach curdle, but I forced myself to keep going. I wanted to sit fully upright.

I brought my right hand to my face and found bandages wrapped over my palm. When I inspected my left arm, I found it wasn't bandaged; but the skin was scraped off—as if I'd fallen and tried to catch myself.

No. Not fallen. *Propelled.*

And then I remembered everything. A fresh set of sobs erupted from my chest. My heart was ripped in two all over again. I started to shiver uncontrollably.

Clarence . . . Clarence . . . poor Clarence. And Elijah—oh God, Elijah. It couldn't be. This nightmare would end. It had to end!

Make it stop, make it stop!

I called out, but my voice sounded faint, as if miles away. The explosion must have damaged my hearing.

I called again and again, sobbing and desperate, but no one came.

At last I fell back onto the bed and cried until sleep and exhaustion overtook me.

"Eleanor."

Mama's voice. I could hear Mama. I could *hear.*

"Eleanor. Are you awake?"

"Yes," I breathed. I snapped my eyelids up. Mama was there, her face eaten by exhaustion. Heavy pockets were beneath her eyes, wrinkles lined her mouth, and her skin was papery.

"Why are you crying?" I asked. Did she know of Elijah?

"Because you are all right, my darling. You are all right." She laid a cool hand on my brow. "Oh, my Eleanor, I was so frightened."

I moistened my lips, which were cracked and raw. "What day is it?"

"Wednesday. You have been asleep for two days. Doctor Mitchell said you must rest to heal. He thinks you might have suffered a mild concussion."

"Oh." I lolled my head to the side and tried to swallow. "I'm thirsty."

"Yes. Mary will be here any moment with soup." Mama tipped her head and caught my gaze. "What happened? Why were you at the Exhibition, Eleanor?"

I grunted. I didn't want to think about it ever again. And I never, *never* wanted to talk of it. If I stayed in bed forever, I wouldn't have to.

"That blond man brought you home again," Mama said. Her voice was calm, but I sensed a tightness there. She was gauging my reaction. "He said things."

"That's nice." I twisted my head as far from her as possible and stared at the wall. "Can I be left alone now?"

"No." Her voice turned hard, and she wrenched me by the chin back toward her. "You must eat, and you must answer me. How do you know that young man?"

She had been mulling this question for the last two days. I could see it in her frayed desperation. Without answers or understanding, she had driven herself to hysteria.

"I don't know that young man," I said.

"You do. He called you Eleanor, he knew how you'd been hurt, and he cried—are you listening?" Mama squeezed my chin with her fingernails. "Were you seeing that man?"

"No." I lowered my eyelids in a slow blink. A tiny spark of anger ignited between my shoulders. "If I had, though, why would it matter? Especially now?"

"Because Clarence Wilcox is dead."

"I know." I held my breath and forced my mind into submission. I would not think of it. I would not let my thoughts go to that darkness. I must stay in this lethargic apathy. But the anger was growing, spreading from my shoulders into my neck.

"You do not care?" she asked.

"Of course I care."

"Well, you should care a little more, Eleanor. He was your best chance at marriage, and now he's gone. If anyone should find out about you and that man"—she thrust her finger in the direction of the Exhibition—"all your chances—*our* chances—will be ruined."

I laughed. It was a bitter rasp filled with disgust. "Is that all you care about, Mama? Clarence was murdered. I was in an explosion. Still, all you can think about is marriage? Money?"

"This is not funny." Her nostrils flared. "We can't afford the cost of your treatment. Doctor Mitchell was kind enough to allow us to pay later." She glared down her nose at me. "When you are better, when your wounds have healed, you will realize exactly how dire this situation is."

"How dire?" I screeched. "You're the one who wasted our money on curtains and dresses, so I want to know *how dire* you think it is, Mama!"

"Dire enough that we will have to secure an engagement with someone—anyone! And soon." Mama peered at me through half-closed eyes, her lips pursed. "And dire enough that we may need to silence that young man somehow. Your reputation is at stake here. Wounds will heal, grief will pass, but a reputation can never be recovered."

I squeezed my eyes shut and in a stilted voice quoted Shakespeare. "Reputation is an idle and most false imposition." I clung to the memorized words to keep my temper cool and my thoughts clear. "Oft got without merit and lost without deserving."

Mama ignored me. "Your father did enough damage to our family's standing, Eleanor, when he tried to save his company. Your brother only worsened it when he ran off. Without a good reputation, you will not make a suitable match. We will be on the streets soon!"

I opened my eyes and watched her. What an empty shell of a woman she was.

"I was too lax with you before," she continued, "and do not think I will make that same mistake again." She pressed her hands to her forehead and massaged the lines. "I shudder to think why that man brought you home the first time—"

"Because you care nothing for the truth. Listen to yourself!

Listen to your absurd ideas!"

"You are a Fitt, Eleanor. You are Miss Fitt of the Philadelphia Fitts, and I will see that you behave as your class demands."

"Miss Fitt? Miss Fitt? I'm a *misfit*, Mama—that's what I am!" How had I never noticed my name before? I didn't fit with my family, with my class, with the Spirit-Hunters—with anyone.

"Calm yourself."

"No. I don't want you here," I growled. "Leave."

Her body tensed, and her lips thinned.

"Leave!" I shrieked.

At last she stood. "As you wish."

With Mama gone, my ire only grew. And I let it. I relished the way it burned through my body.

A knock sounded at my door, and Mary came in with a tray.

I sat up taller. "I need a favor."

She gave a wary glance toward the door and then nodded.

"Can you tell me what's happening?"

"What d'you mean, Miss Fitt?" She sat on the edge of the bed and arranged the tray in my lap.

"Don't call me that."

"What?"

"Miss . . ." I gulped. "Miss Fitt. Just call me Eleanor. Or nothing at all. What's happened with the Dead and the Spirit-Hunters?"

She winced. "I'm not supposed to talk about that."

"Why?" I sipped my soup.

"Your ma knows," Mary whispered. "About the man—the one that brought you home. She knows he's one of them Spirit-Hunters."

"How?"

"It's all over the papers. His face. He's wanted for two murders."

I choked and fumbled for my tea. It sloshed onto my bed, and tea stains bloomed on the beige sheet. "Who did he kill?"

"One was some old case." She dabbed her apron at the tea stains.

"And the second?"

Her voice dropped to a whisper. "Clarence Wilcox."

"Oh no." I slumped back against my pillow. How the blazes had that been pinned on Daniel?

"Tell me," I demanded. "Tell me everything about Dan—" I broke off. I couldn't say his name or our intimacy would be obvious. "About that man and the Spirit-Hunters."

Mary's lips puckered. "Your mama won't like that."

"If you tell me what the newspapers are saying, I'll give you my Parisian hairpiece."

The edges of her lips curled up. "Well, last night's *Bulletin* said the Spirit-Hunters are responsible for lettin' the Dead get out of hand and destroyin' the Exhibition. The mayor has issued warrants for their arrest."

I sucked in a long, desperate breath. "And what else?"

"It said this Sheridan fellow is dangerous. And the Wilcox family is offering a right *enormous* reward for his capture."

It was far worse than anything I could have imagined. The Spirit-Hunters were being blamed for the Dead—for the havoc Elijah had wrought. Poor, poor Joseph. He'd done nothing but the right thing, and this was how the city had repaid him. I doubted Jie or Daniel much cared, but I knew Joseph did.

Mary wasn't finished. "Three people were killed and twelve injured by these fast Dead. No one's allowed in East Fairmount Park or on the Schuylkill River no more."

I squeezed my eyes shut. I didn't know if Elijah had intentionally killed these people or if some of his army had turned Hungry and escaped to Laurel Hill. But does the source of a man's death matter when the root is evil? I knew Elijah had to be stopped, and I knew *I* had to stop him.

"Miss—er, Eleanor, are you ah'right?" Mary laid a hand on my arm. "Should I get your ma?"

I shook my head violently and flashed my eyes open. "No. I need another favor."

She lifted an eyebrow. "I'm not sure I can do that."

"You can."

"I dunno. Your ma—"

"Enough silly games." I grasped her arm and tugged her close. "I need trousers, a shirt, and sturdy boots, and if you help me, I'll give you my amethyst earrings."

She sucked in a breath, her eyes darting between my face and the hand that gripped her. "I could get fired if your ma finds out."

"I won't tell if you don't. I'll take the secret to my grave." I tugged the maid closer. "Will you help me or not?"

Her eyes ran over my face. "And you just want some trousers, a shirt, and boots?"

"That will fit me, yes."

She licked her lips. "Ah'right then."

I released her and dropped back onto the bed. Sweat beaded on my lip, and I wiped my sleeve over my face.

"I need the clothes by tonight," I said.

Mary squinted. "What are you plannin', Eleanor?"

"That's none of your funeral," I snapped. What a strange way to tell people to mind their own business. And oddly appropriate since tonight could very well be *my* funeral.

Several hours later, as the sun was setting bright orange outside my window, she brought me my requested items with my dinner. She watched me expectantly.

"What is it?" I asked through a mouthful of bread. I swallowed and tipped my head toward the dressing table. "The earrings are over there. Left drawer. In the jewelry box."

She hesitated, but only for a moment. Then she skipped across the room and flung out the drawer. With a small squeal, she yanked the dangling amethysts out and inspected them in the setting sun's glow. "Wait . . . ain't these the ones Master Elijah gave ya?"

My stomach clenched at his name. "Yes," I muttered before tearing off more bread.

"You don't want 'em?"

I shook my head sharply.

She shoved the earrings in her pocket and avoided my eyes. "Tell me what you're planning."

"No."

"Then I'll rat."

"Take whatever you want." I thrust my left hand toward the dressing table. "Jewelry, bonnets, I don't care. Just shut pan!"

"I want to know what you're plannin'," she repeated, her jaw setting at a stubborn angle. "I think you're up to something dangerous. Your ma can't handle any more shock."

"Like you care. You took the earrings without any argument."

"I *do* care," Mary spat. "She's a good woman, and if you run off with that man and break her heart—"

"I'm not running off with anyone! It's not like that at all." I grabbed a fistful of bread and pitched it at her. "Get out. Just get out!"

"No. I don't want your ma to—"

"Get out or I'll tell Mama you stole my earrings." I launched more bread at her. "I'll tell her you stole my kid gloves and my hairpiece."

Mary scampered from the room, her hands covering her face.

I huffed out a heavy sigh and tossed the remaining bread

back on my plate. My head hurt all the way into my eye sockets, and guilt panged in my chest for being cruel to Mary . . . but I'd spent the day planning, and I couldn't give up now.

I *had* to do this. Mary had given me what I needed, and now nothing stood in my way. I had failed to stop Elijah once, but I would not—*could not*—fail again.

Chapter Twenty-four

When the church bells sang eleven and it seemed the house had gone to sleep, I eased from bed. I hadn't moved much in two days, and my muscles burned. At each wooden creak of the floor, I froze and held my breath. But no one noticed, or else no one cared. So I resumed my careful prowling in the dark.

I dressed. The shirt and trousers Mary had gotten were too big, and I had to tie a ribbon around my waist to keep the pants up. The boots were snug yet manageable.

I tiptoed to the door and pressed my ear against it. No sounds came through.

It was now—I had to do it now, while my courage and resolve were strong. I inhaled until my lungs were fully expanded. Then I ventured out. The hall was empty and dark, and no one met me as I navigated the stairs down. I fumbled with the front door, yet still no one came.

And then the door was cracked. I was squeezing through and racing over the porch and across the front lawn.

The night air was thick and textured as if some damp blanket had been cast over the world. There was no breeze. No movement. The only sounds were the insects, humming and content in their own safe lives.

Above, the moon was only a sliver in the sky, and I found the darkness comforting. Safe.

I stepped into the street and jogged, but I didn't make it far before I had to stop. I scuffed to a streetlamp and leaned. My head spun. I would need to go more slowly if I wanted my body to keep up.

Footsteps pounded to my right. I whipped my head around and saw a man rushing down the street toward me. I sprang forward, ready to flee, but the man slowed and shouted.

"It's me, Eleanor—it's me!"

Daniel!

"You're alive," he said between heavy pants.

"*You're* alive." I chuckled weakly. "I thought you were on the run."

"I am, but I'm not that easy to catch." He moved into the warm glow of the streetlight. He was just two paces from me, and I could see fatigue drawn into his face. "What the hell are you doing out of your house?"

"I have things that need doing. Why are you here?"

"I-I was hoping to see you. Catch a glimpse or something." He slung off his flat cap and ran a hand through his hair. "I wanted to know if you were all right. I . . . I almost killed you—and I'm so sorry and I was awful worried." The words flooded from his mouth. "Your mother, she wouldn't let me in, and I thought maybe you were really hurt and it was all my fault."

I shook my head. "Are you blaming yourself for my injuries?"

"I threw the pulse bomb."

"And I picked it up. *I'm* the one who threw it in the end." I patted my chest. "Don't worry about me, all right? Now . . . I've got to go. I have work to do." I glanced side to side.

Daniel planted his feet and crossed his arms. "I see what you're doing, Empress. I know about your brother—I figured it out when you tried to save his wretched skin. I won't let you see him."

"It's not like that." I sidled past him, but he grabbed my left hand. His fingers scratched at my raw palm.

I groaned and yanked back my arm. His eyes grew wide. "What is it?"

I gritted my teeth. "Nothing. Just some cuts from the explosion."

"You hit the ground real hard." He hung his head. "I thought I'd killed you."

An emptiness eddied through my chest—I didn't want his guilt. I didn't deserve it.

"You did nothing wrong, Daniel." I waved at myself. "See? I'm just fine."

His gaze crept up and met mine. "You also scratched up your . . ." He trailed off and gestured to my face.

"Is it bad?"

"Not so bad." He lifted his free hand to my cheek. "You're still you." His fingers brushed down the line of my jaw.

He set his thumb on my chin and guided my face to the side. His eyes flicked over the skin, and then he tipped my face the other way. "You'll be right as rain after a few days of healing."

I nodded, not trusting myself to speak.

As if scrutinizing the shape of my cheek, he leaned closer until I could feel his breath.

Then his lips touched my skin—only the slightest brush along my cheekbone.

My breath caught, and my heart with it. But I didn't pull away. I couldn't. I knew if I moved, if this moment ended, my chest would ache with this hollowness forever.

He slowly drew back his hand. I twisted my face to his, and before he could retreat, I reached out and pressed my good hand against his stomach.

He sucked in a breath, and I bit back my own gasp. He was the first boy I'd ever touched, and the stiffness of his body through his shirt was unexpected. And wonderful.

"Eleanor." His voice was so low, I could barely hear it. "Eleanor, we can't do this."

"Oh," I breathed, but I didn't move. Nor did he.

He was so near. I couldn't keep my gaze from his face. I wanted to memorize the way his lips shuddered with his breath; the way his tongue was just visible when his lips parted; the way his eyes didn't break from my face; and above all, the way his stomach felt beneath the fabric of his clothes.

Then his body shook—only the slightest tremor—and he lowered his face.

His mouth reached mine, and in an instant I *knew* what the fascination with lips was all about. Even the gentlest touch—for that was all it was—sent my mind reeling and my heart racing. It was sweeter than I'd ever dreamed possible. His scent and his touch overwhelmed my brain, and I could think of nothing but Daniel.

He drew back, and I found I could barely breathe. My chest felt so tight with emotion—so full. His own breaths were short and shallow.

Then suddenly his lips were on mine again. And I kissed back. His hands rose to cradle my head, and he tugged me more tightly into the embrace. He pressed me to the lamppost, his body a shield to the world beyond, and I slipped my hand all the way around his waist.

His stubble scratched my chin, but I didn't care.

Long, hard kisses turned into quick, desperate ones and then back again. This, whatever this was, had flared out of our control. His skin was as salty as it smelled—delicious and intoxicating.

Somewhere, deep in my mind, I knew there would be

consequences. Now was not the time for passion. Yet my body betrayed me by shutting off those worries and taking control.

Think only of Daniel.

The church bells rang half past. They pierced my mind, and reality flew back into focus. Daniel jerked away from me.

His lips were swollen and his cheeks flushed. He panted, "I'm sorry."

"Why?" My lips felt puffy and raw, and my heart banged like a timpani in my ears.

He shook his head. "I shouldn't have done this. I'm sorry."

"I wanted you to . . . I wanted you to kiss me."

He didn't answer, but I knew he wanted it too. I could see it in the way his eyes ran over my face, in the way he leaned toward me, in the way his mouth hovered partly open.

But I could also see his sincere regret.

He slapped his cap on and drew it low over his face. "I made a mistake."

My heart sank into my belly, and the hollowness erupted in my chest. "A mistake?" The words echoed strangely in my ears.

"Yes." He avoided meeting my gaze.

I lowered my chin. His words *hurt.* For all that I knew it was wrong, I never thought he would call it a mistake.

But I didn't want sadness or regret. I'd had enough of those emotions, and they only made me feel weak, helpless. So I let anger come.

I narrowed my eyes into a harsh glare. "You're the first man I've ever kissed, and you've decided I'm a mistake—a *misfit.*"

"Now hold your horses." He straightened, and his eyes locked on mine. "It's not like that."

"No? Then what *is* it like?"

He opened his mouth, but I shot my hand up and cut him off. I didn't want excuses or explanations.

"Actually, Daniel, I don't care. Now is hardly the time for such trivial"—I wrinkled my nose—"such trivial things. I have to go. I have work to do."

His jaw clenched and his nostrils flared. "And if you think I'll let you waltz off to find Elijah, then you're mad. I'm sorry, but he's not your brother anymore, Empress. He's a lunatic, and there's nothing you can do now."

I scoffed derisively. "I'm not meeting him for tea! I'm doing what I should have done in the first place."

"You can't stop him." He thrust his face into mine. "Not like this. Not alone. Think, Empress, think!"

"No!" I shouted, a wave of rage and terror rolling down my body. "No! I can't think. If I think, I'll lose everything. I won't be able to *stop* thinking. Of Clarence, of Elijah, of you, of the walls that surround me everywhere. I can't!"

Daniel's face relaxed, and his eyes held pity. I hated it.

"Empress. You know you're not the only person hurt here. Joseph, Jie, and me? We're all stuck in this cesspool too."

"But I'm the only one to blame."

"No! The necromancer is to blame—not you." He wet his lips. "You're . . . well, you're as good and innocent as they come."

"Enough, Daniel. Just shut pan." I marched away from him.

I pulsed with rejection and fear and a *burn* to do what needed to be done. I had a real, desperate goal to achieve, and I was furious with myself for forgetting. Furious that Daniel had called me a mistake. Furious that Mama cared nothing for my injuries or Clarence's death. Furious that my brother was a monster I could not save.

But I was also strong—stronger than Daniel or Mama or Elijah gave me credit for.

I stalked down the street, my energy high and focus clear. Daniel jogged up beside me.

"Fine," he said. "I can't stop you, and I won't try. But no matter what you say, I'm going with you—to help. We do it together, and we do it as a team."

Joseph and Jie were near Laurel Hill, so Daniel and I left the hired carriage a mile from the cemetery—no driver would go any closer—and walked the rest of the way. We trekked up Ridge Avenue and then into the woods north of Laurel Hill. Daniel's glowworms offered a dim light to see by, and he spent part of the journey explaining all that had happened in two days.

"Mayor Stokely and the Exhibition board were furious on Monday," he said. "Lotta damage to the Exhibition, and a *hell* of a lotta damage to their reputations. It only got worse when they found Junior's body."

I exhaled sharply, keeping my eyes focused on the uneven forest floor. I didn't want to think of Clarence, of his gruesome corpse, of his devastated family. "Then what happened?" I pressed.

"Well, Peger told the mayor that I'd done it—that I had killed Junior. He said the Spirit-Hunters were the hoodlums who'd destroyed the factory, and then to cap the climax, he accused us of bein' the necromancer. Within an hour, warrants were out for the three of us—thank God Jie sniffed the change in the wind. She got all our stuff packed up in a wagon, and when the news broke that we were wanted criminals, we skedaddled."

"To Laurel Hill," I said.

"Yep—watch your step." He guided me over a jutting tree root. "The Hungry have been breaking through the northern gate, but we intercept 'em—most, anyways. Joseph's tired, though. Three times now, the spirit has shown up. Joseph barely managed to fight it off the last time."

I ducked under a low branch and shook my head. "How long will you keep up this ridiculous sentry?"

He didn't answer me. I supposed he had no answer to give. It reinforced my resolve to end this war tonight. To stop Elijah now.

After what felt like hours of walking and tripping over tree roots, we reached the Spirit-Hunters' camp just north of Laurel Hill.

If I'd thought the Spirit-Hunters' accommodations at the Exhibition were crude, it was luxurious compared to their new home. From Daniel's worktable they had crafted a lean-to against a tree, and next to that they'd stacked what remained of their tattered belongings. A table leg was splintered—the work of the spirit, perhaps?—and the same lone lantern from their lab hung on a branch and illuminated the area. There was no camp-fire, and I could see no food.

Joseph staggered from beneath the lean-to. I gawked at his appearance. He wore no gloves, no waistcoat, and no hat. The impeccably dressed gentleman I'd come to know was worn away.

He raised an eyebrow at Daniel. "Dare I ask why she is here?"

"She wants to go into Laurel Hill," Daniel said. He explained to his leader all that had happened since my escape several hours before. Well, not *entirely* all. He skimmed over the kisses—though I did hear a strain in his voice when he described how he had found me.

When Daniel finished his story, Joseph turned to me. "Is all this true, Miss Fitt?"

"Yes. And call me Eleanor." I glanced around the tiny camp. "Where's Jie?"

"Dealing with one of the Dead. It escaped not far from here, and Jie lured it from camp. I . . ." He swallowed. "I was too tired to electrocute it."

"I can see you're exhausted." I gestured to the lean-to. "You live with too few comforts to stay strong. You can't keep fighting the Dead when you're in such bad shape."

"You're one to talk," Daniel retorted. "You were in an explosion!"

"And my injuries are nothing compared to the deaths of

340

the last few days." I set my jaw and turned my hardest stare on Joseph. "We must go in and stop Elijah. Tonight."

"That is not possible. Your brother is too powerful for us."

"So you intend to live here in the woods forever? Protecting a city that hates you?" I snorted, putting as much disgust into the noise as I could. "You'll waste away from overwork."

Joseph lifted a shoulder. "Do you have an alternative?"

"Yes. I can go inside and stop Elijah. He won't hurt me."

"Even if you speak the truth, Eleanor, can you do what is necessary to stop him?" Joseph's voice was low, as if his concerned words were intended for my ears only. Despite all that had happened to him, he was still worried about me.

"Yes."

"How? How do you intend to do it?" His eyelids lowered. "If we go in to stop your brother, we have to be certain we can succeed in destroying both him and his army. If we are killed and fail . . ." He shook his head. "If we fail, there will be no one to stop him. No one in Philadelphia can survive the corpses in this cemetery."

I pushed back my shoulders. "Then I will find Elijah, and I will kill him."

Daniel stomped in front of me. "You don't get it, Empress. You can't just go in and kill him, or we'd have done that a long time ago. The army's gotta be put to rest first. We have to remove all the spiritual energy that animates them."

My eyes flicked to Daniel. The lantern light made bottomless holes where his eyes would be. "Why?"

"If your brother gets killed, then the leash snaps. They need the necromancer to command them. Otherwise, every single corpse in Laurel Hill will turn rabid." His voice dropped. "They will hunt you down and eat you alive. Then those hundreds of Dead will break free from Laurel Hill and ravage the city. We can't stop the Hungry if they're not contained."

"He is right," Joseph said. "Like all cemetery fences, Laurel Hill's iron bars were only constructed to contain the occasional corpse. It cannot withstand an army of violent, powerful, desperate bodies."

The thud of footsteps in the forest hit my ears. I swiveled around, my arms up and ready to fight.

Jie jogged into the clearing. Her black braid was wrapped tightly around her head, and in her hand she held a sword, which flickered in the yellow light.

Her eyes lit on me, and she grinned. "You're alive."

"So are you." I inclined my head toward the sword. It was as long as her arm, two-edged, and tapered to a point. Though it gleamed, I could see it was chipped and dented.

Her smile widened as she moved to my side. "One Hungry corpse is easy, yeah? It's the whole army I can't fight."

"Where'd you get that sword?" I asked. "It looks ancient."

She snickered. "I think it actually *is* ancient. . . . Like, Roman, yeah? It was just lying there with a bunch of other swords, so I took it."

I choked. "You took a sword from the Ancient Rome exhibit? That's . . . Well, somehow that fits."

"It's an *international* exhibition." She shrugged one shoulder. "So a Chinese girl with a Roman sword in an American city. It's perfect, yeah? A little old, but I sharpened it up some, and now it works fine. Don't need a clean cut to stop the Hungry." She popped her knuckles. "As long as you're the closest life around, the corpse'll follow you. When it's more than one chasing you— that's when it gets tricky, yeah?"

I blinked. "Wait." Something about those last words triggered an idea in my mind. I fidgeted with the ribbon around my waist. "So if the Hungry follow the nearest living person, then . . . well, if all the Dead turn Hungry, then all the Dead will chase you."

"Yep." Daniel scratched his jaw. "That's why Philadelphia stands no chance if the fence falls. The Dead will head straight for the city."

"How many pulse bombs are left?" I asked.

"Ten." He cocked his head. "It ain't enough to blow up the whole cemetery. The Dead don't stand in one place—your brother's got 'em shuffling around everywhere."

"Do they go to the river?"

"Some," Jie answered. She wiped her sword with a cloth. "But they don't go all the way to the water because of the steep hill, yeah?"

"And the Hungry?" I looked between the three Spirit-Hunters. "Do they ever go to the shore?"

Joseph cleared his throat and shook his head. "There are no people on the river to attract them. When they breach the fence, they head straight to us."

I cocked my head. "But the water—you could use the water to magnify your power, couldn't you?"

"*Wi*. That much water would enhance my range and power significantly. But without the influence machine to produce a strong electric spark, I would not be able to shock the Dead."

Daniel frowned. "And the influence machine can't go in the water, Empress."

I flashed my eyebrows and bared a wicked grin. "I have a plan. We need a boat."

CHAPTER TWENTY-FIVE

With barely a splash, the oar slid from the Schuylkill's water. Each of Daniel's sure strokes in the stolen rowboat brought the Spirit-Hunters and me through the morning fog and closer to the cemetery's steep, rocky hillside.

Jie and Daniel had commandeered the boat downstream—south near the Girard Avenue Bridge—where simple boats such as this were rented out for pleasure-fishing. We needed the water to magnify Joseph's powers, and we needed the boat to carry the influence machine. If all went according to my plan, we'd end this war today, in this river.

None of us spoke. I sat at the front and imagined the plan over and over. The influence machine was behind me at the boat's center. Its hulking form was as high as my knees, and it was covered with Daniel's coat to protect it from the water. Next to it was a bag of the remaining pulse bombs.

Jie held her sword, and her head swiveled all about. Joseph held his head in hands. His lips moved, and I thought he might be praying.

Behind him were two sturdy tree branches, stripped of leaves and bark—one for Joseph, one for Daniel. Weak defense against savage corpses, yet the best we could do.

When we reached the riverbank, Daniel hopped out and dragged us onto the narrow strip of silty shore. I clambered out and glanced around. My palms were slick with nervous sweat, and I wiped them over and over again on my trousers.

The orange glow of morning hung low on the horizon, and the new light made new shadows. I was scared of those shadows.

"I cannot sense the Dead," Joseph whispered. "But soon the Hungry will sense *us*."

These were the only words spoken before we toiled up the hill. It wasn't a long slope—fifty feet at most—but it was steep and treacherous, with jagged boulders and loose pebbles.

We crested the ridge and reached the forest edge that marked the beginning of the cemetery grounds. A corpse burst from the trees. Its clothes and skin had rotted away long ago, and all that remained was bone and gristle. In moments it was on me—not even giving me time to panic—with its teeth chomping at me faster than I could flee. I staggered back, lifting my hands instinctively to cover my face.

With a crack, the chomping stopped. I lowered my hands to find the skull snapped to the side and detached from the spine.

Another crack, and the skeleton's knees crunched. The monster toppled to the ground. Daniel stood behind it, the branch in his hand and his chest heaving.

I stared in sick fascination. The headless skeleton dug its fingers into the earth and dragged its crippled frame toward me. How could it still move? Truly, the only way to stop these corpses was by stopping the energy that animated them or by annihilating the bodies.

Two more Dead crashed from the brush. Jie and Joseph tackled them head on.

"Run!" Daniel yelled at me. "You have to go now—I'll follow!" He whirled around, and with a loping gate, he dashed to meet the nearest corpse.

Yes. I had to go now. That was my job: to reach Elijah before the Dead reached me.

I bolted from the battle and into the tiny strip of forest. Briars and brambles clawed at me, but I barreled through. The Dead could be anywhere, and speed was a safer option than silence.

In seconds I reached the last tree in the forest fringe and stumbled onto a cemetery plot. A tombstone loomed beside a gaping hole. What had once been a grassy mound was now a pile of disrupted soil and casket splinters.

I scanned the view before me. I had visited Laurel Hill many times over the last six years, and I knew its winding paths well. Yet, for a panicky moment, nothing looked familiar. All the trees, monuments, and open graves looked the same.

Then there, to my right, I saw the carriageway I needed.

Relief flashed through me, and with a long, steeling breath, I clenched my fists and set off toward the path—toward where I knew Elijah would be: our father's grave.

The sun was coming up faster now, and its beams pierced the sky and layered the cemetery in thick shadows. I spun my head side to side, constantly searching for movement. Every grave I passed was open. As Clarence had said all those days ago, *I hear all the corpses in Laurel Hill have come to life.*

Then I heard a distant pounding. Unnaturally quick feet. I spun about until I spotted to my left and down another path the rapid, rolling stride of a Hungry. Still distant, but vicious and bounding toward me.

Panic exploded in my chest. I had no choice now but to run.

I pushed my feet as hard as the terrain and my body would let me—down dirt paths, across grassy plots, over empty graves, and around tombstones. *Faster, Eleanor, faster.* I had to get to Elijah. I had to get away!

The corpse was gaining ground.

I leaped over red zinnias and raced onto a crowded expanse of tombstones. The corpse was so close now I could hear its bones scraping and its teeth gnashing.

God, I wasn't ready to die. In a flash of awareness, I understood Clarence's wild determination to live. It's one thing to fear death, but it's another to fear the Dead.

I reached a marble tombstone topped with an angel. Straight beyond it would lead me to Elijah. I had to get around the damn thing, and that meant I would have to slow.

I hope there's an open grave on the other side.

I aimed my stride for the right edge of the tombstone's marble base. When I reached its corner, I skidded around. Once on the other side, I bolted left. I was directly in front of the tombstone now, and the hole I'd hoped for gaped before me.

I sprang up and sailed through the air. Beneath me, the grave whizzed past. A jagged wooden plank jutted straight up from the overturned soil. My boots barely missed it.

I hit the ground on the other side so hard that my knees popped, but I didn't stop. I staggered upright and ran.

Then came the sounds of slicing flesh and snapping bones. I risked a glance back.

The corpse had impaled itself on the exposed coffin wood. It wore an old Union uniform—I had seen this Hungry once before. But rather than claw at me through iron bars, it now struggled furiously to gain purchase on the loose soil. Eventually its unnatural strength and desperation would pay off, and it would fight itself free.

I wouldn't be around when that happened.

I wove around empty graves and towering stones. My breath burned in my chest, but I was so close to Elijah now.

Even if I hadn't known where in the cemetery he would be, I could have sorted it out by the Dead. The closer I got to Elijah, the more they were lolling about. Some noticed me and adjusted their course to follow, but none were near enough to be a problem.

Yet.

I jumped over more zinnias and hit the gravel running. I was only a hundred feet or so from my destination now.

But it didn't matter. I'd reached the first of Elijah's personal guard.

I skittered to a stop, whipping my head about in search of a way through. But hundreds of Dead stood before me—a wall of gray, rotting flesh. It was like the rows of Dead at the Exhibition, except these were so densely packed, I could never hope to pass.

The nearest ones sensed me. They twisted around, their arms rose up, and they lunged. Behind me I knew more Dead closed in. And somewhere, not far behind, a skeletal Union soldier galloped after me.

I was out of options, and with that realization, trembling overtook me.

"Elijah!" I screamed. "Elijah! Help!" My vocal cords ripped with each frantic shriek, and sobs started, deep in my chest. Each moment, the Dead tumbled closer.

"Elijah! It's me, Eleanor! It's me!" I screamed as loud as I could. Over and over I shouted my brother's name. Still, the Dead closed in.

Then they were on me. Cold, stiff fingers dug into my flesh, and all I wanted to do was squeeze my eyes shut and let them have me. I didn't want to watch their decrepit mouths rip me apart. But I made my eyes stay open. I made myself fight back through my sobs.

Their fingers dug off my blistered skin, and, oh God— it *hurt*! Their lidless eyes were so close I could see the milky haze where their pupils had once been. Carrion breath, numbing and noxious, rolled over me.

I kept screaming. I pawed at the hands—everywhere! The Dead were everywhere! This was not how I wanted to die! They pressed in on me and clawed at my face, at my chest.

I crumpled to the earth beneath their bone fingers.

"Eleanor!"

After what seemed an eternity, I heard my name.

"Eleanor!"

In a great, convulsing wave, the bodies surrounding me tottered back, and footsteps—sure, living footsteps—approached. "Eleanor, let me help you."

I whimpered and lifted my head. My scabs were open and bleeding; the bandages were long gone.

"Elijah," I rasped. Relief shuddered through me. "Y-you heard me?"

He slid a hand beneath my left arm and tugged me into a sitting position. "Yes . . . And I'm sorry my army hurt you." He reached out and stroked the side of my face. "You're bleeding everywhere."

All my resolve, the clarity of my mission, my carefully laid plans—they all vanished when I gazed into Elijah's sea-blue eyes. They were the same eyes they'd always been, with or without his spectacles. I didn't see a monster before me; only my brother. Tender and true.

Tears stung in my eyes. "I missed you."

"I missed you too." He whipped his head around and then

back to me. "Come. One of the Hungry draws near. We will be safer at the grave."

He scooped me up with no effort and carried me through the lines of now-still corpses.

We reached our father's grave. The marble cross that marked it towered high and heavy above me. It was a testament to Father's good character, to the Fitt name, to our eternal lives in heaven—or so I'd always thought.

Now it seemed sinister. Wrong. There was no heaven here. Eternal life meant waking up as a putrid corpse.

The grass that had once adorned the plot was long gone, replaced by mud and exposed roots. A shovel lay nearby.

I avoided looking at the lip of the burial hole. I knew the mahogany coffin lay within, and I didn't think I could stomach the sight of my father—or whatever remained of him.

Elijah set me gently on the dirt and knelt beside me. "Do you need anything? Water, perhaps?"

I swallowed. My mouth tasted like blood and tears. "No. I'm all right."

He eyed me for several long moments. Then he rubbed the bridge of his nose as if his spectacles were still there and misbehaving. "Why are you here, El?"

"I-I wanted to see you. I'm worried. About you. About this."

He stiffened. "I'm fine. You don't have to look after me anymore."

"I didn't mean it like that." Yet as I spoke the words, I realized they weren't true. I *did* want to look after him. I wanted him to need me as much as I needed him.

He rose and dusted off his hands. "I . . . well, I'm sorry, El."

I gulped. "For what?"

"I'm failing at my task. If you're here to see Father then you'll be disappointed."

I clambered to my feet. "You can't bring him back?"

"No."

"Then don't. It's . . ." I reached for his sleeve. "It's all right to stop."

"No, it's not." He hunched over and pressed his palms to his eyes. "Over and over again I've tried, but Father's spirit won't answer my call. It's as if . . . as if there's something in my way. Something in the spirit realm that blocks him."

"So leave it and come home. Please. Mama and I need you." I tilted his chin to look at me. "We're out of money, Elijah. Almost all of it is gone, and we *need* you."

He jerked away from me. "Money won't be a problem. I'll go back to Egypt. I'll resurrect the Black Pullet, and we'll live in wealth for the rest of our days. Everything will be all right. But first, El, I need to bring Father back."

"Please don't!" I cried. "Please come home. *I* need you! If you stop now, we can go home and pretend none of this ever happened. We can climb the tree, read Shakespeare, and—"

"Listen to yourself." His face scrunched up. "We can't go back. Things will never be—*can* never be like they were. I'm not the weakling who left town, and you're not the little girl I left behind."

My breathing turned shallow and fast. I clenched his filthy sleeve in my fist. "Then we'll leave. We'll go abroad and see the world."

He nodded slowly. "Yes, but first Father must see what I have done. What I've accomplished. Nothing stands in his way now! He can run for city council and do all the things he dreamed of." Elijah took my hand in his. "He always said, 'We must show them.' Well, I have. None of those Gas Ring devils will ever trouble him or *me* again."

And that was when it hit me. The full weight of the situation careened back into my mind and my heart. My brother was insane. An army of decayed corpses surrounded me, and the wasted body of my father lay only a few feet away. Elijah had *killed* men—killed Clarence!—with no remorse, and I knew he would do it again. *He* was the devil here, not the Gas Ring.

And I was here to stop him, not to save him.

I licked my cracked lips. "You have to stop," I said with all the authority I could muster. "Now."

He scowled and stomped to the edge of the open grave. "I'm so close, El, I won't turn back. It's that damn spirit," he growled. "It keeps releasing my army from my control. Whatever it is, it knows necromancy, and it knows it better than I do." His eyes fixed on mine, their blue depths murky. "One by one, it releases them from my control, so they turn into those . . ." He waved in the direction from which I'd come. "Into those crazy, desperate Hungry Dead."

"Then why keep trying?" I stalked toward him. "Give up!

Lay the Dead to rest and—"

At that moment thunder boomed. It rattled the earth, and my knees shook. It was one of the pulse bombs.

Elijah lunged at me. "What was that?" He gripped my shirt and heaved me toward his face. "The Spirit-Hunters are here, aren't they? You betrayed me." The edge of his lips twisted up. "Well, there's no escape for them. Not today." He shoved hard, and I tumbled to the earth.

Elijah twirled around to his army. With his arms thrust high, he chanted words I didn't understand or recognize.

The rows of Dead lurched to a start. Ancient feet scuffed and bones creaked, and in seconds the army was shambling away. Toward the river. Toward the Spirit-Hunters.

I heaved myself to my feet but didn't speak. What could I say? Reason would not work, nor would begging. My best option was to stick to my plan.

Elijah snatched me by the shoulder and dragged me to Father's grave. "You're going to help me raise Father."

"No."

He scoffed. "You have very little choice in the matter. I carry the power to raise the Dead, which means you do too. And it's about time you shared."

"Wh-what do you mean I hold the power?" I demanded.

He didn't answer. He just clamped his hands on my shoulders and pivoted me toward the grave.

I balked at the sight before me. The lid to Father's dark mahogany coffin had been shoved partly off, leaving the top half of his body exposed. Other than the tattered black suit, I could see nothing in this skeleton that resembled the man I had loved.

"The power to reach the Dead—it's a special skill that only a select few have." Elijah dug his nails into my arms. "And oftentimes it runs in a family. It runs in a person's blood. Can't you feel it?"

An electric tingle whipped through my body, and as before at the library, I found my muscles locked in place. Behind me Elijah chanted. The current was not strong—it merely tickled and made me want to scratch my insides—yet I could not move or resist it.

A minute of Elijah's murmurs passed. Then he let go, and I stumbled and fell next to the grave. He jostled me aside.

"We did it, El! Look! We did it!" He leaped into the hole.

I looked down and saw the skeleton twitch. Its whole frame rattled.

I recoiled. "How do you know the spell worked?"

"Because the body moves!" Elijah scurried to the coffin. "I must get Father free. Help me push the lid off."

"Father?" I asked. My eyes ran over the skull, searching for something familiar. All I saw were empty sockets and wisps of brittle hair.

A knocking sounded from inside the coffin. The skeleton was trying to get out.

Elijah tugged at the mahogany lid, glee shining on his face and sparkling in his eyes. "Help me, El! Father's here!"

I shook my head and backed away. "No Elijah. This is wrong. That's not . . . I don't think it's Father."

Elijah paused, and his face snapped to me. Our father's skeleton was wrestling inside the coffin now, and the clatter of bone fingers against the wood sounded like thousands of tiny, scuttling feet.

Then the skeleton's toothy mouth started chomping.

Elijah's eyes bulged and he staggered back. He hit the soil wall of the hole. The lid flipped off and slammed against the dirt.

"Get out!" I shrieked. I surged for the shovel and hoisted it, grunting from the weight.

Elijah climbed from the grave and pitched toward me. "The grimoire! I need it—where is it?"

"I don't know! You took it from me!"

The skeleton lurched at Elijah.

With a howl, I flew at it and swung the shovel. It connected with the skull, and painful waves writhed up my arms. The skeleton toppled sideways, but in moments it was up again.

I reared back to attack once more, but its yellow teeth zoomed at my face. I toppled over, dropping the shovel. The skeleton was on me, and I couldn't keep its biting jaws away.

"Eleanor! No!" Elijah charged. He tackled it away from me, Latin bellowing from his mouth. He and the corpse fought in a mass of scratching and biting and shouting.

I rolled to my feet.

"*Dormi!*" Elijah roared, his fists and forearms keeping the vicious jaws from his neck.

I vaulted at the shovel. A scream ripped through the air—
Elijah!

I twisted back to find the skeleton's teeth locked on my brother's throat.

"*Dormi*," Elijah struggled to say. "*Dormi*."

The skeleton collapsed, a heap of bone and suit. I bolted to it. Beneath the monster, blood streamed from my brother's neck. I shoved the corpse off him. On Elijah's throat was a torn, fleshy hole that shot blood out in pulses.

Elijah's eyes were closed, and his chest barely moved. My brother was dying.

"Elijah—oh God, Elijah." I brushed a hand through his auburn hair. "Wake up. Please!"

His eyes fluttered open. I could tell he wanted to speak.

"Shhh. Stay calm, quiet." Tears swelled in my chest, and my breathing picked up. "Shhh, shhh, Elijah."

More blood spurted. It ran down his neck in rivulets and sank into the soil.

"No." My words trembled. "Don't go—please. Hold on." I fumbled for his hand and clasped it in mine.

This was my mission: Elijah's death. I had known it would come to this, and yet now that it was happening, I didn't want it to. I could never *want* him to die.

"Please," I whispered.

Elijah gurgled and shook. "C-cowards die many times before their . . . before their deaths." His eyes rolled back in his head. One more heartbeat of blood oozed from his neck.

Then his body went limp.

The sobs came, and I wailed my mourning to the sky. I hunched over him and draped my arms around his body. Blood smeared onto my clothes, mixing with my own.

My brother—my best friend—was dead. In the end he'd given it all up. He had tackled the Hungry off me.

If he had stayed a murderous monster, then maybe his death wouldn't hurt so much. . . .

I shivered and hugged my arms to my stomach. The air felt frigid and frozen, biting with its chill.

His last words—oh God, they were from Shakespeare. Our shared love and childhood joy.

"Cowards die many times before their deaths," I whispered, tugging at my sleeves. "The valiant never taste of death but once."

Then suddenly, the cold vanished.

Elijah twitched. Then he choked, and blood sputtered from his mouth.

My stomach heaved. "Elijah!" I slid my left hand beneath his neck. His chest moved. The blood started dribbling again, and it was sticky and slick on my fingers.

"You're alive. Oh, thank God. Can you hear me? Elijah?"

A lopsided grin tugged at his lips. "Y-es. Alive."

His eyes whipped open. I sucked in. The irises weren't blue—they were a bright, catlike yellow.

"*Bonjour, Mamzèi,*" he said. The voice was the same timbre as my brother's, but the words were strange and lilting.

I ripped my hand away. It wasn't Elijah. I scuttled back. "What are you?"

"I am alive. That is what I am." He rose gracefully, cracking his neck and rolling his shoulders. He took a step toward me. Then another, as if testing the body's muscles.

I dove for the shovel. Whatever had taken hold of my brother's body, I'd be damned if I'd let it stay alive. That was Elijah's skin—not some container for a filthy . . .

Spirit.

The cold from moments before. It was the spirit, and it had filled my brother's corpse. It was the only explanation.

I heaved the shovel up and turned back to Elijah. He was grinning.

"That's a bad idea." He clucked his tongue and wagged a single finger. "Drop the shovel or I'll kill you."

"No." I foisted the shovel high. "E-even if you wear my brother's body, I'll beat your skull in."

He chuckled and opened his hands. "I very much doubt that, *Mamʒèi*." In a flurry of movement too fast for me to react, my brother's corpse slithered to me and slung the shovel from my hand. His speed was incredible, and I tripped backward.

He gripped my shirt before I could fall, and with no effort, he dragged me to the base of the marble tombstone. He slammed me against it and pinned me there.

I kicked and punched, but it was like beating a statue. It hurt me more than him.

He brought his face close to mine, his yellow eyes glowing.

Blood sputtered from his neck and sprayed my face. It was as frozen as his touch.

"Where is Joseph?" he demanded.

I stopped struggling. "Joseph?"

"*Wi*. Joseph." He spoke the name so fiercely that spittle flew like shards of ice and stabbed into my skin. "He and I have unfinished business, and I intend to settle it."

I gasped. "You're Marcus. From New Orleans."

"*Wi*," Marcus purred in my ear. His breath was damp and frosty. "Joseph stopped me then, but he could not stop me forever. Death only made me stronger, *chéri*. Aware. Joseph and his ridiculous Spirit-Hunters don't stand a chance."

I swallowed back my revulsion. He stank, like blood and sweat and grave dirt, like corruption and decay.

"Joseph will kill you," I croaked. "You've taken my brother's body, and I swear I will take it back. We will send you to the hottest flames in hell to rot for eternity—"

He slapped me hard, and my head snapped to the side. Blinding stars swam through my vision.

"Somehow," I rasped, blinking back unbidden tears, "you will die and never see daylight—"

He grasped my neck with both hands, squeezing and cutting off my words.

The world blurred, and no air came into my lungs. I strained to reach his neck, to claw at his gaping wound, but he merely straightened his arms—his reach was longer than mine.

I couldn't breathe. I needed air.

361

I grabbed his left pinkie and yanked it back as far as it would go. I felt the snap of his knuckle, and then I heard Elijah—no, Marcus—shriek.

His grip released and air slid down my throat. Before he could choke me again, I thrust out my leg and connected with the side of his knee. He howled again, and his face twisted with rage.

I scrambled away from him, but he clutched at my hair and yanked me back. Salty tears burned my eyes.

Then an explosion cracked through the morning air.

Marcus spun toward the sound, hauling me with him. It had come from the river. "So Joseph is that way. Perfect."

Marcus tugged me close, his cold breath rolling over me. "The Hungry come, and I think I will leave you as bait . . . a distraction, if you will. But first I will take the grimoire." He shoved his hands into my pockets, but they were empty.

He gave a strangled cry. "Where is it?" he growled. He glanced in the river's direction, and I followed his gaze. Someone was running, and just behind was a pack of rabid Dead.

"I don't have it." I breathed a weak laugh. "It's gone."

"Liar. Your brother had it just before his death—I saw it! If you don't tell me where—"

I spat in his face, satisfied to see it dribble down his cheek.

His fist connected with my chin. The world flashed with black. I tottered backward. Marcus shoved me, and I fell into the open grave.

Chapter Twenty-Six

I lay on my back on the lid of my father's coffin, the glowing sky above me. The ground shook, dirt rattling beside me. Pain welled from my jaw and cheeks, and my vision swirled with spots and clouds.

My death was approaching. The corpses were coming in a great stampede to kill me. Despite the dizziness, I pushed myself up and drew my legs in to stand. I could hear the clamor of their rancid feet, but I wasn't ready to die. I supposed I never would be.

A body hit the coffin lid. Daniel—it was Daniel. He threw himself on me and shoved me down.

"Don't move," he said, draping his arms around me.

My ears filled with the roar of dynamite, and the earth

quaked. Gray flesh and maggots and soil rained around me, though not *on* me. Daniel kept me safe.

Then came silence, but it was the thick silence that follows pandemonium. The air still vibrated from the explosion.

Daniel moved back. "Empress—oh God." His hands came to my face, and he wiped at my eyes. I hadn't even realized I was crying. "You're cut all over . . . is anything broken? Can you stand? Eleanor, look at me."

"I think." My voice cracked, but with the movement of my vocal cords, some of my dizziness dispersed. "Yes, I can stand."

Daniel slid his hand to the small of my back and helped me rise. His face was smeared with mud and blood and sweat, but his eyes were as sharp as ever. "Where'd your brother go?"

"It's not Elijah anymore. He's dead. The spirit—it took his body, Daniel. I-it was waiting all this time, and it's Marcus—the necromancer Joseph knew."

Daniel's brow wrinkled. "I'm not sure I follow, but now's not the time to figure it out."

He shot up tall and peeped around like a prairie dog. Then he slouched back to my side. "We're outta time. Joseph and Jie are luring the Hungry away."

An explosion from the south made the ground around us crumble.

I gripped Daniel's shirt and forced him to look at me. "I sent the Dead to you like we planned—Elijah sent the army to the river. Why didn't Joseph stop them? Why are you here?"

"I . . . I got separated from them." He shook his head. "And

I said I'd follow you, didn't I? I meant it."

"But that wasn't the plan."

"Damn the plan, Eleanor! You were right. On the bridge when you said I'd do the same, you were right. I would. I am. Now come on." He scrambled out of the grave and towed me out with him.

"Look," I said. "It's the grimoire. Marcus wanted it." It was half buried in the soil at my feet. I swooped it up and passed it to Daniel, who shoved it into his pocket. Then he darted to a familiar sack nearby. It was the pulse bombs.

He slung the bag up. "We're gonna run now, you got it? When the Dead get close, I'll light one of these, but I've only got two left. The rest are with Joseph and Jie. We've gotta get to the river." He pointed toward the Schuylkill, and I scanned the horizon. There were endless tombs and endless bodies between us and the river. And charging around those tombs and corpses were the Dead. Directly in our path.

Daniel and I launched into a gallop. The sun had completely risen behind us, and the blazing light sent our shadows shooting far ahead. The Dead were approaching fast.

We reached a gray granite monument, and Daniel heaved me down before it. He slipped a pulse bomb in my hand and whipped out a match. With a flash and crackle, the dynamite's fuse flared to life.

"Throw it," I said. The Dead were so close now I could hear their gnashing jaws.

Daniel didn't budge, and the fuse blazed on. Now I could

hear the thud of each footfall as the earth soaked it up. The Dead would be on us in a moment.

"Daniel! Throw the damn—"

His arm reeled back and then snapped. The bomb sailed over the monument. He pulled me to his chest and wrapped his arms around me.

The explosion was deafening. It covered all sounds and echoed in my brain. Debris flew and fluttered around us. Then Daniel yanked me to my feet and we pressed on through the smoke and dusty haze. Limp bodies were scattered among the wreckage of blasted tombstones.

Thank God his inventions actually work.

We raced past the coffin on which the Union soldier had impaled himself. I spared a glimpse, but the body wasn't there. Nor was the splintered wood.

Next we came to the main carriageway, and I could see the forest fringe. Beyond those trees was the Schuylkill River. We were close, and we had one bomb left.

Another explosion blasted, but it was far off. I hoped Joseph and Jie had enough pulse bombs. The war wasn't finished yet.

We reached the edge of the cemetery's woods. Daniel grabbed my left arm, and we bounded into the trees. The ground sloped down, and we ran faster now. We were in trouble. The Dead had surrounded us, and I could see their faces in the foliage.

I didn't hear the crack of the match, but I saw the flame and I watched the fuse catch. As before, Daniel lobbed it away and hugged me to his chest.

Something hit us at full speed, knocking us sideways. I landed on my right shoulder. Then the monster was at my throat.

I clawed at its face, but my nails just shredded decomposed skin.

Boom! The shadows of the forest disappeared in a flash of light.

The corpse crumpled onto me. Branches, rocks, and unrecognizable body parts crashed around, but I couldn't hear any of it. The explosion had been too close, and it had blackened my hearing.

Daniel appeared, pushing the corpse to the side. Then he drew me to my feet, and we stumbled onward.

We reached the rocky edge that dropped to the river. It was far too steep to descend. The sun sparkled on the lazy water, but I couldn't see our boat. Daniel pointed north, and I nodded. As we clambered along the bluff, my hearing returned, and with it came the sounds of struggle.

The forest was filled with crashing and beating footsteps.

"How many Dead are there?" I shrieked.

"Too many!" Daniel seized my hand. "We need to get to the water. Now." He shoved me ahead of him, and we bolted down the hill.

Another explosion rang out from the forest while we were tumbling down the jagged hill. Joseph and Jie were heading toward the water too.

We hit the riverbank. So did the Dead. They landed in heaps

of flesh and cloth. Busted knees and broken elbows didn't matter to them—nor did the angle at which they hit the ground. They always bounced back to their feet.

The rowboat was only paces from us. Daniel shouted, "Get in!"

But then dazzling pain blasted through my brain. Red, white, black shards that stabbed everything.

I screamed. One of the corpses had locked its mouth onto my right hand. Teeth shredded through the skin and grated against my bones. A long strip of splintered wood protruded from its chest and sliced at my legs.

It was the Union soldier.

I hit and gouged and bucked, all the while screaming my pain and trying to avoid the swinging coffin wood.

An oar swung through the air—Daniel. It connected with the corpse's head, and the teeth tore free, taking my flesh and sinew with it. The oar hit the soldier again, and this time the head crunched and flopped to the side. It flailed at Daniel, head hanging and teeth still chomping.

Another explosion ripped through the morning. The Dead toppled, and I toppled too. I felt weak and distant, and I knew my hand was bleeding something fierce.

Daniel's arms scooped under me. He hefted me up and trudged toward the boat. Joseph was on the shore beside it—he must have detonated the last pulse bomb. Ragged gashes bled across his face and through his shirt.

"You don't look good," I said.

"Don't talk." Daniel set me on my feet, and Joseph slid his arm beneath me. Then Daniel whirled around. "Jie! Come on!"

Joseph and I sloshed into the river. My hand throbbed with every footstep. It was so mangled—all pulpy muscles and exposed bone. The water was calm as always, but over its lapping flow I heard more Dead on the way.

"Joseph," I said, trying to ignore the pain in my arm. "Marcus is here."

He turned his face toward me, his eyes enormous and bloodshot. "What?"

In as few words as possible, I explained what had happened.

"Marcus used your brother's spell to connect souls to bodies," Joseph said, his face a mask of horror. "And he used it against him. . . . But you say he is gone now?"

"I don't know. He ran off and left me as food for the Hungry." I glanced up the hill. Jie barreled down the slope, the Dead behind her. She held her sword in one hand and a gleaming copper bomb in the other.

She hit the shore screaming, "Matches! I need fire!" Daniel and Joseph lurched for her. The corpses were at her heels.

But suddenly, the Dead stopped moving. With no warning at all and in no time, every single corpse froze its frantic hunt. They straightened like sentries and waited.

I glanced around. Daniel, Joseph, and Jie looked as confused as I.

Then applause began from the top of the hill. I jerked my head up.

My brother's body stood atop the crest, his grin wide and his hands clapping. Though I did notice one finger hanging limp.

"*Bonjour*, Joseph," he called. "Did you miss me?"

In three bounding leaps, Marcus cleared the rocky bluff and hit the riverbank. Somehow the wound on his neck was already smaller and scabbing over.

Daniel and Jie skittered back.

"My friend," Marcus said. He advanced along the shore. The hordes of Dead moved with him, mimicking his stride and speed.

Joseph sped from the water, his movements sluggish but determined. He clenched his fists at his side and tipped his chin high. "Stealing souls was not enough, Marcus? You had to start stealing bodies too?"

Marcus spread his hands, palms up. His movements were far more elegant than Elijah's had ever been. "After six years in death, I'd say I deserve a new home." He flexed his arms and smiled. "This one serves me quite well. Strong, young, and—"

"Not yours!" I shouted. Fresh rage pulsed in my chest. With my bloodied hand held to my heart, I splashed from the water and stomped toward Marcus. I craved violence. "It's not your body. It's not yours!" I bolted over the shore, picking up speed. "I said you would die, and I meant it!"

I lunged. Daniel sprang forward and grabbed me by the waist, but I kept screaming. "I promise, I won't let you live! I'll kill you and send your soul back to where it belongs!"

I wanted to rip the satisfaction off this monster's face—a face that looked less like Elijah's as my fury grew. I wanted Marcus dead, and I wanted to be the one to do it. "It's not your body!"

"Enough," Marcus spat. He arched a single eyebrow. "You're hardly in a position for such threats, and I'm growing rather sick of your antics." He pointed at me, his mouth moved with silent words, and the corpses convulsed to life. They hitched forward, hands up, and flowed around Marcus and Joseph. More started tumbling down the hill. I was their target.

Daniel yanked me toward the boat. The shuffling feet weren't far behind. Daniel shoved me into the boat, and Jie followed. Then he climbed in with us, and we pushed from shore. Daniel rowed full force.

"Why are we leaving?" I had blood all down my chest— some of it from my cuts, some of it from Elijah's dying wound, and most of it from my still-oozing hand. "We have to get Joseph. We have to stop Marcus."

"We won't be any help if we're dead," Daniel said. "The Dead aren't hurting Joseph or Marcus right now." He pointed to the riverbank.

I followed his finger. The sun burned in my eyes, but I could see the corpses raging down the slope. Hundreds of backlit silhouettes. They splashed into the river, unhampered by the water. I could just make out Joseph's tall form in the mass of stumbling figures.

"What the hell is happening?" Jie demanded. "I thought that was your brother."

"Not anymore," Daniel said. He stopped rowing. We were in the middle of the river, and we watched the fight onshore. My hand shot pulses of pain through my arm and stars through my vision, but I couldn't tear my eyes from Marcus and Joseph.

"Do you have any pulse bombs left?" Daniel asked Jie.

"Just the one," she said.

"Shit." His head spun left and right. "What do we do?"

"Go back!" I yelled. "We go back. We can throw the bomb."

"That'll kill Joseph, Empress."

"Look!" Jie said.

The Dead had cleared a space around the fighters, and Marcus was beating the life out of Joseph. He flung Joseph around like a loose puppet. Marcus's fists connected with Joseph's jaw, nose, stomach. Then the Dead swarmed too thickly around the fight, and I couldn't see them anymore.

"Go back!" I shrieked. The current had picked us up and was pulling us away from the cemetery.

"Yes!" Jie grabbed Daniel's sleeve. "Row us back!"

"How?" he demanded. "We can't get through that!"

He was right. What remained of the army—likely half the cemetery—was either marching through the river or stepping into it. Decrepit, waterlogged bodies.

"He'll die if we leave him." My voice cracked.

"We'll get through another way," Jie said. "Just row back to the shore *somewhere*."

I watched the Dead and strained to see Marcus and Joseph. When I finally did see, I wished instantly that I hadn't.

"No!" Jie cried.

Marcus had a limp, bloodied Joseph by the collar and was dragging him effortlessly up the hill.

Jie squeezed her eyes shut. "He's gonna sacrifice him."

Daniel grabbed the oars, his face hardened and his lips compressed into a narrow line. "We'll get out over there." He gestured to an empty shore expanse south of us. We slid through the water toward it.

"Once we're there," he continued in a gruff voice, "we'll try to get into Laurel Hill from another point, like maybe the south gate. If we're lucky, we'll find Marcus and—"

His words broke off. The oars had hit something.

Daniel's eyes grew huge. "Shit!"

Fingers, arms, and claws surged from the water, scratching and shaking the boat. The Dead had reached us, and we were surrounded.

Jie burst into action. Her sword sliced into the water while Daniel beat at the hands with his oars, but more hands appeared—faster than they could fight.

All I could do was stare, my hand clutched to my chest and my mind scrambling for a solution.

The boat tipped dangerously. A skeletal hand was latched onto the rim, and Jie darted at it, almost tripping over the influence machine. She hacked at the hand until the fingers were severed.

And then the solution locked into place in my mind. Joseph had power—he was gifted with the ability to touch spirits. Elijah had that gift. *I* had that gift. It was why I could use the earrings, why I could handle electrocution, and why Elijah had used me to resurrect Father.

"I can use the machine!"

Jie and Daniel jerked their heads toward me.

"Start spinning," I cried. "I can use it to stop the Dead—to stop Marcus."

"No!" Daniel rammed his oar into the water, but the splashing and thrashing didn't cease. "That's the stupidest thing—you can't do that!"

"Stupid or not, it might work," Jie interrupted. She dropped to the boat's floor, ripped the jacket off the machine, and gripped the handle firmly. She nodded, intensity and belief bright in her eyes, and before Daniel could stop her, she started turning the wheels.

I scooted toward the machine. I could do this, I knew I could—and I really had no choice but to try.

"Clear a spot in the water," I yelled at Daniel. The boat was pitching and rolling all around. We'd topple to a death of drowning at any moment. "I need to touch the water, Daniel—clear it!"

He grabbed Jie's sword, and without another word, he chopped at the corpses closest to me.

Crack! Blue sparks flew from the machine.

"Go," Jie said.

I shoved my mutilated hand into the river. Then I leaned forward and thrust my left hand into the popping electricity.

The electricity hit me with a crack. It was like at the library but tenfold stronger. The current raced through my body. The bubbling heat poured through me and into the water.

Millions of worms crawled beneath my skin, and I could smell burning flesh and hair. Then a light erupted all around. Behind my eyes, in my eyes, through my chest. A sapphire light brighter than the sun. With it came a thunder that shook my soul.

With it came power.

It felt like eternity. Like the world spun and spun. I was the river, I was the fish, I was the soil and the roots and the sea, and then I was Jie and I was Daniel. I was Joseph. I felt as large as the entire planet and as small as the tiniest cell.

And then I understood how Joseph could use the water to affect the Dead. I could *feel* the corpses and their corrupt energy. I focused on their hungry souls and the tethers that connected them to Marcus.

The leashes looked like glowing blue strands of spiderweb, wispy yet strong. I began with the corpse closest to me, though I'd no idea what to do. I didn't know how to blast the tethers like a cue ball; and when I concentrated on the single thread, nothing happened. I tried to touch it, but I had no physical control. I moved my senses closer to the thread. It was rather beautiful, the pieces of spiritual energy. Beautiful, but wrong. It didn't belong in this world.

What had Elijah said to the Hungry? *Dormi*. Sleep.

"Go back," I sang. "Go back to your realm, and sleep."

The line grew taut and then broke in the middle. Like a fuse, it shortened in both directions. It shivered and shrank; and when it reached the corpse, the final drops of energy disappeared.

I moved to the next corpse and repeated the technique. After ten or so, the process grew easier. After thirty, I was adept enough to do more than one at a time. How the dickens Joseph could do *all* of them at once was unfathomable to me, but my method worked, so I kept going.

When the last corpse was sent to the spirit realm and I could no longer sense corruption, I searched—or rather I groped much like one does in the pitch of night—for Marcus.

I found him far away. He was running, and his soul slithered and slid from my grasp. He must have felt the breaking ties and fled the scene. Even if I had been able to grab him, he had fully bonded with my brother's body, and I didn't think I could banish his energy so easily—or perhaps at all. The farther he ran, the more my ability to even sense him dwindled. Then he vanished entirely.

I turned my attention to Joseph. He was still alive. Good.

Then I noticed the curtain. It was a shimmery, hazy thing that hung before me. Thick like velvet but opaque like prisms. Elijah was there, at the edge, and watching me. I saw his soul. It sparkled like the sun on the river, and warmth washed over me. It was the smile after the storm. He was no longer tormented, but the boy I'd always known. Beside him was a fainter light. A tender, bearlike glow. My father.

It was right. *That* was right.

Then I was Eleanor again. I slammed back into my body

and into my own awareness.

I gasped. I was on the ground, and the stench of rotting flesh was everywhere. I gulped and coughed, and my lungs screamed for breath.

"Empress," someone called.

I panted and panted, my eyes clenched shut. I felt like a big, scratched bruise.

"Eleanor," Daniel said. "Miss Fitt! Wake up!"

I fluttered my eyelids open. "I'm not a misfit anymore," I rasped. "I thought I told you that."

CHAPTER TWENTY-SEVEN

The Spirit-Hunters wound up bringing me to Philadelphia's Pennsylvania Hospital. My right hand, the one the corpse had bitten, was a bloody pulp and had grown foul quickly. Infection was imminent. Joseph had fared a little better than I, but he couldn't enter the hospital because of his criminal status. Jie had promised she could heal him, though.

They'd left me with a strict but able nurse and then departed. I didn't know if I would see them again.

I was in a large room in the women's wing of the hospital, and at least fifteen other patients were with me. Mama couldn't afford a private room, but I hardly cared. If anything, I enjoyed the companionable pain of the ill. Their hacking coughs were pleasant music to the wretchedness in my right wrist. To the grief in my heart.

I lost my right hand. The doctor was forced to amputate.

I'd heard stories after the war with the South. Stories about broken men. So many soldiers came home without legs or forearms or fingers, and I'd always thought that was what "broken" meant. Now I knew it wasn't the physical pain that had shattered the soldiers' hearts but everything else. The death and the loss and the constant, heavy choice to keep fighting or give up.

The days passed, and when I thought of Clarence, I forced my mind to see his beautiful smile. I also clung to my final vision of Elijah and Father. At times I imagined I could see them still, watching me from the spirit realm.

I knew there would be no going back to the way things were. No more sitting in the cherry tree, no more playing chess, and no more dreaming of a world with Elijah. So I spent the long, empty moments considering what I wanted now. What I would do when I left the hospital. Blazes, I longed to find Marcus and shred his soul to pieces, but first . . . first I had things in Philadelphia that needed doing.

It was Sunday, June the eighteenth, three days after I'd destroyed my own brother. Half a week since the final dregs of my old life, of the old Eleanor had been erased.

At that moment Mary sat on the end of my hospital bed reading *Twelfth Night* to me. I half listened, my left fingers scrubbing gently at my face. My right cheek constantly begged for scratching. The doctor swore I would have no scars so long as I left the scabs alone.

The murmur of Mary's words echoed like a soothing wind through the hospital wing. Mary visited daily since Mama would not. I suspected guilt ate at Mary's insides for letting me leave the house.

I cleared my throat, and Mary stopped reading.

"If we sell the piano, we can afford to keep the house. For a while at least. Have you told her that?" I eased myself into a sitting position.

"Aye, and your ma won't let me sell it." She closed the Shakespeare volume and looked at me warily.

"Do it anyway. Tell her I told you to." I massaged the nape of my neck. "And sell all my evening gowns and jewelry. The gowns alone should cover the hospital bill."

"True." A flush grew on Mary's cheeks, and she picked at the book's spine. "I've got some amethyst earrings that . . . well, if you're willing, I could sell them."

I laughed, a hollow sound. "Keep them, Mary. I doubt you'll get paid for a long time. Hell, I don't even know why you're still working for us."

"You oughtn't cuss, Eleanor." She wagged a finger at me. "Anyway, I got nowhere else to go, and your ma's always treated me right. And . . . and you too. You don't deserve all this." She waved around the room.

"Oh, I deserve it. Trust me."

"I find that hard to believe. Nobody deserves what that reporter's gone and done to ya."

My throat tightened, and I clenched the cotton sheet in my

left fist. Mary had brought me the paper the day before, and it hadn't been pleasant reading.

Once the amazement had worn off over Laurel Hill's ruins and the hundreds of corpses floating in the Schuylkill, and once people had realized the Dead would no longer plague the city or Exhibition, the *Philadelphia Bulletin*—or rather Nick Peger—had latched onto a new campaign: me. It had somehow reached his ears that Clarence was with me the night of his death, and Peger had bitten into this juicy news with rabid, Deadlike ferocity.

Though the speculation did not spread to other newspapers, the damage was done. Mrs. Wilcox and Allison publicly denounced my family. I knew it was the final blow for my dragon-mother. If Mama had ever intended to swallow her devastation and leave her bedroom, she certainly wouldn't now.

I rather thought my family deserved the Wilcoxes' hatred. Though no one knew the exact truth, my family *was* the cause of Clarence's death.

Of course, Peger could prove none of his accusations against me. Soon enough, some other story would come along to replace me. I hoped.

I settled back onto my pillow. "You don't have to stay, Mary. I'm tired now, and I think I'll sleep."

"Ah'right."

"Don't forget what I said about the gowns. There must be someone who will buy them."

She nodded.

382

"And," I added, my voice tight, "if she'll listen, tell Mama I love her."

"Wake up," said a voice. "Eleanor, wake up."

I opened my eyes, groggy and confused. The room was dark, and except for the heavy breaths of slumber, it was a silent Sunday night.

Someone sat on my bed, much like Mary had, but this person was small, and her voice was like a sharp-edged music box.

"Jie," I breathed. "How'd you get in?"

She grinned, a flash of white in the dark. "The window by your bed."

"But I'm on the second story."

"And that's what trees are for, yeah?" She helped me sit up.

"Why are you here? Have you found Marcus?"

"No, but we think we know where he's gone, so we're leaving town."

"To be honest," I said with a sad twist to my lips, "I thought you'd be long gone by now."

"Nothing personal, Eleanor, but I would have. It's not safe for us, yeah?" She cracked her knuckles against her jaw. "But Daniel wouldn't go until one of us had gotten in here to see you."

My heart twisted, and I turned away. "Ah."

"We also wanted to give you this." She set a fat, dirty envelope on my bedside table. "It was in the grimoire pages. It's full of letters . . . from your brother. To you. We thought you might want them."

383

My throat stung. "Thanks," I whispered. "S-so where are you going?"

"Chicago. A headless corpse was found there. It must be Marcus's work."

"Was the corpse walking?"

"Naw. Marcus probably sacrificed someone for the power. We're not completely sure it was him, but chances are pretty high it is." She scooted closer to me. "I wish you could come with us."

A breathy laugh broke through my lips, and tears glossed over my eyes. "I wish that too, Jie, but I can barely walk."

"We could wait a little longer." She opened her hands wide. "There's nothing but hate left for you in this town."

"I know." I sniffled and wiped my nose on my sleeve. "But I can't leave. I have to take care of my mother."

"Have you told her about your brother?"

"N-no." My voice broke. If I wasn't careful, I would be crying soon. "Not yet, but I will."

Jie grunted. "Well, if you change your mind about staying, you come find us, yeah?"

"How will I know where you are?"

"I'll write to you. Every city we visit, I'll send you a letter."

A grin tugged at my lips. "All right."

Jie slid off the bed. "I should go now. There's a big reward out for me." She smiled, her eyes gleaming with wicked pleasure. "Besides, I still gotta let Daniel in."

"Huh?"

"He's at the front door." She rolled her eyes. "He's too

clumsy to climb trees, yeah?" She gave me a quick hug. "See you around, Eleanor." Then she scampered silently through the room and disappeared into the hall.

Brittle minutes passed, and my heart started banging uncomfortably. After a few days in bed, all my anger at Daniel's rejection had faded into a tender regret.

He appeared in the doorway, a shadowy figure. He crept toward my bed, and once he reached my side, he gazed down at me for several moments. His eyes ran over my lacerated arms, flicked to my bandaged stump, and then paused at my face.

"Can I sit?" he whispered, waving to the bed.

"Yes, of course."

He perched on the edge. Then he tugged off his cap and squeezed it in his hands. "I wanted to say good-bye . . . and tell you sorry."

"For what?"

"For everything. Your brother, your hand, me . . ." He swallowed, and his Adam's apple bobbed. "When you first came to our lab, I thought you were a snobby princess who only cared about herself. Just the sort of person I hate."

I bit the inside of my mouth, trying to keep the thirsty ache away. "A-and now?"

"Now . . ." He shook his head and gazed at his cap. "Well, you're none of that. I was wrong. You're an empress with grit and brains, and I wish . . ."

"What?" My voice was so low it could barely be heard. "You wish what?"

"That we could have helped you more."

My breath shot out. Silly, Eleanor—what had I thought he would say? That he wished we could be together? What a ninny I was. And yet, despite my best attempts to stifle it, the hollowness was still strong inside.

I forced a soft chuckle. "You saved my life—the three of you saved me over and over again. There was nothing more you could have done."

"Maybe." His gaze lingered on my bandaged wrist, and he dipped his head toward it. "There are, uh, ways to make fake hands, you know . . . mechanical ones."

I tilted my head to one side. "Are you offering?"

"I can always try." He shrugged one shoulder, his cheeks reddening, and he picked at a threadbare spot on his cap. At last, he cleared his throat. "Well, um, that's all I wanted to say. I don't want you to think that just 'cause everything seems bad that it is." He rubbed his knees and glanced at me. "I should go now."

My lips went dry, and without thinking I leaned forward and gripped his sleeve. "Wait."

He kept his eyes locked on mine. Their emerald sheen was invisible in the dark.

"Daniel . . . you don't . . . or, that is to say, you're not . . ." I licked my lips and gulped. "You're not in love with me, are you." I spoke it as a statement and tried to ignore my pounding heart.

He twisted his head away. "It's not that simple."

"It's a yes or no." I pulled back my hand.

"Then . . ." He set his cap on his head. "Then no. No, I'm not."

My stomach clenched painfully. But it was all right; it would be all right. Better to know than to wonder.

He rose and gave me a final stare. "Please, Empress, take care of yourself. I won't be here to rescue you."

I let a weak grin pass over my lips. I refused to let him see how heartsick I was at his words. "Of course. I'll be careful. Best of luck to you, Mr. Sheridan."

He winced at the name. His mouth bobbed, and he inhaled as if to speak, but then he shook his head and pressed his lips tightly together.

He doffed his hat. "Take care, Empress." Then he tiptoed from the room.

Once he was out of sight, I eased myself from the bed. I hadn't walked in several days without someone assisting me, but I managed to stumble to the window and lean out. I wanted to see the Spirit-Hunters go.

Daniel and Jie soon scurried from the front door beneath me. They hit the grass and jogged over the yard toward the road—toward Market Street. Below a streetlamp I could see a poised, top-hatted figure. I was glad Joseph was back to his usual elegance, though I was certain he bore permanent scars too.

Just before Jie and Daniel reached the street, Daniel stopped. He twirled around and gazed up at me, as if he had sensed my eyes on his back. He strode a few steps toward me, paused, and then strode two more.

He slung off his cap and pressed it to his chest. Then, with the casual grace that marked all of his movements, he dropped to one knee and bowed his head.

He was declaring fealty to his empress.

I laughed—I couldn't help it. The absurdity of it all. The bittersweet sting. When he lifted back up, I saw he too wore a smile. He waved with his cap, and after flopping it back on his head, he swiveled and trotted to the street. Then, without another look back, the Spirit-Hunters left.

I limped to my bed, exhausted from my standing stint. I wanted to leave this hospital soon, but I needed more time to recover. Eventually, I would be out. Mama needed me, and I had a new life to create. New dreams to dream. A left hand to learn to use.

I would see the Spirit-Hunters again. I was certain of it. There was an enormous world out there, filled with Josephs and Jies and Daniels—and I wanted to see it and to meet them. I wanted to experience *everything*.

Mama had been right. Wounds would heal, grief would pass, but a reputation could never be recovered—and in my case, nor could innocence. But that was perfectly fine.

"The fault is not in our stars," I whispered to the ceiling. "But in ourselves. This was my choice."

I drifted into a healing sleep and dreamed of Elijah's smile.